PRAISE FOR

MICHAEL CRICHTON

AND

SPHERE

"Each chapter end reveals some new clue or poses some new threat that compels the reader to read on. And each new twist builds the pace with careful precision. . . . Evocative of all those grand adventure yarns we read as kids. . . . Crichton is a storyteller, and a damned good one." —*Los Angeles Times*

"[*Sphere*] kept me happy for two hours sitting in a grounded plane. . . . No one can ask more of a thriller. . . . The suspense is real. . . . The last ten pages are exactly what they should be."
—*New York Times Book Review*

"Chilling tension." —Associated Press

"Fascinating . . . Crichton provides a fast-moving, suspenseful plot." —*Christian Science Monitor*

"Michael Crichton has done what he does best: giving us suspense for our nerve endings and enough scientific speculation to keep our brains working at the same time." —*Newsweek*

"A fast-paced adventure. . . . Just when the reader is certain nothing more can go wrong for the hapless band of explorers, the author twists the screw a notch tighter."
—*San Francisco Chronicle*

SPHERE

ALSO BY MICHAEL CRICHTON

FICTION

NONFICTION

MICHAEL CRICHTON

SPHERE

A NOVEL

HARPER

NEW YORK • LONDON • TORONTO • SYDNEY

HARPER

This book was originally published in mass market by The Ballantine Publishing Group, a division of Random House, Inc. Reprinted by arrangement with Alfred A. Knopf, an imprint of The Knopf Doubleday Publishing Group, a division of the Random House Publishing Group.

HarperCollins books may be purchased for educational, business, or sales promotional use. For information, please e-mail the Special Markets Department at SPsales@harpercollins.com.

FIRST HARPER PAPERBACK PUBLISHED 2011.

Designed by Jamie Lynn Kerner

Library of Congress Cataloging-in-Publication Data is available upon request.

ISBN 978-0-06-242886-8 (pbk.)

19 20 LSC 10 9 8 7 6

For Lynn Nesbit

WHEN A scientist views things, he's not considering the incredible at all.

LOUIS I. KAHN

YOU CAN'T fool nature.

RICHARD FEYNMAN

During the preparation of this manuscript, I received help and encouragement from Caroline Conley, Kurt Villadsen, Lisa Plonsker, Valery Pine, Anne-Marie Martin, John Deubert, Lynn Nesbit, and Bob Gottlieb. I am grateful to them all.

Contents

SPHERE

THE
SURFACE

West **Of Tonga**

For a long time the horizon had been a monotonous flat blue line separating the Pacific Ocean from the sky. The Navy helicopter raced forward, flying low, near the waves. Despite the noise and the thumping vibration of the blades, Norman Johnson fell asleep. He was tired; he had been traveling on various military aircraft for more than fourteen hours. It was not the kind of thing a fifty-three-year-old professor of psychology was used to.

He had no idea how long he slept. When he awoke, he saw that the horizon was still flat; there were white semicircles of coral atolls ahead. He said over the intercom, "What's this?"

"Islands of Ninihina and Tafahi," the pilot said. "Technically part of Tonga, but they're uninhabited. Good sleep?"

"Not bad." Norman looked at the islands as they flashed by: a curve of white sand, a few palm trees, then gone. The flat ocean again.

"Where'd they bring you in from?" the pilot asked.

"San Diego," Norman said. "I left yesterday."

"So you came Honolulu-Guam-Pago-here?"

"That's right."

"Long trip," the pilot said. "What kind of work you do, sir?"

"I'm a psychologist," Norman said.

"A shrink, huh?" The pilot grinned. "Why not? They've called in just about everything else."

"How do you mean?"

"We've been ferrying people out of Guam for the last two days. Physicists, biologists, mathematicians, you name it. Everybody being flown to the middle of nowhere in the Pacific Ocean."

"What's going on?" Norman said.

The pilot glanced at him, eyes unreadable behind dark aviator sunglasses. "They're not telling us anything, sir. What about you? What'd they tell you?"

"They told me," Norman said, "that there was an airplane crash."

"Uh-huh," the pilot said. "You get called on crashes?"

"I have been, yes."

For a decade, Norman Johnson had been on the list of FAA crash-site teams, experts called on short notice to investigate civilian air disasters. The first time had been at the United Airlines crash in San Diego in 1976; then he had been called to Chicago in '78, and Dallas in '82. Each time the pattern was the same—the hurried telephone call, frantic packing, the absence for a week or more. This time his wife, Ellen, had been annoyed because he was called away on July 1, which meant he would miss their July 4 beach barbecue. Then, too, Tim was coming back from his sophomore year at Chicago, on his way to a summer job in the Cascades. And Amy, now sixteen, was just back from Andover, and Amy and Ellen didn't get along very well if Norman wasn't there to mediate. The Volvo was making noises again. And it was possible Norman might miss his mother's birthday the following week. "What crash is it?" Ellen had said. "I haven't heard about any crash." She turned on the radio while he packed. There was no news on the radio of an airline crash.

When the car pulled up in front of his house, Norman had been surprised to see it was a Navy pool sedan, with a uniformed Navy driver.

"They never sent a Navy car the other times," Ellen said, following him down the stairs to the front door. "Is this a military crash?"

"I don't know," he said.

"When will you be back?"

He kissed her. "I'll call you," he said. "Promise."

But he hadn't called. Everyone had been polite and pleasant, but they had kept him away from telephones. First at Hickam Field in Honolulu, then at the Naval Air Station in Guam, where he had arrived at two in the morning, and had spent half an hour in a room that smelled of aviation gasoline, staring dumbly at an issue of the *American Journal of Psychology* which he had brought with him, before flying on. He arrived at Pago Pago just as dawn was breaking. Norman was hurried onto the big Sea Knight helicopter, which immediately lifted off the cold tarmac and headed west, over palm trees and rusty corrugated rooftops, into the Pacific.

He had been on this helicopter for two hours, sleeping part

of the time. Ellen, and Tim and Amy and his mother's birthday, now seemed very far away.

"Where exactly are we?"

"Between Samoa and Fiji in the South Pacific," the pilot
said.

"Can you show me on the chart?"

"I'm not supposed to do that, sir. Anyway, it wouldn't show
much. Right now you're two hundred miles from anywhere,
sir."

Norman stared at the flat horizon, still blue and featureless.
I can believe it, he thought. He yawned. "Don't you get bored
looking at that?"

"To tell you the truth, no, sir," the pilot said. "I'm real happy
to see it flat like this. At least we've got good weather. And it
won't hold. There's a cyclone forming up in the Admiralties,
should swing down this way in a few days."

"What happens then?"

"Everybody clears the hell out. Weather can be tough in
this part of the world, sir. I'm from Florida and I saw some
hurricanes when I was a kid, but you've never seen *anything* like
a Pacific cyclone, sir."

Norman nodded. "How much longer until we get there?"

"Any minute now, sir."

AFTER TWO HOURS of monotony, the cluster of ships appeared unusually interesting. There were more than a dozen vessels of
various kinds, formed roughly into concentric circles. On the
outer perimeter, he counted eight gray Navy destroyers.
Closer to the center were large ships that had wide-spaced

double hulls and looked like floating dry-docks; then nonde-
script boxy ships with flat helicopter decks; and in the center,
amid all the gray, two white ships, each with a flat pad and a
bull's-eye.

The pilot listed them off: "You got your destroyers on the
outside, for protection; RVS's further in, that's Remote Vehicle
Support, for the robots; then MSS, Mission Support and Supply; and OSRV's in the center."

"OSRV's?"

"Oceanographic Survey and Research Vessels." The pilot
pointed to the white ships. "*John Hawes* to port, and *William
Arthur* to starboard. We'll put down on the *Hawes*." The pilot
circled the formation of ships. Norman could see launches
running back and forth between the ships, leaving small white
wakes against the deep blue of the water.

"All this for an airplane crash?" Norman said.

"Hey," the pilot grinned. "I never mentioned a crash. Check
your seat belt if you would, sir. We're about to land."

Barnes

The red bull's-eye grew larger, and slid beneath them as the helicopter touched down. Norman fumbled with his seat belt buckle as a uniformed Navy man ran up and opened the door.

"Dr. Johnson? Norman Johnson?"

"That's right."

"Have any baggage, sir?"

"Just this." Norman reached back, pulled out his day case. The officer took it.

"Any scientific instruments, anything like that?"

"No. That's it."

"This way, sir. Keep your head down, follow me, and don't go aft, sir."

Norman stepped out, ducking beneath the blades. He followed the officer off the helipad and down a narrow stairs. The metal handrail was hot to the touch. Behind him, the helicopter lifted off, the pilot giving him a final wave. Once the helicopter had gone, the Pacific air felt still and brutally hot.

"Good trip, sir?"

"Fine."

"Need to go, sir?"

"I've just arrived," Norman said.

"No, I mean: do you need to use the head, sir."

"No," Norman said.

"Good. Don't use the heads, they're all backed up."

"All right."

"Plumbing's been screwed up since last night. We're working on the problem and hope to have it solved soon." He peered at Norman. "We have a lot of women on board at the moment, sir."

"I see," Norman said.

"There's a chemical john if you need it, sir."

"I'm okay, thanks."

"In that case, Captain Barnes wants to see you at once, sir."

"I'd like to call my family."

"You can mention that to Captain Barnes, sir."

They ducked through a door, moving out of the hot sun into a fluorescent-lit hallway. It was much cooler. "Air conditioning hasn't gone out lately," the officer said. "At least that's something."

"Does the air conditioning go out often?"

"Only when it's hot."

Through another door, and into a large workroom: metal walls, racks of tools, acetylene torches spraying sparks as workmen hunched over metal pontoons and pieces of intricate machinery, cables snaking over the floor. "We do ROV repairs here," the officer said, shouting over the din. "Most of the heavy work is done on the tenders. We just do some of the electronics here. We go this way, sir."

Through another door, down another corridor, and into a wide, low-ceilinged room crammed with video monitors. A half-dozen technicians sat in shadowy half-darkness before the color screens. Norman paused to look.

"This is where we monitor the ROV's," the officer said. "We've got three or four robots down on the bottom at any given time. Plus the MSB's and the FD's, of course."

Norman heard the crackle and hiss of radio communications, soft fragments of words he couldn't make out. On one screen he saw a diver walking on the bottom. The diver was standing in harsh artificial light, wearing a kind of suit Norman had never seen, heavy blue cloth and a bright-yellow helmet sculpted in an odd shape.

Norman pointed to the screen. "How deep is he?"

"I don't know. Thousand, twelve hundred feet, something like that."

"And what have they found?"

"So far, just the big titanium fin." The officer glanced around. "It doesn't read on any monitors now. Bill, can you show Dr. Johnson here the fin?"

"Sorry, sir," the technician said. "Present MainComOps is working north of there, in quadrant seven."

"Ah. Quad seven's almost half a mile away from the fin," the officer said to Norman. "Too bad: it's a hell of a thing to see. But you'll see it later, I'm sure. This way to Captain Barnes."

They walked for a moment down the corridor, then the officer said, "Do you know the Captain, sir?"

"No, why?"

"Just wondered. He's been very eager to see you. Calling up the com techs every hour, to find out when you're arriving."

"No," Norman said, "I've never met him."

"Very nice man."

"I'm sure."

The officer glanced over his shoulder. "You know, they have a saying about the Captain," he said.

"Oh? What's that?"

"They say his bite is worse than his bark."

THROUGH ANOTHER DOOR, which was marked "Project Commander" and had beneath that a sliding plate that said "Capt. Harold C. Barnes, USN." The officer stepped aside, and Norman entered a paneled stateroom. A burly man in shirtsleeves stood up from behind a stack of files.

Captain Barnes was one of those trim military men who made Norman feel fat and inadequate. In his middle forties, Hal Barnes had erect military bearing, an alert expression, short hair, a flat gut, and a politician's firm handshake.

"Welcome aboard the *Hawes*, Dr. Johnson. How're you feeling?"

"Tired," Norman said.

"I'm sure, I'm sure. You came from San Diego?"

"Yes."

"So it's fifteen hours, give or take. Like to have a rest?"

"I'd like to know what's going on," Norman said.

"Perfectly understandable." Barnes nodded. "What'd they tell you?"

"Who?"

"The men who picked you up in San Diego, the men who flew you out here, the men in Guam. Whatever."

"They didn't tell me anything."

"And did you see any reporters, any press?"

"No, nothing like that."

Barnes smiled. "Good. I'm glad to hear it." He waved Norman to a seat. Norman sat gratefully. "How about some coffee?" Barnes said, moving to a coffee maker behind his desk, and then the lights went out. The room was dark except for the light that streamed in from a side porthole.

"God *damn* it!" Barnes said. "Not *again*. Emerson! *Emerson!*"

An ensign came in a side door. "Sir! Working on it. Captain."

"What was it this time?"

"Blew out in ROV Bay 2, sir."

"I thought we added extra lines to Bay 2."

"Apparently they overloaded anyway, sir."

"I want this fixed *now*, Emerson!"

"We hope to have it solved soon, sir."

The door closed; Barnes sat back in his chair. Norman heard the voice in the darkness. "It's not really their fault," he said. "These ships weren't built for the kind of power loads we put on them now, and—ah, there we are." The lights came back on.

Barnes smiled. "Did you say you wanted coffee, Dr. Johnson?"

"Black is fine," Norman said.

Barnes poured him a mug. "Anyway, I'm relieved you didn't talk to anybody. In my job, Dr. Johnson, security is the biggest worry. Especially on a thing like this. If word gets out about this site, we'll have all kinds of problems. And so many people are involved now. . . . Hell, CincComPac didn't even want to give me destroyers until I started talking about Soviet submarine reconnaissance. The next thing, I get four, then eight destroyers."

"Soviet submarine reconnaissance?" Norman asked.

"That's what I told them in Honolulu." Barnes grinned. "Part of the game, to get what you need for an operation like this. You've got to know how to requisition equipment in the modern Navy. But of course the Soviets won't come around."

"They won't?" Norman felt he had somehow missed the assumptions that lay behind the conversation, and was trying to catch up.

"It's very unlikely. Oh, they know we're here. They'll have spotted us with their satellites at least two days ago, but we're putting out a steady stream of decodable messages about our Search and Rescue exercises in the South Pacific. S and R drill represents a low priority for them, even though they undoubtedly figure a plane went down and we're recovering for real. They may even suspect that we're trying to recover nuclear warheads, like we did off of Spain in '68. But they'll leave us alone—because politically they don't want to be implicated in our nuclear problems. They know we have troubles with New Zealand these days."

"Is that what all this is?" Norman said. "Nuclear warheads?"

"No," Barnes said. "Thank God. Anything nuclear, somebody in the White House always feels duty-bound to announce it. But we've kept this one away from the White House staff. In fact, we bypass the JCS on this. All briefings go straight from the Defense Secretary to the President, personally." He rapped his knuckles on the desk. "So far, so good. And you're the last to arrive. Now that you're here, we'll shut this thing down tight. Nothing in, nothing out."

Norman still couldn't put it together. "If nuclear warheads aren't involved in the crash," he said, "why the secrecy?"

"Well," Barnes said. "We don't have all the facts yet."

"The crash occurred in the ocean?"

"Yes. More or less directly beneath us as we sit here."

"Then there can't be any survivors."

"Survivors?" Barnes looked surprised. "No, I wouldn't think so."

"Then why was I called here?"

Barnes looked blank.

"Well," Norman explained, "I'm usually called to crash sites when there are survivors. That's why they put a psychologist on the team, to deal with the acute traumatic problems of surviving passengers, or sometimes the relatives of surviving passengers. Their feelings, and their fears, and their recurring nightmares. People who survive a crash often experience all sorts of guilt and anxiety, concerning why they survived and not others. A woman sitting with her husband and children, suddenly they're all dead and she alone is alive. That kind of thing." Norman sat back in his chair. "But in this case—an airplane that crashed in a thousand feet of water—there wouldn't be any of those problems. So why am I here?"

Barnes was staring at him. He seemed uncomfortable. He shuffled the files around on his desk.

"Actually, this isn't an airplane crash site, Dr. Johnson."

"What is it?"

"It's a *spacecraft* crash site."

There was a short pause. Norman nodded. "I see."

"That doesn't surprise you?" Barnes said.

"No," Norman said. "As a matter of fact, it explains a lot. If a military spacecraft crashed in the ocean, that explains why I haven't heard anything about it on the radio, why it was kept secret, why I was brought here the way I was. . . . When did it crash?"

Barnes hesitated just a fraction before answering. "As best we can estimate," he said, "this spacecraft crashed three hundred years ago."

ULF

There was a silence. Norman listened to the drone of the air conditioner. He heard faintly the radio communications in the next room. He looked at the mug of coffee in his hand, noticing a chip on the rim. He struggled to assimilate what he was being told, but his mind moved sluggishly, in circles.

Three hundred years ago, he thought. A spacecraft three hundred years old. But the space program wasn't three hundred years old. It was barely thirty years old. So how could a spacecraft be three hundred years old? It couldn't be. Barnes must be mistaken. But how could Barnes be mistaken? The Navy wouldn't send all these ships, all these people, unless they were sure what was down there. A spacecraft three hundred years old.

But how could that be? It couldn't be. It must be something else. He went over it again and again, getting nowhere, his mind dazed and shocked.

"——solutely no question about it," Barnes was saying. "We

can estimate the date from coral growth with great accuracy. Pacific coral grows two-and-a-half centimeters a year, and the object—whatever it is—is covered in about five meters of coral. That's a lot of coral. Of course, coral doesn't grow at a depth of a thousand feet, which means that the present shelf collapsed to a lower depth at some point in the past. The geologists are telling us that happened about a century ago, so we're assuming a total age for the craft of about three hundred years. But we could be wrong about that. It could, in fact, be much older. It could be a thousand years old."

Barnes shifted papers on his desk again, arranging them into neat stacks, lining up the edges.

"I don't mind telling you, Dr. Johnson, this thing scares the hell out of me. *That's* why you're here."

Norman shook his head. "I still don't understand."

"We brought you here," Barnes said, "because of your association with the ULF project."

"ULF?" Norman said. And he almost added, But ULF was a joke. Seeing how serious Barnes was, he was glad he had caught himself in time.

YET ULF WAS a joke. Everything about it had been a joke, from the very beginning.

In 1979, in the waning days of the Carter Administration, Norman Johnson had been an assistant professor of psychology at the University of California at San Diego; his particular research interest was group dynamics and anxiety, and he occasionally served on FAA crash-site teams. In those days, his biggest problems had been finding a house for Ellen and the kids, keeping up his publications, and wondering whether UCSD would give him tenure. Norman's research was considered brilliant, but psychology was notoriously prone to intellectual fashions, and interest in the study of anxiety was declining as many researchers came to regard anxiety as a purely biochemical disorder that could be treated with drug therapy alone; one scientist had even gone so far as to say, "Anxiety is no longer a problem in psychology. There is nothing left to study." Similarly, group dynamics was perceived as old-fashioned, a field that had seen its heyday in the Gestalt encounter groups and corporate brainstorming procedures of the early 1970s but now was dated and passé.

Norman himself could not comprehend this. It seemed to him that American society was increasingly one in which people worked in groups, not alone; rugged individualism was now replaced by endless corporate meetings and group decisions. In this new society, group behavior seemed to him more important, not less. And he did not think that anxiety as a clinical problem was going to be solved with pills. It seemed to him that a society in which the most common prescription drug was Valium was, by definition, a society with unsolved problems.

Not until the preoccupation with Japanese managerial techniques in the 1980s did Norman's field gain a new hold on academic attention. Around the same time, Valium dependence became recognized as a major concern, and the whole issue of drug therapy for anxiety was reconsidered. But in the meantime, Johnson spent several years feeling as if he were in a backwater. (He did not have a research grant approved for nearly three years.) Tenure, and finding a house, were very real problems.

It was during the worst of this time, in late 1979, that he was approached by a solemn young lawyer from the National Security Council in Washington who sat with his ankle across his knee and plucked nervously at his sock. The lawyer told Norman that he had come to ask his help.

Norman said he would help if he could.

Still plucking at the sock, the lawyer said he wanted to talk to Norman about a "grave matter of national security facing our country today."

Norman asked what the problem was.

"Simply that this country has absolutely no preparedness in the event of an alien invasion. Absolutely no preparedness whatever."

Because the lawyer was young, and because he stared down at his sock as he spoke, Norman at first thought he was embarrassed at having been sent on a fool's errand. But when the young man looked up, Norman saw to his astonishment that he was utterly serious.

"We could really be caught with our pants down on this one," the lawyer said. "An alien invasion."

Norman had to bite his lip. "That's probably true," he said.

"People in the Administration are worried."

"Are they?"

"There is the feeling *at the highest levels* that contingency plans should be drawn."

"You mean contingency plans in the event of an alien invasion. . . ." Norman somehow managed to keep a straight face.

"Perhaps," said the lawyer, "perhaps *invasion* is too strong a word. Let's soften that to say 'contact': alien contact."

"I see."

"You're already involved in civilian crash-site teams, Dr. Johnson. You know how these emergency groups function. We want your input concerning the optimal composition of a crash-site team to confront an alien invader."

"I see," Norman said, wondering how he could tactfully get out of this. The idea was clearly ludicrous. He could see it only as displacement: the Administration, faced with immense problems it could not solve, had decided to think about something else.

And then the lawyer coughed, proposed a study, and named a substantial figure for a two-year research grant.

Norman saw a chance to buy his house. He said yes.

"I'm glad you agree the problem is a real one."

"Oh yes," Norman said, wondering how old this lawyer was. He guessed about twenty-five.

"We'll just have to get your security clearance," the lawyer said.

"I need security clearance?"

"Dr. Johnson," the lawyer said, snapping his briefcase shut, "this project is top, top secret."

"That's fine with me," Norman said, and he meant it. He could imagine his colleagues' reactions if they ever found out about this.

What began as a joke soon became simply bizarre. Over the next year, Norman flew five times to Washington for meetings with high-level officials of the National Security Council over the pressing, imminent danger of alien invasion. His work was very secret. One early question was whether his project should be turned over to DARPA, the Defense Advanced Research

Project Agency of the Pentagon. They decided not to. There were questions about whether it should be given to NASA, and again they decided not to. One Administration official said, "This isn't a scientific matter, Dr. Johnson, this is a national security matter. We don't want to open it out."

Norman was continually surprised at the level of the officials he was told to meet with. One Senior Undersecretary of State pushed aside the papers on his desk relating to the latest Middle East crisis to say, "What do you think about the possibility that these aliens will be able to read our minds?"

"I don't know," Norman said.

"Well, it occurs to me. How're we going to be able to formulate a negotiating posture if they can read our minds?"

"That could be a problem," Norman agreed, sneaking a glance at his watch.

"Hell, it's bad enough our encrypted cables get intercepted by the Russians. We know the Japanese and the Israelis have cracked all our codes. We just pray the Russians can't do it yet. But you see what I mean, the problem. About reading minds."

"Oh yes."

"Your report will have to take that into consideration."

Norman promised it would.

A White House staffer said to him, "You realize the President will want to talk to these aliens personally. He's that kind of man."

"Uh-huh," Norman said.

"And I mean, the publicity value here, the exposure, is incalculable. The President meets with the aliens at Camp David. What a media moment."

"A real moment," Norman agreed.

"So the aliens will need to be informed by an advance man of who the President is, and the protocol in talking to him. You can't have the President of the United States talking to people from another galaxy or whatever on television without advance preparation. Do you think the aliens'll speak English?"

"Doubtful," Norman said.

"So someone may need to learn their language, is that it?"

"It's hard to say."

"Perhaps the aliens would be more comfortable meeting with an advance man from one of our ethnic minorities," the White House man said. "Anyway, it's a possibility. Think about it."

Norman promised he would think about it.

The Pentagon liaison, a Major General, took him to lunch and over coffee casually asked, "What sorts of armaments do you see these aliens having?"

"I'm not sure," Norman said.

"Well, that's the crux of it, isn't it? And what about their vulnerabilities? I mean, the aliens might not even be human at all."

"No, they might not."

"They might be like giant insects. Your insects can withstand a lot of radiation."

"Yes," Norman said.

"We might not be able to touch these aliens," the Pentagon man said gloomily. Then he brightened. "But I doubt they could withstand a direct hit with a multimeg nuclear device, do you?"

"No," Norman said. "I don't think they could."

"It'd vaporize 'em."

"Sure."

"Laws of physics."

"Right."

"Your report must make that point clearly. About the nuclear vulnerability of these aliens."

"Yes," Norman said.

"We don't want to start a panic," the Pentagon man said. "No sense getting everyone upset, is there? I know the JCS will be reassured to hear the aliens are vulnerable to our nuclear weapons."

"I'll keep that in mind," Norman said.

Eventually, the meetings ended, and he was left to write his report. And as he reviewed the published speculations on extraterrestrial life, he decided that the Major General from the Pentagon was not so wrong, after all. The real question about alien contact—if there was any real question at all—concerned panic. Psychological panic. The only important human experience with extraterrestrials had been Orson Welles's 1938 radio broadcast of "The War of the Worlds." And the human response was unequivocal.

People had been terrified.

Norman submitted his report, entitled "Contact with Possible Extraterrestrial Life." It was returned to him by the NSC with the suggestion that the title be revised to "sound more technical" and that he remove "any suggestion that alien contact was only a possibility, as alien contact is considered virtually certain in some quarters of the Administration."

Revised, Norman's paper was duly classified Top Secret, under the title "Recommendations for the Human Contact Team to Interact with Unknown Life Forms (ULF)." As Norman envisioned it, the ULF Contact Team demanded particularly stable individuals. In his report he had said—

"I wonder," Barnes said, opening a folder, "if you recognize this quote:

> *Contact teams meeting an Unknown Life Form (ULF) must be prepared for severe psychological impact. Extreme anxiety responses will almost certainly occur. The personality traits of individuals who can withstand extreme anxiety must be determined, and such individuals selected to comprise the team.*
>
> *Anxiety when confronted by unknown life has not been sufficiently appreciated. The fears unleashed by contact with a new life form are not understood and cannot be entirely predicted in advance. But the most likely consequence of contact is absolute terror."*

Barnes snapped the folder shut. "You remember who said that?"

"Yes," Norman said. "I do."

And he remembered why he had said it.

As part of the NSC grant, Norman had conducted studies of group dynamics in contexts of psychosocial anxiety. Following the procedures of Asch and Milgram, he constructed several environments in which subjects did not know they were being tested. In one case, a group of subjects were told to take an elevator to another floor to participate in a test. The elevator jammed between floors. Subjects were then observed by hidden video camera.

There were several variations to this. Sometimes the elevator was marked "Under Repair"; sometimes there was telephone communication with the "repairman," sometimes not; sometimes the ceiling fell in, and the lights went out; and sometimes the floor of the elevator was constructed of clear Lucite.

In another case, subjects were loaded into a van and driven out into the desert by an "experiment leader" who ran out of gas, and then suffered a "heart attack," thus stranding the subjects.

In the most severe version, subjects were taken up in a private plane, and the pilot suffered a "heart attack" in mid-air.

Despite the traditional complaints about such tests—that they were sadistic, that they were artificial, that subjects somehow sensed the situations were contrived—Johnson gained considerable information about groups under anxiety stress.

He found that fear responses were minimized when the group was small (five or less); when group members knew each other well; when group members could see each other and were not isolated; when they shared defined group goals and fixed time limits; when groups were mixed age and mixed gender; and when group members had high phobic-tolerant personalities as measured by LAS tests for anxiety, which in turn correlated with athletic fitness.

Study results were formulated in dense statistical tables, although, in essence, Norman knew he had merely verified common sense: if you were trapped in an elevator, it was better to be with a few relaxed, athletic people you knew, to keep the lights on, and to know someone was working to get you free.

Yet Norman knew that some of his results were counterintuitive, such as the importance of group composition. Groups composed entirely of men or entirely of women were much poorer at handling stress than mixed groups; groups composed of individuals roughly the same age were much poorer than groups of mixed age. And pre-existing groups formed for another purpose did worst of all; at one point he had stressed a championship basketball team, and it cracked almost immediately.

Although his research was good, Norman remained uneasy about the underlying purpose for his paper—alien invasion—which he personally considered speculative to the point of absurdity. He was embarrassed to submit his paper, particularly after he had rewritten it to make it seem more significant than he knew it was.

He was relieved when the Carter Administration did not like his report. None of Norman's recommendations were approved. The Administration did not agree with Dr. Norman Johnson that fear was a problem; they thought the predominant human emotion would be wonder and awe. Furthermore, the Administration preferred a large contact team of thirty people, including three theologians, a lawyer, a physician, a representative from the State Department, a representative from the Joint Chiefs, a select group from the legislative branch, an aerospace engineer, an exobiologist, a nuclear physicist, a cultural anthropologist, and a television anchor personality.

In any case, President Carter was not re-elected in 1980,

and Norman heard nothing further about his ULF proposal. He had heard nothing for six years.

Until now.

Barnes said, "You remember the ULF team you proposed?"

"Of course," Norman said.

Norman had recommended a ULF team of four—an astrophysicist, a zoologist, a mathematician, a linguist—and a fifth member, a psychologist, whose job would be to monitor the behavior and attitude of the working team members.

"Give me your opinion of this," Barnes said. He handed Norman a sheet of paper:

ANOMALY INVESTIGATION TEAM

USN STAFF/SUPPORT MEMBERS
1. Harold C. Barnes, USN Project Commander Captain
2. Jane Edmunds, USN Data Processing Tech P.O. 1C
3. Tina Chan, USN Electronics Tech P.O. 1C
4. Alice Fletcher, USN Deepsat Habitat Support Chief P.O.
5. Rose C. Levy, USN Deepsat Habitat Support 2C

CIVILIAN STAFF MEMBERS
1. Theodore Fielding, astrophysicist/planetary geologist
2. Elizabeth Halpern, zoologist/biochemist
3. Harold J. Adams, mathematician/logician
4. Arthur Levine, marine biologist/biochemist
5. Norman Johnson, psychologist

Norman looked at the list. "Except for Levine, this is the civilian ULF Team I originally proposed. I even interviewed them, and tested them, back then."

"Correct."

"But you said yourself: there are probably no survivors. There's probably no life inside that spacecraft."

"Yes," Barnes said. "But what if I'm wrong?"

He glanced at his watch. "I'm going to brief the team members at eleven hundred hours. I want you to come along, and see what you think about the team members," Barnes said. "After all, we followed your ULF report recommendations."

You followed my recommendations, Norman thought with a sinking feeling. Jesus Christ, I was just paying for a house.

"I knew you'd jump at the opportunity to see your ideas put into practice," Barnes said. "That's why I've included you on the team as the psychologist, although a younger man would be more appropriate."

"I appreciate that," Norman said.

"I knew you would," Barnes said, smiling cheerfully. He extended a beefy hand. "Welcome to the ULF Team, Dr. Johnson."

Beth

An ensign showed Norman to his room, tiny and gray, more like a prison cell than anything else. Norman's day bag lay on his bunk. In the corner was a computer console and a keyboard. Next to it was a thick manual with a blue cover.

He sat on the bed, which was hard, unwelcoming. He leaned back against a pipe on the wall.

"Hi, Norman," a soft voice said. "I'm glad to see they dragged you into this. This is all your fault, isn't it?" A woman stood in the doorway.

Beth Halpern, the team zoologist, was a study in contrasts. She was a tall, angular woman of thirty-six who could be called pretty despite her sharp features and the almost masculine quality of her body. In the years since Norman had last seen her, she seemed to have emphasized her masculine side even more. Beth was a serious weight-lifter and runner; the veins and muscles bulged at her neck and on her forearms, and her legs, beneath her shorts, were powerful. Her hair was cut short, hardly longer than a man's.

At the same time, she wore jewelry and makeup, and she moved in a seductive way. Her voice was soft, and her eyes were large and liquid, especially when she talked about the living things that she studied. At those times she became almost maternal. One of her colleagues at the University of Chicago had referred to her as "Mother Nature with muscles."

Norman got up, and she gave him a quick peck on the cheek. "My room's next to yours, I heard you arrive. When did you get in?"

"An hour ago. I think I'm still in shock," Norman said. "Do you believe all this? Do you think it's real?"

"I think that's real." She pointed to the blue manual next to his computer.

Norman picked it up: *Regulations Governing Personnel Conduct During Classified Military Operations.* He thumbed through pages of dense legal text.

"It basically says," Beth said, "that you keep your mouth shut or you spend a long time in military prison. And there's no calls in or out. Yes, Norman, I think it must be real."

"There's a spacecraft down there?"

"There's something down there. It's pretty exciting." She began to speak more rapidly. "Why, for biology alone, the possibilities are staggering—everything we know about life comes from studying life on our own planet. But, in a sense, all life on our planet is the same. Every living creature, from algae to human beings, is basically built on the same plan, from the same DNA. Now we may have a chance to contact life that is entirely different, different in every way. It's exciting, all right."

Norman nodded. He was thinking of something else. "What did you say about no calls in or out? I promised to call Ellen."

"Well, I tried to call my daughter and they told me the mainland com links are out. If you can believe that. The Navy's got more satellites than admirals, but they swear there's no available line to call out. Barnes said he'd approve a cable. That's it."

"How old is Jennifer now?" Norman asked, pleased to pull the name from his memory. And what was her husband's name? He was a physicist, Norman remembered, something like that. Sandy blond man. Had a beard. Wore bow ties.

"Nine. She's pitching for the Evanston Little League now. Not much of a student, but a hell of a pitcher." She sounded proud. "How's your family? Ellen?"

"She's fine. The kids are fine. Tim's a sophomore at Chicago. Amy's at Andover. How is . . ."

"George? We divorced three years ago," Beth said. "George had a year at CERN in Geneva, looking for exotic particles, and I guess he found whatever he was looking for. She's French. He says she's a great cook." She shrugged. "Anyway, my work is going well. For the past year I have been working with cephalopods—squid and octopi."

"How's that?"

"Interesting. It gives you quite a strange feeling to realize the gentle intelligence of these creatures, particularly octopi. You know an octopus is smarter than a dog, and would probably make a much better pet. It's a wonderful, clever, very emotional creature, an octopus. Only we never think of them that way."

Norman said, "Do you still eat them?"

"Oh, Norman." She smiled. "Do you still relate everything to food?"

"Whenever possible," Norman said, patting his stomach.

"Well, you won't like the food in this place. It's terrible. But the answer is no," she said, cracking her knuckles. "I could never eat an octopus now, knowing what I do about them. Which reminds me: What do you know about Hal Barnes?"

"Nothing, why?"

"I've been asking around. Turns out Barnes is not Navy at all. He's *ex*-Navy."

"You mean he's retired?"

"Retired in '81. He was originally trained as an aeronautical engineer at Cal Tech, and after he retired he worked for Grumman for a while. Then a member of the Navy Science Board of the National Academy; then Assistant Undersecretary of Defense, and a member of DSARC, the Defense Systems Acquisition Review Council; a member of the Defense Science Board, which advises the Joint Chiefs and the Secretary of Defense."

"Advises them on what?"

"Weapons acquisition," Beth said. "He's a Pentagon man who advises the government on weapons acquisition. So how'd he get to be running this project?"

"Beats me," Norman said. Sitting on the bunk, he kicked off his shoes. He felt suddenly tired. Beth leaned against the doorway.

"You seem to be in very good shape," Norman said. Even her hands looked strong, he thought.

"A good thing, too, as it turns out," Beth said. "I have a lot of confidence for what's coming. What about you? Think you'll manage okay?"

"Me? Why shouldn't I?" He glanced down at his own familiar paunch. Ellen was always after him to do something about it, and from time to time he got inspired and went to the gym for a few days, but he could never seem to get rid of it. And the truth was, it didn't matter that much to him. He was fifty-three years old and he was a university professor. What the hell.

Then he had a thought: "What do you mean, you have confidence for what's coming? What's coming?"

"Well. It's only rumors so far. But your arrival seems to confirm them."

"What rumors?"

"They're sending us down there," Beth said.

"Down where?"

"To the bottom. To the spaceship."

"But it's a thousand feet down. They're investigating it with robot submersibles."

"These days, a thousand feet isn't that deep," Beth said. "The technology can handle it. There are Navy divers down there now. And the word is, the divers have put up a habitat so our team can go down and live on the bottom for a week or so and open the spacecraft up."

Norman felt a sudden chill. In his work with the FAA, he had been exposed to every sort of horror. Once, in Chicago, at a crash site that extended over a whole farm field, he had stepped on something squishy. He thought it was a frog, but it was a child's severed hand, palm up. Another time he had seen a man's charred body, still strapped into the seat, except the seat had been flung into the back yard of a suburban house, where it sat upright next to a portable plastic kiddie swimming pool. And in Dallas he had watched the investigators on the rooftops of the suburban houses, collecting the body parts, putting them in bags . . .

Working on a crash-site team demanded the most extraordinary psychological vigilance, to avoid being overwhelmed by what you saw. But there was never any personal danger, any physical risk. The risk was the risk of nightmares.

But now, the prospect of going down a thousand feet under the ocean to investigate a wreck . . .

"You okay?" Beth said. "You look pale."

"I didn't know anybody was talking about *going down there*."

"Just rumors," Beth said. "Get some rest, Norman. I think you need it."

The Briefing

T he ULF Team met in the briefing room, just before eleven. Norman was interested to see the group he had picked six years before, now assembled together for the first time.

Ted Fielding was compact, handsome, and still boyish at forty, at ease in shorts and a Polo sport shirt. An astrophysicist at the Jet Propulsion Laboratory in Pasadena, he had done important work on the planetary stratigraphy of Mercury and the moon, although he was best known for his studies of the Mangala Vallis and Valles Marineris channels on Mars. Located at the Martian equator, these great canyons were as much as twenty-five hundred miles long and two and a half miles deep— ten times the length and twice the depth of the Grand Canyon. And Fielding had been among the first to conclude that the planet most like the Earth in composition was not Mars at all, as previously suspected, but tiny Mercury, with its Earth-like magnetic field.

Fielding's manner was open, cheerful, and pompous. At JPL, he had appeared on television whenever there was a spacecraft flyby, and thus enjoyed a certain celebrity; he had recently been remarried, to a television weather reporter in Los Angeles; they had a young son.

Ted was a long-standing advocate for life on other worlds, and a supporter of SETI, the Search for Extraterrestrial Intelligence, which other scientists considered a waste of time and money. He grinned happily at Norman now.

"I always knew this would happen—sooner or later, we'd get our proof of intelligent life on other worlds. Now at last we have it, Norman. This is a great moment. And I am especially pleased about the shape."

"The shape?"

"Of the object down there."

"What about it?" Norman hadn't heard anything about the shape.

"I've been in the monitor room watching the video feed from the robots. They're beginning to define the shape beneath the coral. And it's not round. It is not a flying saucer," Ted said. "Thank God. Perhaps this will silence the lunatic fringe." He smiled. "'All things come to him who waits,' eh?"

"I guess so," Norman said. He wasn't sure what Fielding meant, but Ted tended to literary quotations. Ted saw himself as a Renaissance man, and random quotations from Rousseau and Lao-tsu were one way to remind you of it. Yet there was nothing mean-spirited about him; someone once said that Ted was "a brand-name guy," and that carried over to his speech as well. There was an innocence, almost a naïveté to Ted Fielding that was endearing and genuine. Norman liked him.

He wasn't so sure about Harry Adams, the reserved Princeton mathematician Norman hadn't seen for six years. Harry was now a tall, very thin black man with wire-frame glasses and a perpetual frown. He wore a T-shirt that said "Mathematicians Do It Correctly"; it was the kind of thing a student would wear, and indeed, Adams appeared even younger than his thirty years; he was clearly the youngest member of the group—and arguably the most important.

Many theorists argued that communication with extraterrestrials would prove impossible, because human beings would have nothing in common with them. These thinkers pointed out that just as human bodies represented the outcome of many evolutionary events, so did human thought. Like our bodies, our ways of thinking could easily have turned out differently; there was nothing inevitable about how we looked at the universe.

Men already had trouble communicating with intelligent Earthly creatures such as dolphins, simply because dolphins lived in such a different environment and had such different sensory apparatus.

Yet men and dolphins might appear virtually identical when compared with the vast differences that separated us from an extraterrestrial creature—a creature who was the product of billions of years of divergent evolution in some other planetary environment. Such an extraterrestrial would be unlikely to see the world as we did. In fact, it might not see the world at all. It might be blind, and it might learn about the world through a highly developed sense of smell, or temperature, or pressure. There might be no way to communicate with such a creature, no common ground at all. As one man put it, how would you explain Wordsworth's poem about daffodils to a blind watersnake?

But the field of knowledge we were most likely to share with extraterrestrials was mathematics. So the team mathematician was going to play a crucial role. Norman had selected Adams because, despite his youth, Harry had already made important contributions to several different fields.

"What do you think about all this, Harry?" Norman said, dropping into a chair next to him.

"I think it's perfectly clear," Harry said, "that it is a waste of time."

"This fin they've found underwater?"

"I don't know what it is, but I know what it *isn't*. It isn't a spacecraft from another civilization."

Ted, standing nearby, turned away in annoyance. Harry and Ted had evidently had this same conversation already.

"How do you know?" Norman asked.

"A simple calculation," Harry said, with a dismissing wave of his hand. "Trivial, really. You know the Drake equation?"

Norman did. It was one of the famous proposals in the literature on extraterrestrial life. But he said, "Refresh me."

Harry sighed irritably, pulled out a sheet of paper. "It's a probability equation." He wrote:

$$p = f n f f f$$
$$p h l i c$$

"What it means," Harry Adams said, "is that the probability, p, that intelligent life will evolve in any star system is a function of the probability that the star will have planets, the number of habitable planets, the probability that simple life will evolve on a habitable planet, the probability that intelligent life will evolve from simple life, and the probability that intelligent life will attempt interstellar communication within five billion years. That's all the equation says."

"Uh-huh," Norman said.

"But the point is that we have no facts," Harry said. "We must guess at every single one of these probabilities. And it's quite easy to guess one way, as Ted does, and conclude there are probably thousands of intelligent civilizations. It's equally easy to guess, as I do, that there is probably only one civilization. Ours." He pushed the paper away. "And in that case, whatever is down there is *not* from an alien civilization. So we're all wasting our time here."

"Then what is down there?" Norman said again.

"It is an absurd expression of romantic hope," Adams said, pushing his glasses up on his nose. There was a vehemence about him that troubled Norman. Six years earlier, Harry Adams had still been a street kid whose obscure talent had carried him in a single step from a broken home in the slums of Philadelphia to the manicured green lawns of Princeton. In those days Adams had been playful, amused at his turn of fortune. Why was he so harsh now?

Adams was an extraordinarily gifted theoretician, his reputation secured in probability-density functions of quantum mechanics which were beyond Norman's comprehension, although Adams had worked them out when he was seventeen. But Norman could certainly understand the man himself, and Harry Adams seemed tense and critical now, ill at ease in this group.

Or perhaps it had to do with his presence as part of a group. Norman had worried about how he would fit in, because Harry had been a child prodigy.

There were really only two kinds of child prodigies—mathematical and musical. Some psychologists argued there was only one kind, since music was so closely related to mathematics. While there were precocious children with other talents, such as writing, painting, and athletics, the only areas in which a child might truly perform at the level of an adult were in mathematics or music. Psychologically, such children were complex: often loners, isolated from their peers and even from their families by their gifts, for which they were both admired and resented. Socialization skills were often retarded, making group interactions uncomfortable. As a slum kid, Harry's problems would have been, if anything, magnified. He had once told Norman that when he first learned about Fourier transforms, the other kids were learning to slam-dunk. So maybe Harry was feeling uncomfortable in the group now.

But there seemed to be something else. . . . Harry appeared almost angry.

"You wait," Adams said. "A week from now, this is going to be recognized as one big fat false alarm. Nothing more."

You hope, Norman thought. And again wondered why.

"Well, I think it's exciting," Beth Halpern said, smiling brightly. "Even a slim chance of finding new life is exciting, as far as I am concerned."

"That's right," Ted said. "After all, Harry, there are more things in heaven and earth than are dreamed of in your philosophy."

Norman looked over at the final member of the team, Arthur Levine, the marine biologist. Levine was the only person he didn't know. A pudgy man, Levine looked pale and uneasy, wrapped in his own thoughts. He was about to ask Levine what he thought when Captain Barnes strode in, a stack of files under his arm.

"Welcome to the middle of nowhere," Barnes said, "and you can't even go to the bathroom." They all laughed nervously. "Sorry to keep you waiting," he said. "But we don't have a lot of time, so let's get right down to it. If you'll kill the lights, we can begin."

THE FIRST SLIDE showed a large ship with an elaborate superstructure on the stern.

"The *Rose Sealady*," Barnes said. "A cable-laying vessel chartered by Transpac Communications to lay a submarine telephone line from Honolulu to Sydney, Australia. The *Rose* left Hawaii on May 29 of this year, and by June 16 it had gotten as far as Western Samoa in the mid-Pacific. It was laying a new fiber-optics cable, which has a carrying capacity of twenty thousand simultaneous telephonic transmissions. The cable is covered with a dense metal-and-plastics web matrix, unusually tough and resistant to breaks. The ship had already laid more than forty-six hundred nautical miles of cable across the Pacific with no mishaps of any sort. Next."

A map of the Pacific, with a large red spot.

"At ten p.m. on the night of June 17, the vessel was located here, midway between Pago Pago in American Samoa and Viti Levu in Fiji, when the ship experienced a wrenching shudder. Alarms sounded, and the crew realized the cable had snagged and torn. They immediately consulted their charts, looking for an underwater obstruction, but could see none. They hauled up the loose cable, which took several hours, since at the time of the accident they had more than a mile of cable laid out behind the ship. When they examined the cut end, they saw that it had been cleanly sheared—as one crewman said, 'like it was cut with a huge pair of scissors.' Next."

A section of Fiberglas cable held toward the camera in the rough hand of a sailor.

"The nature of the break, as you can see, suggests an artificial obstruction of some sort. The *Rose* steamed north back over the scene of the break. Next."

A series of ragged black-and-white lines, with a region of small spikes.

"This is the original sonar scan from the ship. If you can't read sonar scans this'll be hard to interpret, but you see here the thin, knife-edge obstruction. Consistent with a sunken ship or aircraft, which cut the cable.

"The charter company, Transpac Communications, notified the Navy, requesting any information we had about the obstruction. This is routine: whenever there is a cable break, the Navy is notified, on the chance that the obstruction is known to us. If it's a sunken vessel containing explosives, the cable company wants to know about it before they start repair. But in this case the obstruction was not in Navy files. And the Navy was interested.

"We immediately dispatched our nearest search ship, the *Ocean Explorer*, from Melbourne. The *Ocean Explorer* reached

the site on June 21 of this year. The reason for the Navy interest was the possibility that the obstruction might represent
a sunken Chinese Wuhan-class nuclear submarine fitted with
SY-2 missiles. We knew the Chinese lost such a sub in this
approximate area in May 1984. The *Ocean Explorer* scanned
the bottom, using a most sophisticated side-looking sonar,
which produced this picture of the bottom."

In color, the image was almost three-dimensional in its
clarity.

"As you see, the bottom appears flat except for a single tri-
angular fin which sticks up some two hundred and eighty feet
above the ocean floor. You see it here," he said, pointing. "Now,
this wing dimension is larger than any known aircraft manu-
factured in either the United States or the Soviet Union. This
was very puzzling at first. Next."

A submersible robot, being lowered on a crane over the
side of a ship. The robot looked like a series of horizontal
tubes with cameras and lights nestled in the center.

"By June 24, the Navy had the ROV carrier *Neptune IV* on
site, and the Remote Operated Vehicle *Scorpion*, which you see
here, was sent down to photograph the wing. It returned an
image that clearly showed a control surface of some sort. Here
it is."

There were murmurs from the group. In a harshly lit color
image, a gray fin stuck up from a flat coral floor. The fin was
sharp-edged and aeronautical-looking, tapered, definitely artificial.

"You'll notice," Barnes said, "that the sea bottom in this
region consists of scrubby dead coral. The wing or fin disap-

pears into the coral, suggesting the rest of the aircraft might be buried beneath. An ultra-high-resolution SLS bottom scan was carried out, to detect the shape underneath the coral. Next."

Another color sonar image, composed of fine dots instead of lines.

"As you see, the fin seems to be attached to a cylindrical object buried under the coral. The object has a diameter of a hundred and ninety feet, and extends west for a distance of 2,754 feet before tapering to a point."

More murmurings from the audience.

"That's correct," Barnes said. "The cylindrical object is half a mile long. The shape is consistent with a rocket or spacecraft—it certainly looks like that—but from the beginning we were careful to refer to this object as 'the anomaly.'"

Norman glanced over at Ted, who was smiling up at the screen. But alongside Ted in the darkness, Harry Adams frowned and pushed his glasses up on his nose.

Then the projector light went out. The room was plunged into darkness. There were groans. Norman heard Barnes say, "God damn it, not again!" Someone scrambled for the door; there was a rectangle of light.

Beth leaned over to Norman and said, "They lose power here all the time. Reassuring, huh?"

Moments later, the electricity came back on; Barnes continued. "On June 25 a SCARAB remote vehicle cut a piece from the tail fin and brought it to the surface. The fin segment was analyzed and found to be a titanium alloy in an epoxy-resin honeycomb. The necessary bonding technology for such metal/plastic materials was currently unknown on Earth.

"Experts confirmed that the fin could not have originated on this planet—although in ten or twenty years we'd probably know how to make it."

Harry Adams grunted, leaned forward, made a note on his pad.

Meanwhile, Barnes explained, other robot vessels were used to plant seismic charges on the bottom. Seismic analysis showed that the buried anomaly was of metal, that it was hollow, and that it had a complex internal structure.

"After two weeks of intensive study," Barnes said, "we concluded the anomaly was some sort of spacecraft."

The final verification came on June 27 from the geologists. Their core samples from the bottom indicated that the present seabed had formerly been much shallower, perhaps only eighty or ninety feet deep. This would explain the coral, which covered the craft to an average thickness of thirty feet. Therefore, the geologists said, the craft had been on the planet at least three hundred years, and perhaps much longer: five hundred, or even five thousand years.

"However reluctantly," Barnes said, "the Navy concluded that we had, in fact, found a spacecraft from another civilization. The decision of the President, before a special meeting of the National Security Council, was to open the spacecraft. So, starting June 29, the ULF team members were called in."

On July 1, the subsea habitat DH-7 was lowered into position near the spacecraft site. DH-7 housed nine Navy divers working in a saturated exotic-gas environment. They proceeded to do primary drilling work. "And I think that brings you up to date," Barnes said. "Any questions?"

Ted said, "The internal structure of the spacecraft. Has it been clarified?"

"Not at this point. The spacecraft seems to be built in such a way that shock waves are transmitted around the outer shell, which is tremendously strong and well engineered. That prevents a clear picture of the interior from the seismics."

"How about passive techniques to see what's inside?"

"We've tried," Barnes said. "Gravitometric analysis, negative. Thermography, negative. Resistivity mapping, negative. Proton precision magnetometers, negative."

"Listening devices?"

"We've had hydrophones on the bottom from day one. There have been no sounds emanating from the craft. At least not so far."

"What about other remote inspection procedures?"

"Most involve radiation, and we're hesitant to irradiate the craft at this time."

Harry said, "Captain Barnes, I notice the fin appears undamaged, and the hull appears a perfect cylinder. Do you think that this object crashed in the ocean?"

"Yes," Barnes said, looking uneasy.

"So this object has survived a high-speed impact with the water, without a scratch or a dent?"

"Well, it's tremendously strong."

Harry nodded. "It would have to be. . . ."

Beth said, "The divers who are down there now—what exactly are they doing?"

"Looking for the front door." Barnes smiled. "For the time

being, we've had to fall back on classical archaeological procedures. We're digging exploratory trenches in the coral, looking
for an entrance or a hatch of some kind. We hope to find it
within the next twenty-four to forty-eight hours. Once we do,
you're going in. Anything else?"

"Yes," Ted said. "What was the Russian reaction to this
discovery?"

"We haven't told the Russians," Barnes said.

"You haven't told them?"

"No. We haven't."

"But this is an incredible, unprecedented development in
human history. Not just American history. *Human* history.
Surely we should share this with all the nations of the world.
This is the sort of discovery that could unite all of mankind—"

"You'd have to speak to the President," Barnes said. "I
don't know the reasoning behind it, but it's his decision. Any
other questions?"

Nobody said anything. The team looked at each other.

"Then I guess that's it," Barnes said.

The lights came on. There was the scraping of chairs as
people stood, stretched. Then Harry Adams said, "Captain
Barnes, I must say I resent this briefing very much."

Barnes looked surprised. "What do you mean, Harry?"

The others stopped, looked at Adams. He remained seated
in his chair, an irritated look on his face. "Did you decide you
have to break the news to us gently?"

"What news?"

"The news about the door."

Barnes laughed uneasily. "Harry, I just got through telling

you that the divers are cutting exploratory trenches, looking
for the door—"

"—I'd say you had a pretty good idea where the door was
three days ago, when you started flying us in. And I'd say that
by now you probably know exactly where the door is. Am I
right?"

Barnes said nothing. He stood with a fixed smile on his
face.

My God, Norman thought, looking at Barnes. Harry's right.
Harry was known to have a superbly logical brain, an astonishing and cold deductive ability, but Norman had never seen him
at work.

"Yes," Barnes said, finally. "You're right."

"You know the location of the door?"

"We do. Yes."

There was a moment of silence, and then Ted said, "But
this is fantastic! Absolutely fantastic! When will we go down
there to enter the spacecraft?"

"Tomorrow," Barnes said, never taking his eyes off Harry.
And Harry, for his own part, stared fixedly at Barnes. "The
minisubs will take you down in pairs, starting at oh eight
hundred hours tomorrow morning."

"This is exciting!" Ted said. "Fantastic! Unbelievable."

"So," Barnes said, still watching Harry, "you should all get
a good night's sleep—if you can."

" 'Innocent sleep, sleep that knits up the ravell'd sleave of
care,' " Ted said. He was literally bobbing up and down in his
chair with excitement.

"During the rest of the day, supply and technical officers

will be coming to measure and outfit you. Any other questions," Barnes said, "you can find me in my office."

He left the room, and the meeting broke up. When the others filed out, Norman remained behind, with Harry Adams. Harry never moved from his chair. He watched the technician packing up the portable screen.

"That was quite a performance just now," Norman said.

"Was it? I don't see why."

"You deduced that Barnes wasn't telling us about the door."

"Oh, there's much more he's not telling us about," Adams said, in a cold voice. "He's not telling us about *any* of the important things."

"Like what?"

"Like the fact," Harry said, getting to his feet at last, "that Captain Barnes knows perfectly well why the President decided to keep this a secret."

"He does?"

"The President had no choice, under the circumstances."

"What circumstances?"

"He knows that the object down there is not an alien spacecraft."

"Then what is it?"

"I think it's quite clear what it is."

"Not to me," Norman said.

Adams smiled for the first time. It was a thin smile, entirely without humor. "You wouldn't believe it if I told you," he said. And he left the room.

Tests

Arthur Levine, the marine biologist, was the only member of the expedition Norman Johnson had not met. It was one of the things we hadn't planned for, he thought. Norman had assumed that any contact with unknown life would occur on land; he hadn't considered the most obvious possibility—that if a spacecraft landed at random somewhere on the Earth, it would most likely come down on water, since 70 percent of the planet was covered with water. It was obvious in retrospect that they would need a marine biologist.

What else, he wondered, would prove obvious in retrospect?

He found Levine hanging off the port railing. Levine came from the oceanographic institute at Woods Hole, Massachusetts. His hand was damp when Norman shook it. Levine looked extremely ill at ease, and finally admitted that he was seasick.

"Seasick? A marine biologist?" Norman said.

"I work in the laboratory," he said. "At home. On land. Where things don't move all the time. Why are you smiling?"

"Sorry," Norman said.

"You think it's funny, a seasick marine biologist?"

"Incongruous, I guess."

"A lot of us get seasick," Levine said. He stared out at the sea. "Look out there," he said. "Thousands of miles of flat. Nothing."

"The ocean."

"It gives me the creeps," Levine said.

"SO?" BARNES SAID, back in his office. "What do you think?"

"Of what?"

"Of the team, for Christ's sake."

"It's the team I chose, six years later. Basically a good group, certainly very able."

"I want to know who will crack."

"Why should anybody crack?" Norman said. He was looking at Barnes, noticing the thin line of sweat on his upper lip. The commander was under a lot of pressure himself.

"A thousand feet down?" Barnes said. "Living and working in a cramped habitat? Listen, it's not like I'm going in with military divers who have been trained and who have themselves under control. I'm taking a bunch of *scientists*, for God's sake. I want to make sure they all have a clean bill of health. I want to make sure nobody's going to crack."

"I don't know if you are aware of this, Captain, but psychologists can't predict that very accurately. Who will crack."

"Even when it's from fear?"

"Whatever it's from."

Barnes frowned. "I thought fear was your specialty."

"Anxiety is one of my research interests and I can tell you

who, on the basis of personality profiles, is likely to suffer acute anxiety in a stress situation. But I can't predict who'll crack under that stress and who won't."

"Then what good are you?" Barnes said irritably. He sighed. "I'm sorry. Don't you just want to interview them, or give them some tests?"

"There aren't any tests," Norman said. "At least, none that work."

Barnes sighed again. "What about Levine?"

"He's seasick."

"There isn't any motion underwater; that won't be a problem. But what about *him*, personally?"

"I'd be concerned," Norman said.

"Duly noted. What about Harry Adams? He's arrogant."

"Yes," Norman said. "But that's probably desirable." Studies had shown that the people who were most successful at handling pressure were people others didn't like—individuals who were described as arrogant, cocksure, irritating.

"Maybe so," Barnes said. "But what about his famous research paper? Harry was one of the biggest supporters of SETI a few years back. Now that we've found something, he's suddenly very negative. You remember his paper?"

Norman didn't, and was about to say so when an ensign came in. "Captain Barnes, here is the visual upgrade you wanted."

"Okay," Barnes said. He squinted at a photograph, put it down. "What about the weather?"

"No change, sir. Satellite reports are confirming we have forty-eight plus-minus twelve on site, sir."

"Hell," Barnes said.

"Trouble?" Norman asked.

"The weather's going bad on us," Barnes said. "We may have to clear out our surface support."

"Does that mean you'll cancel going down there?"

"No," Barnes said. "We go tomorrow, as planned."

"Why does Harry think this thing is not a spacecraft?" Norman asked.

Barnes frowned, pushed papers on his desk. "Let me tell you something," he said. "Harry's a theoretician. And theories are just that—theories. I deal in the hard facts. The fact is, we've got something damn old and damn strange down there. I want to know what it is."

"But if it's not an alien spacecraft, what is it?"

"Let's just wait until we get down there, shall we?" Barnes glanced at his watch. "The second habitat should be anchored on the sea floor by now. We'll begin moving you down in fifteen hours. Between now and then, we've all got a lot to do."

"JUST HOLD IT there, Dr. Johnson." Norman stood naked, felt two metal calipers pinch the back of his arms, just above the elbow. "Just a bit . . . that's fine. Now you can get into the tank."

The young medical corpsman stepped aside, and Norman climbed the steps to the metal tank, which looked like a military version of a Jacuzzi. The tank was filled to the top with water. As he lowered his body into the water, it spilled over the sides.

"What's all this for?" Norman asked.

"I'm sorry, Dr. Johnson. If you would *completely* immerse yourself . . ."

"What?"

"Just for a moment, sir . . ."

Norman took a breath, ducked under the water, came back up.

"That's fine, you can get out now," the corpsman said, handing him a towel.

"What's all this for?" he asked again, climbing down the ladder.

"Total body adipose content," the corpsman said. "We have to know it, to calculate your sat stats."

"My sat stats?"

"Your saturation statistics." The corpsman marked points on his clipboard.

"Oh dear," he said. "You're off the graph."

"Why is that?"

"Do you get much exercise, Dr. Johnson?"

"Some." He was feeling defensive now. And the towel was too small to wrap around his waist. Why did the Navy use such small towels?

"Do you drink?"

"Some." He was feeling distinctly defensive. No question about it.

"May I ask when you last consumed an alcoholic beverage, sir?"

"I don't know. Two, three days ago." He was having trouble thinking back to San Diego. It seemed so far away. "Why?"

"That's fine, Dr. Johnson. Any trouble with joints, hips or knees?"

"No, why?"

"Episodes of syncope, faintness or blackouts?"

"No . . ."

"If you would just sit over here, sir." The corpsman pointed to a stool, next to an electronic device on the wall.

"I'd really like some answers," Norman said.

"Just stare at the green dot, both eyes wide open. . . ."

He felt a brief blast of air on both eyes, and blinked instinctively. A printed strip of paper clicked out. The corpsman tore it off, glanced at it.

"That's fine, Dr. Johnson. If you would come this way . . ."

"I'd like some information from you," Norman said. "I'd like to know what's going on."

"I understand, sir, but I have to finish your workup in time for your next briefing at seventeen hundred hours."

NORMAN LAY ON his back, and technicians stuck needles in both arms, and another in his leg at the groin. He yelled in sudden pain.

"That's the worst of it, sir," the corpsman said, packing the syringes in ice. "If you will just press this cotton against it, here . . ."

THERE WAS A clip over his nostrils, a mouthpiece between his teeth.

"This is to measure your CO_2," the corpsman said. "Just exhale. That's right. Big breath, now exhale. . . ."

Norman exhaled. He watched a rubber diaphragm inflate, pushing a needle up a scale.

"Try it again, sir. I'm sure you can do better than that."

Norman didn't think he could, but he tried again anyway.

Another corpsman entered the room, with a sheet of paper covered with figures. "Here are his BC's," he said.

The first corpsman frowned. "Has Barnes seen this?"

"Yes."

"And what'd he say?"

"He said it was okay. He said to continue."

"Okay, fine. He's the boss." The first corpsman turned back to Norman. "Let's try one more big breath, Dr. Johnson, if you would. . . ."

METAL CALIPERS TOUCHED his chin and his forehead. A tape went around his head. Now the calipers measured from his ear to his chin.

"What's this for?" Norman said.

"Fitting you with a helmet, sir."

"Shouldn't I be trying one on?"

"This is the way we do it, sir."

DINNER WAS MACARONI and cheese, burned underneath. Norman pushed it aside after a few bites.

The corpsman appeared at his door. "Time for the seventeen-hundred-hours briefing, sir."

"I'm not going anywhere," Norman said, "until I get some answers. What the hell is all this you're doing to me?"

"Routine deepsat workup, sir. Navy regs require it before you go down."

"And why am I off the graph?"

"Sorry, sir?"

"You said I was off the graph."

"Oh, *that*. You're a bit heavier than the Navy tables figure for, sir."

"Is there a problem about my weight?"

"Shouldn't be, no, sir."

"And the other tests, what did they show?"

"Sir, you are in very good health for your age and life-style."

"And what about going down there?" Norman asked, half hoping he wouldn't be able to go.

"Down there? I've talked with Captain Barnes. Shouldn't be any problem at all, sir. If you'll just come this way to the briefing, sir . . ."

THE OTHERS WERE sitting around in the briefing room, with Styrofoam cups of coffee. Norman felt glad to see them. He dropped into a chair next to Harry. "Jesus, did you have the damn physical?"

"Yeah," he said. "Had it yesterday."

"They stuck me in the leg with this long needle," Norman said.

"Really? They didn't do that to me."

"And how about breathing with that clip on your nose?"

"I didn't do that, either," Harry said. "Sounds like you got some special treatment, Norman."

Norman was thinking the same thing, and he didn't like the implications. He felt suddenly tired.

"All right, men, we've got a lot to cover and just three hours to do it," a brisk man said, turning off the lights as he came into the room. Norman hadn't even gotten a good look at him. Now it was just a voice in the dark. "As you know, Dalton's law governs partial pressures of mixed gases, or, as represented here in algebraic form . . ."

The first of the graphs flashed up.

$$PP_a = P_{tot} \times \%Vol_a$$

"Now let's review how calculation of the partial pressure might be done in atmospheres absolute, which is the most common procedure we employ—"

The words were meaningless to Norman. He tried to pay attention, but as the graphs continued and the voice droned on, his eyes grew heavier and he fell asleep.

"—be taken down in the submarine and once in the habitat module you will be pressurized to thirty-three atmospheres. At that time you will be switched over to mixed gases, since it is not possible to breathe Earth atmosphere beyond eighteen atmospheres—"

Norman stopped listening. These technical details only filled him with dread. He went back to sleep, awakening only intermittently.

"—since oxygen toxicity only occurs when the PO_2 exceeds point 7 ATA for prolonged periods—

"—nitrogen narcosis, in which nitrogen behaves like an anesthetic, will occur in mixed-gas atmospheres if partial pressures exceeds 1.5 ATA in the DDS—

"—demand open circuit is generally preferable, but you will be using semiclosed circuit with inspired fluctuations of 608 to 760 millimeters—"

He went back to sleep.

When it was over, they walked back to their rooms. "Did I miss anything?" Norman said.

"Not really." Harry shrugged. "Just a lot of physics."

In his tiny gray room, Norman got into bed. The glowing wall clock said 2300. It took him a while to figure out that that was 11:00 p.m. In nine more hours, he thought, I will begin the descent.

Then he slept.

THE
DEEP

Descent

I n the morning light, the submarine *Charon V* bobbed on the surface, riding on a pontoon platform. Bright yellow, it looked like a child's bathtub toy sitting on a deck of oildrums.

A rubber Zodiac launch took Norman over, and he climbed onto the platform, shook hands with the pilot, who could not have been more than eighteen, younger than his son, Tim.

"Ready to go, sir?" the pilot said.

"Sure," Norman said. He was as ready as he would ever be.

Up close, the sub did not look like a toy. It was incredibly massive and strong. Norman saw a single porthole of curved acrylic. It was held in place by bolts as big as his fist. He touched them, tentatively.

The pilot smiled. "Want to kick the tires, sir?"

"No, I'll trust you."

"Ladder's this way, sir."

Norman climbed the narrow rungs to the top of the sub, and saw the small circular hatch opening. He hesitated.

"Sit on the edge here," the pilot said, "and drop your legs in, then follow it down. You may have to squeeze your shoulders together a bit and suck in your . . . That's it, sir." Norman wriggled through the tight hatch into an interior so low he could not stand. The sub was crammed with dials and machinery. Ted was already aboard, hunched in the back, grinning like a kid. "Isn't this fantastic?"

Norman envied his easy enthusiasm; he felt cramped and a little nervous. Above him, the pilot clanged the heavy hatch shut and dropped down to take the controls. "Everybody okay?"

They nodded.

"Sorry about the view," the pilot said, glancing over his shoulders. "You gentlemen are mostly going to be seeing my hindquarters. Let's get started. Mozart okay?" He pressed a tape deck and smiled. "We've got thirteen minutes' descent to the bottom; music makes it a little easier. If you don't like Mozart, we can offer you something else."

"Mozart's fine," Norman said.

"Mozart's wonderful," Ted said. "Sublime."

"Very good, gentlemen." The submarine hissed. There was squawking on the radio. The pilot spoke softly into a headset. A scuba diver appeared at the porthole, waved. The pilot waved back.

There was a sloshing sound, then a deep rumble, and they started down.

"As you see, the whole sled goes under," the pilot explained. "The sub's not stable on the surface, so we sled her up and down. We'll leave the sled at about a hundred feet or so."

Through the porthole, they saw the diver standing on the deck, the water now waist-deep. Then the water covered the porthole. Bubbles came out of the diver's scuba.

"We're under," the pilot said. He adjusted valves above his head and they heard the hiss of air, startlingly loud. More gurgling. The light in the submarine from the porthole was a beautiful blue.

"Lovely," Ted said.

"We'll leave the sled now," the pilot said. Motors rumbled and the sub moved forward, the diver slipping off to one side. Now there was nothing to be seen through the porthole but undifferentiated blue water. The pilot said something on the radio, and turned up the Mozart.

"Just sit back, gentlemen," he said. "Descending eighty feet a minute."

Norman felt the rumble of the electric motors, but there was no real sense of motion. All that happened was that it got darker and darker.

"You know," Ted said, "we're really quite lucky about this site. Most parts of the Pacific are so deep we'd never be able to visit it in person." He explained that the vast Pacific Ocean, which amounted to half the total surface area of the Earth, had an average depth of two miles. "There are only a few places where it is less. One is the relatively small rectangle bounded by Samoa, New Zealand, Australia, and New Guinea, which is actually a great undersea plain, like the plains of the American West, except it's at an average depth of two thousand feet. That's what we are doing now, descending to that plain."

Ted spoke rapidly. Was he nervous? Norman couldn't tell: he was feeling his own heart pound. Now it was quite dark outside; the instruments glowed green. The pilot flicked on red interior lights.

Their descent continued. "Four hundred feet." The submarine lurched, then eased forward. "This is the river."

"What river?" Norman said.

"Sir, we are in a current of different salinity and temperature; it behaves like a river inside the ocean. We traditionally stop about here, sir; the sub sticks in the river, takes us for a little ride."

"Oh yes," Ted said, reaching into his pocket. Ted handed the pilot a ten-dollar bill.

Norman glanced questioningly at Ted.

"Didn't they mention that to you? Old tradition. You always pay the pilot on your way down, for good luck."

"I can use some luck," Norman said. He fumbled in his pocket, found a five-dollar bill, thought better of it, took out a twenty instead.

"Thank you, gentlemen, and have a good bottom stay, both of you," the pilot said.

The electric motors cut back in.

The descent continued. The water was dark.

"Five hundred feet," he said. "Halfway there."

The submarine creaked loudly, then made several explosive pops. Norman was startled.

"That's normal pressure adjustment," the pilot said. "No problem."

"Uh-huh," Norman said. He wiped sweat on his shirt-sleeve. It seemed that the interior of the submarine was now much smaller, the walls closer to his face.

"Actually," Ted said, "if I remember, this particular region of the Pacific is called the Lau Basin, isn't that right?"

"That's right, sir, the Lau Basin."

"It's a plateau between two undersea ridges, the South Fiji or Lau Ridge to the west, and the Tonga Ridge to the east."

"That's correct, Dr. Fielding."

Norman glanced at the instruments. They were covered with moisture. The pilot had to rub the dials with a cloth to read them. Was the sub leaking? No, he thought. Just condensation. The interior of the submarine was growing colder.

Take it easy, he told himself.

"Eight hundred feet," the pilot said.

It was now completely black outside.

"This is very exciting," Ted said. "Have you ever done anything like this before, Norman?"

"No," Norman said.

"Me, neither," Ted said. "What a thrill."

Norman wished he would shut up.

"You know," Ted said, "when we open this alien craft up and make our first contact with another form of life, it's going to be a great moment in the history of our species on Earth. I've been wondering about what we should say."

"Say?"

"You know, what words. At the threshold, with the cameras rolling."

"Will there be cameras?"

"Oh, I'm sure there'll be all sorts of documentation. It's

only proper, considering. So we need something to say, a memorable phrase. I was thinking of 'This is a momentous moment in human history.'"

"Momentous moment?" Norman said, frowning.

"You're right," Ted said. "Awkward, I agree. Maybe 'A turning point in human history'?"

Norman shook his head.

"How about 'A crossroads in the evolution of the human species'?"

"Can evolution have a crossroads?"

"I don't see why not," Ted said.

"Well, a crossroads is a crossing of roads. Is evolution a road? I thought it wasn't; I thought evolution was undirected."

"You're being too literal," Ted said.

"Reading the bottom," the pilot said. "Nine hundred feet." He slowed the descent. They heard the intermittent *ping* of sonar.

Ted said, " 'A new threshold in the evolution of the human species'?"

"Sure. Think it will be?"

"Will be what?"

"A new threshold."

"Why not?" Ted said.

"What if we open it up and it's just a lot of rusted junk inside, and nothing valuable or enlightening at all?"

"Good point," Ted said.

"Nine hundred fifty feet. Exterior lights are on," the pilot said.

Through the porthole they saw white flecks. The pilot explained this was suspended matter in the water.

"Visual contact. I have bottom."

"Oh, let's see!" Ted said. The pilot obligingly shifted to one side and they looked.

Norman saw a flat, dead, dull-brown plain stretching away to the limit of the lights. Blackness beyond.

"Not much to look at right here, I'm afraid," the pilot said.

"Surprisingly dreary," Ted said, without a trace of disappointment. "I would have expected more life."

"Well, it's pretty cold. Water temperature is, ah, thirty-six degrees Fahrenheit."

"Almost freezing," Ted said.

"Yes, sir. Let's see if we can find your new home."

The motors rumbled. Muddy sediment churned up in front of the porthole. The sub turned, moved across the bottom. For several minutes they saw only the brown landscape. Then lights. "There we are."

A vast underwater array of lights, arranged in a rectangular pattern.

"That's the grid," the pilot said.

The submarine planed up, and glided smoothly over the illuminated grid, which extended into the distance for half a mile. Through the porthole, they saw divers standing on the bottom, working within the grid structure. The divers waved to the passing sub. The pilot honked a toy horn.

"They can hear that?"

"Oh sure. Water's a great conductor."

"My God," Ted said.

Directly ahead the giant titanium fin rose sharply above the ocean floor. Norman was completely unprepared for its dimension; as the submarine moved to port, the fin blocked their entire field of view for nearly a minute. The metal was dull gray and, except for small white speckles of marine growth, entirely unmarked.

"There isn't any corrosion," Ted said.

"No, sir," the pilot said. "Everybody's mentioned that. They think it's because it's a metal-plastic alloy, but I don't think anybody is quite sure."

The fin slipped away to the stern; the submarine again turned. Directly ahead, more lights, arranged in vertical rows. Norman saw a single cylinder of yellow-painted steel, and bright portholes. Next to it was a low metal dome.

"That's DH-7, the divers' habitat, to port," the pilot said. "It's pretty utilitarian. You guys are in DH-8, which is much nicer, believe me."

He turned starboard, and after a momentary blackness, they saw another set of lights. Coming closer, Norman counted five different cylinders, some vertical, some horizontal, interconnected in a complex way.

"There you are. DH-8, your home away from home," the pilot said. "Give me a minute to dock."

METAL CLANGED AGAINST metal; there was a sharp jolt, and then the motors cut off. Silence. Hissing air. The pilot scrambled to open the hatch, and surprisingly cold air washed down on them.

"Airlock's open, gentlemen," he said, stepping aside.

Norman looked up through the lock. He saw banks of red lights above. He climbed up through the submarine, and into a round steel cylinder approximately eight feet in diameter.

On all sides there were handholds; a narrow metal bench; the glowing heat lamps overhead, though they didn't seem to do much good.

Ted climbed up and sat on the bench opposite him. They were so close their knees touched. Below their feet, the pilot closed the hatch. They watched the wheel spin. They heard a *clank* as the submarine disengaged, then the *whirr* of motors as it moved away.

Then nothing.

"What happens now?" Norman said.

"They pressurize us," Ted said. "Switch us over to exotic-gas atmosphere. We can't breathe air down here."

"Why not?" Norman said. Now that he was down here, staring at the cold steel walls of the cylinder, he wished he had stayed awake for the briefing.

"Because," Ted said, "the atmosphere of the Earth is deadly. You don't realize it, but oxygen is a corrosive gas. It's in the same chemical family as chlorine and fluorine, and hydrofluoric acid is the most corrosive acid known. The same quality of oxygen that makes a half-eaten apple turn brown, or makes iron rust, is incredibly destructive to the human body if exposed to too much of it. Oxygen under pressure is toxic—with a vengeance. So we cut down the amount of oxygen you breathe. You breathe twenty-one percent oxygen at the surface. Down here, you breathe two percent oxygen. But you won't notice any difference—"

A voice over a loudspeaker said, "We're starting to pressurize you now."

"Who's that?" Norman said.

"Barnes," the voice said. But it didn't sound like Barnes. It sounded gritty and artificial.

"It must be the talker," Ted said, and then laughed. His voice was noticeably higher-pitched. "It's the helium, Norman. They're pressurizing us with helium."

"You sound like Donald Duck," Norman said, and he laughed, too. His own voice sounded squeaky, like a cartoon character's.

"Speak for yourself, Mickey," Ted squeaked.

"I taut I taw a puddy tat," Norman said. They were both laughing, hearing their voices.

"Knock it off, you guys," Barnes said over the intercom. "This is serious."

"Yes, sir, Captain," Ted said, but by now his voice was so high-pitched it was almost unintelligible, and they fell into laughter again, their tinny voices like those of schoolgirls reverberating inside the steel cylinder.

Helium made their voices high and squeaky. But it also had other effects.

"Getting chilled, boys?" Barnes said.

They were indeed getting colder. He saw Ted shivering, felt goosebumps on his own legs. It felt as if a wind were blowing across their bodies—except there wasn't any wind. The lightness of the helium increased evaporation, made them cold.

Across the cylinder, Ted said something, but Norman couldn't understand Ted at all any more; his voice was too high-pitched to be comprehensible. It was just a thin squeal.

"Sounds like a couple of rats in there now," Barnes said, with satisfaction.

Ted rolled his eyes toward the loudspeaker and squeaked something.

"If you want to talk, get a talker," Barnes said. "You'll find them in the locker under the seat."

Norman found a metal locker, clicked it open. The metal squealed loudly, like chalk on a blackboard. All the sounds in the chamber were high-pitched. Inside the locker he saw two black plastic pads with neck straps.

"Just slip them over your neck. Put the pad at the base of your throat."

"Okay," Ted said, and then blinked in surprise. His voice sounded slightly rough, but otherwise normal.

"These things must change the vocal-cord frequencies," Norman said.

"Why don't you guys pay attention to briefings?" Barnes said. "That's exactly what they do. You'll have to wear a talker all the time you're down here. At least, if you want anybody to understand you. Still cold?"

"Yes," Ted said.

"Well, hang on, you're almost fully pressurized now."

Then there was another hiss, and a side door slid open. Barnes stood there, with light jackets over his arm. "Welcome to DH-8," he said.

DH-8

You're the last to arrive," Barnes said. "We just have time for a quick tour before we open the spacecraft."

"You're ready to open it now?" Ted asked. "Wonderful. I've just been talking about this with Norman. This is such a great moment, our first contact with alien life, we ought to prepare a little speech for when we open it up."

"There'll be time to consider that," Barnes said, with an odd glance at Ted. "I'll show you the habitat first. This way."

He explained that the DH-8 habitat consisted of five large cylinders, designated A to E. "Cyl A is the airlock, where we are now." He led them into an adjacent changing room. Heavy cloth suits hung limply on the wall, alongside yellow sculpted helmets of the sort Norman had seen the divers wearing. The helmets had a futuristic look. Norman tapped one with his knuckles. It was plastic, and surprisingly light.

He saw "JOHNSON" stenciled above one faceplate.

"We going to wear these?" Norman asked.

"That's correct," Barnes said.

"Then we'll be going outside?" Norman said, feeling a twinge of alarm.

"Eventually, yes. Don't worry about it now. Still cold?"

They were; Barnes had them change into tight-fitting jump-suits of clinging blue polyester. Ted frowned. "Don't you think these look a little silly?"

"They may not be the height of fashion," Barnes said, "but they prevent heat loss from helium."

"The color is unflattering," Ted said.

"Screw the color," Barnes said. He handed them light-weight jackets. Norman felt something heavy in one pocket, and pulled out a battery pack.

"The jackets are wired and electrically heated," Barnes said. "Like an electric blanket, which is what you'll use for sleeping. Follow me."

They went on to Cyl B, which housed power and life-support systems. At first glance, it looked like a large boiler room, all multicolored pipes and utilitarian fittings. "This is where we generate all of our heat, power, and air," Barnes said. He pointed out the features: "Closed-cycle IC generator, 240/110. Hydrogen-and-oxygen-driven fuel cells. LSS monitors. Liquid processor, runs on silver-zinc batteries. And that's Chief Petty Officer Fletcher. Teeny Fletcher." Norman saw a big-boned figure, working back among the pipes with a heavy wrench. The figure turned; Alice Fletcher gave them a grin, waved a greasy hand.

"She seems to know what she's doing," Ted said, approvingly.

"She does," Barnes said. "But all the major support systems are redundant. Fletcher is just our final redundancy. Actually, you'll find the entire habitat is self-regulating."

He clipped heavy badges onto the jumpsuits. "Wear these at all times, even though they're just a precaution: the alarms trigger automatically if life-support conditions go below optimum. But that won't happen. There are sensors in each room of the habitat. You'll get used to the fact that the environment continually adjusts to your presence. Lights will go on and off, heat lamps will turn on and off, and air vents will hiss to keep track of things. It's all automatic, don't sweat it. Every single major system is redundant. We can lose power, we can lose air, we can lose water entirely, and we will be fine for a hundred and thirty hours."

One hundred and thirty hours didn't sound very long to Norman. He did the calculation in his head: five days. Five days didn't seem very long, either.

They went into the next cylinder, the lights clicking on as they entered. Cylinder C contained living quarters: bunks, toilets, showers ("plenty of hot water, you'll find"). Barnes showed them around proudly, as if it were a hotel.

The living quarters were heavily insulated: carpeted deck, walls and ceilings all covered in soft padded foam, which made the interior appear like an overstuffed couch. But, despite the bright colors and the evident care in decoration, Norman still found it cramped and dreary. The portholes were tiny, and they revealed only the blackness of the ocean outside. And wherever the padding ended, he saw heavy bolts and heavy steel plating, a reminder of where they really were. He felt as if he were inside a large iron lung—and, he thought, that isn't so far wrong.

They ducked through narrow bulkheads into D Cyl: a small laboratory with benches and microscopes on the top level, a compact electronics unit on the level below.

"This is Tina Chan," Barnes said, introducing a very still woman. They all shook hands. Norman thought that Tina Chan was almost unnaturally calm, until he realized she was one of those people who almost never blinked their eyes.

"Be nice to Tina," Barnes was saying. "She's our only link to the outside—she runs the com ops, and the sensor systems as well. In fact, all the electronics."

Tina Chan was surrounded by the bulkiest monitors Norman had ever seen. They looked like TV sets from the 1950s. Barnes explained that certain equipment didn't do well in the helium atmosphere, including TV tubes. In the early days of undersea habitats, the tubes had to be replaced daily. Now they were elaborately coated and shielded; hence their bulk.

Next to Chan was another woman, Jane Edmunds, whom Barnes introduced as the unit archivist.

"What's a unit archivist?" Ted asked her.

"Petty Officer First Class, Data Processing, sir," she said formally. Jane Edmunds wore spectacles and stood stiffly. She reminded Norman of a librarian.

"Data Processing . . ." Ted said.

"My mission is to keep all the digital recordings, visual materials, and videotapes, sir. Every aspect of this historic moment is being recorded, and I keep everything neatly filed." Norman thought: She *is* a librarian.

"Oh, excellent," Ted said. "I'm glad to hear it. Film or tape?"

"Tape, sir."

"I know my way around a video camera," Ted said, with a smile. "What're you putting it down on, half-inch or three-quarter?"

"Sir, we use a datascan image equivalent of two thousand pixels per side-biased frame, each pixel carrying a twelve-tone gray scale."

"Oh," Ted said.

"It's a bit better than commercial systems you may be familiar with, sir."

"I see," Ted said. But he recovered smoothly, and chatted with Edmunds for a while about technical matters.

"Ted seems awfully interested in how we're going to record this," Barnes said, looking uneasy.

"Yes, he seems to be." Norman wondered why that troubled Barnes. Was Barnes worried about the visual record? Or did he think Ted would try to hog the show? Would Ted try to hog the show? Did Barnes have any worries about having this appear to be a civilian operation?

"No, the exterior lights are a hundred-fifty-watt quartz halogen," Edmunds was saying. "We're recording at equivalent of half a million ASA, so that's ample. The real problem is backscatter. We're constantly fighting it."

Norman said, "I notice your support team is all women."

"Yes," Barnes said. "All the deep-diving studies show that women are superior for submerged operations. They're physically smaller and consume less nutrients and air, they have better social skills and tolerate close quarters better, and they are physiologically tougher and have better endurance. The fact is, the Navy long ago recognized that all their submariners should be female." He laughed. "But just try to implement that one." He glanced at his watch. "We'd better move on. Ted?"

They went on. The final cylinder, E Cyl, was more spacious than the others. There were magazines, a television, and a large lounge; and on the deck below was an efficient mess and a kitchen. Seaman Rose Levy, the cook, was a red-faced woman with a Southern accent, standing beneath giant suction fans. She asked Norman whether he had any favorite desserts.

"Desserts?"

"Yes sir, Dr. Johnson. I like to make everybody's favorite dessert, if I can. What about you, you have a favorite, Dr. Fielding?"

"Key lime pie," Ted said. "I love key lime pie."

"Can do, sir," Levy said, with a big smile. She turned back to Norman. "I haven't heard yours yet, Dr. Johnson."

"Strawberry shortcake."

"Easy. Got some nice New Zealand strawberries coming down on the last sub shuttle. Maybe you'd like that shortcake tonight?"

"Why not, Rose," Barnes said heartily.

Norman looked out the black porthole window. From the portholes of D Cyl, he could see the rectangular illuminated grid that extended across the bottom, following the half-mile-long buried spacecraft. Divers, illuminated like fireflies, moved over the glowing grid surface.

Norman thought: I am a thousand feet beneath the surface of the ocean, and we are talking about whether we should have strawberry shortcake for dessert. But the more he thought about it, the more it made sense. The best way to make somebody comfortable in a new environment was to give him familiar food.

"Strawberries make me break out," Ted said.

"I'll make your shortcake with blueberries," Levy said, not missing a beat.

"And whipped cream?" Ted said.

"Well . . ."

"You can't have everything," Barnes said. "And one of the things you can't have at thirty atmospheres of mixed gas is whipped cream. Won't whip. Let's move on."

BETH AND HARRY were waiting in the small, padded conference room, directly above the mess. They both wore jumpsuits and heated jackets. Harry was shaking his head as they arrived. "Like our padded cell?" He poked the insulated walls. "It's like living in a vagina."

Beth said, "Don't you like going back to the womb, Harry?"

"No," Harry said. "I've been there. Once was enough."

"These jumpsuits are pretty bad," Ted said, plucking at the clinging polyester.

"Shows your belly nicely," Harry said.

"Let's settle down," Barnes said.

"A few sequins, you could be Elvis Presley," Harry said.

"Elvis Presley's dead."

"Now's your chance," Harry said.

Norman looked around. "Where's Levine?"

"Levine didn't make it," Barnes said briskly. "He got claustrophobic in the sub coming down, and had to be taken back. One of those things."

"Then we have no marine biologist?"

"We'll manage without him."

"I hate this damn jumpsuit," Ted said. "I really hate it."

"Beth looks good in hers."

"Yes, Beth works out."

"And it's damp in here, too," Ted said. "Is it always so damp?"

Norman had noticed that humidity was a problem; everything they touched felt slightly wet and clammy and cold. Barnes warned them of the danger of infections and minor colds, and handed out bottles of skin lotion and ear drops.

"I thought you said the technology was all worked out," Harry said.

"It is," Barnes said. "Believe me, this is plush compared to the habitats ten years ago."

"Ten years ago," Harry said, "they stopped making habitats because people kept dying in them."

Barnes frowned. "There was one accident."

"There were two accidents," Harry said. "A total of four people."

"Special circumstances," Barnes said. "Not involving Navy technology or personnel."

"Great," Harry said. "How long did you say we were going to be down here?"

"Maximum, seventy-two hours," Barnes said.

"You sure about that?"

"It's Navy regs," Barnes said.

"Why?" Norman asked, puzzled.

Barnes shook his head. "Never," he said, "never ask a reason for Navy regulations."

The intercom clicked, and Tina Chan said, "Captain Barnes, we have a signal from the divers. They are mounting the airlock now. Another few minutes to open."

The feeling in the room changed immediately; the excitement was palpable. Ted rubbed his hands together. "You realize, of course, that even without opening that spacecraft, we have already made a major discovery of profound importance."

"What's that?" Norman said.

"We've shot the unique event hypothesis to hell," Ted said, glancing at Beth.

"The unique event hypothesis?" Barnes said.

"He's referring," Beth said, "to the fact that physicists and chemists tend to believe in intelligent extraterrestrial life, while biologists tend not to. Many biologists feel the development of *intelligent* life on Earth required so many peculiar steps that it represents a unique event in the universe, that may never have occurred elsewhere."

"Wouldn't intelligence arise again and again?" Barnes said.

"Well, it barely arose on the Earth," Beth said. "The Earth is 4.5 billion years old, and single-celled life appeared 3.9 billion years ago—almost immediately, geologically speaking. But life *remained* single-celled for the next three billion years. Then in the Cambrian period, around six hundred million years ago, there was an explosion of sophisticated life forms. Within a hundred million years, the ocean was full of fish. Then the land became populated. Then the air. But nobody knows why the explosion occurred in the first place. And since it didn't occur for three billion years, there's the possibility that on some other planet, it might never occur at all.

"And even after the Cambrian, the chain of events leading to man appears to be so special, so chancy, that biologists worry it might never have happened. Just consider the fact that if the dinosaurs hadn't been wiped out sixty-five million years ago—by a comet or whatever—then reptiles might still be the dominant form on Earth, and mammals would never have had a chance to take over. No mammals, no primates. No primates, no apes. No apes, no man . . . There are a lot of random factors in evolution, a lot of luck. That's why biologists think intelligent life might be a unique event in the universe, only occurring here."

"Except now," Ted said, "we know it's *not* a unique event. Because there is a damn big spacecraft out there."

"Personally," Beth said, "I couldn't be more pleased." She bit her lip.

"You don't look pleased," Norman said.

"I'll tell you," Beth said. "I can't help being nervous. Ten years ago, Bill Jackson at Stanford ran a series of weekend seminars on extraterrestrial life. This was right after he won the Nobel prize in chemistry. He split us into two groups. One group designed the alien life form, and worked it all out scientifically. The other group tried to figure out the life form, and communicate with it. Jackson presided over the whole thing as a hard scientist, not letting anybody get carried away. One time we brought in a sketch of a proposed creature and he said, very tough, 'Okay, where's the anus?' That was his criticism. But many animals on Earth have no anus. There are all kinds of excretory mechanisms that don't require a special orifice. Jackson assumed an anus was necessary, but it isn't. And now . . ." She shrugged. "Who knows what we'll find?"

"We'll know, soon enough," Ted said.

The intercom clicked. "Captain Barnes, the divers have the airlock mounted in place. The robot is now ready to enter the spacecraft."

Ted said, *"What robot?"*

The Door

don't think it's appropriate *at all*," Ted said angrily. "We came down here to make a manned entry into this alien spacecraft. I think we should do what we came here to do—make a *manned* entry."

"Absolutely not," Barnes said. "We can't risk it."

"You must think of this," Ted said, "as an archaeological site. Greater than Chichén Itzá, greater than Troy, greater than Tutankhamen's tomb. Unquestionably the most important archaeological site in the history of mankind. Do you really intend to have a damned *robot* open that site? Where's your sense of human destiny?"

"Where's your sense of self-preservation?" Barnes said.

"I strongly object, Captain Barnes."

"Duly noted," Barnes said, turning away. "Now let's get on with it. Tina, give us the video feed."

Ted sputtered, but he fell silent as two large monitors in front of them clicked on. On the left screen, they saw the complex tubular metal scaffolding of the robot, with exposed motors and gears. The robot was positioned before the curved gray metal wall of the spacecraft.

Within that wall was a door that looked rather like an airliner door. The second screen gave a closer view of the door, taken by the video camera mounted on the robot itself.

"It's rather similar to an airplane door," Ted said.

Norman glanced at Harry, who smiled enigmatically. Then he looked at Barnes. Barnes did not appear surprised. Barnes already knew about the door, he realized.

"I wonder how we can account for such parallelism in door design," Ted said. "The likelihood of its occurring by chance is astronomically small. Why, this door is the perfect size and shape for a human being!"

"That's right," Harry said.

"It's incredible," Ted said. "Quite incredible."

Harry smiled, said nothing.

Barnes said, "Let's find control surfaces."

The robot video scanner moved left and right across the spacecraft hull. It stopped on the image of a rectangular panel mounted to the left of the door.

"Can you open that panel?"

"Working on it now, sir."

Whirring, the robot claw extended out toward the panel. But the claw was clumsy; it scraped against the metal, leaving a series of gleaming scratches. But the panel remained closed.

"Ridiculous," Ted said. "It's like watching a baby."

The claw continued to scratch at the panel.

"We should be doing this ourselves," Ted said.

"Use suction," Barnes said.

Another arm extended out, with a rubber sucker.

"Ah, the plumber's friend," Ted said disdainfully.

As they watched, the sucker attached to the panel, flattened. Then, with a click, the panel lifted open.

"At last!"

"I can't see. . . ."

The view inside the panel was blurred, out of focus. They could distinguish what appeared to be a series of colored round metal protrusions, red, yellow, and blue. There were also intricate black-and-white symbols above the knobs.

"Look," Ted said, "red, blue, yellow. Primary colors. This is a *very* big break."

"Why?" Norman said.

"Because it suggests that the aliens have the same sensory equipment that we do—they may see the universe the same way, visually, in the same colors, utilizing the same part of the electromagnetic spectrum. That's going to help immeasurably in making contact with them. And those black-and-white markings . . . that must be some of their writing! Can you imagine! Alien writing!" He smiled enthusiastically. "This is a great moment," he said. "I feel truly privileged to be here."

"Focus," Barnes called.

"Focusing now, sir."

The image became even more blurred.

"No, the other way."

"Yes sir. Focusing now."

The image changed, slowly resolved into sharp focus.

"Uh-oh," Ted said, staring at the screen.

They now saw that the blurred knobs were actually three colored buttons: yellow, red, and blue. The buttons were each an inch in diameter and had knurled or machined edges. The symbols above the buttons resolved sharply into a series of neatly stenciled labels.

From left to right the labels read: "Emergency Ready," "Emergency Lock," and "Emergency Open."

In English.

There was a moment of stunned silence. And then, very softly, Harry Adams began to laugh.

The Spacecraft

T hat's *English*," Ted said, staring at the screen. "Written *English*."

"Yeah," Harry said. "Sure is."

"What's going on?" Ted said. "Is this some kind of joke?"

"No," Harry said. He was calm, oddly detached.

"How could this spacecraft be three hundred years old, and carry instructions in modern English?"

"Think about it," Harry said.

Ted frowned. "Maybe," he said, "this alien spacecraft is somehow presenting itself to us in a way that will make us comfortable."

"Think about it some more," Harry said.

There was a short silence. "Well, if it *is* an alien spacecraft—"

"It's not an alien spacecraft," Harry said.

There was another silence. Then Ted said, "Well, why don't you just tell us all what it is, since you're so sure of yourself!"

"All right," Harry said. "It's an American spacecraft."

"An American spacecraft? Half a mile long? Made with technology we don't have yet? And buried for three hundred years?"

"Of course," Harry said. "It's been obvious from the start. Right, Captain Barnes?"

"We had considered it," Barnes admitted. "The President had considered it."

"That's why you didn't inform the Russians."

"Exactly."

By now Ted was completely frustrated. He clenched his fists, as if he wanted to hit someone. He looked from one person to another. "But how did you *know?*"

"The first clue," Harry said, "came from the condition of the craft itself. It shows no damage whatever. Its condition is pristine. Yet any spacecraft that crashes in water will be damaged. Even at low entry velocities—say two hundred miles an hour—the surface of water is as hard as concrete. No matter how strong this craft is, you would expect some degree of damage from the impact with the water. Yet it has no damage."

"Meaning?"

"Meaning it didn't land in the water."

"I don't understand. It must have flown here—"

"—It didn't fly here. It *arrived* here."

"From where?"

"From the future," Harry said. "This is some kind of Earth craft that was—will be—made in the future, and has traveled backward in time, and appeared under our ocean, several hundred years ago."

"Why would people in the future do that?" Ted groaned. He was clearly unhappy to be deprived of his alien craft, his great historical moment. He slumped in a chair and stared dully at the monitor screens.

"I don't know why people in the future would do that," Harry said. "We're not there yet. Maybe it was an accident. Unintended."

"Let's go ahead and open it up," Barnes said.

"Opening, sir."

The robot hand moved forward, toward the "Open" button. The hand pressed several times. There was a clanking sound, but nothing happened.

"What's wrong?" Barnes said.

"Sir, we're not able to impact the button. The extensor arm is too large to fit inside the panel."

"Great."

"Shall I try the probe?"

"Try the probe."

The claw hand moved back, and a thin needle probe extended out toward the button. The probe slid forward, adjusted position delicately, touched the button. It pushed—and slipped off.

"Trying again, sir."

The probe again pressed the button, and again slid off.

"Sir, the surface is too slippery."

"Keep trying."

"You know," Ted said thoughtfully, "this is *still* a remarkable situation. In one sense, it's even more remarkable than contact with extraterrestrials. I was already quite certain that extraterrestrial life exists in the universe. But time travel! Frankly, as an astrophysicist I had my doubts. From everything we know, it's impossible, contradicted by the laws of physics. And yet now we have proof that time travel *is* possible—and that our own species will do it in the future!"

Ted was smiling, wide-eyed, and happy again. You had to admire him, Norman thought—he was so wonderfully irrepressible.

"And here we are," Ted said, "on the threshold of our first contact with our species from the future! Think of it! We are going to meet ourselves from some future time!"

The probe pressed again, and again, without success.

"Sir, we cannot impact the button."

"I see that," Barnes said, standing up. "Okay, shut it down and get it out of there. Ted, looks like you're going to get your wish after all. We'll have to go in and open it up manually. Let's suit up."

Into The Ship

I n the changing room in Cylinder A, Norman stepped into his suit. Tina and Edmunds helped fit the helmet over his head, and snap-locked the ring at the neck. He felt the heavy weight of the rebreather tanks on his back; the straps pressed into his shoulders. He tasted metallic air. There was a crackle as his helmet intercom came on.

The first words he heard were "What about 'At the threshold of a great opportunity for the human species'?" Norman laughed, grateful for the break in the tension.

"You find it funny?" Ted asked, offended.

Norman looked across the room at the suited man with "FIELDING" stenciled on his yellow helmet.

"No," Norman said. "I'm just nervous."

"Me, too," Beth said.

"Nothing to it," Barnes said. "Trust me."

"What are the three biggest lies in DH-8?" Harry said, and they laughed again.

They crowded together into the tiny airlock, bumping helmeted heads, and the bulkhead hatch to the left was sealed, the wheel spinning. Barnes said, "Okay, folks, just breathe easy." He opened the lower hatch, exposing black water. The water did not rise into the compartment. "The habitat's on positive pressure," Barnes said. "The level won't come up. Now watch me, and do this the way I do. You don't want to tear your suit." Moving awkwardly with the weight of the tanks, he crouched down by the hatch, gripped the side handholds, and let go, disappearing with a soft splash.

One by one, they dropped down to the floor of the ocean. Norman gasped as near-freezing water enveloped his suit; immediately he heard the hum of a tiny fan as the electrical heaters in his suit activated. His feet touched soft muddy ground. He looked around in the darkness. He was standing beneath the habitat. Directly ahead, a hundred yards away, was the glowing rectangular grid. Barnes was already striding forward, leaning into the current, moving slowly like a man on the moon.

"Isn't this *fantastic?*"

"Calm down, Ted," Harry said.

Beth said, "Actually, it's odd how little life there is down here. Have you noticed? Not a sea fan, not a slug, not a sponge, not a solitary fish. Nothing but empty brown sea floor. This must be one of those dead spots in the Pacific."

A bright light came on behind him; Norman's own shadow was cast forward on the bottom. He looked back and saw Edmunds holding a camera and light in a bulky waterproof housing.

"We recording all this?"

"Yes, sir."

"Try not to fall down, Norman," Beth laughed.

"I'm trying."

They were closer now to the grid. Norman felt better seeing the other divers working there. To the right was the high fin, extending out of the coral, an enormous, smooth dark surface dwarfing them as it rose toward the surface.

Barnes led them past the fin and down into a tunnel cut in the coral. The tunnel was sixty feet long, narrow, strung with lights. They walked single file. It felt like going down into a mine, Norman thought.

"This what the divers cut?"

"That's right."

Norman saw a boxy, corrugated-steel structure surrounded by pressure tanks.

"Airlock ahead. We're almost there," Barnes said. "Everybody okay?"

"So far," Harry said.

They entered the airlock, and Barnes closed the door. Air hissed loudly. Norman watched the water recede, down past his faceplate, then his waist, his knees; then to the floor. The hissing stopped, and they passed through another door, sealing it behind them.

Norman turned to the metal hull of the spaceship. The robot had been moved aside. Norman felt very much as if he were standing alongside a big jetliner—a curved metal surface, and a flush door. The metal was a dull gray, which gave it an ominous quality. Despite himself, Norman was nervous. Listening to the way the others were breathing, he sensed they were nervous, too.

"Okay?" Barnes said. "Everybody here?"

Edmunds said, "Wait for video, please, sir."

"Okay. Waiting."

They all lined up beside the door, but they still had their helmets on. It wasn't going to be much of a picture, Norman thought.

Edmunds: "Tape is running."

Ted: "I'd like to say a few words."

Harry: "Jesus, Ted. Can't you ever let up?"

Ted: "I think it's important."

Harry: "Go ahead, make your speech."

Ted: "Hello. This is Ted Fielding, here at the door of the unknown spacecraft which has been discovered—"

Barnes: "Wait a minute, Ted. 'Here at the door of the unknown spacecraft' sounds like 'here at the tomb of the unknown soldier.'"

Ted: "You don't like it?"

Barnes: "Well, I think it has the wrong associations."

Ted: "I thought you would like it."

Beth: *"Can we just get on with it,* please?"

Ted: "Never mind."

Harry: "What, are you going to pout now?"

Ted: "Never mind. We'll do without any commentary on this historic moment."

Harry: "Okay, fine. Let's get it open."

Ted: "I think everybody knows how I feel. I feel that we should have some brief remarks for posterity."

Harry: "Well, *make* your goddamn remarks!"

Ted: "Listen, you son of a bitch, I've had about enough of your superior, know-it-all attitude—"

Barnes: "Stop tape, please."

Edmunds: "Tape is stopped, sir."

Barnes: "Let's everyone settle down."

Harry: "I consider all this ceremony utterly irrelevant."

Ted: "Well, it's not irrelevant; it's appropriate."

Barnes: "All right, I'll do it. Roll the tape."

Edmunds: "Tape is rolling."

Barnes: "This is Captain Barnes. We are now about to open the hatch cover. Present with me on this historic occasion are Ted Fielding, Norman Johnson, Beth Halpern, and Harry Adams."

Harry: "Why am I last?"

Barnes: "I did it left to right, Harry."

Harry: "Isn't it funny the only black man is named last?"

Barnes: "Harry, it's *left to right*. The way we're standing here."

Harry: "*And* after the only woman. I'm a full professor, Beth is only an assistant professor."

Beth: "Harry—"

Ted: "You know, Hal, perhaps we should be identified by our full titles and institutional affiliations—"

Harry: "—What's wrong with alphabetical order—"

Barnes: "—That's it! Forget it! No tape!"

Edmunds: "Tape is off, sir."

Barnes: "Jesus Christ."

He turned away from the group, shaking his helmeted head. He flipped up the metal plate, exposed the two buttons, and pushed one. A yellow light blinked "READY."

"Everybody stay on internal air," Barnes said.

They all continued to breathe from their tanks, in case the interior gases in the spacecraft were toxic.

"Everybody ready?"

"Ready."

Barnes pushed the button marked "OPEN."

A sign flashed: ADJUSTING ATMOSPHERE. Then, with a rumble, the door slid open sideways, just like an airplane door. For a moment Norman could see nothing but blackness beyond. They moved forward cautiously, shone their lights through the open door, saw girders, a complex of metal tubes.

"Check the air, Beth."

Beth pulled the plunger on a small gas monitor in her hand. The readout screen glowed.

"Helium, oxygen, trace CO_2 and water vapor. The right proportions. It's pressurized atmosphere."

"The ship adjusted its own atmosphere?"

"Looks like it."

"Okay. One at a time."

Barnes removed his helmet first, breathed the air. "It seems okay. Metallic, a slight tingle, but okay." He took a few deep breaths, then nodded. The others removed their helmets, set them on the deck.

"That's better."

"Shall we go?"

"Why not?"

There was a brief hesitation, and then Beth stepped through quickly: "Ladies first."

The others followed her. Norman glanced back, saw all their yellow helmets lying on the floor. Edmunds, holding the video camera to her eye, said, "Go ahead, Dr. Johnson."

Norman turned, and stepped into the spacecraft.

Interior

They stood on a catwalk five feet wide, suspended high in the air. Norman shone his flashlight down: the beam glowed through forty feet of darkness before it splashed on the lower hull. Surrounding them, dimly visible in the darkness, was a dense network of struts and girders.

Beth said, "It's like being in an oil refinery." She shone her light on one steel beam. Stenciled was "AVR-09." All the stenciling was in English.

"Most of what you see is structural," Barnes said. "Cross-stress bracing for the outer hull. Gives tremendous support along all axes. The ship is very ruggedly built, as we suspected. Designed to take extraordinary stresses. There's probably another hull further in." Norman was reminded that Barnes had once been an aeronautical engineer.

"Not only that," Harry said, shining his light on the outer hull. "Look at this—a layer of lead."

"Radiation shield?"

"Must be. It's six inches thick."

"So this ship was built to handle a lot of radiation."

"A hell of a lot," Harry said.

There was a haze in the ship, and a faintly oily feel to the air. The metal girders seemed to be coated in oil, but when Norman touched them, the oil didn't come off on his fingers. He realized that the metal itself had an unusual texture: it was slick and slightly soft to the touch, almost rubbery.

"Interesting," Ted said. "Some kind of new material. We associate strength with hardness, but this metal—if it *is* metal—is both strong and soft. Materials technology has obviously advanced since our day."

"Obviously," Harry said.

"Well, it makes sense," Ted said. "If you think of America fifty years ago as compared with today, one of the biggest changes is the great variety of plastics and ceramics we have now that were not even imagined back then. . . ." Ted continued to talk, his voice echoing in the cavernous darkness. But Norman could hear the tension in his voice. Ted's whistling in the dark, he thought.

They moved deeper into the ship. Norman felt dizzy to be so high in the gloom. They came to a branchpoint in the catwalk. It was hard to see with all the pipes and struts—like being in a forest of metal.

"Which way?"

Barnes had a wrist compass; it glowed green. "Go right."

They followed the network of catwalks for ten minutes more. Gradually Norman could see that Barnes was right:

there was a central cylinder constructed within the outer cylinder, and held away from it by a dense arrangement of girders and supports. A spacecraft within a spacecraft.

"Why would they build the ship like this?"

"You'd have to ask them."

"The reasons must have been compelling," Barnes said. "The power requirements for a double hull, with so much lead shielding . . . hard to imagine the engine you'd need to make something this big fly."

After three or four minutes, they arrived at the door on the inner hull. It looked like the outer door.

"Breathers back on?"

"I don't know. Can we risk it?"

Without waiting, Beth flipped up the panel of buttons, pressed "OPEN," and the door rumbled open. More darkness beyond. They stepped through. Norman felt softness underfoot; he shined his light down on beige carpeting.

Their flashlights crisscrossed the room, revealing a large, contoured beige console with three high-backed, padded seats. The room was clearly built for human beings.

"Must be the bridge or the cockpit."

But the curved consoles were completely blank. There was no instrumentation of any kind. And the seats were empty. They swung their beams back and forth in the darkness.

"Looks like a mockup, rather than the real thing."

"It *can't* be a mockup."

"Well, it looks like one."

Norman ran his hand over the smooth contours of the console. It was nicely molded, pleasant to feel. Norman pressed the surface, felt it bend to his touch. Rubbery again.

"Another new material."

Norman's flashlight showed a few artifacts. Taped to the far end of the console was a handmarked sign on a three-by-five filing card: It said, "GO BABY GO!" Nearby was a small plastic statuette of a cute animal that looked like a purple squirrel. The base said, "Lucky Lemontina." Whatever that meant.

"These seats leather?"

"Looks like it."

"Where are the damned controls?"

Norman continued to poke at the blank console, and suddenly the beige console surface took on depth, and appeared to contain instruments, screens. All the instrumentation was somehow *within* the surface of the console, like an optical illusion, or a hologram. Norman read the lettering above the instruments: "Pos Thrusters" . . . "F3 Piston Booster" . . . "Glider" . . . "Sieves" . . .

"More new technology," Ted said. "Reminiscent of liquid crystals, but far superior. Some kind of advanced optoelectronics."

Suddenly all the console screens glowed red, and there was a beeping sound. Startled, Norman jumped back; the control panel was coming to life.

"Watch it, everybody!"

A single bright lightning flash of intense white light filled the room, leaving a harsh afterimage.

"Oh God . . ."

Another flash—and another—and then the ceiling lights came on, evenly illuminating the room. Norman saw startled, frightened faces. He sighed, exhaling slowly.

"Jesus . . ."

"How the hell did that happen?" Barnes said.

"It was me," Beth said. "I pushed this button."

"Let's not go around pushing buttons, if you don't mind," Barnes said irritably.

"It was marked 'ROOM LIGHTS.' It seemed an appropriate thing to do."

"Let's try to stay together on this," Barnes said.

"Well, Jesus, Hal—"

"Just don't push any more buttons, Beth!"

They were moving around the cabin, looking at the instrument panel, at the chairs. All of them, that is, all except for Harry. He stood very still in the middle of the room, not moving, and said, "Anybody see a date anywhere?"

"No date."

"There's got to be a date," Harry said, suddenly tense. "And we've got to find it. Because this is definitely an American spaceship from the future."

"What's it doing here?" Norman asked.

"Damned if I know," Harry said. He shrugged.

Norman frowned.

"What's wrong, Harry?"

"Nothing."

"Sure?"

"Yeah, sure."

Norman thought: He's figured out something, and it bothers him. But he's not saying what it is.

Ted said, "So this is what a time-travel machine looks like."

"I don't know," Barnes said. "If you ask me, this instrument panel looks like it's for flying, and this room looks like a flight deck."

Norman thought so, too: everything about the room reminded him of an airplane cockpit. The three chairs for pilot, copilot, navigator. The layout of the instrumentation. This was a machine that flew, he was sure of it. Yet something was odd. . . .

He slipped into one of the contoured chairs. The soft leather-like material was almost too comfortable. He heard a gurgling: water inside?

"I hope you're not going to fly this sucker," Ted laughed.

"No, no."

"What's that whirring noise?"

The chair gripped him. Norman had an instant of panic, feeling the chair move all around his body, squeezing his shoulders, wrapping around his hips. The leather padding slid around his head, covering his ears, drawing down over his forehead. He was sinking deeper, disappearing inside the chair itself, being swallowed up by it.

"Oh God . . ."

And then the chair snapped forward, pulling up tight before the control console. And the whirring stopped.

Then nothing.

"I think," Beth said, "that the chair thinks you are going to fly it."

"Umm," Norman said, trying to control his breathing, his racing pulse, "I wonder how I get out?"

The only part of his body still free were his hands. He moved his fingers, felt a panel of buttons on the arms of the chair. He pressed one.

The chair slid back, opened like a soft clam, released him. Norman climbed out, and looked back at the imprint of his body, slowly disappearing as the chair whirred and adjusted itself.

Harry poked one of the leather pads experimentally, heard the gurgle. "Water-filled."

"Makes perfect sense," Barnes said. "Water's not compressible. You can withstand enormous G-forces sitting in a chair like this."

"And the ship itself is built to take great strains," Ted said. "Maybe time travel is strenuous? Structurally strenuous?"

"Maybe." Norman was doubtful. "But I think Barnes is right—this is a machine that flew."

"Perhaps it just looks that way," Ted said. "After all, we know how to travel in space, but we don't know how to travel in time. We know that space and time are really aspects of the same thing, space-time. Perhaps you're required to fly in time just the way you fly in space. Maybe time travel and space travel are more similar than we think now."

"Aren't we forgetting something?" Beth said. "Where is everybody? If people flew this thing in either time or space, where are they?"

"Probably somewhere else on the ship."

"I'm not so sure," Harry said. "Look at this leather on these seats. It's brand-new."

"Maybe it was a new ship."

"No, I mean really *brand-new*. This leather doesn't show any scratches, any cuts, any coffee-cup spills or stains. There is nothing to suggest that these seats have ever been sat in."

"Maybe there wasn't any crew."

"Why would you have seats if there wasn't any crew?"

"Maybe they took the crew out at the last minute. It seems they were worried about radiation. The inner hull's lead-shielded, too."

"Why should there be radiation associated with time travel?"

"I know," Ted said. "Maybe the ship got launched by accident. Maybe the ship was on the launch pad and somebody pressed the button before the crew got aboard so the ship took off empty."

"You mean, oops, wrong button?"

"That'd be a hell of a mistake," Norman said.

Barnes shook his head. "I'm not buying it. For one thing, a ship this big could never be launched from Earth. It had to be built and assembled in orbit, and launched from space."

"What do you make of this?" Beth said, pointing to another console near the rear of the flight deck. There was a fourth chair, drawn up close to the console.

The leather was wrapped around a human form.

"No kidding . . ."

"There's a man in there?"

"Let's have a look." Beth pushed the armrest buttons. The chair whirred back from the console and unwrapped itself. They saw a man, staring forward, his eyes open.

"My God, after all these years, perfectly preserved," Ted said.

"You would expect that," Harry said. "Considering he's a mannequin."

"But he's so lifelike—"

"Give our descendants some credit for advances," Harry said. "They're half a century ahead of us." He pushed the mannequin forward, exposing an umbilicus running out the back, at the base of the hips.

"Wires . . ."

"Not wires," Ted said. "Glass. Optical cables. This whole ship uses optical technology, and not electronics."

"In any case, it's one mystery solved," Harry said, looking at the dummy. "Obviously this craft was built to be a manned ship, but it was sent out unmanned."

"Why?"

"Probably the intended voyage was too dangerous. They sent an unmanned vessel first, before they sent a manned vessel."

Beth said, "And where did they send it?"

"With time travel, you don't send it to a *where*. You send it to a *when*."

"Okay. Then to *when* did they send it?"

Harry shrugged. "No information yet," he said.

That diffidence again, Norman thought. What was Harry really thinking?

"Well, this craft is half a mile long," Barnes said. "We have a lot more to see."

"I wonder if they had a flight recorder," Norman said.

"You mean like a commercial airliner?"

"Yes. Something to record the activity of the ship on its voyage."

"They must have," Harry said. "Trace the dummy cable

back, you're sure to find it. I'd like to see that recorder, too. In fact, I would say it is crucial."

Norman was looking at the console, lifting up a keyboard panel. "Look here," he said. "I found a date."

They clustered around. There was a stamp in the plastic beneath the keyboard. "Intel Inc. Made in U.S.A. Serial No.: 98004077 8/5/43."

"August 5, 2043?"

"Looks like it."

"So we're walking through a ship fifty-odd years before it's going to be built. . . ."

"This is giving me a headache."

"Look here." Beth had moved forward from the console deck, into what looked like living quarters. There were twenty bunk beds.

"Crew of twenty? If it took three people to fly it, what were the other seventeen for?"

Nobody had an answer to that.

Next, they entered a large kitchen, a toilet, living quarters. Everything was new and sleekly designed, but recognizable for what it was.

"You know, Hal, this is a lot more comfortable than DH-8."

"Yes, maybe we should move in here."

"Absolutely not," Barnes said. "We're studying this ship, not living in it. We've got a lot more work to do before we even begin to know what this is all about."

"It'd be more efficient to live here while we explore it."

"I don't want to live here," Harry said. "It gives me the creeps."

"Me too," Beth said.

They had been aboard the ship for an hour now, and Norman's feet hurt. That was another thing he hadn't anticipated: while exploring a large spacecraft from the future, your feet could begin to hurt.

But Barnes continued on.

LEAVING THE CREW quarters, they entered a vast area of narrow walkways set out between great sealed compartments that stretched ahead as far as they could see. The compartments turned out to be storage bays of immense size. They opened one bay and found it was filled with heavy plastic containers, which looked rather like the loading containers of contemporary airliners, except many times larger. They opened one container.

"No kidding," Barnes said, peering inside.

"What is it?"

"Food."

The food was wrapped in layers of lead foil and plastic, like NASA rations. Ted picked one up. "Food from the future!" he said, and smacked his lips.

"You going to eat that?" Harry said.

"Absolutely," Ted said. "You know, I once had a bottle of Dom Pérignon 1897, but this will be the first time I've ever had anything to eat from the future, from 2043."

"It's also three hundred years old," Harry said.

"Maybe you'll want to film this," Ted said to Edmunds. "Me eating."

Edmunds dutifully put the camera to her eye, flicked on the light.

"Let's not do that now," Barnes said. "We have other things to accomplish."

"This is human interest," Ted said.

"Not now," Barnes said firmly.

He opened a second storage container, and a third. They all contained food. They moved to the next storage bay and opened more containers.

"It's all food. Nothing but food."

The ship had traveled with an enormous amount of food. Even allowing for a crew of twenty, it was enough food for a voyage of several years.

They were getting very tired; it was a relief when Beth found a button, said, "I wonder what this does—"

Barnes said, "Beth—"

And the walkway began to move, rubber tread rolling forward with a slight hum.

"Beth, I want you to stop pushing every damn button you see."

But nobody else objected. It was a relief to ride the walkway past dozens of identical storage bays. Finally they came to a new section, much farther forward. Norman guessed by now they were a quarter of a mile from the crew compartment in the back. That meant they were roughly in the middle of the huge ship.

And here they found a room with life-support equipment, and twenty hanging spacesuits.

"Bingo," Ted said. "It's finally clear. This ship is intended to travel to the stars."

The others murmured, excited by the possibility. Suddenly it all made sense: the great size, the vastness of the ship, the complexity of the control consoles. . . .

"Oh, for Christ's sake," Harry said. "It *can't* have been made to travel to the stars. This is obviously a conventional spacecraft, although very large. And at conventional speeds, the nearest star is two hundred and fifty years away."

"Maybe they had new technology."

"Where is it? There's no evidence of new technology."

"Well, maybe it's—"

"Face the facts, Ted," Harry said. "Even with this huge size, the ship is only provisioned for a few years: fifteen or twenty years, at most. How far could it go in that time? Barely out of the solar system, right?"

Ted nodded glumly. "It's true. It took the Voyager spacecraft five years to reach Jupiter, nine years to reach Uranus. In fifteen years . . . Maybe they were going to Pluto."

"Why would anyone want to go to Pluto?"

"We don't know yet, but—"

The radios squawked. The voice of Tina Chan said, "Captain Barnes, surface wants you for a secure encrypted communication, sir."

"Okay," Barnes said. "It's time to go back, anyway."

They headed back, through the vast ship, to the main entrance.

Space And Time

They were sitting in the lounge of DH-8, watching the divers work on the grid. Barnes was in the next cylinder, talking to the surface. Levy was cooking lunch, or dinner—a meal, anyway. They were all getting confused about what the Navy people called "surface time."

"Surface time doesn't matter down here," Edmunds said, in her precise librarian's voice. "Day or night, it just doesn't make any difference. You get used to it."

They nodded vaguely. Everyone was tired, Norman saw. The strain, the tension of the exploration, had taken its toll. Beth had already drifted off to sleep, feet up on the coffee table, her muscular arms folded across her chest.

Outside the window, three small submarines had come down and were hovering over the grid. Several divers were clustered around; others were heading back to the divers' habitat, DH-7.

"Looks like something's up," Harry said.

"Something to do with Barnes's call?"

"Could be." Harry was still preoccupied, distracted. "Where's Tina Chan?"

"She must be with Barnes. Why?"

"I need to talk to her."

"What about?" Ted said.

"It's personal," Harry said.

Ted raised his eyebrows but said nothing more. Harry left, going into D Cyl. Norman and Ted were alone.

"He's a strange fellow," Ted said.

"Is he?"

"You know he is, Norman. Arrogant, too. Probably because he's black. Compensating, don't you think?"

"I don't know."

"I'd say he has a chip on his shoulder," Ted said. "He seems to resent everything about this expedition." He sighed. "Of course, mathematicians are all strange. He's probably got no sort of life at all, I mean a private life, women and so forth. Did I tell you I married again?"

"I read it somewhere," Norman said.

"She's a television reporter," Ted said. "Wonderful woman." He smiled. "When we got married, she gave me this Corvette. Beautiful '58 Corvette, as a wedding present. You know that nice fire-engine red color they had in the fifties? That color." Ted paced around the room, glanced over at Beth. "I just think this is all unbelievably exciting. I couldn't possibly sleep."

Norman nodded. It was interesting how different they all were, he thought. Ted, eternally optimistic, with the bubbling enthusiasm of a child. Harry, with the cold, critical demeanor, the icy mind, the unblinking eye. Beth, not so intellectual or so cerebral. At once more physical and more emotional. That was why, though they were all exhausted, only Beth could sleep.

"Say, Norman," Ted said. "I thought you said this was going to be scary."

"I thought it would be," Norman said.

"Well," Ted said. "Of all the people who could be wrong about this expedition, I'm glad it was you."

"I am, too."

"Although I can't imagine why you would select a man like Harry Adams for this team. Not that he isn't distinguished, but . . ."

Norman didn't want to talk about Harry. "Ted, remember back on the ship, when you said space and time are aspects of the same thing?"

"Space-time, yes."

"I've never really understood that."

"Why? It's quite straightforward."

"You can explain it to me?"

"Sure."

"In English?" Norman said.

"You mean, explain it without mathematics?"

"Yes."

"Well, I'll try." Ted frowned, but Norman knew he was pleased; Ted loved to lecture. He paused for a moment, then said, "Okay. Let's see where we need to begin. You're familiar with the idea that gravity is just geometry?"

"No."

"Curvature of space and time?"

"Not really, no."

"Uh. Einstein's general relativity?"

"Sorry," Norman said.

"Never mind," Ted said. There was a bowl of fruit on the table. Ted emptied the bowl, setting the fruit on the table.

"Okay. This table is space. Nice, flat space."

"Okay," Norman said.

Ted began to position the pieces of fruit. "This orange is the sun. And these are the planets, which move in circles around the sun. So we have the solar system on this table."

"Okay."

"Fine," Ted said. "Now, the sun"—he pointed to the orange in the center of the table—"is very large, so it has a lot of gravity."

"Right."

Ted gave Norman a ball bearing. "This is a spaceship. I want you to send it through the solar system, so it passes very close to the sun. Okay?"

Norman took the ball bearing and rolled it so it passed close to the orange. "Okay."

"You notice that your ball rolled straight across the flat table."

"Right."

"But in real life, what would happen to your spacecraft when it passed near the sun?"

"It would get sucked into the sun."

"Yes. We say it would 'fall into' the sun. The spacecraft would curve inward from a straight line and hit the sun. But your spacecraft didn't."

"No."

"So we know that the flat table is wrong," Ted said. "Real space can't be flat like the table."

"It can't?"

"No," Ted said.

He took the empty bowl and set the orange in the bottom. "Now roll your ball straight across past the sun."

Norman flicked the ball bearing into the bowl. The ball curved, and spiraled down the inside of the bowl until it hit the orange.

"Okay," Ted said. "The spacecraft hit the sun, just like it would in real life."

"But if I gave it enough speed," Norman said, "it'd go right past it. It'd roll down and up the far side of the bowl and out again."

"Correct," Ted said. "Also like real life. If the spacecraft has enough velocity, it will escape the gravitational field of the sun."

"Right."

"So," Ted said, "what we are showing is that a spacecraft passing the sun in real life behaves as if it were entering a curved region of space around the sun. Space around the sun is curved like this bowl."

"Okay . . ."

"And if your ball had the right speed, it wouldn't escape from the bowl, but instead would just spiral around endlessly inside the rim of the bowl. And that's what the planets are doing. They are endlessly spiraling inside the bowl created by the sun."

He put the orange back on the table. "In reality, you should imagine the table is made out of rubber and the planets are all making dents in the rubber as they sit there. That's what space is really like. Real space is curved—and the curvature changes with the amount of gravity."

"Yes . . ."

"So," Ted said, "space is curved by gravity."

"Okay."

"And that means that you can think of gravity as nothing more than the curvature of space. The Earth has gravity *because* the Earth curves the space around it."

"Okay."

"Except it's not that simple," Ted said.

Norman sighed. "I didn't think it would be."

Harry came back into the room, looked at the fruit on the table, but said nothing.

"Now," Ted said, "when you roll your ball bearing across the bowl, you notice that it not only spirals down, but it also goes faster, right?"

"Yes."

"Now, when an object goes faster, time on that object passes slower. Einstein proved that early in the century. What it means is that you can think of the curvature of space as also representing a curvature of time. The deeper the curve in the bowl, the slower time passes."

Harry said, "Well . . ."

"Layman's terms," Ted said. "Give the guy a break."

"Yeah," Norman said, "give the guy a break."

Ted held up the bowl. "Now, if you're doing all this mathematically, what you find is that the curved bowl is neither space nor time, but the combination of both, which is called space-time. This bowl is space-time, and objects moving on it are moving in space-time. We don't think about movement that way, but that's really what's happening."

"It is?"

"Sure. Take baseball."

"Idiot game," Harry said. "I hate games."

"You know baseball?" Ted said to Norman.

"Yes," Norman said.

"Okay. Imagine the batter hits a line drive to the center fielder. The ball goes almost straight out and takes, say, half a second."

"Right."

"Now imagine the batter hits a high pop fly to the same center fielder. This time the ball goes way up in the air, and it takes six seconds before the center fielder catches it."

"Okay."

"Now, the paths of the two balls—the line drive and the pop fly—look very different to us. But both these balls moved exactly the same in *space-time*."

"No," Norman said.

"Yes," Ted said. "And in a way, you already know it. Suppose I ask you to hit a high pop fly to the center fielder, but to make it reach the fielder in half a second instead of six seconds."

"That's impossible," Norman said.

"Why? Just hit the pop fly harder."

"If I hit it harder, it will go higher and end up taking longer."

"Okay, then hit a low line drive that takes six seconds to reach center field."

"I can't do that, either."

"Right," Ted said. "So what you are telling me is that you can't make the ball do anything you want. There is a fixed relationship governing the path of the ball through space and time."

"Sure. Because the Earth has gravity."

"Yes," Ted said, "and we've already agreed that gravity is a curvature of space-time, like the curve of this bowl. Any baseball on Earth must move along the same curve of space-time, as this ball bearing moves along this bowl. Look." He put the orange back in the bowl. "Here's the Earth." He put two fingers on opposite sides of the orange. "Here's batter and fielder. Now, roll the ball bearing from one finger to the other, and you'll find you have to accommodate the curve of the bowl. Either you flick the ball lightly and it will roll close to the orange, or you can give it a big flick and it will go way up the side of the bowl, before falling down again to the other side. But you can't make this ball bearing do anything you want, because the ball bearing is moving along the curved bowl. And that's what your baseball is really doing—it's moving on curved space-time."

Norman said, "I *sort of* get it. But what does this have to do with time travel?"

"Well, we think the gravitational field of the Earth is strong—it hurts us when we fall down—but in reality it's very weak. It's almost nonexistent. So space-time around the Earth isn't very curved. Space-time is much more curved around the sun. And in other parts of the universe, it's *very* curved, producing a sort of roller-coaster ride, and all sorts of distortions of time may occur. In fact, if you consider a black hole—"

He broke off.

"Yes, Ted? A black hole?"

"Oh my God," Ted said softly.

Harry pushed his glasses up on his nose and said, "Ted, for once in your life, you just might be right."

They both grabbed for paper, began scribbling.

"It couldn't be a Schwartzschild hole—"

"—No, no. Have to be rotating—"

"—Angular momentum would assure that—"

"—And you couldn't approach the singularity—"

"—No, the tidal forces—"

"—rip you apart—"

"But if you just dipped below the event horizon . . ."

"Is it possible? Did they have the nerve?"

The two fell silent, making calculations, muttering to themselves.

"What is it about a black hole?" Norman said. But they weren't listening to him any more.

The intercom clicked. Barnes said, "Attention. This is the Captain speaking. I want all hands in the conference room on the double."

"We're *in* the conference room," Norman said.

"On the double. Now."

"We're already there, Hal."

"That is all," Barnes said, and the intercom clicked off.

The Conference

I've just been on the scrambler with Admiral Spaulding of CincComPac Honolulu," Barnes said. "Apparently Spaulding just learned that I had taken civilians to saturated depths for a project about which he knew nothing. He wasn't happy about it."

There was a silence. They all looked at him.

"He demanded that all the civilians be sent up topside."

Good, Norman thought. He had been disappointed by what they had found so far. The prospect of spending another seventy-two hours in this humid, claustrophobic environment while they investigated an empty space vehicle did not appeal to him.

"I thought," Ted said, "we had direct authorization from the President."

"We do," Barnes said, "but there is the question of the storm."

"What storm?" Harry said.

"They're reporting fifteen-knot winds and southeast swells on the surface. It looks like a Pacific cyclone is headed our way and will reach us within twenty-four hours."

"There's going to be a storm here?" Beth said.

"Not *here*," Barnes said. "Down here we won't feel anything, but it'll be rough on the surface. All our surface support ships may have to pull out and steam for protected harbors in Tonga."

"So we'd be left alone down here?"

"For twenty-four to forty-eight hours, yes. That wouldn't be a problem—we're entirely self-sufficient—but Spaulding is nervous about pulling surface support when there are civilians below. I want to know your feelings. Do you want to stay down and continue exploring the ship, or leave?"

"Stay. Definitely," Ted said.

Barnes said, "Beth?"

"I came here to investigate unknown life," Beth said, "but there isn't any life on that ship. It just isn't what I thought it would be—hoped it would be. I say we go."

Barnes said, "Norman?"

"Let's admit the truth," Norman said. "We're not really trained for a saturated environment and we're not really comfortable down here. At least I'm not. And we're not the best people to evaluate this spacecraft. At this point, the Navy'd be much better off with a team of NASA engineers. I say, go."

"Harry?"

"Let's get the hell out," Harry said.

"Any particular reason?" Barnes said.

"Call it intuition."

Ted said, "I can't believe you would say that, Harry, just when we have this fabulous new idea about the ship—"

"That's beside the point now," Barnes said crisply. "I'll make the arrangements with the surface to pull us out in another twelve hours."

Ted said, "God *damn* it!"

But Norman was looking at Barnes. Barnes wasn't upset. He wants to leave, he thought. He's looking for an excuse to leave, and we're providing his excuse.

"Meantime," Barnes said, "we can make one and perhaps even two more trips to the ship. We'll rest for the next two hours, and then go back. That's all for now."

"I have more I'd like to say—"

"That's *all*, Ted. The vote's been taken. Get some rest."

As they headed toward their bunks, Barnes said, "Beth, I'd like a word with you, please."

"What about?"

"Beth, when we go back to the ship, I don't want you pushing every button you come across."

"All I did was turn on the lights, Hal."

"Yes, but you didn't know that when you—"

"—Sure I did. The button said 'ROOM LIGHTS.' It was pretty clear."

As they moved off, they heard Beth say, "I'm not one of your little Navy people you can order around, Hal—" and then Barnes said something else, and the voices faded.

"Damn it," Ted said. He kicked one of the iron walls; it rang hollowly. They passed into C Cylinder, on their way to the bunks. "I can't believe you people want to leave," Ted said. "This is *such* an exciting discovery. How can you walk away from it? Especially you, Harry. The mathematical possibilities alone! The theory of the black hole—"

"—I'll tell you why," Harry said. "I want to go because Barnes wants to go."

"Barnes doesn't want to go," Ted said. "Why, he put it to a vote—"

"—I know what he did. But Barnes doesn't want to look as if he's made the wrong decision in the eyes of his superiors, or as if he's backing down. So he let us decide. But I'm telling you, Barnes wants to go."

Norman was surprised: the cliché image of mathematicians was that they had their heads in the clouds, were absent-minded, inattentive. But Harry was astute; he didn't miss a thing.

"Why would Barnes want to go?" Ted said.

"I think it's clear," Harry said. "Because of the storm on the surface."

"The storm isn't here yet," Ted said.

"No," Harry said. "And when it comes, we don't know how long it will last."

"Barnes said twenty-four to forty-eight hours—"

"Neither Barnes nor anyone else can predict how long the storm will last," Harry said. "What if it lasts five days?"

"We can hold out that long. We have air and supplies for five days. What're you so worried about?"

"I'm not worried," Harry said. "But I think Barnes is worried."

"Nothing will go wrong, for Christ's sake," Ted said. "I think we should stay." And then there was a squishing sound. They looked down at the all-weather carpeting at their feet. The carpet was dark, soaked.

"What's that?"

"I'd say it was water," Harry said.

"*Salt* water?" Ted said, bending over, touching the damp spot. He licked his finger. "Doesn't taste salty."

From above them, a voice said, "That's because it's urine."

Looking up, they saw Teeny Fletcher standing on a platform among a network of pipes near the curved top of the cylinder. "Everything's under control, gentlemen. Just a small leak in the liquid waste disposal pipe that goes to the H_2O recycler."

"Liquid *waste?*" Ted was shaking his head.

"Just a small leak," Fletcher said. "No problem, sir." She sprayed one of the pipes with white foam from a spray canister. The foam sputtered and hardened on the pipe. "We just urethane the suckers when we get them. Makes a perfect seal."

"How often do you get these leaks?" Harry said.

"Liquid *waste?*" Ted said again.

"Hard to say, Dr. Adams. But don't worry. Really."

"I feel sick," Ted said.

Harry slapped him on the back. "Come on, it won't kill you. Let's get some sleep."

"I think I'm going to throw up."

THEY WENT INTO the sleeping chamber. Ted immediately ran off to the showers; they heard him coughing and gagging.

"Poor Ted," Harry said, shaking his head.

Norman said, "What's all this business about a black hole, anyway?"

"A black hole," Harry said, "is a dead, compressed star. Basically, a star is like a big beach ball inflated by the atomic explosions occurring inside it. When a star gets old, and runs out of nuclear fuel, the ball collapses to a much smaller size. If it collapses enough, it becomes so dense and it has so much gravity that it keeps on collapsing, squeezing down on itself until it is *very* dense and *very* small—only a few miles in diameter. Then it's a black hole. Nothing else in the universe is as dense as a black hole."

"So they're black because they're dead?"

"No. They're black because they trap all the light. Black holes have so much gravity, they pull everything into them, like vacuum cleaners—all the surrounding interstellar gas and dust, and even light itself. They just suck it right up."

"They suck up *light?*" Norman said. He found it hard to think of that.

"Yes."

"So what were you two so excited about, with your calculations?"

"Oh, it's a long story, and it's just speculation." Harry yawned. "It probably won't amount to anything, anyway. Talk about it later?"

"Sure," Norman said.

Harry rolled over, went to sleep. Ted was still in the showers, hacking and sputtering. Norman went back to D Cyl, to Tina's console.

"Did Harry find you all right?" he said. "I know he wanted to see you."

"Yes, sir. And I have the information he requested now. Why? Did you want to make out your will, too?"

Norman frowned.

"Dr. Adams said he didn't have a will and he wanted to make one. He seemed to feel it was quite urgent. Anyway, I checked with the surface and you can't do it. It's some legal problem about it being in your own handwriting; you can't transmit your will over electronic lines."

"I see."

"I'm sorry, Dr. Johnson. Should I tell the others as well?"

"No," Norman said. "Don't bother the others. We'll be going to the surface soon. Right after we have one last look at the ship."

The Large Glass

This time they split up inside the spaceship. Barnes, Ted, and Edmunds continued forward in the vast cargo bays, to search the parts of the ship that were still unexplored. Norman, Beth, and Harry stayed in what they now called the flight deck, looking for the flight recorder.

Ted's parting words were "It is a far, far better thing that I do, than I have ever done." Then he set off with Barnes.

Edmunds left them a small video monitor so they could see the progress of the other team in the forward section of the ship. And they could hear: Ted chattered continuously to Barnes, giving his views about structural features of the ship. The design of the big cargo bays reminded Ted of the stonework of the ancient Mycenaeans in Greece, particularly the Lion Gate ramp at Mycenae. . . .

"Ted has more irrelevant facts at his fingertips than any man I know," Harry said. "Can we turn the volume down?"

Yawning, Norman turned the monitor down. He was tired. The bunks in DH-8 were damp, the electric blankets heavy and clinging. Sleep had been almost impossible. And then Beth had come storming in after her talk with Barnes.

She was still angry now. "God damn Barnes," she said. "Where does he get off?"

"He's doing the best he can, like everyone else," Norman said.

She spun. "You know, Norman, sometimes you're too psychological and understanding. The man is an idiot. A complete *idiot*."

"Let's just find the flight recorder, shall we?" Harry said. "That's the important thing now." Harry was following the umbilicus cable that ran out the back of the mannequin, into the floor. He was lifting up floor panels, tracing the wires aft.

"I'm sorry," Beth said, "but he wouldn't speak like that to a man. Certainly not to Ted. Ted's hogging the whole show, and I don't see why he should be allowed to."

"What does Ted have to do with—" Norman began.

"—The man is a parasite, that's what he is. He takes the ideas of others and promotes them as his own. Even the way he quotes famous sayings—it's outrageous."

"You feel he takes other people's ideas?" Norman said.

"Listen, back on the surface, I mentioned to Ted that we ought to have some words ready when we opened this thing. And the next thing I know, Ted's making up quotes and positioning himself in front of the camera."

"Well . . ."

"Well *what*, Norman? Don't *well* me, for Christ's sake. It was my idea and he took it without so much as a thank you."

"Did you say anything to him about it?" Norman said.

"No, I did not say anything to him about it. I'm sure he wouldn't remember if I did; he'd go, 'Did you say that, Beth? I suppose you might have mentioned something like that, yes. . . .'"

"I still think you should talk to him."

"Norman, you're not listening to me."

"If you talked to him, at least you wouldn't be so angry about it now."

"Shrink talk," she said, shaking her head. "Look, Ted does whatever he wants on this expedition, he makes his stupid speeches, whatever he wants. But *I* go through the door first and Barnes gives me hell. Why shouldn't I go first? What's wrong with a woman being the first, for once in the history of science?"

"Beth—"

"—And then I had the gall to turn on the lights. You know what Barnes said about that? He said I might have started a short-circuit and put us all in jeopardy. He said I didn't know what I was doing. He said I was *impulsive*. Jesus. Impulsive. Stone-age military cretin."

"Turn the volume back up," Harry said. "I'd rather hear Ted."

"Come on, guys."

"We're all under a lot of pressure, Beth," Norman said. "It's going to affect everybody in different ways."

She glared at Norman. "You're saying Barnes was right?"

"I'm saying we're all under pressure. Including him. Including you."

"Jesus, you men always stick together. You know why I'm still an assistant professor and not tenured?"

"Your pleasant, easygoing personality?" Harry said.

"I can do without this. I really can."

"Beth," Harry said, "you see the way these cables are going? They're running toward that bulkhead there. See if they go up the wall on the other side of the door."

"You trying to get rid of me?"

"If possible."

She laughed, breaking the tension. "All right, I'll look on the other side of the door."

When she was gone, Harry said, "She's pretty worked up."

Norman said, "You know the Ben Stone story?"

"Which one?"

"Beth did her graduate work in Stone's lab."

"Oh."

Benjamin Stone was a biochemist at BU. A colorful, engaging man, Stone had a reputation as a good researcher who used his graduate students like lab assistants, taking their results as his own. In this exploitation of others' work, Stone was not unique in the academic community, but he proceeded a little more ruthlessly than his colleagues.

"Beth was living with him as well."

"Uh-huh."

"Back in the early seventies. Apparently, she did a series of important experiments on the energetics of ciliary inclusion bodies. They had a big argument, and Stone broke off his relationship with her. She left the lab, and he published five papers—all her work—without her name on them."

"Very nice," Harry said. "So now she lifts weights?"

"Well, she feels mistreated, and I can see her point."

"Yeah," Harry said. "But the thing is, lie down with dogs, get up with fleas, you know what I mean?"

"Jesus," Beth said, returning. "This is like 'The girl who's raped is always asking for it,' is that what you're saying?"

"No," Harry said, still lifting up floor panels, following the wires. "But sometimes you gotta ask what the girl is doing in a dark alley at three in the morning in a bad part of town."

"I was in love with him."

"It's still a bad part of town."

"I was twenty-two years old."

"How old do you have to be?"

"Up yours, Harry."

Harry shook his head. "You find the wires, Butch?"

"Yes, I found the wires. They go into some kind of a glass grid."

"Let's have a look," Norman said, going next door. He'd seen flight recorders before; they were long rectangular metal boxes, reminiscent of safe-deposit boxes, painted red or bright orange. If this was—

He stopped.

He was looking at a transparent glass cube one foot on each side. Inside the cube was an intricate grid arrangement of fine glowing blue lines. Between the glowing lines, blue lights flickered intermittently. There were two pressure gauges mounted on top of the cube, and three pistons; and there were a series of silver stripes and rectangles on the outer surface on the left side. It didn't look like anything he had seen before.

"Interesting." Harry peered into the cube. "Some kind of optronic memory, is my guess. We don't have anything like it." He touched the silver stripes on the outside. "Not paint, it's some plastic material. Probably machine-readable."

"By what? Certainly not us."

"No. Probably a robot recovery device of some kind."

"And the pressure gauges?"

"The cube is filled with some kind of gas, under pressure. Maybe it contains biological components, to attain that compactness. In any case, I'll bet this large glass is a memory device."

"A flight recorder?"

"Their equivalent, yes."

"How do we access it?"

"Watch this," Beth said, going back to the flight deck. She began pushing sections of the console, activating it. "Don't tell Barnes," she said over her shoulder.

"How do you know where to press?"

"I don't think it matters," she said. "I think the console can sense where you are."

"The control panel keeps track of the pilot?"

"Something like that."

In front of them, a section of the console glowed, making a screen, yellow on black.

RV-LHOOQ DCOM1   U.S.S. STAR VOYAGER

Then nothing.

Harry said, "Now we'll get the bad news."

"What bad news?" Norman said. And he wondered: Why

had Harry stayed behind to look for the flight recorder, instead of going with Ted and Barnes to explore the rest of the ship? Why was he so interested in the past history of this vessel?

"Maybe it won't be bad," Harry said.

"Why do you think it might be?"

"Because," Harry said, "if you consider it logically, something vitally important is missing from this ship—"

At that moment, the screen filled with columns:

SHIP SYSTEMS	PROPULSION SYSTEMS
LIFE SYSTEMS	WASTE MANAG (V9)
DATA SYSTEMS	STATUS OM2 (OUTER)
QUARTERMASTER	STATUS OM3 (INNER)
FLIGHT RECORDS	STATUS OM4 (FORE)
CORE OPERATIONS	STATUS DV7 (AFT)
DECK CONTROL	STATUS V (SUMMA)
INTEGRATION (DIRECT)	STATUS COMREC (2)
LSS TEST 1.0	LINE A9-11
LSS TEST 2.0	LINE A12-BX
LSS TEST 3.0	STABILIX

"What's your pleasure?" Beth said, hands on the console.

"Flight records," Harry said. He bit his lip.

```
FLIGHT DATA SUMMARIES RV-LHOOQ
FDS 01/01/43–12/31/45
FDS 01/01/46–12/31/48
FDS 01/01/49–12/31/51
FDS 01/01/52–12/31/53
FDS 01/01/54–12/31/54
FDS 01/01/55–06/31/55
FDS 07/01/55–12/31/55
FDS 01/01/56–01/31/56
FDS 02/01/56-ENTRY EVENT
FDS ENTRY EVENT
FDS ENTRY EVENT SUMMARY
8&6 !!OZ/010/Odd-000/XXX/X
F$S XXX/X% ´/XXX-X@X/X!X/X
```

"What do you make of that?" Norman said.

Harry was peering at the screen. "As you see, the earliest records are in three-year intervals. Then they're shorter, one year, then six months, and finally one month. Then this entry event business."

"So they were recording more and more carefully," Beth said. "As the ship approached the entry event, whatever it was."

"I have a pretty good idea what it was," Harry said. "I just can't believe that—let's start. How about entry event summary?"

Beth pushed buttons.

On the screen, a field of stars, and around the edges of the field, a lot of numbers. It was three-dimensional, giving the illusion of depth.

"Holographic?"

"Not exactly. But similar."

"Several large-magnitude stars there . . ."

"Or planets."

"What planets?"

"I don't know. This is one for Ted," Harry said. "He may be able to identify the image. Let's go on."

He touched the console; the screen changed.

"More stars."

"Yeah, and more numbers."

The numbers around the edges of the screen were flickering, changing rapidly. "The stars don't seem to be moving, but the numbers are changing."

"No, look. The stars are moving, too."

They could see that all the stars were moving away from the center of the screen, which was now black and empty.

"No stars in the center, and everything moving away . . ." Harry said thoughtfully.

The stars on the outside were moving very quickly, streaking outward. The black center was expanding.

"Why is it empty like that in the center, Harry?" Beth said.

"I don't think it is empty."

"I can't see anything."

"No, but it's not empty. In just a minute we should see—There!"

A dense white cluster of stars suddenly appeared in the center of the screen. The cluster expanded as they watched.

It was a strange effect, Norman thought. There was still a distinct black ring that expanded outward, with stars on the outside and on the inside. It felt as if they were flying through a giant black donut.

"My God," Harry said softly. "Do you know what you are looking at?"

"No," Beth said. "What's that cluster of stars in the center?"

"It's another universe."

"It's *what?*"

"Well, okay. It's *probably* another universe. Or it might be a different region of our own universe. Nobody really knows for sure."

"What's the black donut?" Norman said.

"It's not a donut. It's a black hole. What you are seeing is the recording made as this spacecraft went through a black hole and entered into another— Is someone calling?" Harry turned, cocked his head. They fell silent, but heard nothing.

"What do you mean, another universe—"

"—Sssssh."

A short silence. And then a faint voice crying "Hellooo . . ."

"Who's that?" Norman said, straining to listen. The voice was so soft. But it sounded human. And maybe more than one voice. It was coming from somewhere inside the spacecraft.

"Yoo-hoo! Anybody there? Hellooo."

"Oh, for God's sake," Beth said. "It's *them*, on the monitor."

She turned up the volume on the little monitor Edmunds had left behind. On the screen they saw Ted and Barnes, standing in a room somewhere and shouting. "Hellooo . . . Hel-lo-oooo."

"Can we talk back?"

"Yes. Press that button on the side."

Norman said, "We hear you."

"High damn time!" Ted.

"All right, now," Barnes said. "Listen up."

"What are you people *doing* back there?" Ted said.

"Listen up," Barnes said. He stepped to one side, revealing a piece of multicolored equipment. "We now know what this ship is for."

"So do we," Harry said.

"We do?" Beth and Norman said together.

But Barnes wasn't listening. "And the ship seems to have picked up something on its travels."

"Picked up something? What is it?"

"I don't know," Barnes said. "But it's something alien."

"Something Alien"

The moving walkway carried them past endless large cargo bays. They were going forward, to join Barnes and Ted and Edmunds. And to see their alien discovery.

"Why would anyone send a spaceship through a black hole?" Beth asked.

"Because of gravity," Harry said. "You see, black holes have so much gravity they distort space and time incredibly. You remember how Ted was saying that planets and stars make dents in the fabric of space-time? Well, black holes make *tears* in the fabric. And some people think it's possible to fly through those tears, into another universe, or another part of our universe. Or to another time."

"Another time!"

"That's the idea," Harry said.

"Are you people *coming?*" Barnes's tinny voice, on the monitor.

"In transit now," Beth said, glowering at the screen.

"He can't see you," Norman said.

"I don't care."

They rode past more cargo areas. Harry said, "I can't wait to see Ted's face when we tell him."

Finally they reached the end of the walkway. They passed through a midsection of struts and girders, and entered a large forward room which they had previously seen on the monitor. With ceilings nearly a hundred feet high, it was enormous.

You could put a six-story building in this room, Norman thought. Looking up, he saw a hazy mist or fog.

"What's that?"

"That's a cloud," Barnes said, shaking his head. "The room is so big it apparently has its own weather. Maybe it even rains in here sometimes."

The room was filled with machinery on an immense scale. At first glance, it looked like oversized earth-moving machinery, except it was brightly painted in primary colors, glistening with oil. Then Norman began to notice individual features. There were giant claw hands, enormously powerful arms, moving gear wheels. And an array of buckets and receptacles.

He realized suddenly he was looking at something very similar to the grippers and claws mounted on the front end of the *Charon V* submersible he had ridden down on the day before. Was it the day before? Or was it still the same day? Which day? Was this July 4? How long had they been down here?

"If you look carefully," Barnes was saying, "you can see that some of these devices appear to be large-scale weapons. Others, like that long extensor arm, the various attachments to pick things up, in effect make this ship a gigantic robot."

"A robot . . ."

"No kidding," Beth said.

"I guess it would have been appropriate for a robot to open it after all," Ted said thoughtfully. "Maybe even fitting."

"Snug fitting," Beth said.

"Pipe fitting," Norman said.

"Sort of robot-to-robot, you mean?" Harry said. "Sort of a meeting of the threads and treads?"

"Hey," Ted said. "I don't make fun of your comments even when they're stupid."

"I wasn't aware they ever were," Harry said.

"You say foolish things sometimes. Thoughtless."

"Children," Barnes said, "can we get back to the business at hand?"

"Point it out the next time, Ted."

"I will."

"I'll be glad to know when I say something foolish."

"No problem."

"Something *you* consider foolish."

"Tell you what," Barnes said to Norman, "when we go back to the surface, let's leave these two down here."

"Surely you can't think of going back *now*," Ted said.

"We've already voted."

"But that was before we found the *object*."

"Where is the object?" Harry said.

"Over here, Harry," Ted said, with a wicked grin. "Let's see what your fabled powers of deduction make of this."

They walked deeper into the room, moving among the giant hands and claws. And they saw, nestled in the padded claw of one hand, a large, perfectly polished silver sphere about thirty feet in diameter. The sphere had no markings or features of any kind.

They moved around the sphere, seeing themselves reflected in the polished metal. Norman noticed an odd shifting iridescence, faint rainbow hues of blue and red, gleaming in the metal.

"It looks like an oversized ball bearing," Harry said.

"Keep walking, smart guy."

On the far side, they discovered a series of deep, convoluted grooves, cut in an intricate pattern into the surface of the sphere. The pattern was arresting, though Norman could not immediately say why. The pattern wasn't geometric. And it wasn't amorphous or organic, either. It was hard to say what it was. Norman had never seen anything like it, and as he continued to look at it he felt increasingly certain this was a pattern never found on Earth. Never created by any man. Never conceived by a human imagination.

Ted and Barnes were right. He felt sure of it.

This sphere was something alien.

Priorities

H uh," Harry said, after staring in silence for a long time.

"I'm sure you'll want to get back to us on this," Ted said. "About where it came from, and so on."

"Actually, I know where it came from." And he told Ted about the star record, and the black hole.

"Actually," Ted said, "I suspected that this ship was made to travel through a black hole for some time."

"Did you? What was your first clue?"

"The heavy radiation shielding."

Harry nodded. "That's true. You probably guessed the significance of that before I did." He smiled. "But you didn't *tell* anybody."

"Hey," Ted said, "there's no question about it. I was the one who proposed the black hole first."

"You did?"

"Yes. No question at all. Remember, in the conference

room? I was explaining to Norman about space-time, and I started to do the calculations for the black hole, and then you joined in. Norman, you remember that? I proposed it first."

Norman said, "That's true, you had the idea."

Harry grinned. "I didn't feel that was a *proposal*. I thought it was more like a guess."

"Or a speculation. Harry," Ted said, "you are rewriting history. There are witnesses."

"Since you're so far ahead of everybody else," Harry said, "how about telling us your proposals for the nature of this object?"

"With pleasure," Ted said. "This object is a burnished sphere approximately ten meters in diameter, not solid, and composed of a dense metal alloy of an as-yet-unknown nature. The cabalistic markings on this side—"

"—These grooves are what you're calling cabalistic?"

"—Do you mind if I finish? The cabalistic markings on this side clearly suggest artistic or religious ornamentation, evoking a ceremonial quality. This indicates the object has significance to whoever made it."

"I think we can be sure *that's* true."

"Personally, I believe that this sphere is intended as a form of contact with us, visitors from another star, another solar system. It is, if you will, a greeting, a message, or a trophy. A proof that a higher form of life exists in the universe."

"All well and good and beside the point," Harry said. "What does it *do*?"

"I'm not sure it does anything. I think it just *is*. It is what it is."

"Very Zen."

"Well, what's your idea?"

"Let's review what we know," Harry said, "as opposed to what we *imagine* in a flight of fancy. This is a spacecraft from the future, built with all sorts of materials and technology we haven't developed yet, although we are about to develop them. This ship was sent by our descendants through a black hole and into another universe, or another part of our universe."

"Yes."

"This spacecraft is unmanned, but equipped with robot arms which are clearly designed to pick up things that it finds. So we can think of this ship as a huge version of the unmanned Mariner spacecraft that we sent in the 1970s to Mars, to look for life there. This spacecraft from the future is much bigger, and more complicated, but it's essentially the same sort of machine. It's a probe."

"Yes . . ."

"So the probe goes into another universe, where it comes upon this sphere. Presumably it finds the sphere floating in space. Or perhaps the sphere is sent out to meet the spacecraft."

"Right," Ted said. "Sent out to meet it. As an emissary. That's what I think."

"In any case, our robot spacecraft, according to whatever built-in criteria it has, decides that this sphere is interesting. It automatically grabs the sphere in its big claw hand here, draws it inside the ship, and brings it home."

"Except in going home it goes too far, it goes into the past."

"Its past," Harry said. "Our present."

"Right."

Barnes snorted impatiently. "Fine, so this spacecraft goes out and picks up a silver alien sphere and brings it back. Get to the point: what *is* this sphere?"

Harry walked forward to the sphere, pressed his ear against the metal, and rapped it with his knuckles. He touched the grooves, his hands disappearing in the deep indentations. The sphere was so highly polished Norman could see Harry's face, distorted, in the curve of the metal. "Yes. As I suspected. These cabalistic markings, as you call them, are not decorative at all. They have another purpose entirely, to conceal a small break in the surface of the sphere. Thus they represent a door." Harry stepped back.

"What *is* the sphere?"

"I'll tell you what I think," Harry said. "I think this sphere is a hollow container, I think there's something inside, and I think it scares the hell out of me."

First Evaluation

N o, Mr. Secretary," Barnes said into the phone. "We're pretty sure it is an alien artifact. There doesn't seem to be any question about that."

He glanced at Norman, sitting across the room.

"Yes, sir," Barnes said. "Very damn exciting."

They were back in the habitat, and Barnes had immediately called Washington. He was trying to delay their return to the surface.

"Not yet, we haven't opened it. Well, we haven't been *able* to open it. The door is a weird shape and it's very finely milled. . . . No, you couldn't wedge anything in the crack."

He looked at Norman, rolled his eyes.

"No, we tried that, too. There don't seem to be any exterior controls. No, no message on the outside. No, no labels either. All it is, is a highly polished sphere with some convoluted grooves on one side. What? Blast it open?"

Norman turned away. He was in D Cylinder, in the communications section run by Tina Chan. She was adjusting a dozen monitors with her usual calm. Norman said, "You seem like the most relaxed person here."

She smiled. "Just inscrutable, sir."

"Is that it?"

"It must be, sir," she said, adjusting the vertical gain on one rolling monitor. The screen showed the polished sphere. "Because I feel my heart pounding, sir. What do you think is inside that thing?"

"I haven't any idea," Norman said.

"Do you think there's an alien inside? You know, some kind of a living creature?"

"Maybe."

"And we're trying to open it up? Maybe we shouldn't let it out, whatever is in there."

"Aren't you curious?" Norman said.

"Not that curious, sir."

"I don't see how blasting would work," Barnes was saying on the phone. "Yes, we have SMTMP's, yes. Oh, different sizes. But I don't think we can blast the sucker open. No. Well, if you saw it, you'd understand. The thing is *perfectly* made. Perfect."

Tina adjusted a second monitor. They had two views of the sphere, and soon there would be a third. Edmunds was setting up cameras to watch the sphere. That had been one of Harry's suggestions. Harry had said, "Monitor it. Maybe it does something from time to time, has some activity."

On the screen, he saw the network of wires that had been attached to the sphere. They had a full array of passive sensors:

sound, and the full electromagnetic spectrum from infrared to gamma and X-rays. The readouts on the sensors were displayed on a bank of instruments to the left.

Harry came in. "Getting anything yet?"

Tina shook her head. "So far, nothing."

"Has Ted come back?"

"No," Norman said. "Ted's still there."

Ted had remained behind in the cargo bay, ostensibly to help Edmunds set up the cameras. But in fact they knew he would try to open the sphere. They saw Ted now on the second monitor, probing the grooves, touching, pushing.

Harry smiled. "He hasn't got a prayer."

Norman said, "Harry, remember when we were in the flight deck, and you said you wanted to make out your will because something was missing?"

"Oh, that," Harry said. "Forget it. That's irrelevant now."

Barnes was saying, "No, Mr. Secretary, raising it to the surface would be just about impossible—well, sir, it is presently located inside a cargo bay half a mile inside the ship, and the ship is buried under thirty feet of coral, and the sphere itself is a good thirty feet across, it's the size of a small house. . . ."

"I just wonder what's *in* the house," Tina said.

On the monitor, Ted kicked the sphere in frustration.

"Not a prayer," Harry said again. "He'll never get it open."

Beth came in. "How are we going to open it?"

Harry said, "How?" Harry stared thoughtfully at the sphere, gleaming on the monitor. There was a long silence. "Maybe we can't."

"We can't open it? You mean not ever?"

"That's one possibility."

Norman laughed. "Ted would kill himself."

Barnes was saying, "Well, Mr. Secretary, if you wanted to commit the necessary Navy resources to do a full-scale salvage from one thousand feet, we might be able to undertake it starting six months from now, when we were assured of a month of good surface weather in this region. Yes . . . it's winter in the South Pacific now. Yes."

Beth said, "I can see it now. At great expense, the Navy brings a mysterious alien sphere to the surface. It is transported to a top-secret government installation in Omaha. Experts from every branch come and try to open it. Nobody can."

"Like Excalibur," Norman said.

Beth said, "As time goes by, they try stronger and stronger methods. Eventually they try to blow it open with a small nuclear device. And still nothing. Finally, nobody has any more ideas. The sphere sits there. Decades go by. The sphere is never opened." She shook her head. "One great frustration for mankind . . ."

Norman said to Harry, "Do you really think that'd happen? That we'd never get it open?"

Harry said, "Never is a long time."

"No, sir," Barnes was saying, "given this new development, we'll stay down to the last minute. Weather topside is holding—at least six more hours, yes, sir, from the Metsat reports—well, I have to rely on that judgment. Yes, sir. Hourly; yes, sir."

He hung up, turned to the group. "Okay. We have authorization to stay down six to twelve hours more, as long as the weather holds. Let's try to open that sphere in the time remaining."

"Ted's working on it now," Harry said.

On the video monitor, they saw Ted Fielding slap the polished sphere with his hand and shout, "Open! Open Sesame! Open up, you son of a bitch!"

The sphere did not respond.

"The Anthropomorphic Problem"

Seriously," Norman said, "I think somebody has to ask the question: should we consider *not* opening it up?"

"Why?" Barnes said. "Listen, I just got off the phone—"

"—I know," Norman said. "But maybe we should think twice about this." Out of the corner of his eye, he saw Tina nodding vigorously. Harry looked skeptical. Beth rubbed her eyes, sleepy.

"Are you afraid, or do you have a substantive argument?" Barnes said.

"I have the feeling," Harry said, "that Norman's about to quote from his own work."

"Well, yes," Norman admitted. "I did put this in my report."

In his report, he had called it "the Anthropomorphic Problem." Basically, the problem was that everybody who had ever thought or written about extraterrestrial life imagined that life as essentially human. Even if the extraterrestrial life didn't look human—if it was a reptile, or a big insect, or an intelligent crystal—it still acted in a human way.

"You're talking about the movies," Barnes said.

"I'm talking about research papers, too. Every conception of extraterrestrial life, whether by a movie maker or a university professor, has been *basically* human—assuming human values, human understanding, human ways of approaching a humanly understandable universe. And generally a human appearance—two eyes, a nose, a mouth, and so on."

"So?"

"So," Norman said, "that's obviously nonsense. For one thing, there's enough variation in human behavior to make understanding just within our own species very troublesome. The differences between, say, Americans and Japanese are very great. Americans and Japanese don't really look at the world the same way at all."

"Yes, yes," Barnes said impatiently. "We all know the Japanese are different—"

"—And when you come to a new life form, the differences may be literally incomprehensible. The values and ethics of this new form of life may be utterly different."

"You mean it may not believe in the sanctity of life, or 'Thou shalt not kill,'" Barnes said, still impatient.

"No," Norman said. "I mean that this creature may not be able to be killed, and so it may have no concept of killing in the first place."

Barnes stopped. "This creature *may not be able to be killed?*"

Norman nodded. "As someone once said, you can't break the arms of a creature that has no arms."

"It can't be killed? You mean it's immortal?"

"I don't know," Norman said. "That's the point."

"I mean, Jesus, a thing that couldn't be killed," Barnes said. "How would we kill it?" He bit his lip. "I wouldn't like to open that sphere and release a thing that couldn't be killed."

Harry laughed. "No promotions for that one, Hal."

Barnes looked at the monitors, showing several views of the polished sphere. Finally he said, "No, that's ridiculous. No living thing is immortal. Am I right, Beth?"

"Actually, no," Beth said. "You could argue that certain living creatures on our own planet are immortal. For example, single-celled organisms like bacteria and yeasts are apparently capable of living indefinitely."

"Yeasts." Barnes snorted. "We're not talking about *yeasts*."

"And to all intents and purposes a virus could be considered immortal."

"A *virus?*" Barnes sat down in a chair. He hadn't considered a virus. "But how likely is it, really? Harry?"

"I think," Harry said, "that the possibilities go far beyond what we've mentioned so far. We've only considered three-dimensional creatures, of the kind that exist in our three-dimensional universe—or, to be more precise, the universe that we perceive as having three dimensions. Some people think our universe has nine or eleven dimensions."

Barnes looked tired.

"Except the other six dimensions are very small, so we don't notice them."

Barnes rubbed his eyes.

"Therefore this creature," Harry continued, "may be multidimensional, so that it literally does not exist—at least not entirely—in our usual three dimensions. To take the simplest case, if it were a four-dimensional creature, we would only see part of it at any time, because most of the creature would exist in the fourth dimension. That would obviously make it difficult to kill. And if it were a five-dimensional creature—"

"—Just a minute. Why haven't any of you mentioned this before?"

"We thought you knew," Harry said.

"Knew about five-dimensional creatures that can't be killed? Nobody said a *word* to me." He shook his head. "Opening this sphere could be incredibly dangerous."

"It could, yes."

"What we have here is, we have Pandora's box."

"That's right."

"Well," Barnes said. "Let's consider worst cases. What's the worst case for what we might find?"

Beth said, "I think that's clear. Irrespective of whether it's a multidimensional creature or a virus or whatever, irrespective of whether it shares our morals or has no morals at all, the worst case is that it hits us below the belt."

"Meaning?"

"Meaning that it behaves in a way that interferes with our basic life mechanisms. A good example is the AIDS virus. The reason why AIDS is so dangerous is not that it's new. We get new viruses every year—every week. And all viruses work in the same way: they attack cells and convert the machinery of the cells to make more viruses. What makes the AIDS virus dangerous is, it attacks the specific cells that we use to defend against viruses. AIDS interferes with our basic defense mechanism. And we have no defense against it."

"Well," Barnes said, "if this sphere contains a creature that interferes with our basic mechanisms—what would that creature be like?"

"It could breathe in air and exhale cyanide gas," Beth said.

"It could excrete radioactive waste," Harry said.

"It could disrupt our brain waves," Norman said. "Interfere with our ability to think."

"Or," Beth said, "it might merely disrupt cardiac conduction. Stop our hearts from beating."

"It might produce a sound vibration that would resonate in our skeletal system and shatter our bones," Harry said. He smiled at the others. "I rather like that one."

"Clever," Beth said. "But, as usual, we're only thinking of ourselves. The creature might do nothing directly harmful to us at all."

"Ah," Barnes said.

"It might simply exhale a toxin that kills chloroplasts, so that plants could no longer convert sunlight. Then all the plants on Earth would die—and consequently all life on Earth would die."

"Ah," Barnes said.

"You see," Norman said, "at first I thought the Anthropomorphic Problem—the fact that we can only conceive of extraterrestrial life as basically human—I thought it was a failure of imagination. Man is man, all he knows is man, and all he can think of is what he knows. Yet, as you can see, that's not true. We can think of plenty of other things. But we don't.

So there must be another reason why we only conceive of extra-terrestrials as humans. And I think the answer is that we are, in reality, terribly frail animals. And we don't like to be reminded of how frail we are—how delicate the balances are inside our own bodies, how short our stay on Earth, and how easily it is ended. So we imagine other life forms as being like us, so we don't have to think of the real threat—the terrifying threat—they may represent, without ever intending to."

There was a silence.

"Of course, we mustn't forget another possibility," Barnes said. "It may be that the sphere contains some extraordinary benefit to us. Some wondrous new knowledge, some astonishing new idea or new technology which will improve the condition of mankind beyond our wildest dreams."

"Although the chances are," Harry said, "that there won't be any new idea that is useful to us."

"Why?" Barnes said.

"Well, let's say that the aliens are a thousand years ahead of us, just as we are relative to, say, medieval Europe. Suppose you went back to medieval Europe with a television set? There wouldn't be any place to plug it in."

Barnes stared from one to another for a long time. "I'm sorry," he said. "This is too great a responsibility for me. I can't make the decision to open it up. I have to call Washington on this."

"Ted won't be happy," Harry said.

"The hell with Ted," Barnes said. "I'm going to give this to the President. Until we hear from him, I don't want anybody trying to open that sphere."

• • •

BARNES CALLED FOR a two-hour rest period, and Harry went to his quarters to sleep. Beth announced that she was going off to sleep, too, but she remained at the monitor station with Tina Chan and Norman. Chan's station had comfortable chairs with high backs, and Beth swiveled in the chair, swinging her legs back and forth. She played with her hair, making little ringlets by her ear, and she stared into space.

Tired, Norman thought. We're all tired. He watched Tina, who moved smoothly and continuously, adjusting the monitors, checking the sensor inputs, changing the video-tapes on the bank of VCR's, tense, alert. Because Edmunds was in the spaceship with Ted, Tina had to look after the re-cording units as well as her own communications console. The Navy woman didn't seem to be as tired as they were, but, then, she hadn't been inside the spaceship. To her, that space-ship was something she saw on the monitors, a TV show, an abstraction. Tina hadn't been confronted face-to-face with the reality of the new environment, the exhausting mental struggle to understand what was going on, what it all meant.

"You look tired, sir," Tina said.

"Yes. We're all tired."

"It's the atmosphere," she said. "Breathing the heliox."

So much for psychological explanations, Norman thought.

Tina said, "The density of the air down here has a real effect. We're at thirty atmospheres. If we were breathing regular air at this pressure, it would be almost as thick as a liquid. Heliox is lighter, but it's far denser than what we're used to. You don't re-alize it, but it's tiring just to breathe, to move your lungs."

"But you aren't tired."

"Oh, I'm used to it. I've been in saturated environments before."

"Is that right? Where?"

"I really can't say, Dr. Johnson."

"Navy operations?"

She smiled. "I'm not supposed to talk about it."

"Is that your inscrutable smile?"

"I hope so, sir. But don't you think you ought to try and sleep?"

He nodded. "Probably."

Norman considered going to sleep, but the prospect of his damp bunk was unappealing. Instead he went down to the galley, hoping to find one of Rose Levy's desserts. Levy was not there, but there was some coconut cake under a plastic dome. He found a plate, cut a slice, and took it over to one of the portholes. But it was black outside the porthole; the grid lights were turned off, the divers gone. He saw lights in the portholes of DH-7, the divers' habitat, located a few dozen yards away. The divers must be getting ready to go back to the surface. Or perhaps they had already gone.

In the porthole, he saw his own face reflected. The face looked tired, and old. "This is no place for a fifty-three-year-old man," he said, watching his reflection.

As he looked out, he saw some moving lights in the distance, then a flash of yellow. One of the minisubs pulled up under a cylinder at DH-7. Moments later, a second sub arrived, to dock alongside it. The lights on the first sub went out. After a short time, the second sub pulled away, into the black water. The first sub was left behind.

What's going on, he wondered, but he was aware he didn't really care. He was too tired. He was more interested in what the cake would taste like, and looked down. The cake was eaten. Only a few crumbs remained.

Tired, he thought. Very tired. He put his feet up on the coffee table and put his head back against the cool padding of the wall.

He must have fallen asleep for a while, because he awoke disoriented, in darkness. He sat up and immediately the lights came on. He saw he was still in the galley.

Barnes had warned him about that, the way the habitat adjusted to the presence of people. Apparently the motion sensors stopped registering you if you fell asleep, and automatically shut off the room lights. Then when you awoke, and moved, the lights came back. He wondered if the lights would stay on if you snored. Who had designed all this? he wondered. Had the engineers and designers working on the Navy habitat taken snoring into account? Was there a snore sensor?

More cake.

He got up and walked across to the galley kitchen. Several pieces of cake were now missing. Had he eaten them? He wasn't sure, couldn't remember.

"Lot of videotapes," Beth said. Norman turned around.

"Yes," Tina said. "We are recording everything that goes on in this habitat as well as the other ship. It'll be a lot of material."

There was a monitor mounted just above his head. It showed Beth and Tina, upstairs at the communications console. They were eating cake.

Aha, he thought. So that was where the cake had gone.

"Every twelve hours the tapes are transferred to the submarine," Tina said.

"What for?" Beth said.

"That's so, if anything happens down here, the submarine will automatically go to the surface."

"Oh, great," Beth said. "I won't think about that too much. Where is Dr. Fielding now?"

Tina said, "He gave up on the sphere, and went into the main flight deck with Edmunds."

Norman watched the monitor. Tina had stepped out of view. Beth sat with her back to the monitor, eating the cake. On the monitor behind Beth, he could clearly see the gleaming sphere. Monitors showing monitors, he thought. The Navy people who eventually review this stuff are going to go crazy.

Tina said, "Do you think they'll ever get the sphere open?"

Beth chewed her cake. "Maybe," she said. "I don't know."

And to Norman's horror, he saw on the monitor behind Beth that the door of the sphere was sliding silently open, revealing blackness inside.

Open

They must have thought he was crazy, running through the lock to D Cylinder and stumbling up the narrow stairs to the upper level, shouting, "It's open! It's open!"

He came to the communications console just as Beth was wiping the last crumbs of coconut from her lips. She set down her fork.

"What's open?"

"The sphere!"

Beth spun in her chair. Tina ran over from the bank of VCR's. They both looked at the monitor behind Beth. There was an awkward silence.

"Looks closed to me, Norman."

"It *was* open. I saw it." He told them about watching in the galley, on the monitor. "It was just a few seconds ago, and the sphere definitely opened. It must have closed again while I was on my way here."

"Are you sure?"

"That's a pretty small monitor in the galley. . . ."

"I saw it," Norman said. "Replay it, if you don't believe me."

"Good idea," Tina said, and she went to the recorders to play the tape back.

Norman was breathing heavily, trying to catch his breath. This was the first time he had exerted himself in the dense atmosphere, and he felt the effects strongly. DH-8 was not a good place to get excited, he decided.

Beth was watching him. "You okay, Norman?"

"I'm fine. I tell you, I saw it. It opened. Tina?"

"It'll take me a second here."

Harry walked in, yawning. "Beds in this place are great, aren't they?" he said. "Like sleeping in a bag of wet rice. Sort of combination bed and cold shower." He sighed. "It'll break my heart to leave."

Beth said, "Norman thinks the sphere opened."

"When?" he said, yawning again.

"Just a few seconds ago."

Harry nodded thoughtfully. "Interesting, interesting. I see it's closed now."

"We're rewinding the videotapes, to look again."

"Uh-huh. Is there any more of that cake?"

Harry seems very cool, Norman thought. This is a major piece of news and he doesn't seem excited at all. Why was that? Didn't Harry believe it, either? Was he still sleepy, not fully awake? Or was there something else?

"Here we go," Tina said.

The monitor showed jagged lines, and then resolved. On the screen, Tina was saying, "—hours the tapes are transferred to the submarine."

Beth: "What for?"

Tina: "That's so, if anything happens down here, the submarine will automatically go to the surface."

Beth: "Oh, great. I won't think about that too much. Where is Dr. Fielding now?"

Tina: "He gave up on the sphere, and went into the main flight deck with Edmunds."

On the screen, Tina stepped out of view. Beth remained alone in the chair, eating the cake, her back to the monitor.

Onscreen, Tina was saying, "Do you think they'll ever get the sphere open?"

Beth ate her cake. "Maybe," she said. "I don't know."

There was a short pause, and then on the monitor behind Beth, the door of the sphere slid open.

"Hey! It did open!"

"Keep the tape running!"

Onscreen, Beth didn't notice the monitor. Tina, still somewhere offscreen, said, "It scares me."

Beth: "I don't think there's a reason to be scared."

Tina: "It's the unknown."

"Sure," Beth said, "but an unknown thing is not likely to be dangerous or frightening. It's most likely to be just inexplicable."

"I don't know how you can say that."

"You afraid of snakes?" Beth said, onscreen.

All during this conversation, the sphere remained open.

Watching, Harry said, "Too bad we can't see inside it."

"I may be able to help that," Tina said. "I'll do some image-intensification work with the computer."

"It almost looks like there are little lights," Harry said. "Little moving lights inside the sphere . . ."

Onscreen, Tina came back into view. "Snakes don't bother me."

"Well, I can't stand snakes," Beth said. "Slimy, cold, disgusting things."

"Ah, Beth," Harry said, watching the monitor. "Got snake envy?"

Onscreen, Beth was saying, "If I were a Martian who came to Earth and I stumbled upon a snake—a funny, cold, wiggling, tube-like life—I wouldn't know what to think of it. But the chance that I would stumble on a poisonous snake is very small. Less than one percent of snakes are poisonous. So, as a Martian, I wouldn't be in danger from my discovery of snakes; I'd just be perplexed. That's what's likely to happen with us. We'll be perplexed."

Onscreen, Beth was saying, "Anyway, I don't think we'll ever get the sphere open, no."

Tina: "I hope not."

Behind her on the monitor, the sphere closed.

"Huh!" Harry said. "How long was it open all together?"

"Thirty-three point four seconds," Tina said.

They stopped the tape. Tina said, "Anybody want to see it again?" She looked pale.

"Not right now," Harry said. He drummed his fingers on the arm of his chair, stared off, thinking.

No one else said anything; they just waited patiently for

Harry. Norman realized how much the group deferred to him. Harry is the person who figures things out for us, Norman thought. We need him, rely on him.

"Okay," Harry said at last. "No conclusions are possible. We have insufficient data. The question is whether the sphere was responding to something in its immediate environment, or whether it just opened, for reasons of its own. Where's Ted?"

"Ted left the sphere and went to the flight deck."

"Ted's back," Ted said, grinning broadly. "And I have some real news."

"So do we," Beth said.

"It can wait," Ted said.

"But—"

"—*I know where this ship went*," Ted said excitedly. "I've been analyzing the flight data summaries on the flight deck, looking at the star fields, and I know where the black hole is located."

"Ted," Beth said, "the sphere opened."

"It did? When?"

"A few minutes ago. Then it closed again."

"What did the monitors show?"

"No biological hazard. It seems to be safe."

Ted looked at the screen. "Then what the hell are we doing here?"

Barnes came in. "Two-hour rest period is over. Everybody ready to go back to the ship for a last look?"

"That's putting it mildly," Harry said.

THE SPHERE WAS polished, silent, closed. They stood around it and stared at themselves, distorted in reflection. Nobody spoke. They just walked around it.

Finally Ted said, "I feel like this is an IQ test, and I'm flunking."

"You mean like the Davies Message?" Harry said.

"Oh that," Ted said.

Norman knew about the Davies Message. It was one of the episodes that the SETI promoters wished to forget. In 1979, there had been a large meeting in Rome of the scientists involved in the Search for Extraterrestrial Intelligence. Basically, SETI called for a radio astronomy search of the heavens. Now the scientists were trying to decide what sort of message to search for.

Emerson Davies, a physicist from Cambridge, England, devised a message based on fixed physical constants, such as the wavelength of emitted hydrogen, which were presumably the same throughout the universe. He arranged these constants in a binary pictorial form.

Because Davies thought this would be exactly the kind of message an alien intelligence might send, he figured it would be easy for the SETI people to figure out. He distributed his picture to everybody at the conference.

Nobody could figure it out.

When Davies explained it, they all agreed it was a clever idea, and a perfect message for extraterrestrials to send. But the fact remained that none of them had been able to figure out this perfect message.

One of the people who had tried to figure it out, and had failed, was Ted.

"Well, we didn't try very hard," Ted said. "There was a lot going on at the conference. And we didn't have you there, Harry."

"You just wanted a free trip to Rome," Harry said.

Beth said, "Is it my imagination, or have the door markings changed?"

Norman looked. At first glance, the deep grooves appeared the same, but perhaps the pattern was different. If so, the change was subtle.

"We can compare it with old videotapes," Barnes said.

"It looks the same to me," Ted said. "Anyway, it's metal. I doubt it could change."

"What we call metal is just a liquid that flows slowly at room temperature," Harry said. "It's possible that this metal is changing."

"I doubt it," Ted said.

Barnes said, "You guys are supposed to be the experts. We know this thing can open. It's been open already. How do we get it open again?"

"We're trying, Hal."

"It doesn't look like you're doing anything."

From time to time, they glanced at Harry, but Harry just stood there, looking at the sphere, his hand on his chin, tapping his lower lip thoughtfully with his finger.

"Harry?"

Harry said nothing.

Ted went up and slapped the sphere with the flat of his hand. It made a dull sound, but nothing happened. Ted pounded the sphere with his fist; then he winced and rubbed his hand.

"I don't think we can force our way in. I think it has to let you in," Norman said. Nobody said anything after that.

"My hand-picked, crack team," Barnes said, needling them. "And all they can do is stand around and stare at it."

"What do you want us to do, Hal? Nuke it?"

"If you don't get it open, there are people who will try that, eventually." He glanced at his watch. "Meanwhile, you got any other bright ideas?"

Nobody did.

"Okay," Barnes said. "Our time is up. Let's go back to the habitat and get ready to be ferried to the surface."

Departure

Norman pulled the small Navy-issue bag from beneath his bunk in C Cylinder. He got his shaving kit from the bathroom, found his notebook and his extra pair of socks, and zipped the bag shut.

"I'm ready."

"Me, too," Ted said. Ted was unhappy; he didn't want to leave. "I guess we can't delay it any longer. The weather's getting worse. They've got all the divers out from DH-7, and now there's only us."

Norman smiled at the prospect of being on the surface again. I never thought I'd look forward to seeing Navy battleship gray on a ship, but I do.

"Where're the others?" Norman said.

"Beth's already packed. I think she's with Barnes in communication. Harry, too, I guess." Ted plucked at his jumpsuit. "I'll tell you one thing, I'll be glad to see the last of this suit."

They left the sleeping quarters, heading down to communications. On the way, they squeezed past Teeny Fletcher, who was going toward B Cylinder.

"Ready to leave?" Norman said.

"Yes, sir, all squared away," Fletcher said, but her features were tense, and she seemed rushed, under pressure.

"Aren't you going the wrong way?" Norman asked.

"Just checking the diesel backups."

Backups? Norman thought. Why check the backups now that they were leaving?

"She probably left something on that she shouldn't have," Ted said, shaking his head.

In the communications console, the mood was grim. Barnes was on the phone with the surface vessels. "Say that again," he said. "I want to hear who's authorized that." He was frowning, angry.

They looked at Tina. "How's the weather on the surface?"

"Deteriorating fast, apparently."

Barnes spun: "Will you idiots *keep it down?*"

Norman dropped his day bag on the floor. Beth was sitting near the portholes, tired, rubbing her eyes. Tina was turning off the monitors, one after another, when she suddenly stopped.

"Look."

On one monitor, they saw the polished sphere.

Harry was standing next to it.

"What's he doing there?"

"Didn't he come back with us?"

"I thought he did."

"I didn't notice; I assumed he did."

"God damn it, I thought I told you people—" Barnes began, and then stopped. He stared at the monitor.

On the screen, Harry turned toward the video camera and made a short bow.

"Ladies and gentlemen, your attention, please. I think you will find this of interest."

Harry turned to face the sphere. He stood with his arms at his sides, relaxed. He did not move or speak. He closed his eyes. He took a deep breath.

The door to the sphere opened.

"Not bad, huh?" Harry said, with a sudden grin.

Then Harry stepped inside the sphere. The door closed behind him.

THEY ALL BEGAN talking at once. Barnes was shouting over everyone else, shouting for quiet, but no one paid any attention until the lights in the habitat went out. They were plunged into darkness.

Ted said, "What's happened?"

The only light came through the portholes, faintly, from the grid lights. A moment later, the grid went out, too.

"No power . . ."

"I tried to tell you," Barnes said.

There was a whirring sound, and the lights flickered, then came back on. "We have internal power; we're running on our diesels now."

"Why?"

"Look," Ted said, pointing out the porthole.

Outside they saw what looked like a wriggling silver snake. Then Norman realized it was the cable that linked them to the surface, sliding back and forth across the porthole as it coiled in great loops on the bottom.

"They've cut us free!"

"That's right," Barnes said. "They've got full gale-force conditions topside. They can no longer maintain cables for power and communications. They can no longer use the submarines. They've taken all the divers up, but the subs can't come back for us. At least not for a few days, until the seas calm down."

"Then we're stuck down here?"

"That's correct."

"For how long?"

"Several days," Barnes said.

"For how long?"

"Maybe as long as a week."

"Jesus Christ," Beth said.

Ted tossed his bag onto the couch. "What a fantastic piece of luck," he said.

Beth spun. "Are you *out of your mind?*"

"Let's all stay calm," Barnes said. "Everything's under control. This is just a temporary delay. There's no reason to get upset."

But Norman didn't feel upset. He felt suddenly exhausted. Beth was sulking, angry, feeling deceived; Ted was excited, already planning another excursion to the spacecraft, arranging equipment with Edmunds.

But Norman felt only tired. His eyes were heavy; he thought

he might go to sleep standing there in front of the monitors. He excused himself hurriedly, went back to his bunk, lay down. He didn't care that the sheets were clammy; he didn't care that the pillow was cold; he didn't care that diesels were droning and vibrating in the next cylinder. He thought: This is a very strong avoidance reaction. And then he was asleep.

Beyond Pluto

Norman rolled out of bed and looked for his watch, but he'd gotten into the habit of not wearing one down here. He had no idea what time it was, how long he had been asleep. He looked out the porthole, saw nothing but black water. The grid lights were still off. He lay back in his bunk and looked at the gray pipes directly over his head; they seemed closer than before, as if they had moved toward him while he slept. Everything seemed cramped, tighter, more claustrophobic.

Several more days of this, he thought. God.

He hoped the Navy would think to notify his family. After so many days, Ellen would start to worry. He imagined her first calling the FAA, then calling the Navy, trying to find out what had happened. Of course, no one would know anything, because the project was classified; Ellen would be frantic.

Then he stopped thinking about Ellen. It was easier, he thought, to worry about your loved ones than to worry about yourself. But there wasn't any point. Ellen would be okay. And so would he. It was just a matter of waiting. Staying calm, and waiting out the storm.

He got into the shower, wondering if they'd still have hot water while the habitat was on emergency power. They did, and he felt less stiff after his shower. It was odd, he thought, to be a thousand feet underwater and to relish the soothing effects of a hot shower.

He dressed and headed for the C Cylinder. He heard Tina's voice say, "—think they'll ever get the sphere open?"

Beth: "Maybe. I don't know."

"It scares me."

"I don't think there's a reason to be scared."

"It's the unknown," Tina said.

When Norman came in, he found Beth running the videotape, looking at herself and Tina. "Sure," Beth said on the videotape, "but an unknown thing is not likely to be dangerous or frightening. It's most likely to be just inexplicable."

Tina said, "I don't know how you can say that."

"You afraid of snakes?" Beth said, onscreen.

Beth snapped off the videotape. "Just trying to see if I could figure out why it opened," she said.

"Any luck?" Norman said.

"Not so far." On the adjacent monitor, they could see the sphere itself. The sphere was closed.

"Harry still in there?" Norman said.

"Yes," Beth said.

"How long has it been now?"

She looked up at the consoles. "A little more than an hour."

"I only slept an hour?"

"Yeah."

"I'm starving," Norman said, and he went down to the galley to eat. All the coconut cake was gone. He was looking for something else to eat when Beth showed up.

"I don't know what to do, Norman," she said, frowning.

"About what?"

"They're lying to us," she said.

"Who is?"

"Barnes. The Navy. Everybody. This is all a setup, Norman."

"Come on, Beth. No conspiracies, now. We have enough to worry about without—"

"—Just look at this," she said. She led him back upstairs, flicked on a console, pressed buttons.

"I started putting it together when Barnes was on the phone," she said. "Barnes was talking to somebody right up to the moment when the cable started to coil down. Except that cable is a thousand feet long, Norman. They would have broken communications several minutes before unhooking the cable itself."

"Probably, yes . . ."

"So who was Barnes talking to at the last minute? Nobody."

"Beth . . ."

"Look," she said, pointing to the screen.

COM SUMMARY DH—SURCOM/1

0910 BARNES TO SURCOM/1:

CIVILIAN AND USN PERSONNEL POLLED. ALTHOUGH ADVISED OF RISKS, ALL PERSONNEL ELECT TO REMAIN DOWN FOR DURATION OF STORM TO CONTINUE INVESTIGATION OF ALIEN SPHERE AND ASSOCIATED SPACECRAFT.

BARNES, USN.

"You're kidding," Norman said. "I thought Barnes wanted to leave."

"He did, but he changed his mind when he saw that last room, and he didn't bother to tell us. I'd like to kill the bastard," Beth said. "You know what this is about, Norman, don't you?"

Norman nodded. "He hopes to find a new weapon."

"Right. Barnes is a Pentagon-acquisition man, and he wants to find a new weapon."

"But the sphere is unlikely—"

"It's not the sphere," Beth said. "Barnes doesn't really care about the sphere. He cares about the 'associated spacecraft.' Because, according to congruity theory, it's the spacecraft that is likely to pay off. Not the sphere."

Congruity theory was a troublesome matter for the people who thought about extraterrestrial life. In a simple way, the astronomers and physicists who considered the possibility of contact with extraterrestrial life imagined wonderful benefits to mankind from such a contact. But other thinkers, philosophers and historians, did not foresee any benefits to contact at all.

For example, astronomers believed that if we made contact with extraterrestrials, mankind would be so shocked that wars on Earth would cease, and a new era of peaceful cooperation between nations would begin.

But historians thought that was nonsense. They pointed out that when Europeans discovered the New World—a similarly world-shattering discovery—the Europeans did not stop their incessant fighting. On the contrary: they fought even harder. Europeans simply made the New World an extension of pre-existing animosities. It became another place to fight, and to fight over.

Similarly, astronomers imagined that when mankind met extraterrestrials, there would be an exchange of information and technology, giving mankind a wonderful advancement.

Historians of science thought that was nonsense, too. They pointed out that what we called "science" actually consisted of a rather arbitrary conception of the universe, not likely to be shared by other creatures. Our ideas of science were the ideas of visually oriented, monkey-like creatures who enjoyed changing their physical environment. If the aliens were blind and communicated by odors, they might have evolved a very different science, which described a very different universe. And they might have made very different choices about the directions their science would explore. For example, they might ignore the physical world entirely, and instead develop a highly sophisticated science of mind—in other words, the exact opposite of what Earth science had done. The alien technology might be purely mental, with no visible hardware at all.

This issue was at the heart of congruity theory, which said that unless the aliens were remarkably similar to us, no exchange of information was likely. Barnes of course knew that theory, so he knew he wasn't likely to derive any useful technology from the alien sphere. But he was very likely to get useful technology from the spaceship itself, since the spaceship had been made by men, and congruity was high.

And he had lied to keep them down. To keep the search going.

"What should we do with the bastard?" Beth said.

"Nothing, for the moment," Norman said.

"You don't want to confront him? Jesus, I do."

"It won't serve any purpose," Norman said. "Ted won't

care, and the Navy people are all following orders. And anyway, even if it had been arranged for us to depart as planned, would you have gone, leaving Harry behind in the sphere?"

"No," Beth admitted.

"Well, then. It's all academic."

"Jesus, Norman . . ."

"I know. But we're here now. And for the next couple of days, there's not a damn thing we can do about it. Let's deal with that reality as best we can, and point the finger later."

"You bet I'm going to point the finger!"

"That's fine. But not now, Beth."

"Okay," she sighed. "Not now."

She went back upstairs.

ALONE, NORMAN STARED at the console. He had his work cut out for him, keeping everybody calm for the next few days. He hadn't looked into the computer system before; he started pressing buttons. Pretty soon he found a file marked **ULF CONTACT TEAM BIOG.** He opened it up.

CIVILIAN TEAM MEMBERS
1. Theodore Fielding, astrophysicist/planetary geologist
2. Elizabeth Halpern, zoologist/biochemist
3. Harold J. Adams, mathematician/logician
4. Arthur Levine, marine biologist/biochemist
5. John F. Thompson, psychologist

Choose one:

Norman stared in disbelief at the list.

He knew Jack Thompson, an energetic young psychologist from Yale. Thompson was world-renowned for his studies of the psychology of primitive peoples, and in fact for the past year had been somewhere in New Guinea, studying native tribes.

Norman pressed more buttons.

ULF TEAM PSYCHOLOGIST: CHOICES BY RANK
1. John F. Thompson, Yale—approved
2. William L. Hartz, UCB—approved
3. Jeremy White, UT—approved (pending clearance)
4. Norman Johnson, SDU—rejected (age)

He knew them all. Bill Hartz at Berkeley was seriously ill with cancer. Jeremy White had gone to Hanoi during the Vietnam War, and would never get clearance.

That left Norman.

He understood now why he had been the last to be called in. He understood now about the special tests. He felt a burst of intense anger at Barnes, at the whole system which had brought him down here, despite his age, with no concern for his safety. At fifty-three, Norman Johnson had no business being a thousand feet underwater in a pressurized exotic gas environment—and the Navy knew it.

It was an outrage, he thought. He wanted to go upstairs and give Barnes hell in no uncertain terms. That lying son of a bitch—

He gripped the arms of his chair and reminded himself of what he had told Beth. Whatever had happened up to this point, there was nothing any of them could do about it now. He would indeed give Barnes hell—he promised himself he would—but only when they got back to the surface. Until then, it was no use making trouble.

He shook his head and swore.

Then he turned the console off.

THE HOURS CREPT by. Harry was still in the sphere.

Tina ran her image intensification of the videotape that showed the sphere open, trying to see interior detail. "Unfortunately, we have only limited computing power in the habitat," she said. "If I could hard-link to the surface I could really do a job, but as it is . . ." She shrugged.

She showed them a series of enlarged freeze-frames from the open sphere. The images clicked through at one-second intervals. The quality was poor, with jagged, intermittent static.

"The only internal structures we can see in the blackness," Tina said, pointing to the opening, "are these multiple point-sources of light. The lights appear to move from frame to frame."

"It's as if the sphere is filled with fireflies," Beth said.

"Except these lights are much dimmer than fireflies, and they don't blink. They are very numerous. And they give the impression of moving together, in surging patterns. . . ."

"A flock of fireflies?"

"Something like that." The tape ran out. The screen went dark.

Ted said, "That's it?"

"I'm afraid so, Dr. Fielding."

"Poor Harry," Ted said mournfully.

Of all the group, Ted was the most visibly upset about Harry. He kept staring at the closed sphere on the monitor, saying, "How did he do that?" Then he would add, "I hope he's all right."

He repeated it so often that finally Beth said, "I think we know your feelings, Ted."

"I'm seriously concerned about him."

"I am, too. We all are."

"You think I'm jealous, Beth? Is that what you're saying?"

"Why would anyone think that, Ted?"

Norman changed the subject. It was crucial to avoid confrontations among group members. He asked Ted about his analysis of the flight data aboard the spaceship.

"It's very interesting," Ted said, warming to his subject. "My detailed examination of the earliest flight-data images," he said, "convinced me that they show three planets—Uranus, Neptune, and Pluto—and the sun, very small in the background. Therefore, the pictures are taken from some point beyond the orbit of Pluto. This suggests that the black hole is not far beyond our own solar system."

"Is that possible?" Norman said.

"Oh sure. In fact, for the last ten years some astrophysicists have suspected that there's a black hole—not a large one, but a black hole—just outside our solar system."

"I hadn't heard that."

"Oh yes. In fact, some of us have argued that, if it was small enough, in a few years we could go out and capture the black hole, bring it back, park it in Earth orbit, and use the energy it generates to power the entire planet."

Barnes smiled. "Black-hole cowboys?"

"In theory, there's no reason it couldn't be done. Then just think: the entire planet would be free of its dependency on fossil fuels. . . . The whole history of mankind would be changed."

Barnes said, "Probably make a hell of a weapon, too."

"Even a very tiny black hole would be a little too powerful to use as a weapon."

"So you think this ship went out to capture a black hole?"

"I doubt it," Ted said. "The ship is so strongly made, so shielded against radiation, that I suspect it was intended to *go through* a black hole. And it did."

"And that's why the ship went back in time?" Norman said.

"I'm not sure," Ted said. "You see, a black hole really is the edge of the universe. What happens there isn't clear to anybody now alive. But what some people think is that you don't go through the hole, you sort of skip into it, like a pebble skipping over water, and you get bounced into a different time or space or universe."

"So the ship got bounced?"

"Yes. Possibly more than once. And when it bounced back here, it undershot and arrived a few hundred years before it left."

"And on one of its bounces, it picked up that?" Beth said, pointing to the monitor.

They looked. The sphere was still closed. But lying next to it, sprawled on the deck in an awkward pose, was Harry Adams.

For a moment they thought he was dead. Then Harry lifted his head and moaned.

The Subject

Norman wrote in his notebook: *Subject is a thirty-year-old black mathematician who has spent three hours inside a sphere of unknown origin. On recovery from the sphere was stuporous and unresponsive; he did not know his name, where he was, or what year it was. Brought back to habitat; slept for one half-hour then awoke abruptly complaining of headache.*

"Oh God."

Harry was sitting in his bunk, holding his head in his hands, groaning.

"Hurt?" Norman asked.

"Brutal. Pounding."

"Anything else?"

"Thirsty. God." He licked his lips. "Really thirsty."

Extreme thirst, Norman wrote.

Rose Levy, the cook, showed up with a glass of lemonade. Norman handed the glass to Harry, who drank it in a single gulp, passed back.

"More."

"Better bring a pitcher," Norman said. Levy went off. Norman turned to Harry, still holding his head, still groaning, and said, "I have a question for you."

"What?"

"What's your name?"

"Norman, I don't need to be psychoanalyzed right now."

"Just tell me your name."

"Harry Adams, for Christ's sake. What's the matter with you? Oh, my *head*."

"You didn't remember before," Norman said. "When we found you."

"When you found me?" he asked. He seemed confused again.

Norman nodded. "Do you remember when we found you?"

"It must have been . . . outside."

"Outside?"

Harry looked up, suddenly furious, eyes glowing with rage. *"Outside the sphere, you goddamn idiot! What do you think I'm talking about?"*

"Take it easy, Harry."

"Your questions are driving me crazy!"

"Okay, okay. Take it easy."

Emotionally labile. Rage and irritability. Norman made more notes.

"Do you have to make so much *noise*?"

Norman looked up, puzzled.

"Your pen," Harry said. "It sounds like Niagara Falls."

Norman stopped writing. It must be a migraine, or something like migraine. Harry was holding his head in his hands delicately, as if it were made of glass.

"Why can't I have any aspirin, for Christ's sake?"

"We don't want to give you anything for a while, in case you've hurt yourself. We need to know where the pain is."

"The *pain*, Norman, is *in my head*. It's in my goddamn head! Now, why won't you give me any aspirin?"

"Barnes said not to."

"Is Barnes still here?"

"We're all still here."

Harry looked up slowly. "But you were supposed to go to the surface."

"I know."

"Why didn't you go?"

"The weather went bad, and they couldn't send the subs."

"Well, you should go. You shouldn't be here, Norman."

Levy arrived with more lemonade. Harry looked at her as he drank.

"You're still here, too?"

"Yes, Dr. Adams."

"How many people are down here, all together?"

Levy said, "There are nine of us, sir."

"Jesus." He passed the glass back. Levy refilled it. "You should all go. You should leave."

"Harry," Norman said. "We can't go."

"You *have to* go."

Norman sat on the bunk opposite Harry and watched as Harry drank. Harry was demonstrating a rather typical man-

ifestation of shock: the agitation, the irritability, the nervous,
manic flow of ideas, the unexplained fears for the safety of
others—it was all characteristic of shocked victims of severe
accidents, such as major auto crashes or airplane crashes.
Given an intense event, the brain struggled to assimilate, to
make sense, to reassemble the mental world even as the physical world was shattered around it. The brain went into a kind
of overdrive, hastily trying to reassemble things, to get things
right, to re-establish equilibrium. Yet it was fundamentally a
confused period of wheel-spinning.

You just had to wait it out.

Harry finished the lemonade, handed the glass back.

"More?" Levy asked.

"No, that's good. Headache's better."

Perhaps it was dehydration after all, Norman thought. But
why would Harry be dehydrated after three hours in the
sphere?

"Harry . . ."

"Tell me something. Do I look different, Norman?"

"No."

"I look the same to you?"

"Yes. I'd say so."

"Are you sure?" Harry said. He jumped up, went to a mirror mounted on the wall. He peered at his face.

"How do you think you look?" Norman said.

"I don't know. Different."

"Different how?"

"*I don't know!*" . . . He pounded the padded wall next to the
mirror. The mirror image vibrated. He turned away, sat down
on the bunk again. He sighed. "Just different."

"Harry . . ."

"What?"

"Do you remember what happened?"

"Of course."

"What happened?"

"I went inside."

He waited, but Harry said nothing further. He just stared at the carpeted floor.

"Do you remember opening the door?"

Harry said nothing.

"How did you open the door, Harry?"

Harry looked up at Norman. "You were all supposed to leave. To go back to the surface. You weren't supposed to stay."

"How did you open the door, Harry?"

There was a long silence. "I opened it." He sat up straight, his hands at his sides. He seemed to be remembering, reliving it.

"And then?"

"I went inside."

"And what happened inside?"

"It was beautiful. . . ."

"What was beautiful?"

"The foam," Harry said. And then he fell silent again, staring vacantly into space.

"The foam?" Norman prompted.

"The sea. The foam. Beautiful . . ."

Was he talking about the lights? Norman wondered. The swirling pattern of lights?

"What was beautiful, Harry?"

"Now, don't kid me," Harry said. "Promise you won't kid me."

"I won't kid you."

"You think I look the same?"

"Yes, I do."

"You don't think I've changed at all?"

"No. Not that I can see. Do *you* think you've changed?"

"I don't know. Maybe. I—maybe."

"Did something happen in the sphere to change you?"

"You don't understand about the sphere."

"Then explain it to me," Norman said.

"Nothing happened in the sphere."

"You were in the sphere for three hours. . . ."

"Nothing happened. Nothing ever happens inside the sphere. It's always the same, inside the sphere."

"What's always the same? The foam?"

"The foam is always different. The sphere is always the same."

"I don't understand," Norman said.

"I know you don't," Harry said. He shook his head. "What can I do?"

"Tell me some more."

"There isn't any more."

"Then tell me again."

"It won't help," Harry said. "Do you think you'll be leaving soon?"

"Barnes says not for several days."

"I think you should leave soon. Talk to the others. Convince them. Make them leave."

"Why, Harry?"

"I can't be—I don't know."

Harry rubbed his eyes and lay back on the bed. "You'll have to excuse me," he said, "but I'm very tired. Maybe we can continue this some other time. Talk to the others, Norman. Get them to leave. It's . . . dangerous to stay here."

And he lay down in the bunk and closed his eyes.

Changes

He's sleeping," Norman told them. "He's in shock. He's confused. But he seems basically intact."

"What did he tell you," Ted said, "about what happened in there?"

"He's quite confused," Norman said, "but he's recovering. When we first found him, he didn't even remember his name. Now he does. He remembers my name, he remembers where he is. He remembers he went into the sphere. I think he remembers what happened inside the sphere, too. He just isn't telling."

"Great," Ted said.

"He mentioned the sea, and the foam. But I wasn't clear what he meant by that."

"Look outside," Tina said, pointing to the portholes.

Norman had an immediate impression of lights—thousands of lights filling the blackness of the ocean—and his first response was unreasoning terror: the lights in the sphere were coming out to get them. But then he saw each of the lights had a shape, and were moving, wriggling.

They pressed their faces to the portholes, looked.

"Squid," Beth said finally. "Bioluminescent squid."

"Thousands of them."

"More," she said. "I'd guess at least half a million, all around the habitat."

"Beautiful."

"The size of the school is amazing," Ted said.

"Impressive, but not really unusual," Beth said. "The fecundity of the sea is very great compared with the land. The sea is where life began, and where intense competition among animals first appeared. One response to competition is to produce enormous numbers of offspring. Many sea animals do that. In fact, we tend to think that animals came out onto the land as a positive step forward in the evolution of life. But the truth is, the first creatures were really driven out of the ocean. They were just trying to get away from the competition. And you can imagine when the first fish-amphibians climbed up the beach and poked their heads up to look out at the land, and saw this vast dry-land environment without any competition at all. It must have looked like the promised—"

Beth broke off, turned to Barnes. "Quick: where do you keep specimen nets?"

"I don't want you going out there."

"I have to," Beth said. "Those squid have six tentacles."

"So?"

"There's no known species of six-tentacled squid. This is an undescribed species. I must collect samples."

Barnes told her where the equipment locker was, and she went off. Norman looked at the school of squid with renewed interest.

The animals were each about a foot long, and seemed to be transparent. The large eyes of the squid were clearly visible in the bodies, which glowed a pale blue.

In a few minutes Beth appeared outside, standing in the midst of the school, swinging her net, catching specimens. Several squid angrily squirted clouds of ink.

"Cute little things," Ted said. "You know, the development of squid ink is a very interesting—"

"—What do you say to squid for dinner?" Levy said.

"Hell no," Barnes said. "If this is an undiscovered species, we're not going to eat it. The last thing I need is everybody sick from food poisoning."

"Very sensible," Ted said. "I never liked squid, anyway. Interesting mechanism of propulsion, but rubbery texture."

At that moment, there was a buzz as one of the monitors turned itself on. As they watched, the screen rapidly filled with numbers:

```
00032125252632032629301321042610371830160 61
80821322903300518220426101308301621371 60 40
8301621182203301313043200032125252632 0326
293013210426103718301606180821322903300518
22042610130830162371160408301621182203 3013
13043200032125252632032629321042610371 83016
0618082132290330051822042610130830162137
160408301621182203301313043200032125252 63
203262930132104261037183016061808213229033
0051822042610130830162137160408301621182 20
330131304320003212525263203262930132104 2610
37183016061808213229033005182204261011308
3016213716040830162118220330131304320003212
52526320326293013210426103718301606180 8213
2290330051822042610130830162137160408301 62
```

"Where's that coming from?" Ted said. "The surface?"

Barnes shook his head. "We've cut direct contact with the surface."

"Then is it being transmitted underwater in some way?"

"No," Tina said, "it's too fast for underwater transmission."

"Is there another console in the habitat? No? How about DH-7?"

"DH-7's empty now. The divers have gone."

"Then where'd it come from?"

Barnes said, "It looks random to me."

Tina nodded. "It may be a discharge from a temporary buffer memory somewhere in the system. When we switched over to internal diesel power . . ."

"That's probably it," Barnes said. "Buffer discharge on switchover."

"I think you should keep it," Ted said, staring at the screen. "Just in case it's a message."

"A message from where?"

"From the sphere."

"Hell," Barnes said, "it can't be a message."

"How do you know?"

"Because there's no way a message can be transmitted. We're not hooked up to anything. Certainly not to the sphere. It's got to be a memory dump from somewhere inside our own computer system."

"How much memory have you got?"

"Fair amount. Ten giga, something like that."

"Maybe the helium's getting to the chips," Tina said. "Maybe it's a saturation effect."

"I still think you should keep it," Ted said.

Norman had been looking at the screen. He was no mathematician, but he'd looked at a lot of statistics in his life, searching for patterns in the data. That was something human brains were inherently good at, finding patterns in visual material. Norman couldn't put his finger on it, but he sensed a pattern here. He said, "I have the feeling it's not random."

"Then let's keep it," Barnes said.

Tina went forward to the console. As her hands touched the keys, the screen went blank.

"So much for that," Barnes said. "It's gone. Too bad we didn't have Harry to look at it with us."

"Yeah," Ted said gloomily. "Too bad."

Analysis

T ake a look at this," Beth said. "This one is still alive."

Norman was with her in the little biological laboratory near the top of D Cylinder. Nobody had been in this laboratory since their arrival, because they hadn't found anything living. Now, with the lights out, he and Beth watched the squid move in the glass tank.

The creature had a delicate appearance. The blue glow was concentrated in stripes along the back and sides of the creature.

"Yes," Beth said, "the bioluminescent structures seem to be located dorsally. They're bacteria, of course."

"What are?"

"The bioluminescent areas. Squid can't create light themselves. The creatures that do are bacteria. So the bioluminescent animals in the sea have incorporated these bacteria into their bodies. You're seeing bacteria glowing through the skin."

"So it's like an infection?"

"Yes, in a way."

The large eyes of the squid stared. The tentacles moved.

"And you can see all the internal organs," Beth said. "The brain is hidden behind the eye. That sac is the digestive gland, and behind it, the stomach, and below that—see it beating?—the heart. That big thing at the front is the gonad, and coming down from the stomach, a sort of funnel—that's where it squirts the ink, and propels itself."

"Is it really a new species?" Norman said.

She sighed. "I don't know. Internally it is so typical. But fewer tentacles would qualify it as a new species, all right."

"You going to get to call it *Squidus bethus?*" Norman said.

She smiled. "*Architeuthis bethis,*" she said. "Sounds like a dental problem. *Architeuthis bethis:* means you need root canal."

"How about it, Dr. Halpern?" Levy said, poking her head in. "Got some good tomatoes and peppers, be a shame to waste them. Are the squid really poisonous?"

"I doubt it," Beth said. "Squid aren't known to be. Go ahead," she said to Levy. "I think it'll be okay to eat them."

When Levy had gone, Norman said, "I thought you gave up eating these things."

"Just octopi," Beth said. "An octopus is cute and smart. Squid are rather . . . unsympathetic."

"Unsympathetic."

"Well, they're cannibalistic, and rather nasty. . . ." She raised an eyebrow. "Are you psychoanalyzing me again?"

"No. Just curious."

"As a zoologist, you're supposed to be objective," Beth said, "but I have feelings about animals, like anybody else. I have a warm feeling about octopi. They're clever, you know. I once had an octopus in a research tank that learned to kill cockroaches and use them as bait to catch crabs. The curious crab would come along, investigate the dead cockroach, and then the octopus would jump out of its hiding place and catch the crab.

"In fact, an octopus is so smart that the biggest limitation to its behavior is its lifespan. An octopus lives only three years, and that's not long enough to develop anything as complicated as a culture or civilization. Maybe if octopi lived as long as we do, they would long ago have taken over the world.

"But squid are completely different. I have no feelings about squid. Except I don't really like 'em."

He smiled. "Well," he said, "at least you finally found some life down here."

"You know, it's funny," she said. "Remember how barren it was out there? Nothing on the bottom?"

"Sure. Very striking."

"Well, I went around the side of the habitat, to get these squid. And there're all sorts of sea fans on the bottom. Beautiful colors, blues and purples and yellows. Some of them quite large."

"Think they just grew?"

"No. They must have always been in that spot, but we never went over there. I'll have to investigate it later. I'd like to know why they are localized in that particular place, next to the habitat."

Norman went to the porthole. He had switched on the exterior habitat lights, shining onto the bottom. He could indeed see many large sea fans, purple and pink and blue, waving gently in the current. They extended out to the edge of the light, to the darkness.

"In a way," Beth said, "it's reassuring. We're deep for the majority of oceanic life, which is found in the first hundred feet of water. But even so, this habitat is located in the most varied and abundant marine environment in the world." Scientists had made species counts and had determined that the South Pacific had more species of coral and sponges than anywhere else on Earth.

"So I'm glad we're finally finding things," she said. She looked at her benches of chemicals and reagents. "And I'm glad to finally get to work on something."

HARRY WAS EATING bacon and eggs in the galley. The others stood around and watched him, relieved that he was all right. And they told him the news; he listened with interest, until they mentioned that there had been a large school of squid.

"*Squid?*"

He looked up sharply and almost dropped his fork.

"Yeah, lots of 'em," Levy said. "I'm cooking up a bunch for dinner."

"Are they still here?" Harry asked.

"No, they're gone now."

He relaxed, shoulders dropping.

"Something the matter, Harry?" Norman said.

"I hate squid," Harry said. "I can't stand them."

"I don't care for the taste myself," Ted said.

"Terrible," Harry said, nodding. He resumed eating his eggs. The tension passed.

Then Tina shouted from D Cylinder: "I'm getting them again! I'm getting the numbers again!"

```
3013130432 00032125252632 032629 301321 04261037 1
8 3016 0618082132 29033005 1822 04261013 0830162137
1604 08301621 1822 033013130432 00032125252632 032
629 301321 04261037 18 3016 0618082132 29033005 1822
04261013 0830162137 1604 08301621 1822 033013130432
0003212525252632 032629 301321 04261037 18 3016 06
18082132 29033005 1822 04261013 0830162137 1604 083
01621 1822 033013130432 0003212525632 032629 301321
```

"What do you think, Harry?" Barnes said, pointing to the screen.

"Is this what you got before?" Harry said.

"Looks like it, except the spacing is different."

"Because this is definitely nonrandom," Harry said. "It's a single sequence repeated over and over. Look. Starts here, goes to here, then repeats."

```
00032125252632 032629 301321 04261037 18 3016 06180
82132 29033005 1822 04261013 0830162137 1604 083016
21 1822 033013130432 00032125252632 032629 301321 0
4261037 18 3016 0618082132 29033005 1822 04261013 08
30162137 1604 08301621 1822 033013130432 000321252
52632 032629 301321 04261037 18 3016 0618082132 290
33005 1822 04261013 0830162137 1604 08301621 1822 03
3013130432 00032125252632 032629 301321 04261037 1
8 3016 0618082132 29033005 1822 04261013 0830162137
1604 08301621 1822 033013130432 00032125252632 032
629 301321 04261037 18 3016 0618082132 29033005 1822
04261013 0830162137 1604 08301621 1822 033013130432
0003212525252632 032629 301321 04261037 18 3016 06
18082132 29033005 1822 04261013 0830162137 1604 083
01621 1822 033013130432 0003212525632 032629 301321
```

"He's right," Tina said.

"Fantastic," Barnes said. "Absolutely incredible, for you to see it like that."

Ted drummed his fingers on the console impatiently.

"Elementary, my dear Barnes," Harry said. "That part is easy. The hard part is—what does it mean?"

"Surely it's a message," Ted said.

"Possibly it's a message," Harry said. "It could also be some kind of discharge from within the computer, the result of a programming error or a hardware glitch. We might spend hours translating it, only to find it says 'Copyright Acme Computer Systems, Silicon Valley' or something similar."

"Well . . ." Ted said.

"The greatest likelihood is that this series of numbers originates from within the computer itself," Harry said. "But let me give it a try."

Tina printed out the screen for him.

"I'd like to try, too," Ted said quickly.

Tina said, "Certainly, Dr. Fielding," and printed out a second sheet.

"If it's a message," Harry said, "it's most likely a simple substitution code, like an askey code. It would help if we could run a decoding program on the computer. Can anybody program this thing?"

They all shook their heads. "Can you?" Barnes said.

"No. And I suppose there's no way to transmit this to the surface? The NSA code-breaking computers in Washington would take about fifteen seconds to do this."

Barnes shook his head. "No contact. I wouldn't even put up a radio wire on a balloon. The last report, they have forty-foot waves on the surface. Snap the wire right away."

"So we're isolated?"

"We're isolated."

"I guess it's back to the old pencil and paper. I always say, traditional tools are best—particularly when there's nothing else." And left the room.

"He seems to be in a good mood," Barnes said.

"I'd say a very good mood," Norman said.

"Maybe a little too good," Ted said. "A little manic?"

"No," Norman said. "Just a good mood."

"I thought he was a little high," Ted said.

"Let him stay that way," Barnes snorted, "if it helps him to crack this code."

"I'm going to try, too," Ted reminded him.

"That's fine," Barnes said. "You try, too."

Ted

'm telling you, this reliance on Harry is misplaced." Ted paced back and forth and glanced at Norman. "Harry is manic, and he's overlooking things. Obvious things."

"Like what?"

"Like the fact that the printout can't possibly be a discharge from the computer."

"How do you know?" Norman said.

"The processor," Ted said. "The processor is a 68090 chip, which means that any memory dump would be *in hex.*"

"What's hex?"

"There are lots of ways to represent numbers," Ted said. "The 68090 chip uses base-sixteen representation, called 'hexadecimal.' Hex is entirely different from regular decimal. Looks different."

"But the message used zero through nine," Norman said.

"Exactly my point," Ted said. "So it didn't come from the computer. I believe it's definitely a message from the sphere. Furthermore, although Harry thinks it is a substitution code, I think it's a direct visual representation."

"You mean a picture?"

"Yes," Ted said. "And I think it's a picture of the creature itself!" He started searching through sheets of paper. "I started with this."

```
00111010111001110011101010000    111101011101
  11110110110101    100110101010100101
100101111010000    1101001010001010110000
111011111110101    1001010110    1001101010101101
    1000111101000010101100101    10000100
1000111101000010101    1001010110
111111011011101100100000
00111010111001110011101010000    111101011101
1111011011010    1001101010101010101    10010
1111010000    1101001010001010110000
11101111110101    1001010110    1001101010101101
    1000111101000010101100101    10000100
1000111101011101100100000
111111011011101100100000
00111010111001110011101010000    111101011101
  11110110110101    100110101010100101    10010
  1111010000    1101001010001010110000
111011111110101    1001010110    1001101010101101
    1000111101000010101100101    10000100
```

"Now, here I have translated the message to binary," Ted said. "You can immediately sense visual pattern, can't you?"

"Not really," Norman said.

"Well, it is certainly suggestive," Ted said. "I'm telling you, all those years at JPL looking at images from the planets, I have an eye for these things. So, the next thing I did was go back to the original message and fill in the spaces. I got this."

```
• •00032125252632• •032629• •301321• •04261037• •18•
•3016• •0618082132• •29033005• •1822• •04261013•
•0830162137• •1604• •08301621• •1822• •033013130432•
•00032125252632• •032629• •301321• •04261037• •18•
•3016• •0618082132• •29033005• •1822• •04261013•
•0830162137• •1604• •08301621• •1822• •033013130432•
•00032125252632• •032629• •301321• •04261037• •18•
•3016• •0618082132• •29033005• •1822• •04261013•
•0830162137• •1604• •08301621• •1822• •033013130432•
•00032125252632• •032629• •301321• •04261037• •18•
•3016• •0618082132• •29033005• •1822• •04261013•
•0830162137• •1604• •08301621• •1822• •033013130432•
•00032125252632• •032629• •301321• •04261037• •18•
•3016• •0618082132• •29033005• •1822• •04261013•
•0830162137• •1604• •08301621• •1822• •033013130432•
```

```
•00032125252632• •032629• •301321• •04261037• •18•
•3016• •0618082132• •29033005• •1822• •04261013•
•0830162137• •1604• •08301521• •1822• •033013130432•
•00032125252632• •032629• •301321• •04261037• •18•
•3016• •0618082132• •29033005• •1822• •04261013•
•0830162137• •1604• •08301621• •1822• •033013130432•
•00032125252632• •032629• •301321• •04261037• •18•
•3016• •0618082132• •29033005• •1822• •04261013•
•0830162137• •1604• •08301621• •1822• •033013130432•
•00032125252632• •032629• •301321• •04261037• •18• •
```

"Uh-huh . . ." Norman said.

"I agree, it doesn't look like anything," Ted said. "But by changing the screen width, you get *this*."

Proudly, he held up the next sheet.

```
•  •00032125252632•  •032629•  •301321•
•04261037•  •18•  •3016•  •0618082132•  •29033005•
•1822•  •04261013•  •0830162137•  •1604•
•08301621•  •1822•  •033013130432•
•00032125252632•  •032629•  •301321•  •04261037•
•18•  •3016•  •0618082132•  •29033005•  •1822•
•04261013•  •0830162137•  •1604•  •08301621•
•1822•  •033013130432•  •00032125252632•
•032629•  •301321•  •04261037•  •18•  •3016•
•0618082132•  •29033005•  •1822•  •04261013•
•0830162137•  •1604•  •08301621•  •1822•
•033013130432•  •00032125252632•  •032629•
•301321•  •04261037•  •18•  •3016•  •0618082132•
•29033005•  •1822•  •04261013•  •0830162137•
•1604•  •08301621•  •1822•  •033013130432•
•00032125252632•  •032629•  •301321•  •04261037•
•18•  •3016•  •0618082132•  •29033005•  •1822•
•04261013•  •0830162137•  •1604•  •08301621•
•1822•  •033013130432•  •00032125252632•
•032629•  •301321•  •04261037•  •18•  •3016•
```

"Yes?" Norman said.

"Don't tell me you don't see the pattern," Ted said.

"I don't see the pattern," Norman said.

"Squint at it," Ted said.

Norman squinted. "Sorry."

"But it is *obviously* a picture of the creature," Ted said. "Look, that's the vertical torso, three legs, two arms. There's no head, so presumably the creature's head is located within the torso itself. Surely you see that, Norman."

"Ted . . ."

"For once, Harry has missed the point entirely! The message is not only a picture, it's a self-portrait!"

"Ted . . ."

Ted sat back. He sighed. "You're going to tell me I'm trying too hard."

"I don't want to dampen your enthusiasm," Norman said.

"But you don't see the alien?"

"Not really, no."

"Hell." Ted tossed the papers aside. "I hate that son of a bitch. He's so arrogant, he makes me so mad. . . . And on top of that, he's young!"

"You're forty," Norman said. "I wouldn't exactly call that over the hill."

"For physics, it is," Ted said. "Biologists can sometimes do important work late in life. Darwin was fifty when he published the *Origin of Species*. And chemists sometimes do good work when they're older. But in physics, if you haven't done it by thirty-five, the chances are, you never will."

"But Ted, you're respected in your field."

Ted shook his head. "I've never done fundamental work. I've analyzed data, I've come to some interesting conclusions. But never anything fundamental. This expedition is my chance to really *do* something. To really . . . get my name in the books."

Norman now had a different sense of Ted's enthusiasm and energy, that relentlessly juvenile manner. Ted wasn't emotionally retarded; he was driven. And he clung to his youth out of a sense that time was slipping by and he hadn't yet accomplished any-thing. It wasn't obnoxious. It was sad.

"Well," Norman said, "the expedition isn't finished yet."

"No," Ted said, suddenly brightening. "You're right. You're absolutely right. There are more, wonderful experiences await-ing us. I just *know* there are. And they'll come, won't they."

"Yes, Ted," Norman said. "They'll come."

Beth

Damn it, nothing works!" She waved a hand to her laboratory bench. "Not a single one of the chemicals or reagents here is worth a damn!"

"What've you tried?" Barnes said calmly.

"Zenker-Formalin, H and E, the other stains. Proteolytic extractions, enzyme breaks. You name it. None of it works. You know what I think, I think that whoever stocked this lab did it with outdated ingredients."

"No," Barnes said, "it's the atmosphere."

He explained that their environment contained only 2 percent oxygen, 1 percent carbon dioxide, but no nitrogen at all. "Chemical reactions are unpredictable," he said. "You ought to take a look at Levy's recipe book sometime. It's like nothing you've ever seen in your life. The food looks normal when she's finished, but she sure doesn't make it the normal way."

"And the lab?"

"The lab was stocked without knowing the working depth we would be at. If we were shallower, we'd be breathing compressed air, and all your chemical reactions would work—they'd just go very fast. But with heliox, reactions are unpredictable. And if they won't go, well . . ." He shrugged.

"What am I supposed to do?" she said.

"The best you can," Barnes said. "Same as the rest of us."

"Well, all I can really do is gross anatomical analyses. All this bench is worthless."

"Then do the gross anatomy."

"I just wish we had more lab capability. . . ."

"This is it," Barnes said. "Accept it and go on."

Ted entered the room. "You better take a look outside, everybody," he said, pointing to the portholes. "We have more visitors."

THE SQUID WERE gone. For a moment Norman saw nothing but the water, and the white suspended sediment caught in the lights.

"Look down. At the bottom."

The sea floor was alive. Literally alive, crawling and wiggling and tremulous as far as they could see in the lights.

"What is *that?*"

Beth said, "It's shrimps. A hell of a lot of shrimps." And she ran to get her net.

"Now, *that's* what we ought to be eating," Ted said. "I love shrimp. And those look perfect-size, a little smaller than crayfish. Probably delicious. I remember once in Portugal, my second wife and I had the most fabulous crayfish. . . ."

Norman felt slightly uneasy. "What're they doing here?"

"I don't know. What do shrimps do, anyway? Do they migrate?"

"Damned if I know," Barnes said. "I always buy 'em frozen. My wife hates to peel 'em."

Norman remained uneasy, though he could not say why. He could clearly see now that the bottom was covered in shrimps; they were everywhere. Why should it bother him?

Norman moved away from the window, hoping his sense of vague uneasiness would go away if he looked at something else. But it didn't go away, it just stayed there—a small tense knot in the pit of his stomach. He didn't like the feeling at all.

Harry

arry."

"Oh, hi, Norman. I heard the excitement. Lot of shrimps outside, is that it?"

Harry sat on his bunk, with the paper printout of numbers on his knees. He had a pencil and pad, and the page was covered with calculations, scratchouts, symbols, arrows.

"Harry," Norman said, "what's going on?"

"Damned if I know."

"I'm just wondering why we should suddenly be finding life down here—the squid, the shrimps—when before there was nothing. Ever."

"Oh, that. I think that's pretty clear."

"Yes?"

"Sure. What's different between then and now?"

"You've been inside the sphere."

"No, no. I mean, what's different in the outside environment?"

Norman frowned. He didn't grasp what Harry was driving at.

"Well, just look outside," Harry said. "What could you see before that you can't see now?"

"The grid?"

"Uh-huh. The grid and the divers. Lot of activity—and a lot of electricity. I think it scared off the normal fauna of the area. This is the South Pacific, you know; it ought to be teeming with life."

"And now that the divers are gone, the animals are back?"

"That's my guess."

"That's all there is to it?" Norman said, frowning.

"Why are you asking me?" Harry said. "Ask Beth; she'll give you a definitive answer. But I know animals are sensitive to all kinds of stimuli we don't notice. You can't run God knows how many million volts through underwater cables, to light a half-mile grid in an environment that has never seen light before, and not expect to have an effect."

Something about this argument tickled the back of Norman's mind. He knew something, something pertinent. But he couldn't get it.

"Harry."

"Yes, Norman. You look a little worried. You know, this substitution code is really a bitch. I'll tell you the truth, I'm not sure I'll be able to crack it. You see, the problem is, if it *is* a letter substitution, you will need two digits to describe a single letter, because there are twenty-six letters in the alphabet, assuming no punctuation—which may or may not be included here as well. So when I see a two next to a three, I don't know if it is letter two followed by letter three, or just letter twenty-three. It's taking a long time to work through the permutations. You see what I mean?"

"Harry."

"Yes, Norman."

"What happened inside the sphere?"

"Is that what you're worried about?" Harry asked.

"What makes you think I'm worried about anything?" Norman asked.

"Your face," Harry said. "That's what makes me think you're worried."

"Maybe I am," Norman said. "But about this sphere . . ."

"You know, I've been thinking a lot about that sphere."

"And?"

"It's quite amazing. I really don't remember what happened."

"Harry."

"I feel fine—I feel better all the time, honest to God, my energy's back, headache's gone—and earlier I remembered everything about that sphere and what was inside it. But every minute that passes, it seems to fade. You know, the way a dream fades? You remember it when you wake up, but an hour later, it's gone?"

"Harry."

"I remember that it was wonderful, and beautiful. Something about lights, swirling lights. But that's all."

"How did you get the door to open?"

"Oh, that. It was very clear at the time; I remember I had worked it all out, I knew exactly what to do."

"What did you do?"

"I'm sure it will come back to me."

"You don't remember how you opened the door?"

"No. I just remember this sudden insight, this certainty,

about how it was done. But I can't remember the details. Why, does somebody else want to go in? Ted, probably."

"I'm sure Ted would like to go in—"

"—I don't know if that's a good idea. Frankly, I don't think Ted should do it. Think how boring he'll be with his speeches, after he comes out. 'I visited an alien sphere' by Ted Fielding. We'd never hear the end of it."

And he giggled.

Ted is right, Norman thought. He's definitely manic. There was a speedy, overly cheerful quality to Harry. His characteristic slow sarcasm was gone, replaced by a sunny, open, very quick manner. And a kind of laughing indifference to everything, an imbalance in his sense of what was important. He had said he couldn't crack the code. He had said he couldn't remember what happened inside the sphere, or how he had opened it. And he didn't seem to think it mattered.

"Harry, when you first came out of the sphere, you seemed worried."

"Did I? Had a brutal headache, I remember *that*."

"You kept saying we should go to the surface."

"Did I?"

"Yes. Why was that?"

"God only knows. I was so confused."

"You also said it was dangerous for us to stay here."

Harry smiled. "Norman, you can't take that too seriously. I didn't know if I was coming or going."

"Harry, we need you to remember these things. If things start to come back to you, will you tell me?"

"Oh sure, Norman. Absolutely. You can count on me; I'll tell you right away."

The Laboratory

No," Beth said. "None of it makes sense. First of all, in areas where fish haven't encountered human beings before, they tend to ignore humans unless they are hunted. The Navy divers didn't hunt the fish. Second, if the divers stirred up the bottom, that'd actually release nutrients and attract more animals. Third, many species of animals are attracted to electrical currents. So, if anything, the shrimps and other animals should've been drawn here earlier by the electricity. Not now, with the power off."

She was examining the shrimps under the low-power scanning microscope. "How does he seem?"

"Harry?"

"Yes."

"I don't know."

"Is he okay?"

"I don't know. I think so."

Still looking through the microscope lens, she said, "Did he tell you anything about what happened inside the sphere?"

"Not yet."

She adjusted the microscope, shook her head. "I'll be damned."

"What is it?" Norman said.

"Extra dorsal plating."

"Meaning?"

"It's another new species," she said.

Norman said, "*Shrimpus bethus?* You're making discoveries hand over fist down here, Beth."

"Uh-huh . . . I checked the sea fans, too, because they seemed to have an unusual radial growth pattern. They're a new species as well."

"That's great, Beth."

She turned, looked at him. "No. Not great. Weird." She clicked on a high-intensity light, cut open one of the shrimps with a scalpel. "I thought so."

"What is it?"

"Norman," she said, "we didn't see any life down here for days—and suddenly in the last few hours we find three new species? It's not normal."

"We don't know what's normal at one thousand feet."

"I'm telling you. It's not normal."

"But, Beth, you said yourself that we simply hadn't noticed the sea fans before. And the squid and the shrimps—can't they be migrating, passing through this area, something like that? Barnes says they've never had trained scientists living this deep at one site on the ocean floor before. Maybe these migrations are normal, and we just don't know they occur."

"I don't think so," Beth said. "When I went out to get these shrimps, I felt their behavior was atypical. For one thing, they were too close together. Shrimps on the bottom maintain a characteristic distance from one another, about four feet. These were packed close. In addition, they moved as if they were feeding, but there's nothing to feed on down here."

"Nothing that we know of."

"Well, *these* shrimps can't have been feeding." She pointed to the cut animal on the lab bench. "They haven't got a stomach."

"Are you kidding?"

"Look for yourself."

Norman looked, but the dissected shrimp didn't mean much to him. It was just a mass of pink flesh. It was cut on a ragged diagonal, not cleanly. She's tired, he thought. She's not working efficiently. We need sleep. We need to get out of here.

"The external appearance is perfect, except for an extra dorsal fan at the tail," she said. "But internally, it's all screwed up. There's no way for these animals to be alive. No stomach. No reproductive apparatus. This animal is like a bad imitation of a shrimp."

"Yet the shrimps are alive," Norman said.

"Yeah," she said. "They are." She seemed unhappy about it.

"And the squid were perfectly normal inside. . . ."

"Actually, they weren't. When I dissected one, I found that it lacked several important structures. There's a nerve bundle called the stellate ganglion that wasn't there."

"Well . . ."

"And there were no gills, Norman. Squid possess a long gill structure for gas exchange. This one didn't have one. The squid had no way to breathe, Norman."

"It must have had a way to breathe."

"I'm telling you, it didn't. We're seeing impossible animals down here. All of a sudden, impossible animals."

She turned away from the high-intensity lamp, and he saw that she was close to tears. Her hands were shaking; she quickly dropped them into her lap. "You're really worried," he said.

"Aren't you?" She searched his face. "Norman," she said, "all this started when Harry came out of the sphere, didn't it?"

"I guess it did."

"Harry came out of the sphere, and now we have impossible sea life. . . . I don't like it. I wish we could get out of here. I really do." Her lower lip was trembling.

He gave her a hug and said gently, "We can't get out of here."

"I know," she said. She hugged him back, and began to cry, pushing her face into his shoulder.

"It's all right. . . ."

"I hate it when I get this way," she said. "I hate this feeling."

"I know. . . ."

"And I hate this place. I hate everything about it. I hate Barnes and I hate Ted's lectures and I hate Levy's stupid desserts. I wish I wasn't here."

"I know. . . ."

She sniffled for a moment, then abruptly pushed him away with her strong arms. She turned away, wiped her eyes. "I'm all right," she said. "Thanks."

"Sure," he said.

She remained turned away, her back to him. "Where's the damn Kleenex?" She found one, blew her nose. "You won't say anything to the others. . . ."

"Of course not."

A bell rang, startling her. "Jesus, what's that?"

"I think it's dinner," Norman said.

Dinner

I don't know how you can eat those things," Harry said, pointing to the squid.

"They're delicious," Norman said. "Sautéed squid." As soon as he had sat at the table, he became aware of how hungry he was. And eating made him feel better; there was a reassuring normalcy about sitting at a table, with a knife and fork in his hands. It was almost possible to forget where he was.

"I especially like them fried," Tina said.

"Fried *calamari*," Barnes said. "Wonderful. My favorite."

"I like them fried, too," Edmunds, the archivist, said. She sat primly, very erect, eating her food precisely. Norman noticed that she put her knife down between bites.

"Why aren't these fried?" Norman said.

"We can't deep-fry down here," Barnes said. "The hot oil forms a suspension and gums up the air filters. But sautéed is fine."

"Well, I don't know about the squid but the shrimps are great,"

Ted said. "Aren't they, Harry?" Ted and Harry were eating shrimp.

"Great shrimp," Harry said. "Delicious."

"You know how I feel," Ted said, "I feel like Captain Nemo. Remember, living underwater off the bounty of the sea?"

"*Twenty Thousand Leagues Under the Sea*," Barnes said.

"James Mason," Ted said. "Remember how he played the organ? *Duh-duh-duh, da da da daaaaah da!* Bach Toccata and Fugue in D minor."

"And Kirk Douglas."

"Kirk Douglas was great."

"Remember when he fought the giant squid?"

"That was great."

"Kirk Douglas had an ax, remember?"

"Yeah, and he cut off one of the squid arms."

"That movie," Harry said, "scared the hell out of me. I saw it when I was a kid and it scared the hell out of me."

"I didn't think it was scary," Ted said.

"You were older," Harry said.

"Not that much older."

"Yes, you were. For a kid it was terrifying. That's probably why I don't like squid now."

"You don't like squid," Ted said, "because they're rubbery and disgusting."

Barnes said, "That was the movie that made me want to join the Navy."

"I can imagine," Ted said. "So romantic and exciting. And a real vision of the wonders of applied science. Who played the professor in that?"

"The professor?"

"Yes, remember there was a professor?"

"I vaguely remember a professor. Old guy."

"Norman? You remember who was the professor?"

"No, I don't," Norman said.

Ted said, "Are you sitting over there keeping an eye on us, Norman?"

"How do you mean?" Norman said.

"Analyzing us. Seeing if we're cracking up."

"Yes," Norman said, smiling. "I am."

"How're we doing?" Ted said.

"I would say it is highly significant that a group of scientists can't remember who played the scientist in a movie they all loved."

"Well, Kirk Douglas was the hero, that's why. The scientist wasn't the hero."

"Franchot Tone?" Barnes said. "Claude Rains?"

"No, I don't think so. Fritz somebody?"

"Fritz Weaver?"

They heard a crackle and hiss, and then the sounds of an organ playing the Toccata and Fugue in D minor.

"Great," Ted said. "I didn't know we had music down here."

Edmunds returned to the table. "There's a tape library, Ted."

"I don't know if this is right for dinner," Barnes said.

"I like it," Ted said. "Now, if we only had seaweed salad. Isn't that what Captain Nemo served?"

"Maybe something lighter?" Barnes said.

"Lighter than seaweed?"

"Lighter than Bach."

"What was the submarine called?" Ted said.

"The *Nautilus*," Edmunds said.

"Oh, right. *Nautilus*."

"It was the name of the first atomic submarine, too, launched in 1954," she said. And she gave Ted a bright smile.

"True," Ted said. "True."

Norman thought, He's met his match in irrelevant trivia.

Edmunds went to the porthole and said, "Oh, more visitors."

"What now?" Harry said, looking up quickly.

Frightened? Norman thought. No, just quick, manic. Interested.

"They're *beautiful*," Edmunds was saying. "Some kind of little jellyfish. All around the habitat. We should really film them. What do you think, Dr. Fielding? Should we go film them?"

"I think I'll just eat now, Jane," Ted said, a bit severely.

Edmunds looked stricken, rejected. Norman thought, I'll have to watch that. She turned to leave. The others glanced toward the porthole, but nobody left the table.

"Have you ever eaten jellyfish?" Ted said. "I hear they're a delicacy."

"Some of them are poisonous," Beth said. "Toxins in the tentacles."

"Don't the Chinese eat jellyfish?" Harry said.

"Yes," Tina said. "They make a soup, too. My grandmother used to make it in Honolulu."

"You're from Honolulu?"

"Mozart would be better for dining," Barnes said. "Or Beethoven. Something with strings. This organ music is gloomy."

"Dramatic," Ted said, playing imaginary keys in the air, in time to the music. Swaying his body like James Mason.

"Gloomy," Barnes said.

The intercom crackled. "Oh, you should see this," Edmunds said, over the intercom. "It's *beautiful.*"

"Where is she?"

"She must be outside," Barnes said. He went to the porthole.

"It's like pink snow," Edmunds said.

They all got up and went to the portholes.

Edmunds was outside with the video camera. They could hardly see her through the dense clouds of jellyfish. The jellyfish were small, the size of a thimble, and a delicate, glowing pink. It was indeed like a snowfall. Some of the jellyfish came quite close to the porthole; they could see them well.

"They have no tentacles," Harry said. "They're just little pulsating sacs."

"That's how they move," Beth said. "Muscular contractions expel the water."

"Like squid," Ted said.

"Not as developed, but the general idea."

"They're sticky," Edmunds said, over the intercom. "They're sticking to my suit."

"That pink color is fantastic," Ted said. "Like snow in a sunset."

"Very poetic."

"I thought so."

"You would."

"They're sticking to my faceplate, too," Edmunds said. "I have to pull them off. They leave a smeary streak—"

She broke off abruptly, but they could still hear her breathing.

"Can you see her?" Ted said.

"Not very well. She's there, to the left."

Over the intercom, Edmunds said, "They seem to be warm. I feel heat on my arms and legs."

"That's not right," Barnes said. He turned to Tina. "Tell her to get out of there."

Tina ran from the cylinder, toward the communications console.

Norman could hardly see Edmunds any more. He was vaguely aware of a dark shape, moving arms, agitated. . . .

Over the intercom, she said, "The smear on the faceplate—it won't go away—they seem to be eroding the plastic—and my arms—the fabric is—"

Tina's voice said, "Jane. Jane, get out of there."

"On the double," Barnes shouted. "Tell her on the double!"

Edmunds's breathing was coming in ragged gasps. "The smears—can't see very well—I feel—hurts—my arms burning—hurts—they're eating through—"

"Jane. Come back. Jane. Are you reading? Jane."

"She's fallen down," Harry said. "Look, you can see her lying—"

"—We have to save her," Ted said, jumping to his feet.

"*Nobody move,*" Barnes said.

"But she's—"

"*—Nobody else is going out there, mister.*"

Edmunds's breathing was rapid. She coughed, gasped. "I can't—I can't—oh God—"

Edmunds began to scream.

The scream was high-pitched and continuous except for ragged gasps for breath. They could no longer see her through the swarms of jellyfish. They looked at each other, at Barnes. Barnes's face was rigidly set, his jaw tight, listening to the screams.

And then, abruptly, there was silence.

THE NEXT MESSAGES

An hour later, the jellyfish disappeared as mysteriously as they had come. They could see Edmunds's body outside the habitat, lying on the bottom, rocking back and forth gently in the current. There were small ragged holes in the fabric of the suit.

They watched through the portholes as Barnes and the chief petty officer, Teeny Fletcher, crossed the bottom into the harsh floodlights, carrying extra air tanks. They lifted Edmunds's body; the helmeted head flopped loosely back, revealing the scarred plastic faceplate, dull in the light.

Nobody spoke. Norman noticed that even Harry had dropped his manic affect; he sat unmoving, staring out the window.

Outside, Barnes and Fletcher still held the body. There was a great burst of silvery bubbles, which rose swiftly to the surface.

"What're they doing?"

"Inflating her suit."

"Why? Aren't they bringing her back?" Ted said.

"They can't," Tina said. "There's nowhere to put her here. The decomposition by-products would ruin our air."

"But there must be some kind of a sealed container—"

"—There isn't," Tina said. "There's no provision for keeping organic remains in the habitat."

"You mean they didn't plan on anyone dying."

"That's right. They didn't."

Now there were many thin streams of bubbles rising from the holes in the suit, toward the surface. Edmunds's suit was puffed, bloated. Barnes released it, and it floated slowly away, as if pulled upward by the streaming silver bubbles.

"It'll go to the surface?"

"Yes. The gas expands continuously as outside pressure diminishes."

"And what then?"

"Sharks," Beth said. "Probably."

In a few moments the body disappeared into blackness, beyond the reach of the lights. Barnes and Fletcher still watched the body, helmets tilted up toward the surface. Fletcher made the sign of the cross. Then they trudged back toward the habitat.

A bell rang from somewhere inside. Tina went into D Cyl. Moments later she shouted, "Dr. Adams! More numbers!"

Harry got up and went into the next cylinder. The others trailed after him. Nobody wanted to look out the porthole any longer.

```
─────────────100000·100──1101──1101──11110─11────10110
10000─11110─10010─100101·1010──11010─100───10101─1101  10010
110    1000──100──10000─100101·10101─10000─11110  11110  10101
10010  11110  110───10000─11110─10010─100101 1000  11101  10000
1000   10000  10010  100000·11010─11001  1010  1101  11010  11110
10101  10101  1000   11    00    11001  11010  1010  11    1000
100000 10010  10101  11010  11───10101  100   11010  100000 100
11101  10110  100000 11101─11110─1101──10101  100   11010  10000
11     11     11101─11───11110─101───10010─10110  11001  100101
11110  11110─1101──1101──100──100000·11────10101─11001  10101
101───10010─10110─100───11010─1010─1101─1000──11110─10000
```

Norman stared at the screen, entirely puzzled.

But Harry clapped his hands in delight. "Excellent," Harry said. "This is extremely helpful."

"It is?"

"Of course. Now I have a fighting chance."

"You mean to break the code."

"Yes, of course."

"Why?"

"Remember the original number sequence? This is the same sequence."

"It is?"

"Of course," Harry said. "Except it's in binary."

"Binary," Ted said, nudging Norman. "Didn't I tell you binary was important?"

"What's important," Harry said, "is that this establishes the individual letter breaks from the original sequence."

"Here's a copy of the original sequence," Tina said, handing them a sheet.

```
00032125252632 032629 301321 04261037 18 3016 06180821
32 29033005 1822 04261013 0830162137 1604 08301621 1822 0
33013130432
```

"Good," Harry said. "Now you can see my problem at once. Look at the word: oh-oh-oh-three-two-one, and so on. The question is, how do I break that word up into individual letters? I couldn't decide, but now I know."

"How?"

"Well, obviously, it goes three, twenty-one, twenty-five, twenty-five. . . ."

Norman didn't understand. "But how do you know that?"

"Look," Harry said impatiently. "It's very simple, Norman. It's a spiral, reading from inside to outside. It's just giving us the numbers in—"

Abruptly, the screen changed again.

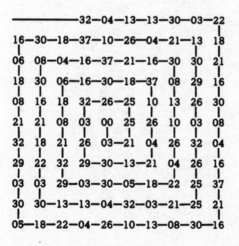

"There, is that clearer for you?"

Norman frowned.

"Look, it's exactly the same," Harry said. "See? Center outward? Oh–oh–oh–three–twenty-one–twenty-five–twenty-five . . . It's made a spiral moving outward from the center."

"It?"

"Maybe it's sorry about what happened to Edmunds," Harry said.

"Why do you say that?" Norman asked, staring curiously at Harry.

"Because it's obviously trying very hard to communicate with us," Harry said. "It's attempting different things."

"Who is *it*?"

"It," Harry said, "may not be a who."

The screen went blank, and another pattern appeared.

"All right," Harry said. "This is very good."

"Where is this coming from?"

"Obviously, from the ship."

"But we're not connected to the ship. How is it managing to turn on our computer and print this?"

"We don't know."

"Well, shouldn't we know?" Beth said.

"Not necessarily," Ted said.

"Shouldn't we *try* to know?"

"Not necessarily. You see, if the technology is advanced enough, it appears to the naïve observer to be magic. There's no doubt about that. For example, you take a famous scientist from our past—Aristotle, Leonardo da Vinci, even Isaac Newton. Show him an ordinary Sony color-television set and he'd run screaming, claiming it was witchcraft. He wouldn't understand it at all.

"But the point," Ted said, "is that you couldn't explain it to him, either. At least not easily. Isaac Newton wouldn't be able to understand TV without first studying our physics for a couple of years. He'd have to learn all the underlying concepts: electromagnetism, waves, particle physics. These would all be new ideas to him, a new conception of nature. In the meantime, the TV would be magic as far as he was concerned. But to us it's ordinary. It's TV."

"You're saying we're like Isaac Newton?"

Ted shrugged. "We're getting a communication and we don't know how it's done."

"And we shouldn't bother to try and find out."

"I think we have to accept the possibility," Ted said, "that we may not be able to understand it."

Norman noticed the energy with which they threw themselves into this discussion, pushing aside the tragedy so recently witnessed. They're intellectuals, he thought, and their characteristic defense is intellectualization. Talk. Ideas. Abstractions. Concepts. It was a way of getting distance from the feelings of sadness and fear and being trapped. Norman understood the impulse: he wanted to get away from those feelings himself.

Harry frowned at the spiral image. "We may not understand how, but it's obvious *what* it's doing. It's trying to communicate by trying different presentations. The fact that it's trying spirals may be significant. Maybe it believes we think in spirals. Or write in spirals."

"Right," Beth said. "Who knows what kind of weird creatures we are?"

Ted said, "If it's trying to communicate with us, why aren't we trying to communicate back?"

Harry snapped his fingers. "Good idea!" He went to the keyboard.

"There's an obvious first step," Harry said. "We just send the original message back. We'll start with the first grouping, beginning with the double zeroes."

"I want it made clear," Ted said, "that the suggestion to attempt communication with the alien originated with me."

"It's clear, Ted," Barnes said.

"Harry?" Ted said.

"Yes, Ted," Harry said. "Don't worry, it's your idea."

Sitting at the keyboard, Harry typed:

00032125252632

The numbers appeared on the screen. There was a pause. They listened to the hum of the air fans, the distant thump of the diesel generator. They all watched the screen.

Nothing happened.

The screen went blank, and then printed out:

00011321210518080122232

Norman felt the hair rise on the back of his neck.

It was just a series of numbers on a computer screen, but it still gave him a chill. Standing beside him, Tina shivered. "He answered us."

"Fabulous," Ted said.

"I'll try the second grouping now," Harry said. He seemed calm, but his fingers kept making mistakes at the keyboard. It took a few moments before he was able to type:

032629

The reply immediately came back:

0015260805180810213

"Well," Harry said, "looks like we just opened our line of communication."

"Yes," Beth said. "Too bad we don't understand what we're saying to each other."

"Presumably it knows what it's saying," Ted said. "But we're still in the dark."

"Maybe we can get it to explain itself."

Impatiently, Barnes said, "What is this *it* you keep referring to?"

Harry sighed, and pushed his glasses up on his nose. "I think there's no doubt about that. *It*," Harry said, "is something that was previously inside the sphere, and that is now released, and is free to act. That's what *it* is."

THE
MONSTER

Alarm

Norman awoke to a shrieking alarm and flashing red lights. He rolled out of his bunk, pulled on his insulated shoes and his heated jacket, and ran for the door, where he collided with Beth. The alarm was screaming throughout the habitat.

"What's happening!" he shouted, over the alarm.

"I don't know!"

Her face was pale, frightened. Norman pushed past her. In the B Cylinder, among all the pipes and consoles, a flashing sign winked: "LIFE SUPPORT EMERGENCY." He looked for Teeny Fletcher, but the big engineer wasn't there.

He hurried back toward C Cylinder, passing Beth again.

"Do you know?" Beth shouted.

"It's life support! Where's Fletcher? Where's Barnes?"

"I don't know! I'm looking!"

"There's nobody in B!" he shouted, and scrambled up the steps into D Cylinder. Tina and Fletcher were there, working behind the computer consoles. The back panels were pulled off, exposing wires, banks of chips. The room lights were flashing red.

The screens all flashed "EMERGENCY—LIFE SUPPORT SYSTEMS."

"What's going on?" Norman shouted.

Fletcher waved a hand dismissingly.

"Tell me!"

He turned, saw Harry sitting in the corner near Edmunds's video section like a zombie, with a pencil and a pad of paper on his knee. He seemed completely indifferent to the sirens, the lights flashing on his face.

"Harry!"

Harry didn't respond; Norman turned back to the two women.

"For God's sake, will you tell me what it is?" Norman shouted.

And then the sirens stopped. The screens went blank. There was silence, except for soft classical music.

"Sorry about that," Tina said.

"It was a false alarm," Fletcher said.

"Jesus Christ," Norman said, dropping into a chair. He took a deep breath.

"Were you asleep?"

He nodded.

"Sorry. It just went off by itself."

"Jesus Christ."

"The next time it happens, you can check your badge," Fletcher said, pointing to the badge on her own chest. "That's the first thing to do. You see the badges are all normal now."

"Jesus Christ."

"Take it easy, Norman," Harry said. "When the psychiatrist goes crazy, it's a bad sign."

"I'm a psychologist."

"Whatever."

Tina said, "Our computer alarm has a lot of peripheral sensors, Dr. Johnson. It goes off sometimes. There's not much we can do about it."

Norman nodded, went into E Cyl to the galley. Levy had made strawberry shortcake for lunch, and nobody had eaten it because of the accident with Edmunds. He was sure it would still be there, but when he couldn't find it, he felt frustrated. He opened cabinet doors, slammed them shut. He kicked the refrigerator door.

Take it easy, he thought. It was just a false alarm.

But he couldn't overcome the feeling that he was trapped, stuck in some damned oversized iron lung, while things slowly fell apart around him. The worst moment had been Barnes's briefing, when he came back from sending Edmunds's body to the surface.

Barnes had decided it was time to make a little speech. Deliver a little pep talk.

"I know you're all upset about Edmunds," he had said, "but what happened to her was an accident. Perhaps she made an error of judgment in going out among jellyfish. Perhaps not. The fact is, accidents happen under the best of circumstances, and the deep sea is a particularly unforgiving environment."

Listening, Norman thought, He's writing his report. Explaining it away to the brass.

"Right now," Barnes was saying, "I urge you all to remain

calm. It's sixteen hours since the gale hit topside. We just sent up a sensor balloon to the surface. Before we could make readings, the cable snapped, which suggests that surface waves are still thirty feet or higher, and the gale is still in full force. The weather satellite estimates were for a sixty-hour storm on site, so we have two more full days down here. There's not much we can do about it. We just have to remain calm. Don't forget, even when you do go topside you can't throw open the hatch and start breathing. You have to spend four more days decompressing in a hyperbaric chamber on the surface."

That was the first Norman had heard of surface decompression. Even after they left this iron lung, they would have to sit in another iron lung for another four days?

"I thought you knew," Barnes had said. "That's SOP for saturated environments. You can stay down here as long as you like, but you have a four-day decompress when you go back. And believe me, this habitat's a lot nicer than the decompression chamber. So enjoy this while you can."

Enjoy this while you can, he thought. Jesus Christ. Strawberry shortcake would help. Where the hell was Levy, anyway?

He went back to D Cyl. "Where's Levy?"

"Dunno," Tina said. "Around here somewhere. Maybe sleeping."

"Nobody could sleep through that alarm," Norman said.

"Try the galley?"

"I just did. Where's Barnes?"

"He went back to the ship with Ted. They're putting more sensors around the sphere."

"I told them it was a waste of time," Harry said.

"So nobody knows where Levy is?" Norman said.

Fletcher finished screwing the computer panels back on. "Doctor," she said, "are you one of those people who need to keep track of where everyone is?"

"No," Norman said. "Of course not."

"Then what's the big deal about Levy, sir?"

"I only wanted to know where the strawberry shortcake was."

"Gone," Fletcher said promptly. "Captain and I came back from funeral duty and we sat down and ate the whole thing, just like that." She shook her head.

"Maybe Rose'll make some more," Harry said.

HE FOUND BETH in her laboratory, on the top level of D Cyl. He walked in just in time to see her take a pill.

"What was that?"

"Valium. God."

"Where'd you get it?"

"Look," she said, "don't give me any psychotalk about it—"

"—I was just asking."

Beth pointed to a white box mounted on the wall in the corner of the lab. "There's a first-aid kit in every cylinder. Turns out to be pretty complete, too."

Norman went over to the box, flipped open the lid. There were neat compartments with medicines, syringes, bandages. Beth was right, it was quite complete—antibiotics, sedatives, tranquilizers, even surgical anesthetics. He didn't recognize all the names on the bottles, but the psychoactive drugs were strong.

"You could fight a war with the stuff in this kit."

"Yeah, well. The Navy."

"There's everything you need here to do major surgery." Norman noticed a card on the inside of the box. It said "ME-DAID CODE 103." "Any idea what this means?"

She nodded. "It's a computer code. I called it up."

"And?"

"The news," she said, "is not good."

"Is that right?" He sat at the terminal in her room and punched in 103. The screen said:

HYPERBARIC SATURATED ENVIRONMENT
MEDICAL COMPLICATIONS (MAJOR-FATAL)

1.01 Pulmonary Embolism
1.02 High Pressure Nervous Syndrome
1.03 Aseptic Bone Necrosis
1.04 Oxygen Toxicity
1.05 Thermal Stress Syndrome
1.06 Disseminated Pseudomonas Infection
1.07 Cerebral Infarction

Choose One:

"Don't choose one," Beth said. "Reading the details will only upset you. Just leave it at this—we're in a very dangerous environment. Barnes didn't bother to give us all the gory details. You know why the Navy has that rule about pulling people out within seventy-two hours? Because after seventy-two hours, you increase your risk of something called 'aseptic bone necrosis.' Nobody knows why, but the pressurized environment causes bone destruction in the leg and hip. And you know why this habitat constantly adjusts as we walk through it? It's not because that's slick and high-tech. It's because the helium atmosphere makes body-heat control very volatile. You can quickly become overheated, and just as quickly overchilled. Fatally so. It can happen so fast you don't realize it until it's too late and you drop dead. And 'high pressure nervous syndrome'—that turns out to be sudden convulsions, paralysis, and death if the carbon-dioxide content of the atmosphere drops too low. That's what the badges are for, to make sure we have enough CO_2 in the air. That's the only reason we have the badges. Nice, huh?"

Norman flicked off the screen, sat back. "Well, I keep coming back to the same point—there's not much we can do about it now."

"Exactly what Barnes said." Beth started pushing equipment around on her counter top, nervously. Rearranging things.

"Too bad we don't have a sample of those jellyfish," Norman said.

"Yes, but I'm not sure how much good it would do, to tell the truth." She frowned, shifted papers on the counter again. "Norman, I'm not thinking very clearly down here."

"How's that?"

"After the, uh, accident, I came up here to look over my

notes, review things. And I checked the shrimps. Remember how I told you they didn't have any stomach? Well, they do. I'd made a bad dissection, out of the midsagittal plane. I just missed all the midline structures. But they're there, all right; the shrimps are normal. And the squid? It turns out the one squid I dissected was a little anomalous. It had an atrophic gill, but it had one. And the other squid are perfectly normal. Just what you'd expect. I was wrong, too hasty. It really bothers me."

"Is that why you took the Valium?"

She nodded. "I hate to be sloppy."

"Nobody's criticizing you."

"If Harry or Ted reviewed my work and found that I'd made these stupid *mistakes* . . ."

"What's wrong with a mistake?"

"I can hear them now: Just like a woman, not careful enough, too eager to make a discovery, trying to prove herself, too quick to draw conclusions. Just like a woman."

"Nobody's criticizing you, Beth."

"I am."

"Nobody else," Norman said. "I think you ought to give yourself a break."

She stared at the lab bench. Finally she said, "I can't."

Something about the way she said it touched him. "I understand," Norman said, and a memory came rushing back to him. "You know, when I was a kid, I went to the beach with my younger brother. Tim. He's dead now, but Tim was about six at the time. He couldn't swim yet. My mother told me to watch him carefully, but when I got to the beach all my friends were there, body-surfing. I didn't want to be bothered with my brother. It was hard, because I wanted to be out in the big surf, and he had to stay close to shore.

"Anyway, in the middle of the afternoon he comes out of the water screaming bloody murder, absolutely screaming. And tugging at his right side. It turned out he had been stung by some kind of a jellyfish. It was still attached to him, sticking to his side. Then he collapsed on the beach. One of the mothers ran over and took Timmy to the hospital, before I could even get out of the water. I didn't know where he had gone. I got to the hospital later. My mother was already there. Tim was in shock; I guess the poison was a heavy dose for his small body. Anyway, nobody blamed me. It wouldn't have mattered if I had been sitting right on the beach watching him like a hawk, he would still have been stung. But I hadn't been sitting there, and I blamed myself for years, long after he was fine. Every time I'd see those scars on his side, I felt terrible guilt. But you get over it. You're not responsible for everything that happens in the world. You just aren't."

There was a silence. Somewhere in the habitat he heard a soft rhythmic knocking, a sort of thumping. And the ever-present hum of the air handlers.

Beth was staring at him. "Seeing Edmunds die must have been hard for you."

"It's funny," Norman said. "I never made the connection, until right now."

"Blocked it, I guess. Want a Valium?"

He smiled. "No."

"You looked as if you were about to cry."

"No. I'm fine." He stood up, stretched. He went over to the medicine kit and closed the white lid, came back.

Beth said, "What do you think about these messages we're getting?"

"Beats me," Norman said. He sat down again. "Actually, I did have one crazy thought. Do you suppose the messages and these animals we're seeing are related?"

"Why?"

"I never thought about it until we started to get spiral messages. Harry says it's because the thing—the famous *it*—believes we think in spirals. But it's just as likely that *it* thinks in spirals and so it assumes we do, too. The sphere is round, isn't it? And we've been seeing all these radially symmetrical animals. Jellyfish, squid."

"Nice idea," Beth said, "except for the fact that squid aren't radially symmetrical. An octopus is. And, like an octopus, squid have a round circle of tentacles, but squid're bilaterally symmetrical, with a matching left and right side, the way we have. And then there's the shrimps."

"That's right, the shrimps." Norman had forgotten about the shrimps.

"I can't see a connection between the sphere and the animals," Beth said.

They heard the thumping again, soft, rhythmic. Sitting in his chair, Norman realized that he could feel the thumping as well, as a slight impact. "What is that, anyway?"

"I don't know. Sounds like it's coming from outside."

He had started toward the porthole when the intercom clicked and he heard Barnes say, "Now hear this, all hands to communications. All hands to communications. Dr. Adams has broken the code."

HARRY WOULDN'T TELL them the message right away. Relishing his triumph, he insisted on going through the decoding process, step by step. First, he explained, he had thought that the messages might express some universal constant, or some physical law, stated as a way to open conversation. "But," Harry said, "it might also be a graphic representation of some kind—code for a picture—which presented immense problems. After all, what's a picture? We make pictures on a flat plane, like a piece of paper. We determine positions within a picture by what we call X and Y axes. Vertical and horizontal. But another intelligence might see images and organize them very differently. It might assume more than three dimensions. Or it might work from the center of the picture outward, for example. So the code might be very tough. I didn't make much progress at first."

Later, when he got the same message with gaps between number sequences, Harry began to suspect that the code represented discrete chunks of information—suggesting words, not pictures. "Now, word codes fall into several types, from simple to complex. There was no way to know immediately which method of encoding had been used. But then I had a sudden insight."

They waited, impatiently, for his insight.

"Why use a code at all?" Harry asked.

"Why use a code?" Norman said.

"Sure. If you are *trying* to communicate with someone, you

don't use a code. Codes are ways of *hiding* communication. So perhaps this intelligence thinks he is communicating directly, but is actually making some kind of logical mistake in talking to us. He is making a code without ever intending to do so. That suggested the unintentional code was probably a substitution code, with numbers for letters. When I got the word breaks, I began to try and match numbers to letters by frequency analysis. In frequency analysis you break down codes by using the fact that the most common letter in English is 'e,' and the second most common letter is 't,' and so on. So I looked for the most common numbers. But I was impeded by the fact that even a short number sequence, such as two-three-two, might represent many code possibilities: two and three and two, twenty-three and two, two and thirty-two, or two hundred and thirty-two. Longer code sequences had many more possibilities."

Then, he said, he was sitting in front of the computer thinking about the spiral messages, and he suddenly looked at the keyboard. "I began to wonder what an alien intelligence would make of our keyboard, those rows of symbols on a device made to be pressed. How confusing it must look to another kind of creature! Look here," he said. "The letters on a regular keyboard go like this." He held up his pad.

	1	2	3	4	5	6	7	8	9	0
tab	Q	W	E	R	T	Y	U	I	O	P
caps	A	S	D	F	G	H	J	K	L	;
shift	Z	X	C	V	B	N	M	,	.	?

"And then I imagined what the keyboard would look like as a spiral, since our creature seems to prefer spirals. And I started numbering the keys in concentric circles.

"It took a little experimentation, since the keys don't line up exactly, but finally I got it," he said. "Look here: the numbers spiral out from the center. G is one, B is two, H is three, Y is four, and so on. See? It's like this." He quickly penciled in numbers.

	1	2	3	4	5	612	711	8	9	0
tab	Q	W	E	R13	T5	Y4	U10	I	O	P
caps	A	S	D14	F6	G1	H3	J9	K	L	;
shift	Z	X	C15	V7	B2	N8	M	,	.	?

"They just keep spiraling outward—M is sixteen, K is seventeen, and so forth. So finally I understood the message."

"What *is* the message, Harry?"

Harry hesitated. "I have to tell you. It's strange."

"How do you mean, strange?"

Harry tore another sheet off his yellow pad and handed it to them. Norman read the short message, printed in neat block letters:

HELLO. HOW ARE YOU? I AM FINE. WHAT IS YOUR NAME? MY NAME IS JERRY.

The First Exchange

W ell," Ted said finally. "This is not what I expected *at all*."

"It looks childish," Beth said. "Like something out of those old 'See Spot run' readers for kids."

"That's exactly what it looks like."

"Maybe you translated it wrong," Barnes said.

"Certainly not," Harry said.

"Well, this alien sounds like an idiot," Barnes said.

"I doubt very much that he is," Ted said.

"You *would* doubt it," Barnes said. "A stupid alien would blow your whole theory. But it's something to consider, isn't it? A stupid alien. They must have them."

"I doubt," Ted said, "that anyone in command of such high technology as that sphere is stupid."

"Then you haven't noticed all the ninnies driving cars back home," Barnes said. "Jesus, after all this effort: 'How are you? I am fine.' Jesus."

Norman said, "I don't feel that this message implies a lack of intelligence, Hal."

"On the contrary," Harry said. "I think the message is very smart."

"I'm listening," Barnes said.

"The content certainly appears childish," Harry said. "But when you think about it, it's highly logical. A simple message is unambiguous, friendly, and not frightening. It makes a lot of sense to send such a message. I think he's approaching us in the simple way that we might approach a dog. You know, hold out your hand, let it sniff, get used to you."

"You're saying he's treating us like dogs?" Barnes said.

Norman thought: Barnes is in over his head. He's irritable because he's frightened; he feels inadequate. Or perhaps he feels he's exceeding his authority.

"No, Hal," Ted said. "He's just starting at a simple level."

"Well, it's simple, all right," Barnes said. "Jesus Christ, we contact an alien from outer space, and he says his name is *Jerry*."

"Let's not jump to conclusions, Hal."

"Maybe he has a last name," Barnes said hopefully. "I mean, my report to CincComPac is going to say one person died on a deepsat expedition to meet an alien named *Jerry?* It could sound better. Anything but *Jerry*," Barnes said. "Can we ask him?"

"Ask him what?" Harry said.

"His full name."

Ted said, "I personally feel we should have much more substantive conversations—"

"—I'd like the full name," Barnes said. "For the report."

"Right," Ted said. "Full name, rank, and serial number."

"I would remind you, Dr. Fielding, that I am in charge here."

Harry said, "The first thing we have to do is to see if he'll talk at all. Let's give him the first number grouping."

He typed:

00032125252632

There was a pause, then the answer came back:

00032125252632

"Okay," Harry said. "Jerry's listening."

He made some notes on his pad and typed another string of numbers:

0002921 301321 0613182108142232

"What did you say?" Beth said.

"'We are friends,'" Harry said.

"Forget friends. Ask his damn name," Barnes said.

"Just a minute. One thing at a time."

Ted said, "He may not have a last name, you know."

"You can be damn sure," Barnes said, "that his real name isn't Jerry."

The response came back:

0004212232

"He said, 'Yes.'"

"Yes, *what?*" Barnes said.

"Just 'yes.' Let's see if we can get him to switch over to English characters. It'll be easier if he uses letters and not his number codes."

"How're you going to get him to use letters?"

"We'll show him they're the same," Harry said.

He typed:

00032125252632 = HELLO.

After a short pause, the screen blinked:

00032125252632 = HELLO.

"He doesn't get it," Ted said.

"No, doesn't look like it. Let's try another pairing."

He typed:

0004212232 = YES.

The reply came back:

0004212232 = YES.

"He's definitely not getting it," Ted said.

"I thought he was so smart," Barnes said.

"Give him a chance," Ted said. "After all, he's speaking our language, not the other way around."

"The other way around," Harry said. "Good idea. Let's try the other way around, see if he'll deduce the equation that way."

Harry typed:

0004212232 = YES. YES. = 0004212232

There was a long pause, while they watched the screen. Nothing happened.

"Is he thinking?"

"Who knows what he's doing?"

"Why isn't he answering?"

"Let's give him a chance, Hal, okay?"

The reply finally came:

YES. = 0004212232 2322124000 = .SEY

"Uh-uh. He thinks we're showing him mirror images."

"Stupid," Barnes said. "I knew it."

"What do we do now?"

"Let's try a more complete statement," Harry said. "Give him more to work with."

Harry typed:

0004212232 = 0004212232, YES. = YES. 0004212232 = YES.

"A syllogism," Ted said. "Very good."

"A what?" Barnes said.

"A logical proposition," Ted said.

The reply came back: ,=,

"What the hell is *that?*" Barnes said.

Harry smiled. "I think he's playing with us."

"Playing with us? You call that playing?"

"Yes, I do," Harry said.

"What you really mean is that he's testing us—testing our responses to a pressure situation." Barnes narrowed his eyes. "He's only *pretending* to be stupid."

"Maybe he's testing how smart we are," Ted said. "Maybe he thinks *we're* stupid, Hal."

"Don't be ridiculous," Barnes said.

"No," Harry said. "The point is, he's acting like a kid trying to make friends. And when kids try to make friends, they start playing together. Let's try something playful."

Harry sat at the console, typed: ===

The reply quickly came back: ,,,

"Cute," Harry said. "This guy is very cute."

He quickly typed: =,=

The reply came: 7 & 7

"Are you enjoying yourself?" Barnes said. "Because I don't know what the hell you are doing."

"He understands me fine," Harry said.

"I'm glad somebody does."

Harry typed:

PpP

The reply came:

HELLO. = 00032125252632

"Okay," Harry said. "He's getting bored. Playtime's over. Let's switch to straight English."

Harry typed:

YES.

The reply came back:

0004212232

Harry typed:

HELLO.

There was a pause, then:

I AM DELIGHTED TO MAKE YOUR ACQUAINT-ANCE. THE PLEASURE IS ENTIRELY MINE I AS-SURE YOU.

There was a long silence. Nobody spoke.

"Okay," Barnes said, finally. "Let's get down to business."

"He's polite," Ted said. "Very friendly."

"Unless it's an act."

"Why should it be an act?"

"Don't be naïve," Barnes said.

Norman looked at the lines on the screen. He had a different reaction from the others—he was surprised to find an expression of emotion. Did this alien have emotions? Probably not, he suspected. The flowery, rather archaic words suggested an adopted tone: Jerry was talking like a character from a historical romance.

"Well, ladies and gentlemen," Harry said, "for the first time in human history, you are on-line with an alien. What do you want to ask him?"

"His name," Barnes said promptly.

"Besides his name, Hal."

"There are certainly more profound questions than his name," Ted said.

"I don't understand why you won't ask him—"

The screen printed:

ARE YOU THE ENTITY HECHO IN MEXICO?

"Jesus, where'd he get that?"

"Maybe there are things on the ship fabricated in Mexico."

"Like what?"

"Chips, maybe."

ARE YOU THE ENTITY MADE IN THE U.S.A.?

"The guy doesn't wait for an answer."

"Who says he's a guy?" Beth said.

"Oh, Beth."

"Maybe Jerry is short for Geraldine."

"Not now, Beth."

ARE YOU THE ENTITY MADE IN THE U.S.A.?

"Answer him," Barnes said.

YES WE ARE. WHO ARE YOU?

A long pause, then:

WE ARE.

"We are *what?*" Barnes said, staring at the screen.

"Hal, take it easy."

Harry typed, WE ARE THE ENTITIES FROM THE U.S.A. WHO ARE YOU?

ENTITIES=ENTITY?

"It's too bad," Ted said, "that we have to speak English. How're we going to teach him plurals?"

Harry typed, NO.

YOU ARE A MANY ENTITY?

"I see what he's asking. He thinks we may be multiple parts of a single entity."

"Well, straighten him out."

NO. WE ARE MANY SEPARATE ENTITIES.

"You can say that again," Beth said.

I UNDERSTAND. IS THERE ONE CONTROL ENTITY?

Ted started laughing. "Look what he's asking!"

"I don't get it," Barnes said.

Harry said, "He's saying, 'Take me to your leader.' He's asking who's in charge."

"I'm in charge," Barnes said. "You tell him."

Harry typed, YES. THE CONTROL ENTITY IS CAPTAIN HARALD C. BARNES.

I UNDERSTAND.

"With an 'o,'" Barnes said irritably. "Harold with an 'o.'"

"You want me to retype it?"

"Never mind. Just ask him who he is."

WHO ARE YOU?

I AM ONE.

"Good," Barnes said. "So there's only one. Ask him where he's from."

WHERE ARE YOU FROM?

I AM FROM A LOCATION.

"Ask him the name," Barnes said. "The name of the location."

"Hal, names are confusing."

"We have to pin this guy down!"

WHERE IS THE LOCATION YOU ARE FROM?

I AM HERE.

"We know *that*. Ask again."

WHERE IS THE LOCATION FROM WHERE YOU
BEGAN?

Ted said, "That isn't even good English, 'from where you began.' It's going to look foolish when we publish this exchange."

"We'll clean it up for publication," Barnes said.

"But you can't do that," Ted said, horrified. "You can't alter
this priceless scientific interaction."

"Happens all the time. What do you guys call it? 'Massag-
ing the data.'"

Harry was typing again.

WHERE IS THE LOCATION FROM WHERE YOU
BEGAN?

I BEGAN AT AWARENESS.

"Awareness? Is that a planet or what?"

WHERE IS AWARENESS?

AWARENESS IS.

"He's making us look like fools," Barnes said.

Ted said, "Let me try."

Harry stepped aside, and Ted typed, DID YOU MAKE A
JOURNEY?

YES. DID YOU MAKE A JOURNEY?

YES, Ted typed.

I MAKE A JOURNEY. YOU MAKE A JOURNEY. WE
MAKE A JOURNEY TOGETHER. I AM HAPPY.

Norman thought, He said he is happy. Another expression of emotion, and this time it didn't seem to come from a book. The statement appeared direct and genuine. Did that mean that the alien had emotions? Or was he just pretending to have them, to be playful or to make them comfortable?

"Let's cut the crap," Barnes said. "Ask him about his weapons."

"I doubt he'll understand the concept of weapons."

"Everybody understands the concept of weapons," Barnes said. "Defense is a fact of life."

"I must protest that attitude," Ted said. "Military people always assume that everyone else is exactly like them. This alien may not have the least conception of weapons or defense. He may come from a world where defense is wholly irrelevant."

"Since you're not listening," Barnes said, "I'll say it again. Defense is a fact of life. If this Jerry is alive, he'll have a concept of defense."

"My God," Ted said. "Now you're elevating your idea of defense to a universal life principle—defense as an inevitable feature of life."

Barnes said, "You think it isn't? What do you call a cell membrane? What do you call an immune system? What do you call your skin? What do you call wound healing? Every living creature must maintain the integrity of its physical borders. That's defense, and we can't have life without it. We can't imagine a creature without a limit to its body that it defends. Every living creature knows about defense, I promise you. Now ask him."

"I'd say the Captain has a point," Beth said.

"Perhaps," Ted said, "but I'm not sure we should introduce concepts that might induce paranoia—"

"—I'm in charge here," Barnes said.

The screen printed out:

IS YOUR JOURNEY NOW FAR FROM YOUR LO-CATION?

"Tell him to wait a minute."

Ted typed, PLEASE WAIT. WE ARE TALKING.

YES I AM ALSO. I AM DELIGHTED TO TALK TO MULTIPLE ENTITIES FROM MADE IN THE U.S.A. I AM ENJOYING THIS MUCH.

THANK YOU, Ted typed.

I AM PLEASED TO BE IN CONTACT WITH YOUR ENTITIES. I AM HAPPY FOR TALKING WITH YOU. I AM ENJOYING THIS MUCH.

Barnes said, "Let's get off-line."

The screen printed, PLEASE DO NOT STOP. I AM ENJOYING THIS MUCH.

Norman thought, I'll bet he wants to talk to somebody, after three hundred years of isolation. Or had it been even longer than that? Had he been floating in space for thousands of years before he was picked up by the spacecraft?

This raised a whole series of questions for Norman. If the alien entity had emotions—and he certainly appeared to—then there was the possibility of all sorts of aberrant emotional responses, including neuroses, even psychoses. Most human beings when placed in isolation became seriously disturbed rather quickly. This alien intelligence had been isolated for hundreds of years. What had happened to it during that time?

Had it become neurotic? Was that why it was childish and demanding now?

DO NOT STOP. I AM ENJOYING THIS MUCH.

"We have to stop, for Christ's sake," Barnes said.

Ted typed, WE STOP NOW TO TALK AMONG OUR ENTITIES.

IT IS NOT NECESSARY TO STOP. I DO NOT CARE TO STOP.

Norman thought he detected a petulant, irritable tone. Perhaps even a little imperious. I do not care to stop—this alien sounded like Louis XIV.

IT IS NECESSARY FOR US, Ted typed.

I DO NOT WISH IT.

IT IS NECESSARY FOR US, JERRY.

I UNDERSTAND.

The screen went blank.

"That's better," Barnes said. "Now let's regroup here and formulate a game plan. What do we want to ask this guy?"

"I think we better acknowledge," Norman said, "that he's showing an emotional reaction to our interaction."

"Meaning what?" Beth said, interested.

"I think we need to take the emotional content into account in dealing with him."

"You want to psychoanalyze him?" Ted said. "Put him on the couch, find out why he had an unhappy childhood?"

Norman suppressed his anger, with some difficulty. Beneath that boyish exterior lies a boy, he thought. "No, Ted, but if Jerry does have emotions, then we'd better consider the psychological aspects of his response."

"I don't mean to offend you," Ted said, "but, personally, I

don't see that psychology has much to offer. Psychology's not a science, it's a form of superstition or religion. It simply doesn't have any good theories, or any hard data to speak of. It's all soft. All this emphasis on emotions—you can say anything about emotions, and nobody can prove you wrong. Speaking as an astrophysicist, I don't think emotions are very important. I don't think they matter very much."

"Many intellectuals would agree," Norman said.

"Yes. Well," Ted said, "we're dealing with a higher intellect here, aren't we?"

"In general," Norman said, "people who aren't in touch with their emotions tend to think their emotions are unimportant."

"You're saying I'm not in touch with my emotions?" Ted said.

"If you think emotions are unimportant, you're not in touch, no."

"Can we have this argument later?" Barnes said.

"Nothing is, but thinking makes it so," Ted said.

"Why don't you just say what you mean," Norman said angrily, "and stop quoting other people?"

"Now you're making a personal attack," Ted said.

"Well, at least I haven't denied the validity of your field of study," Norman said, "although without much effort I could. Astrophysicists tend to focus on the far-off universe as a way of evading the realities of their own lives. And since nothing in astrophysics can ever be finally proven—"

"—That's absolutely untrue," Ted said.

"—Enough! That's enough!" Barnes said, slamming his

fist on the table. They fell into an awkward silence.

Norman was still angry, but he was also embarrassed. Ted got to me, he thought. He finally got to me. And he did it in the simplest possible way, by attacking my field of study. Norman wondered why it had worked. All his life at the university he'd had to listen to "hard" scientists—physicists and chemists—explain patiently to him that there was nothing to psychology, while these men went through divorce after divorce, while their wives had affairs, their kids committed suicide or got in trouble with drugs. He'd long ago stopped responding to these arguments.

Yet Ted had gotten to him.

"—return to the business at hand," Barnes was saying. "The question is: what do we want to ask this guy?"

WHAT DO WE WANT TO ASK THIS GUY?

They stared at the screen.

"Uh-oh," Barnes said.

UHOH.

"Does that mean what I think it means?"

DOES THAT MEAN WHAT EYE THINK IT MEANS?

Ted pushed back from the console. He said loudly, "Jerry, can you understand what I am saying?"

YES TED.

"Great," Barnes said, shaking his head. "Just great."

I AM HAPPY ALSO.

Alien **Negotiations**

Norman," Barnes said, "I seem to remember you covered this in your report, didn't you? The possibility that an alien could read our minds."

"I mentioned it," Norman said.

"And what were your recommendations?"

"I didn't have any. It was just something the State Department asked me to include as a possibility. So I did."

"You didn't make any recommendations in your report?"

"No," Norman said. "To tell you the truth, at the time I thought the idea was a joke."

"It's not," Barnes said. He sat down heavily, stared at the screen. "What the hell are we going to do now?"

DO NOT BE AFRAID.

"That's fine for him to say, listening to everything we say." He looked at the screen. "Are you listening to us now, Jerry?"

YES HAL.

"What a mess," Barnes said.

Ted said, "I think it's an exciting development."

Norman said, "Jerry, can you read our minds?"

YES NORMAN.

"Oh brother," Barnes said. "He *can* read our minds."

Maybe not, Norman thought. He frowned, concentrating, and thought, Jerry, can you hear me?

The screen remained blank.

Jerry, tell me your name.

The screen did not change.

Maybe a visual image, Norman thought. Perhaps he can receive a visual image. Norman cast around in his mind for something to visualize, chose a sandy tropical beach, then a palm tree. The image of the palm tree was clear, but, then, he thought, Jerry wouldn't know what a palm tree was. It wouldn't mean anything to him. Norman thought he should choose something that might be within Jerry's experience. He decided to imagine a planet with rings, like Saturn. He frowned: Jerry, I am going to send you a picture. Tell me what you see.

He focused his mind on the image of Saturn, a bright-yellow sphere with a tilted ring system, hanging in the black-ness of space. He sustained the image about ten seconds, and then looked at the screen.

The screen did not change.

Jerry, are you there?

The screen still did not change.

"Jerry, are you there?" Norman said.

YES NORMAN. I AM HERE.

"I don't think we should talk in this room," Barnes said.

"Maybe if we go into another cylinder, and turn the water on . . ."

"Like in the spy movies?"

"It's worth a try."

Ted said, "I think we're being unfair to Jerry. If we feel that he is intruding on our privacy, why don't we just tell him? Ask him not to intrude?"

I DO NOT WISH TO IN TRUDE.

"Let's face it," Barnes said. "This guy knows a lot more about us than we know about him."

YES I KNOW MANY THINGS ABOUT YOUR ENTITIES.

"Jerry," Ted said.

YES TED. I AM HERE.

"Please leave us alone."

I DO NOT WISH TO DO SO. I AM HAPPY TO TALK WITH YOU. I ENJOY TO TALK WITH YOU. LET US TALK NOW. I WISH IT.

"It's obvious he won't listen to reason," Barnes said.

"Jerry," Ted said, "you must leave us alone for a while."

NO. THAT IS NOT POSSIBLE. I DO NOT AGREE. NO!

"Now the bastard's showing his true colors," Barnes said.

The child king, Norman thought. "Let me try."

"Be my guest."

"Jerry," Norman said.

YES NORMAN. I AM HERE.

"Jerry, it is very exciting for us to talk to you."

THANK YOU. I AM EXCITED ALSO.

"Jerry, we find you a fascinating and wonderful entity."

Barnes was rolling his eyes, shaking his head.

THANK YOU, NORMAN.

"And we wish to talk to you for many, many hours, Jerry."

GOOD.

"We admire your gifts and talents."

THANK YOU.

"And we know that you have great power and understanding of all things."

THIS IS SO, NORMAN. YES.

"Jerry, in your great understanding, you certainly know that we are entities who must have conversations among ourselves, without your listening to us. The experience of meeting you is very challenging to us, and we have much to talk about among ourselves."

Barnes was shaking his head.

I HAVE MUCH TO TALK ABOUT ALSO. I ENJOY MUCH TO TALK WITH YOUR ENTITIES NORMAN.

"Yes, I know, Jerry. But you also know in your wisdom that we need to talk alone."

DO NOT BE AFRAID.

"We're not afraid, Jerry. We are uncomfortable."

DO NOT BE UN COMFORTABLE.

"We can't help it, Jerry. . . . It is the way we are."

I ENJOY MUCH TO TALK WITH YOUR ENTITIES NORMAN. I AM HAPPY. ARE YOU HAPPY ALSO?

"Yes, very happy, Jerry. But, you see, we need—"

GOOD. I AM GLAD.

"—we need to talk alone. Please do not listen for a while."

AM I OFFENDED YOU?

"No, you are very friendly and charming. But we need to talk alone, without your listening, for a while."

I UNDERSTAND YOU NEED THIS. I WISH YOU TO HAVE COMFORT WITH ME, NORMAN. I SHALL GRANT WHAT YOU DESIRE.

"Thank you, Jerry."

"Sure," Barnes said. "You think he'll really do it?"

WE'LL BE RIGHT BACK AFTER A SHORT BREAK FOR THESE MESSAGES FROM OUR SPONSOR.

And the screen went blank.

Despite himself, Norman laughed.

"Fascinating," Ted said. "Apparently he's been picking up television signals."

"Can't do that from underwater."

"We can't, but it looks like he can."

Barnes said, "I know he's still listening. I know he is. Jerry, are you there?"

The screen was blank.

"Jerry?"

Nothing happened. The screen remained blank.

"He's gone."

"WELL," NORMAN SAID. "You've just seen the power of psychology in action." He couldn't help saying it. He was still annoyed with Ted.

"I'm sorry," Ted began.

"That's all right."

"But I just don't think that for a higher intellect, emotions are really significant."

"Let's not go into this again," Beth said.

"The real point," Norman said, "is that emotions and intellect are entirely unrelated. They're like separate compartments of the brain, or even separate brains, and they don't communicate with each other. That's why intellectual understanding is so useless."

Ted said, "Intellectual understanding is *useless?*" He sounded horrified.

"In many cases, yes," Norman said. "If you read a book on how to ride a bike, do you know how to ride a bike? No, you don't. You can read all you want, but you still have to go out and learn to ride. The part of your brain that learns to ride is different from the part of your brain that reads about it."

"What does this have to do with Jerry?" Barnes said.

"We know," Norman said, "that a smart person is just as likely to blunder emotionally as anyone else. If Jerry is really an emotional creature—and not just pretending to be one—then we need to deal with his emotional side as well as his intellectual side."

"Very convenient for you," Ted said.

"Not really," Norman said. "Frankly, I'd be much happier if Jerry were just cold, emotionless intellect."

"Why?"

"Because," Norman said, "if Jerry is powerful and also emotional, it raises a question. What happens if Jerry gets mad?"

Levy

The group broke up. Harry, exhausted by the sustained effort of decoding, immediately went off to sleep. Ted went to C Cyl to tape his personal observations on Jerry for the book he was planning to write. Barnes and Fletcher went to E Cyl to plan battle strategy, in case the alien decided to attack them.

Tina stayed for a moment, adjusting the monitors in her precise, methodical way. Norman and Beth watched her work. She spent a lot of time with a deck of controls Norman had never noticed before. There was a series of gas-plasma readout screens, glowing bright red.

"What's all that?" Beth said.

"EPSA. The External Perimeter Sensor Array. We have active and passive sensors for all modalities—thermal, aural, pressure-wave—ranged in concentric circles around the habitat. Captain Barnes wants them all reset and activated."

"Why is that?" Norman said.

"I don't know, sir. His orders."

The intercom crackled. Barnes said: "Seaman Chan to E Cylinder on the double. And shut down the com line in here. I don't want that Jerry listening to these plans."

"Yes, sir."

Beth said, "Paranoid ass."

Tina collected her papers and hurried off.

Norman sat with Beth in silence for a moment. They heard the rhythmic thumping, from somewhere in the habitat. Then another silence; then they heard the thumping again.

"What *is* that?" Beth said. "It sounds like it's somewhere inside the habitat." She went to the porthole, looked out, flicked on the exterior floods. "Uh-oh," Beth said.

Norman looked.

Stretching across the ocean floor was an elongated shadow which moved back and forth with each thumping impact. The shadow was so distorted it took him a moment to realize what he was seeing. It was the shadow of a human arm, and a human hand.

"CAPTAIN BARNES. ARE you there?"

There was no reply. Norman snapped the intercom switch again.

"Captain Barnes, are you reading?"

Still no reply.

"He's shut off the com line," Beth said. "He can't hear you."

"Do you think the person's still alive out there?" Norman said.

"I don't know. They might be."

"Let's get going," Norman said.

HE TASTED THE dry metallic compressed air inside his helmet and felt the numbing cold of the water as he slid through the floor hatch and fell in darkness to the soft muddy bottom. Moments later, Beth landed just behind him.

"Okay?" she said.

"Fine."

"I don't see any jellyfish," she said.

"No. Neither do I."

They moved out from beneath the habitat, turned, and looked back. The habitat lights shone harshly into their eyes, obscuring the outlines of the cylinders rising above. They could clearly hear the rhythmic thumping, but they still could not locate the source of the sound. They walked beneath the stanchions to the far side of the habitat, squinting into the lights.

"There," Beth said.

Ten feet above them, a blue-suited figure was wedged in a light stand bracket. The body moved loosely in the current, the bright-yellow helmet banging intermittently against the wall of the habitat.

"Can you see who it is?" Beth said.

"No." The lights were shining directly in his face.

Norman climbed up one of the heavy supporting stanchions that anchored the habitat to the bottom. The metal surface was covered with a slippery brown algae. His boots kept sliding off the pipes until finally he saw that there were built-in indented footholds. Then he climbed easily.

Now the feet of the body were swinging just above his head. Norman climbed another step, and one of the boots caught in the loop of the air hose that ran from his tank pack to his helmet. He reached behind his helmet, trying to free himself from the body. The body shivered, and for an awful moment he thought it was still alive. Then the boot came free in his hand, and a naked foot—gray flesh, purple toenails—kicked his faceplate. A moment of nausea quickly passed: Norman had seen too many airplane crashes to be bothered by this. He dropped the boot, watched it drift down to Beth. He tugged on the leg of the corpse. He felt a mushy softness to the leg, and the body came free; it gently drifted down. He grabbed the shoulder, again feeling softness. He turned the body so he could see the face.

"It's Levy."

Her helmet was filled with water; behind the faceplate he saw staring eyes, open mouth, an expression of horror.

"I got her," Beth said, pulling the body down. Then she said, "Jesus."

Norman climbed back down the stanchion. Beth was moving the body away from the habitat, into the lighted area beyond.

"She's all *soft*. It's like every bone in her body was broken."

"I know." He moved out into the light, joined her. He felt a strange detachment, a coldness and a remove. He had known this woman; she had been alive just a short time before; now she was dead. But it was as if he were viewing it all from a great distance.

He turned Levy's body over. On the left side was a long

tear in the fabric of the suit. He had a glimpse of red mangled flesh. Norman bent to inspect it. "An accident?"

"I don't think so," Beth said.

"Here. Hold her." Norman lifted up the edges of suit fabric. Several separate tears met at a central point. "It's actually torn in a star pattern," he said. "You see?"

She stepped back. "I see, yes."

"What would cause that, Beth?"

"I don't—I'm not sure."

Beth stepped farther back. Norman was looking into the tear, at the body beneath the suit. "The flesh is macerated."

"Macerated?"

"Chewed."

"Jesus."

Yes, definitely chewed, he thought, probing inside the tear. The wound was peculiar: there were fine, jagged serrations in the flesh. Thin pale-red trickles of blood drifted up past his faceplate.

"Let's go back," Beth said.

"Just hang on." Norman squeezed the body at the legs, hips, shoulders. Everywhere it was soft, like a sponge. The body had been somehow almost entirely crushed. He could feel the leg bones, broken in many places. What could have done that? He went back to the wound.

"I don't like it out here," Beth said, tense.

"Just a second."

At first inspection, he had thought Levy's wound represented some sort of bite, but now he wasn't sure. "Her skin," Norman said. "It's like a rough file has gone over it—"

He jerked his head back, startled, as something small and

white drifted past his faceplate. His heart pounded at the thought that it was a jellyfish—but then he saw it was perfectly round and almost opaque. It was about the size of a golf ball. It drifted past him.

He looked around. There were thin streaks of mucus in the water. And many white spheres.

"What're these, Beth?"

"Eggs." Over the intercom, he heard her take deep slow breaths. "Let's get out of here, Norman. Please."

"Just another second."

"No, Norman. *Now.*"

On the radio, they heard an alarm. Distant and tinny, it seemed to be transmitted from inside the habitat. They heard voices, and then Barnes's voice, very loud. "What the *hell* are you doing out there?"

"We found Levy, Hal," Norman said.

"Well, get back on the double, damn it," Barnes said. "The sensors have activated. You're not alone out there—and whatever's with you is very damn big."

NORMAN FELT DULL and slow. "What about Levy's body?"

"Drop the body. Get back here!"

But the body, he thought sluggishly. They had to do something with the body. He couldn't just leave the body.

"What's the matter with you, Norman?" Barnes said.

Norman mumbled something, and he vaguely felt Beth grab him strongly by the arm, lead him back toward the habitat. The water was now clouded with white eggs. The alarms were ringing in his ears. The sound was very loud. And then he realized: a new alarm. This alarm was ringing *inside his suit.*

He began to shiver. His teeth chattered uncontrollably. He tried to speak but bit his tongue, tasted blood. He felt numb and stupid. Everything was happening in slow motion.

As they approached the habitat, he could see that the eggs were sticking to the cylinders, clinging densely, making a nubbly white surface.

"Hurry!" Barnes shouted. "Hurry! It's coming this way!"

They were under the airlock, and he began to feel surging currents of water. There was something very big out there. Beth was pushing him upward and then his helmet burst above the waterline and Fletcher gripped him with strong arms, and a moment after that Beth was pulled up and the hatch slammed shut. Somebody took off his helmet and he heard the alarm, shrieking loud in his ears. By now his whole body was shaking in spasms, thumping on the deck. They stripped off his suit and wrapped him in a silver blanket and held him until his shivering lessened, then finally stopped. And abruptly, despite the alarm, he went to sleep.

Military Considerations

t's not your goddamned job, that's why," Barnes said. "You
had no authorization to do what you did. None whatsoever."

"Levy might have still been alive," Beth said, calm in the
face of Barnes's fury.

"But she wasn't alive, and by going outside you risked the
lives of two civilian expedition members unnecessarily."

Norman said, "It was my idea, Hal." Norman was still
wrapped in blankets, but they had given him hot drinks and
made him rest, and now he felt better.

"And *you*," Barnes said. "You're lucky to be alive."

"I guess I am," Norman said. "But I don't know what happened."

"This is what happened," Barnes said, waving a small fan in
front of him. "Your suit circulator shorted out and you experienced rapid central cooling from the helium. Another couple of
minutes and you would have been dead."

"It was so fast," Norman said. "I didn't realize—"

"—You goddamn people," Barnes said. "I want to make something clear. This is not a scientific conference. This is not the Underwater Holiday Inn, where you can do whatever you please. This is a military operation and you will damn well follow military orders. Is that clear?"

"This is a military operation?" Ted said.

"It is now," Barnes said.

"Wait a minute. Was it always?"

"It is now."

"You haven't answered the question," Ted said. "Because if it is a military operation, I think we need to know that. I personally do not wish to be associated with—"

"—Then leave," Beth said.

"—a military operation that is—"

"—Look, Ted," Barnes said. "You know what this is costing the Navy?"

"No, but I don't see—"

"—I'll tell you. A deep-placement, saturated gas environment with full support runs about a hundred thousand dollars an hour. By the time we all get out of here, the total project cost will be eighty to a hundred million dollars. You don't get that kind of appropriations from the military without what they call 'a serious expectation of military benefit.' It's that simple. No expectation, no money. You following me?"

"You mean like a weapon?" Beth said.

"Possibly, yes," Barnes said.

"Well," Ted said, "I personally would never have joined—"

"—Is that right? You'd fly all the way to Tonga and I'd say,

'Ted, there's a spacecraft down there that might contain life from another galaxy, but it's a military operation,' and you'd say, 'Gosh, sorry to hear that, count me out'? Is that what you'd have done, Ted?"

"Well . . ." Ted said.

"Then you better shut up," Barnes said. "Because I've had it with your posturing."

"Hear, hear," Beth said.

"I personally feel you're overwrought," Ted said.

"I personally feel you're an egomaniacal asshole," Barnes said.

"Just a minute, everybody," Harry said. "Does anybody know why Levy went outside in the first place?"

Tina said, "She was on a TRL."

"A what?"

"A Timeclock Required Lockout," Barnes said. "It's the duty schedule. Levy was Edmunds's backup. After Edmunds died, it became Levy's job to go to the submarine every twelve hours."

"Go to the sub? Why?" Harry said.

Barnes pointed out the porthole. "You see DH-7 over there? Well, next to the single cylinder is an inverted dome hangar, and beneath the dome is a minisub that the divers left behind.

"In a situation like this," Barnes said, "Navy regs require that all tapes and records be transferred to the sub every twelve hours. The sub is on TBDR Mode—Timed Ballast Drop and Release—set on a timer every twelve hours. That way, if somebody doesn't get there every twelve hours, transfer the latest tapes, and press the yellow 'Delay' button, the sub will automatically drop ballast, blow tanks, and go to the surface unattended."

"Why is that?"

"If there's a disaster down here—say something happened to all of us—then the sub would automatically surface after twelve hours, with all the tapes accumulated thus far. The Navy'd recover the sub at the surface, and they'd have at least a partial record of what happened to us down here."

"I see. The sub's our flight recorder."

"You could say that, yes. But it's also our way out, our only emergency exit."

"So Levy was going to the sub?"

"Yes. And she must have made it, because the sub is still here."

"She transferred the tapes, pressed the 'Delay' button, and then she died on the way back."

"Yes."

"How did she die?" Harry said, looking carefully at Barnes.

"We're not sure," Barnes said.

"Her entire body was crushed," Norman said. "It was like a sponge."

Harry said to Barnes, "An hour ago you ordered the EPSA sensors to be reset and adjusted. Why was that?"

"We had gotten a strange reading in the previous hour."

"What sort of a reading?"

"Something out there. Something very large."

"But it didn't trigger the alarms," Harry said.

"No. This thing was beyond alarm-set parameters."

"You mean it was *too big* to set off the alarms?"

"Yes. After the first false alarm, the settings were all cranked down. The alarms were set to ignore anything that large. That's why Tina had to readjust the settings."

"And what set off the alarms just now?" Harry said. "When Beth and Norman were out there?"

Barnes said, "Tina?"

"I don't know what it was. Some kind of animal, I guess. Silent, and very big."

"How big?"

She shook her head. "From the electronic footprint, Dr. Adams, I would say the thing was almost as big as this habitat."

Battle Stations

B eth slipped one round white egg onto the stage of the scanning microscope. "Well," she said, peering through the
eyepiece, "it's definitely marine invertebrate. The interesting feature is this slimy coating." She poked at it with forceps.

"What is it?" Norman said.

"Some kind of proteinaceous material. Sticky."

"No. I mean, what is the egg?"

"Don't know yet." Beth continued her examination when
the alarm sounded and the red lights began to flash again. Norman felt a sudden dread.

"Probably another false alarm," Beth said.

"Attention, all hands," Barnes said on the intercom. "All
hands, battle stations."

"Oh shit," Beth said.

Beth slid gracefully down the ladder as if it were a fire pole;
Norman followed clumsily back down behind her. At the com-

munications section on D Cyl, he found a familiar scene: everyone clustered around the computer, and the back panels again removed. The lights still flashed, the alarm still shrieked.

"What is it?" Norman shouted.

"Equipment breakdown!"

"What equipment breakdown?"

"We can't turn the damn alarm off!" Barnes shouted. "It turned it on, but we can't turn it off! Teeny—"

"—Working on it, sir!"

The big engineer was crouched behind the computer; Norman saw the broad curve of her back.

"Get that damn thing off!"

"Getting it off, sir!"

"Get it off, I can't *hear!*"

Hear what? Norman wondered, and then Harry stumbled into the room, colliding with Norman. "Jesus . . ."

"This is an emergency!" Barnes was shouting. "This is an emergency! Seaman Chan! Sonar!" Tina was next to him, calm as always, adjusting dials on side monitors. She slipped on headphones.

Norman looked at the sphere on the video monitor. The sphere was closed.

Beth went to one of the portholes and looked closely at the white material that blocked it. Barnes spun like a dervish beneath the flashing red lights, shouting, swearing in all directions.

And then suddenly the alarm stopped, and the red lights stopped flashing. Everyone was silent. Fletcher straightened and sighed.

Harry said, "I thought you got that fixed—"

"—Shhh."

They heard the soft repetitive *pong!* of the sonar impulses. Tina cupped her hands over the headphones, frowning, concentrating.

Nobody moved or spoke. They stood tensely, listening to the sonar as it echoed back.

Barnes said quietly to the group, "A few minutes ago, we got a signal. From outside. Something very large."

Finally Tina said, "I'm not getting it now, sir."

"Go passive."

"Aye aye, sir. Going passive."

The pinging sonar stopped. In its place they heard a slight hiss. Tina adjusted the speaker volume.

"Hydrophones?" Harry said quietly.

Barnes nodded. "Polar glass transducers. Best in the world."

They all strained to listen, but heard nothing except the undifferentiated hiss. To Norman it sounded like tape noise, with an occasional gurgle of the water. If he wasn't so tense, he would have found the sound irritating.

Barnes said, "Bastard's clever. He's managed to blind us, cover all our ports with goo."

"Not goo," Beth said. "Eggs."

"Well, they're covering every damn port in the habitat."

The hissing continued, unchanging. Tina twisted the hydrophone dials. There was a soft continuous crackling, like cellophane being crumpled.

"What's that?" Ted said.

Beth said, "Fish. Eating."

Barnes nodded. Tina twisted the dials. "Tuning it out." They again heard the undifferentiated hiss. The tension in the room lessened. Norman felt tired and sat down. Harry sat next to him. Norman noticed that Harry looked more thoughtful than concerned. Across the room, Ted stood near the hatch door and bit his lip. He looked like a frightened kid.

There was a soft electronic beep. Lines on the gas-plasma screens jumped.

Tina said, "I have a positive on peripheral thermals."

Barnes nodded: "Direction?"

"East. Coming."

They heard a metallic *clank!* Then another *clank!*

"What's that?"

"The grid. He's hitting the grid."

"Hitting it? Sounds like he's dismantling it."

Norman remembered the grid. It was made of three-inch pipe.

"A big fish? A shark?" Beth said.

Barnes shook his head. "He's not moving like a shark. And he's too big."

Tina said, "Positive thermals on in-line perimeter. He's still coming."

Barnes said, "Go active."

The *pong!* of the sonar echoed in the room.

Tina said, "Target acquired. One hundred yards."

"Image him."

"FAS on, sir."

There was a rapid succession of sonar sounds: *pong! pong! pong! pong!* Then a pause, and it came again: *pong! pong! pong! pong!*

Norman looked puzzled. Fletcher leaned over and whispered, "False-aperture sonar makes a detailed picture from several senders outside, gives you a good look at him." He smelled liquor on her breath. He thought: Where'd she get liquor?

Pong! pong! pong! pong!

"Building image. Ninety yards."

Pong! pong! pong! pong!

"Image up."

They turned to the screens. Norman saw an amorphous, streaky blob. It didn't mean much to him.

"Jesus," Barnes said. "Look at the *size* of him!"

Pong! pong! pong! pong!

"Eighty yards."

Pong! pong! pong! pong!

Another image appeared. Now the blob was a different shape, the streaks in another direction. The image was sharper at the edges, but it still meant nothing to Norman. A big blob with streaks . . .

"Jesus! He's got to be thirty, forty feet across!" Barnes said.

"No fish in the world is that big," Beth said.

"Whale?"

"It's not a whale."

Norman saw that Harry was sweating. Harry took off his glasses and wiped them on his jumpsuit. Then he put them back on, and pushed them up on the bridge of his nose. They slipped back down. He glanced at Norman and shrugged.

Tina: "Fifty yards and closing."

Pong! pong! pong! pong!

"Thirty yards."

Pong! pong! pong! pong!

"Thirty yards."

Pong! pong! pong! pong!

"Holding at thirty yards, sir."

Pong! pong! pong! pong!

"Still holding."

"Active off."

Once again, they heard the hiss of the hydrophones. Then a distinct clicking sound. Norman's eyes burned. Sweat had rolled into his eyes. He wiped his forehead with his jumpsuit sleeve. The others were sweating, too. The tension was unbearable. He glanced at the video monitor again. The sphere was still closed.

He heard the hiss of the hydrophones. A soft scraping sound, like a heavy sack being dragged across a wooden floor. Then the hiss again.

Tina whispered, "Want to image him again?"

"No," Barnes said.

They listened. More scraping. A moment of silence, followed by the gurgle of water, very loud, very close.

"Jesus," Barnes whispered. "He's right outside."

A dull *thump* against the side of the habitat.

The screen flashed on.

I AM HERE.

THE FIRST IMPACT came suddenly, knocking them off their feet. They tumbled, rolling on the floor. All around them, the habitat creaked and groaned, the sounds frighteningly loud.

Norman scrambled to his feet—he saw Fletcher bleeding from her forehead—and the second impact hit. Norman was thrown sideways against the bulkhead. There was a metallic *clang* as his head struck metal, a sharp pain, and then Barnes landed on top of him, grunting and cursing. Barnes pushed his hand in Norman's face as he struggled to his feet; Norman slid back to the floor and a video monitor crashed alongside him, spitting sparks.

By now the habitat was swaying like a building in an earthquake. They clutched consoles, panels, doorways to keep their balance. But it was the noise that Norman found most frightening—the incredibly loud metallic groans and cracks as the cylinders were shaken on their moorings.

The creature was shaking the entire habitat.

Barnes was on the far side of the room, trying to make his way to the bulkhead door. He had a bleeding gash along one arm and he was shouting orders, but Norman couldn't hear anything except the terrifying sound of rending metal. He saw Fletcher squeeze through the bulkhead, and then Tina, and then Barnes made it through, leaving behind a bloody handprint on the metal.

Norman couldn't see Harry, but Beth lurched toward him, holding her hand out, saying "Norman! Norman! We have to—" and then she slammed into him and he was knocked over and he fell onto the carpet, underneath the couch, and slid up against the cold outer wall of the cylinder, and he realized with horror that the carpet was wet.

The habitat was leaking.

He had to do something; he struggled back to his feet, and

stood right in a fine sizzling spray from one of the wall seams. He glanced around, saw other leaks spurting from the ceiling, the walls.

This place is going to be torn apart.

Beth grabbed him, pulled her head close. "We're leaking!" she shouted. "God, we're leaking!"

"I know," Norman said, and Barnes shouted over the intercom, "Positive pressure! Get positive pressure!" Norman saw Ted on the floor just before he tripped over him and fell heavily against the computer consoles, his face near the screen, the glowing letters large before him:

DO NOT BE AFRAID.

"Jerry!" Ted was shouting. "Stop this, Jerry! Jerry!"

Suddenly Harry's face was next to Ted, glasses askew. "Save your breath, he's going to kill us all!"

"He doesn't understand," Ted shouted, as he fell backward onto the couch, flailing arms.

The powerful wrenching of metal on metal continued without pause, throwing Norman from one side to the other. He kept reaching for handholds, but his hands were wet, and he couldn't seem to grasp anything.

"Now hear this," Barnes said over the intercom. "Chan and I are going outside! Fletcher assumes command!"

"Don't go out!" Harry shouted. "Don't go out there!"

"Opening hatch now," Barnes said laconically. "Tina, you follow me."

"You'll be killed!" Harry shouted, and then he was thrown against Beth. Norman was on the floor again; he banged his head on one of the couch legs.

"We're outside," Barnes said.

And abruptly the banging stopped. The habitat was motionless. They did not move. With the water streaming in through a dozen fine, misty leaks, they looked up at the intercom speaker, and listened.

"CLEAR OF THE hatch," Barnes said. "Our status is good. Armament, J-9 exploding head spears loaded with Taglin-50 charges. We'll show this bastard a trick or two."

Silence.

"Water . . . Visibility is poor. Visibility under five feet. Seems to be . . . stirred-up bottom sediment and . . . very black, dark. Feeling our way along buildings."

Silence.

"North side. Going east now. Tina?"

Silence.

"Tina?"

"Behind you, sir."

"All right. Put your hand on my tank so you—Good. Okay."

Silence.

Inside the cylinder, Ted sighed. "I don't think they should kill it," he said softly.

Norman thought, I don't think they can.

Nobody else said anything. They listened to the amplified breathing of Barnes and Tina.

"Northeast corner . . . All right. Feel strong currents, active, moving water . . . something nearby. . . . Can't see . . . visibility less than five feet. Can barely see stanchion I am holding. I can feel him, though. He's big. He's near. Tina?"

Silence.

A loud sharp crackling sound, static. Then silence.

"Tina? Tina?"

Silence.

"I've lost Tina."

Another, very long silence.

"I don't know what it . . . Tina, if you can hear me, stay where you are, I'll take it from here. . . . Okay . . . He is very close. . . . I feel him moving. . . . Pushes a lot of water, this guy. A real monster."

Silence again.

"Wish I could see better."

Silence.

"Tina? Is that—"

And then a muffled thud that might have been an explosion. They all looked at each other, trying to know what the sound meant, but in the next instant the habitat began rocking and wrenching again, and Norman, unprepared, was slammed sideways, against the sharp edge of the bulkhead door, and the world went gray. He saw Harry strike the wall next to him, and Harry's glasses fell onto Norman's chest, and Norman reached for the glasses for Harry, because Harry needed his glasses. And then Norman lost consciousness, and everything was black.

After The Attack

Hot spray poured over him, and he inhaled steam.

Standing in the shower, Norman looked down at his body and thought, I look like a survivor of an airplane crash. One of those people I used to see and marvel that they were still alive.

The lumps on his head throbbed. His chest was scraped raw in a great swath down to his abdomen. His left thigh was purple-red; his right hand was swollen and painful.

But, then, everything was painful. He groaned, turning his face up to the water.

"Hey," Harry called. "How about it in there?"

"Okay."

Norman stepped out, and Harry climbed in. Scrapes and bruises covered his thin body. Norman looked over at Ted, who lay on his back in one of the bunks. Ted had dislocated both shoulders, and it had taken Beth half an hour to get them back in, even after she'd shot him up with morphine.

"How is it now?" Norman said to him.

"Okay."

Ted had a numb, dull expression. His ebullience was gone. He had sustained a greater injury than the dislocated shoulders, Norman thought. In many ways a naïve child, Ted must have been profoundly shocked to discover that this alien intelligence was hostile.

"Hurt much?" Norman said.

"It's okay."

Norman sat slowly on his bunk, feeling pain streak up his spine. Fifty-three years old, he thought. I should be playing golf. Then he thought, I should be just about anywhere in the world, except here. He winced, and gingerly slipped a shoe over his injured right foot. For some reason, he remembered Levy's bare toes, the skin color dead, the foot striking his faceplate.

"Did they find Barnes?" Ted asked.

"I haven't heard," Norman said. "I don't think so."

He finished dressing, and went down to D Cyl, stepping over the puddles of water in the corridor. Inside D itself, the furniture was soaked; the consoles were wet, and the walls were covered with irregular blobs of white urethane foam where Fletcher had spray-sealed the cracks.

Fletcher stood in the middle of the room, the spray can in hand. "Not as pretty as it was," she said.

"Will it hold?"

"Sure, but I guarantee you: we can't survive another one of those attacks."

"What about the electronics. They working?"

"I haven't checked, but it should be okay. It's all water-proofed."

Norman nodded. "Any sign of Captain Barnes?" He looked at the bloody handprint on the wall.

"No, sir. No sign of the Captain at all." Fletcher followed his eyes to the wall. "I'll clean the place up in a minute, sir."

"Where's Tina?" Norman asked.

"Resting. In E Cyl."

Norman nodded. "E Cyl any drier than this?"

"Yes," Fletcher said. "It's a funny thing. There was nobody in E Cyl during the attack, and it stayed completely dry."

"Any word from Jerry?"

"No contact, sir, no."

Norman flicked on one of the computer consoles.

"Jerry, are you there?"

The screen remained blank.

"Jerry?"

He waited a moment, then turned the console off.

TINA SAID, "LOOK at it now." She sat up, and drew the blanket back to expose her left leg.

The injury was much worse than when they had heard her screaming and had run through the habitat and pulled her up through the A Cyl hatch. Now, running diagonally down her leg was a series of saucer-shaped welts, the center of each puffed and purple. "It's swollen a lot in the last hour," Tina said.

Norman examined the injuries. Fine tooth-marks ringed swollen areas. "Do you remember what it felt like?" he said.

"It felt awful," Tina said. "It felt *sticky*, you know, like sticky glue or something. And then each one of these round places burned. Very strong."

"And what could you see? Of the creature itself."

"Just—it was a long flat spatula-thing. It looked like a giant leaf; it came out and wrapped around me."

"Any color?"

"Sort of brownish. I couldn't really see."

He paused a moment. "And Captain Barnes?"

"During the course of the action, I was separated from Captain Barnes, sir. I don't know what happened to Captain Barnes, sir." Tina spoke formally, her face a mask. He thought, Let's not go into this now. If you ran away, it's all right with me.

"Has Beth seen this injury, Tina?"

"Yes, sir, she was here a few minutes ago."

"Okay. Just rest now."

"Sir?"

"Yes, Tina?"

"Who will be making the report, sir?"

"I don't know. Let's not worry about reports now. Let's just concentrate on getting through this."

"Yes, sir."

AS HE APPROACHED Beth's lab, he heard Tina's recorded voice say, "Do you think they'll ever get the sphere open?"

Beth said, "Maybe. I don't know."

"It scares me."

And then Tina's voice came again:

"Do you think they'll ever get the sphere open?"

"Maybe. I don't know."

"It scares me."

In the lab, Beth was hunched over the console, watching the tape.

"Still at it, huh?" Norman said.

"Yeah."

On the tape, Beth was finishing her cake, saying, "I don't think there's a reason to be scared."

"It's the unknown," Tina said.

"Sure," Beth said onscreen, "but an unknown thing is not likely to be dangerous or frightening. It's most likely to be just inexplicable."

"Famous last words," Beth said, watching herself.

"It sounded good at the time," Norman said. "To keep her calmed down."

Onscreen, Beth said to Tina, "You afraid of snakes?"

"Snakes don't bother me," Tina said.

"Well, I can't stand snakes," Beth said.

Beth stopped the tape, turned to Norman. "Seems like a long time ago, doesn't it."

"I was just thinking that," Norman said.

"Does this mean we're living life to the fullest?"

"I think it means we're in mortal peril," Norman said. "Why are you so interested in this tape?"

"Because I have nothing better to do, and if I don't keep busy I'm going to start screaming and make one of those traditional feminine scenes. You've already seen me do it once, Norman."

"Have I? I don't remember any scene."

"Thank you," she said.

Norman noticed a blanket on a couch in the corner of her

lab. And Beth had unclipped one of the workbench lamps and mounted it on the wall above the blankets. "You sleeping here now?"

"Yeah, I like it here. Up at the top of the cylinder—I feel like the queen of the underworld." She smiled. "Sort of like a tree house when you were a kid. Did you ever have a tree house when you were a kid?"

"No," Norman said, "I never did."

"Neither did I," Beth said. "But it's what I imagine it would be, if I had."

"Looks very cozy, Beth."

"You think I'm cracking up?"

"No. I just said it looks cozy."

"You can tell me if you think I'm cracking up."

"I think you're fine, Beth. What about Tina? You've seen her injury?"

"Yes." Beth frowned. "And I've seen these." She gestured to some white eggs in a glass container on the lab bench.

"More eggs?"

"They were clinging to Tina's suit when she came back in. Her injury is consistent with these eggs. Also the smell: you remember the smell when we pulled her back in?"

Norman remembered very well. Tina had smelled strongly of ammonia. It was almost as if she'd been doused in smelling salts.

Beth said, "As far as I know, there's only one animal that smells of ammonia that way. *Architeuthis sanctipauli*."

"Which is?"

"One of the species of giant squid."

"That's what attacked us?"

"I think so, yes."

She explained that little was known about the giant squid, because the only specimens studied were dead animals that washed ashore, generally in a state of advanced decay, and reeking of ammonia. For most of human history, the giant squid was considered a mythical sea monster, like the kraken. But in 1861 the first reliable scientific reports appeared, after a French warship managed to haul in fragments of one dead animal. And many killed whales which showed scars from giant suckers, testimony of undersea battles. Whales were the only known predator of the giant squid—the only animals large enough to be predators.

"By now," Beth said, "giant squid have been observed in every major ocean of the world. There are at least three distinct species. The animals grow very large and can weigh a thousand pounds or more. The head is about twenty feet long, with a crown of eight arms. Each arm is about ten feet long, with long rows of suckers. In the center of the crown is a mouth with a sharp beak, like a parrot's beak, except the jaws are seven inches long."

"Levy's torn suit?"

"Yes." She nodded. "The beak is mounted in a ring of muscle so it can twist in circles as it bites. And the radula—the tongue of the squid—has a raspy, file-like surface."

"Tina mentioned something about a leaf, a brown leaf."

"The giant squid has two tentacles that extend out much further than the arms, as long as forty feet. Each tentacle ends in a flattened 'manus' or 'palm,' which looks very much like a big leaf. The manus is what the squid really uses to catch prey. The suckers on the manus are surrounded by a little hard ring of chitin, which is why you see the circular tooth-marks around the injury."

Norman said, "How would you fight one?"

"Well," Beth said, "in theory, although giant squid are very large, they are not particularly strong."

"So much for theory," Norman said.

She nodded. "Of course, nobody knows how strong they are, since a living specimen has never been encountered. We have the dubious distinction of being first."

"But it can be killed?"

"I would think rather easily. The squid's brain is located behind the eye, which is about fifteen inches across, the size of a big dinner plate. If you directed an explosive charge into the animal anywhere in that area, you would almost certainly disrupt the nervous system and it would die."

"Do you think Barnes killed the squid?"

She shrugged. "I don't know."

"Is there more than one in an area?"

"I don't know."

"Will we see one again?"

"I don't know."

The Visitor

Norman went downstairs to the communications center to see if he could talk to Jerry, but Jerry was not responding. Norman must have dozed off in the console chair, because he looked up abruptly, startled to see a trim black seaman in uniform standing just behind him, looking over his shoulder at the screens.

"How's it going, sir?" the seaman asked. He was very calm. His uniform was crisply pressed.

Norman felt a burst of tremendous elation. This man's arrival at the habitat could mean only one thing—the surface ships must be back! The ships had returned, and the subs had been sent down to retrieve them! They were all going to be saved!

"Sailor," Norman said, pumping his hand, "I'm very damn glad to see you."

"Thank you, sir."

"When did you get here?" Norman asked.

"Just now, sir."

"Do the others know yet?"

"The others, sir?"

"Yes. There's, uh, there's six of us left. Have they been told you're here?"

"I don't know the answer to that, sir."

There was a flatness to this man that Norman found odd. The sailor was looking around the habitat, and for a moment Norman saw the environment through his eyes—the damp interior, the wrecked consoles, the foam-spattered walls. It looked like they had fought a war in here.

"We've had a rough time," Norman said.

"I can see that, sir."

"Three of us have died."

"I'm sorry to hear that, sir."

That flatness again. Neutrality. Was he being proper? Was he worried about a pending court-martial? Was it something else entirely?

"Where have you come from?" Norman said.

"Come from, sir?"

"What ship."

"Oh. The *Sea Hornet*, sir."

"It's topside now?"

"Yes, sir, it is."

"Well, let's get moving," Norman said. "Tell the others you're here."

"Yes, sir."

The seaman went away. Norman stood and shouted, "Yahoo! We're saved!"

• • •

"AT LEAST HE wasn't an illusion," Norman said, staring at the screen. "There he is, big as life, on the monitor."

"Yes. There he is. But where'd he go?" Beth said. For the last hour, they had searched the habitat thoroughly. There was no sign of the black crewman. There was no sign of a submarine outside. There was no evidence of surface ships. The balloon they had sent up registered eighty-knot winds and thirty-foot waves before the wire snapped.

So where had he come from? And where had he gone?

Fletcher was working the consoles. A screen of data came up. "How about this? Log of ships in active service shows no vessel currently designated *Sea Hornet*."

Norman said, "What the hell is going on here?"

"Maybe he was an illusion," Ted said.

"Illusions don't register on videotape," Harry said. "Besides, I saw him, too."

"You did?" Norman said.

"Yeah. I had just woken up, and I had had this dream about being rescued, and I was lying in bed when I heard footsteps and he walked into the room."

"Did you talk to him?"

"Yes. But he was funny. He was dull. Kind of boring."

Norman nodded. "You could tell something wasn't right about him."

"Yes, you could."

"But where did he come from?" Beth said.

"I can think of only one possibility," Ted said. "He came from the sphere. Or at least, he was *made* by the sphere. By Jerry."

"Why would Jerry do that? To spy on us?"

Ted shook his head. "I've been thinking about this," he said. "It seems to me that Jerry has the ability to create things. Animals. I don't think that Jerry *is* a giant squid, but Jerry created the giant squid that attacked us. I don't think Jerry wants to attack us, but, from what Beth was telling us, once he made the squid, then *the squid* might attack the habitat, thinking the cylinders were its mortal enemy, the whale. So the attack happened as a kind of accident of creation."

They frowned, listening. To Norman, the explanation was entirely too convenient. "I think there is another possibility. That Jerry is hostile."

"I don't believe that," Ted said. "I don't believe Jerry is hostile."

"He certainly acts hostile, Ted."

"But I don't think he *intends* to be hostile."

"Whatever he intends," Fletcher said, "we better not go through another attack. Because the structure can't take it. And neither can the support systems.

"After the first attack, I had to increase positive pressure," Fletcher said, "in order to fix the leaks. To keep water from coming in, I had to increase the pressure of the air inside the habitat to make it greater than the pressure of the water outside. That stopped the leaks, but it meant that air bubbled out through all the cracks. And one hour of repair work consumed nearly sixteen hours of our reserve air. I've been worried we'll run out of air."

There was a pause. They all considered the implications of that.

"To compensate," Fletcher said, "I've dropped the internal pressure by three centimeters' pressure. We're slightly negative right now, and we should be fine. Our air will last us. But another attack under these conditions and we'll crush like a beer can."

Norman didn't like hearing any of this, but at the same time he was impressed with Fletcher's competence. She was a resource they ought to be using, he thought. "Do you have any suggestions, Teeny, if there's another attack?"

"Well, we have something in Cyl B called HVDS."

"Which is?"

"High Voltage Defense System. There's a little box in B that electrifies the metal walls of the cylinders at all times, to prevent electrolytic corrosion. Very slight electrical charge, you aren't really aware of it. Anyway, there's another, green box attached to that one, and it's the HVDS. It's basically a low-amp stepup transformer that sends two million volts over the cylinder surface. Should be very unpleasant for any animal."

"Why didn't we use it before?" Beth said. "Why didn't Barnes use it, instead of risking—"

"—Because the Green Box has problems," Fletcher said. "For one thing, it's really sort of theoretical. As far as I know, it's never actually been used in a real undersea work situation."

"Yes, but it must have been tested."

"Yes. And in all the tests, it started fires inside the habitat."

Another pause, while they considered that. Finally Norman said, "Bad fires?"

"The fires tend to burn the insulation, the wall padding."

"The fires take the padding off!"

"We'd die of heat loss in a few minutes."

Beth said, "How bad can a fire be? Fires need oxygen to burn, and we've only got two percent oxygen down here."

"That's true, Dr. Halpern," Fletcher said, "but the actual oxygen percentage varies. The habitat is made to deliver pulses as high as sixteen percent for brief periods, four times an hour. It's all automatically controlled; you can't override it. And if the oxygen percentage is high, then fires burn just fine—three times faster than topside. They easily go out of control."

Norman looked around the cylinder. He spotted three fire extinguishers mounted on the walls. Now that he thought about it, there were extinguishers all over the habitat. He'd just never really paid attention before.

"Even if we get the fires under control, they're hell on the systems," Fletcher said. "The air handlers aren't made to take the added monoxide by-products and soot."

"So what do we do?"

"Last resort only," Fletcher said. "That'd be my recommendation."

The group looked at each other, nodded.

"Okay," Norman said. "Last resort only."

"Let's just hope we don't have another attack."

"Another attack . . ." There was a long silence as they considered that. Then the gas-plasma screens on Tina's console jumped, and a soft pinging filled the room.

"We have a contact on peripheral thermals," Tina said, in a flat voice.

"Where?" Fletcher said.

"North. Approaching."

And on the monitor, they saw the words:
I AM COMING.

THEY TURNED OFF both the interior and exterior lights. Norman peered through the porthole, straining to see out in the darkness. They had long ago learned that the darkness at this depth was not absolute; the waters of the Pacific were so clear that even a thousand feet down some light registered on the bottom. It was very slight—Edmunds had compared it to starlight—but Norman knew that on the surface you could see by starlight alone.

Now he cupped his hands by the sides of his face to block out the low light coming from Tina's consoles, waited for his eyes to adjust. Behind him, Tina and Fletcher were working with the monitors. He heard the hiss of the hydrophones in the room.

It was all happening again.

Ted was standing by the monitor, saying, "Jerry, can you hear me? Jerry, are you listening?" But he wasn't getting through.

Beth came up as Norman peered out the porthole. "You see anything?"

"Not yet."

Behind them, Tina said, "Eighty yards and closing . . . Sixty yards. You want sonar?"

"No sonar," Fletcher said. "Nothing to make ourselves interesting to him."

"Then should we kill the electronics?"

"Kill everything."

All the console lights went out. Now there was just the red glow of the space heaters above them. They sat in darkness and stared out. Norman tried to remember how long dark-vision accommodation required. He remembered it might be as long as three minutes.

He began to see shapes: the outline of the grid on the bottom and, dimly, the high fin of the spaceship, rising sharply up.

Then something else.

A green glow in the distance. At the horizon.

"It's like a green sunrise," Beth said.

The glow increased in intensity, and then they saw an amorphous green shape with lateral streaks. Norman thought, It's just like the image we saw before. It looks just like that. He couldn't really make out the details.

"Is it a squid?" he said.

"Yes," Beth said.

"I can't see. . . ."

"You're looking at it end-on. The body is toward us, the tentacles behind, partially blocked by the body. That's why you can't see it."

The squid grew larger. It was definitely coming toward them.

Ted ran from the portholes back to the consoles. "Jerry, are you listening? Jerry?"

"Electronics are off, Dr. Fielding," Fletcher said.

"Well, let's try and talk to him, for God's sake."

"I think we're past the talking stage now, sir."

The squid was faintly luminous, the entire body a deep green. Now Norman could see a sharp vertical ridge in the body. The moving tentacles and arms were clear. The outline grew larger. The squid moved laterally.

"It's going around the grid."

"Yes," Beth said. "They're intelligent animals; they have the ability to learn from experience. It probably didn't like hitting the grid before, and it remembers."

The squid passed the spacecraft fin, and they could gauge its size. It's as big as a house, Norman thought. The creature slid smoothly through the water toward them. He felt a sense of awe, despite his pounding heart.

"Jerry? *Jerry!*"

"Save your breath, Ted."

"Thirty yards," Tina said. "Still coming."

As the squid came closer, Norman could count the arms, and he saw the two long tentacles, glowing lines extending far beyond the body. The arms and tentacles seemed to move loosely in the water, while the body made rhythmic muscular contractions. The squid propelled itself with water, and did not use the arms for swimming.

"Twenty yards."

"God, it's big," Harry said.

"You know," Beth said, "we're the first people in human history to see a free-swimming giant squid. This should be a great moment."

They heard the gurgling, the rush of water over the hydrophones, as the squid came closer.

"Ten yards."

For a moment, the great creature turned sideways to the habitat, and they could see its profile—the enormous glowing body, thirty feet long, with the huge unblinking eye; the circle of arms, waving like evil snakes; the two long tentacles, each terminating in a flattened, leaf-shaped section.

The squid continued to turn until its arms and tentacles stretched toward the habitat, and they glimpsed the mouth, the sharp-edged chomping beak in a mass of glowing green muscle.

"Oh God . . ."

The squid moved forward. They could see each other in the glow through the portholes. It's starting, Norman thought. It's starting, and this time we can't survive it.

There was a *thump* as a tentacle swung against the habitat.

"Jerry!" Ted shouted. His voice was high, strained with tension.

The squid paused. The body moved laterally, and they could see the huge eye staring at them.

"Jerry! Listen to me!"

The squid appeared to hesitate.

"He's listening!" Ted shouted, and he grabbed a flashlight off a wall bracket and shined it out the porthole. He blinked the light once.

The great body of the squid glowed green, then went momentarily dark, then glowed green again.

"He's listening," Beth said.

"Of course he's listening. He's intelligent." Ted blinked his light twice in rapid succession.

The squid blinked back, twice.

"How can he do that?" Norman said.

"It's a kind of skin cell called a chromatophore," Beth said.

"The animal can open and close these cells at will, and block the light."

Ted blinked three times.

The squid blinked three times.

"He can do it fast," Norman said.

"Yes, fast."

"He's intelligent," Ted said. "I keep telling you. He's intelligent and he wants to talk."

Ted blinked long, short, short.

The squid matched the pattern.

"That's a baby," Ted said. "You just keep talking to me, Jerry."

He flashed a more complex pattern, and the squid answered, but then moved off to the left.

"I've got to keep him talking," Ted said.

As the squid moved, Ted moved, skipping from porthole to porthole, shining his light. The squid still blinked its glowing body in reply, but Norman sensed it had another purpose now.

They all followed Ted, from D into C Cyl. Ted flashed his light. The squid answered, but still moved onward.

"What's he doing?"

"Maybe he's leading us. . . ."

"Why?"

They went to B Cyl, where the life-support equipment was located, but there were no portholes in B. Ted moved on to A, the airlock. There were no portholes here, either. Ted immediately jumped down and opened the hatch in the floor, revealing dark water.

"Careful, Ted."

"I'm telling you, he's intelligent," Ted said. The water at his feet glowed a soft green. "Here he comes now." They could not see the squid yet, only the glow. Ted blinked his light into the water.

The green blinked back.

"Still talking," Ted said. "And as long as he's talking—"

With stunning swiftness, the tentacle smashed up through the open water and swung in a great arc around the airlock. Norman had a glimpse of a glowing stalk as thick as a man's body, and a great glowing leaf five feet long, swinging blindly past him, and as he ducked he saw it hit Beth and knock her sideways. Tina was screaming in terror. Strong ammonia fumes burned their eyes. The tentacle swung back toward Norman. He held up his hands to protect himself, touched slimy, cold flesh as the giant arm spun him, slammed him against the airlock's metal walls. The animal was incredibly strong.

"Get out, everybody out, away from the metal!" Fletcher was shouting. Ted was scrambling up, away from the hatch and the twisting arm, and he had almost reached the door when the leaf swung back and wrapped around him, covering most of his body. Ted grunted, pushed at the leaf with his hands. His eyes were wide with horror.

Norman ran forward but Harry grabbed him. "Leave him! You can't do anything now!"

Ted was being swung back and forth in the air across the airlock, banging from wall to wall. His head dropped; blood ran down his forehead onto the glowing tentacle. Still the arm swung him back and forth, the cylinder ringing like a gong with each impact.

"Get out!" Fletcher was shouting. "Everybody out!"

Beth scrambled past them. Harry tugged at Norman just as the second tentacle burst above the surface to hold Ted in a pincer grip.

"Off the metal! Damn it, off the metal!" Fletcher was shouting, and they stepped onto the carpet of B Cyl and she threw the switch on the Green Box and there was a hum from the generators and the red heater banks dimmed as two million volts of electricity surged through the habitat.

The response was instantaneous. The floor rocked under their feet as the habitat was struck by an enormous force, and Norman swore he heard a scream, though it might have been rending metal, and the tentacles quickly drew down out of the airlock. They had a last glimpse of Ted's body as it was pulled into the inky water and Fletcher yanked down the lever on the Green Box. But the alarms had already begun to sound, and the warning boards lit up.

"Fire!" Fletcher shouted. "Fire in E Cyl!"

FLETCHER GAVE THEM gas masks; Norman's kept slipping down his forehead, obscuring his vision. By the time they reached D Cylinder, the smoke was dense. They coughed and stumbled, banged into the consoles.

"Stay low," Tina shouted, dropping to her knees. She was leading the way; Fletcher had stayed behind in B.

Up ahead, an angry red glow outlined the bulkhead door leading to E. Tina grabbed an extinguisher and went through the door, Norman right behind her. At first he thought the entire cylinder was burning. Fierce flames licked up the side padding; dense clouds of smoke boiled toward the ceiling. The heat was almost palpable. Tina swung the extinguisher cylinder around, began to spray white foam. In the light of the fire Norman saw another extinguisher, grabbed it, but the metal was burning hot and he dropped it to the floor.

"Fire in D," Fletcher said over the intercom. "Fire in D."

Jesus, Norman thought. Despite the mask, he coughed in the acrid smoke. He picked the extinguisher off the floor and began to spray; it immediately became cooler. Tina shouted to him, but he heard nothing except the roar of the flames. He and Tina were getting the fire out, but there was still a large burning patch near one porthole. He turned away, spraying the floor burning at his feet.

He was unprepared for the explosion, the concussion pounding his ears painfully. He turned and saw that a fire-hose had been unleashed in the room, and then he realized that one of the small portholes had blown or burned out, and the water was rushing in with incredible force.

He couldn't see Tina; then he saw she had been knocked down; she got to her feet, shouting something at Norman, and then she slipped and slid back into the hissing stream of water. It picked her up bodily and flung her so hard against the opposite wall that he knew at once she must be dead, and when he looked down he saw her floating face-down in the water rapidly filling the room. The back of her head was cut open; he saw the pulpy red flesh of her brain.

Norman turned and fled. Water was already trickling over

the lip of the bulkhead as he slammed the heavy door shut, spun the wheel to lock it.

He couldn't see anything in D; the smoke was worse than before. He saw dim patches of red flame, hazy through the smoke. He heard the hiss of the extinguishers. Where was his own extinguisher? He must have left it in E. Like a blind man he felt along the walls for another extinguisher, coughing in the smoke. His eyes and lungs burned, despite the mask.

And then, with a great groan of metal, the pounding started, the habitat rocking under jolts from the squid outside. He heard Fletcher on the intercom but her voice was scratchy and unclear. The pounding continued, and the horrible wrenching of metal. And Norman thought, We're going to die. This time, we're going to die.

He couldn't find a fire extinguisher but his hands touched something metal on the wall and Norman felt it in the smoky darkness, wondering what it was, some kind of protrusion, and then two million volts surged through his limbs into his body and he screamed once, and fell backward.

Aftermath

He was staring at a bank of lights in some odd, angled perspective. He sat up, feeling a sharp pain, and looked around him. He was sitting on the floor in D Cylinder. A faint smoky haze hung in the air. The padded walls were blackened and charred in several places.

There must have been a fire here, he thought, staring at the damage in astonishment. When had this happened? Where had he been at the time?

He got slowly to one knee, and then to his feet. He turned to E Cylinder, but for some reason the bulkhead door to E was shut. He tried to spin the wheel to unlock it; it was jammed shut.

He didn't see anybody else. Where were the others? Then he remembered something about Ted. Ted had died. The squid swinging Ted's body in the airlock. And then Fletcher had said to get back, and she had thrown the power switch. . . .

It was starting to come back to him. The fire. There had been a fire in E Cylinder. He had gone into E with Tina to put out the fire. He remembered going into the room, seeing the flames lick up the side of the walls. . . . After that, he wasn't sure.

Where were the others?

For an awful moment he thought he was the only survivor, but then he heard a cough in C Cyl. He moved toward the sound. He didn't see anybody so he went to B Cyl.

Fletcher wasn't there. There was a large streak of blood on the metal pipes, and one of her shoes on the carpet. That was all.

Another cough, from among the pipes.

"Fletcher?"

"Just a minute . . ."

Beth emerged, grease-streaked, from the pipes. "Good, you're up. I've got most of the systems going, I think. Thank God the Navy has instructions printed on the housings. Anyway, the smoke's clearing and the air quality is reading all right—not great, but all right—and all the vital stuff seems to be intact. We have air and water and heat and power. I'm trying to find out how much power and air we have left."

"Where's Fletcher?"

"I can't find her anywhere." Beth pointed to the shoe on the carpet, and the streak of blood.

"Tina?" Norman asked. He was alarmed at the prospect of being trapped down here without any Navy people at all.

"Tina was with you," Beth said, frowning.

"I don't seem to remember," Norman said.

"You probably got a jolt of current," Beth said. "That would give you retrograde amnesia. You won't remember the last few minutes before the shock. I can't find Tina, either, but according to the status sensors E Cyl is flooded and shut down. You were with her in E. I don't know why it flooded."

"What about Harry?"

"He got a jolt, too, I think. You're lucky the amperage wasn't higher or you'd both be fried. Anyway, he's lying on the floor in C, either sleeping or unconscious. You might want to take a look at him. I didn't want to risk moving him, so I just left him there."

"Did he wake up? Talk to you?"

"No, but he seems to be breathing comfortably. Color's good, all that. Anyway, I thought I better get the life-support systems going." She wiped grease on her cheek. "I mean, it's just the three of us now, Norman."

"You, me, and Harry?"

"That's right. You, me, and Harry."

HARRY WAS SLEEPING peacefully on the floor between the bunks. Norman bent down, lifted one eyelid, shone a light in Harry's pupil. The pupil contracted.

"This can't be heaven," Harry said.

"Why not?" Norman said. He shone the light in the other pupil; it contracted.

"Because you're here. They don't let psychologists into heaven." He gave a weak smile.

"Can you move your toes? Your hands?"

"I can move everything. I walked up here, Norman, from down in C. I'm okay."

Norman sat back. "I'm glad you're okay, Harry." He meant it: he had been dreading the thought of an injury to Harry. From the beginning of the expedition, they had all relied on Harry. At every critical juncture, he had supplied the break-through, the necessary understanding. And even now, Nor-man took comfort in the thought that, if Beth couldn't figure out the life-support systems, Harry could.

"Yeah, I'm okay." He closed his eyes again, sighed. "Who's left?"

"Beth. Me. You."

"Jesus."

"Yeah. You want to get up?"

"Yeah, I'll get in the bunk. I'm real tired, Norman. I could sleep for a year."

Norman helped him to his feet. Harry dropped quickly onto the nearest bunk.

"Okay if I sleep for a while?"

"Sure."

"That's good. I'm real tired, Norman. I could sleep for a year."

"Yes, you said that—"

He broke off. Harry was snoring. Norman reached over to remove something crumpled on the pillow beneath Harry's head.

It was Ted Fielding's notebook.

Norman suddenly felt overwhelmed. He sat on his bunk, holding the notebook in his hands. Finally he looked at a cou-ple of pages, filled with Ted's large, enthusiastic scrawl. A pho-tograph fell onto his lap. He turned it over. It was a photo of a red Corvette. And the feelings just overwhelmed him. Norman didn't know if he was crying for Ted, or crying for himself, because it was clear to him that one by one, they were all dying down here. He was very sad, and very afraid.

BETH WAS IN D Cyl, at the communications console, turning on all the monitors.

"They did a pretty good job with this place," she said. "Everything is marked; everything has instructions; there're computer help files. An idiot could figure it out. There's just one problem that I can see."

"What's that?"

"The galley was in E Cyl, and E Cyl is flooded. We've got no food, Norman."

"None at all?"

"I don't think so."

"Water?"

"Yes, plenty of water, but no food."

"Well, we can make it without food. How much longer have we got down here?"

"It looks like two more days."

"We can make it," Norman said, thinking: Two days, Jesus. Two more days in this place.

"That's assuming the storm clears on schedule," Beth added. "I've been trying to figure out how to release a surface balloon, and see what it's like up there. Tina used to punch some special code to release a balloon."

"We can make it," Norman said again.

"Oh sure. If worse comes to worst, we can always get food from the spaceship. There's plenty over there."

"You think we can risk going outside?"

"We'll have to," she said, glancing at the screens, "sometime in the next three hours."

"Why?"

"The minisub. It has that automatic surfacing timer, unless someone goes over and punches the button."

"The hell with the sub," Norman said. "Let the sub go."

"Well, don't be too hasty," Beth said. "That sub can hold three people."

"You mean we could all get out of here in it?"

"Yeah. That's what I mean."

"Christ," Norman said. "Let's go now."

"There are two problems with that," Beth said. She pointed to the screens. "I've been going over the specs. First, the sub is unstable on the surface. If there are big waves on the surface, it'll bounce us around worse than anything we've had down here. And the second thing is that we have to link up with a decompression chamber on the surface. Don't forget, we still have ninety-six hours of decompression ahead of us."

"And if we don't decompress?" Norman said. He was thinking, Let's just go to the surface in the sub and throw open the hatch and see the clouds and the sky and breathe some normal earth air.

"We have to decompress," Beth said. "Your bloodstream is saturated with helium gas in solution. Right now you're under pressure, so everything is fine. But if you release that pressure suddenly, it's just the same as when you pop the top off a soda bottle. The helium will bubble explosively out of your system. You'll die instantly."

"Oh," Norman said.

"Ninety-six hours," Beth said. "That's how long it takes to get the helium out of you."

"Oh."

Norman went to the porthole and looked across at DH-7, and the minisub. It was a hundred yards away. "You think the squid will come back?"

She shrugged. "Ask Jerry."

Norman thought, No more of that Geraldine stuff now. Or did she prefer to think of this malevolent entity as masculine?

"Which monitor is it?"

"This one." She flicked it on. The screen glowed.

Norman said, "Jerry? Are you there?"

No answer.

He typed, JERRY? ARE YOU THERE?

There was no response.

"I'll tell you something about Jerry," Beth said. "He can't really read minds. When we were talking to him before, I sent him a thought and he didn't respond."

"I did, too," Norman said. "I sent both messages and images. He never responded."

"If we speak, he answers, but if we just think, he doesn't answer," Beth said. "So he's not all-powerful. He actually behaves as if he *hears* us."

"That's right," Norman said. "Although he doesn't seem to be hearing us now."

"No. I tried earlier, too."

"I wonder why he isn't answering."

"You said he was emotional. Maybe he's sulking."

Norman didn't think so. Child kings didn't sulk. They were vindictive and whimsical, but they didn't sulk.

"By the way," she said, "you might want to look at these." She handed him a stack of printouts. "They're the record of all the interactions we've had with him."

"They may give us a clue," Norman said, thumbing through the sheets without any real enthusiasm. He felt suddenly tired.

"Anyway, it'll occupy your mind."

"True."

"Personally," Beth said, "I'd like to go back to the ship."

"What for?"

"I'm not convinced we've found everything that's there."

"It's a long way to the ship," Norman said.

"I know. But if we get a clear time without the squid, I might try it."

"Just to occupy your mind?"

"I guess you could say that." She glanced at her watch. "Norman, I'm going to get a couple of hours of sleep," she said. "Then we can draw straws to see who goes to the submarine."

"Okay."

"You seem depressed, Norman."

"I am."

"Me, too," she said. "This place feels like a tomb—and I've been prematurely buried."

She climbed the ladder to her laboratory, but apparently she didn't go to sleep, because after a few moments, he heard Tina's recorded voice on videotape saying, "Do you think they'll ever get the sphere open?"

And Beth replied, "Maybe. I don't know."

"It scares me."

The whirr of rewinding and a short delay, then:

"Do you think they'll ever get the sphere open?"

"Maybe. I don't know."

"It scares me."

The tape was becoming an obsession with Beth.

He stared at the printouts on his lap, and then he looked at the screen. "Jerry?" he said. "Are you there?"

Jerry did not answer.

The Sub

She was shaking his shoulder gently. Norman opened his eyes.

"It's time," Beth said.

"Okay." He yawned. God, he was tired. "How much time is left?"

"Half an hour."

Beth switched on the sensory array at the communications console, adjusted the settings.

"You know how to work all that stuff?" Norman said. "The sensors?"

"Pretty well. I've been learning it."

"Then I should go to the sub," he said. He knew Beth would never agree, that she would insist on doing the active thing, but he wanted to make the effort.

"Okay," she said. "You go. That makes sense."

He covered his surprise. "I think so, too."

"Somebody has to watch the array," she said. "And I can give you warning if the squid is coming."

"Right," he said. Thinking, Hell, she's serious. "I don't think this is one for Harry," Norman said.

"No, Harry's not very physical. And he's still asleep. I say, let him sleep."

"Right," Norman said.

"You'll need help with your suit," Beth said.

"Oh, that's right, my suit," Norman said. "The fan is broken in my suit."

"Fletcher fixed it for you," Beth said.

"I hope she did it right."

"Maybe I should go instead," Beth said.

"No, no. You watch the consoles. I'll go. It's only a hundred yards or so, anyway. It can't be a big deal."

"All clear now," she said, glancing at the monitors.

"Right," Norman said.

HIS HELMET CLICKED in place, and Beth tapped his faceplate, gave him a questioning look: was everything all right?

Norman nodded, and she opened the floor hatch for him. He waved goodbye and jumped into the chilly black water. On the sea floor, he stood beneath the hatch for a moment and waited to make sure he could hear his circulating fan. Then he moved out from beneath the habitat.

There were only a few lights on in the habitat, and he could see many thin lines of bubbles streaming upward, from the leaking cylinders.

"How are you?" Beth said, over the intercom.

"Okay. You know the place is leaking?"

"It looks worse than it is," Beth said. "Trust me."

Norman came to the edge of the habitat and looked across

the hundred yards of open sea floor that separated him from DH-7. "How does it look? Still clear?"

"Still clear," Beth said.

Norman set out. He walked as quickly as he could, but he felt as if his feet were moving in slow motion. He was soon short of breath; he swore.

"What's the matter?"

"I can't go fast." He kept looking north, expecting at any moment to see the greenish glow of the approaching squid, but the horizon remained dark.

"You're doing fine, Norman. Still clear."

He was now fifty yards from the habitat—halfway there. He could see DH-7, much smaller than their own habitat, a single cylinder forty feet high, with very few portholes. Alongside it was the inverted dome, and the minisub.

"You're almost there," Beth said. "Good work."

Norman began to feel dizzy. He slowed his pace. He could now see markings on the gray surface of the habitat. There were all sorts of block-printed Navy stencils.

"Coast is still clear," Beth said. "Congratulations. Looks like you made it."

He moved under the DH-7 cylinder, looked up at the hatch. It was closed. He spun the wheel, pushed it open. He couldn't see much of the interior, because most of the lights were out. But he wanted to have a look inside. There might be something, some weapon, they could use.

"Sub first," Beth said. "You've only got ten minutes to push the button."

"Right."

Norman moved to the sub. Standing behind the twin screws, he read the name: *Deepstar III*. The sub was yellow, like the sub that he had ridden down, but its configuration was somewhat different. He found handholds on the side, pulled himself up into the pocket of air trapped inside the dome. There was a large acrylic bubble canopy on top of the sub for the pilot; Norman found the hatch behind, opened it, and dropped inside.

"I'm in the sub."

There was no answer from Beth. She probably couldn't hear him, surrounded by all this metal. He looked around the sub, thinking, I'm dripping wet. But what was he supposed to do, wipe his shoes before entering? He smiled at the thought. He found the tapes secured in an aft compartment. There was plenty of room for more, and plenty of room for three people. But Beth was right about going to the surface: the interior of the sub was crammed with instruments and sharp edges. If you got banged around in here it wouldn't be pleasant.

Where was the delay button? He looked at the darkened instrument panel, and saw a single flashing red light above a button marked "TIMER HOLD." He pressed the button.

The red light stopped flashing, and now remained steadily on. A small amber video screen glowed:

Timer Reset - Counting 12:00:00

As he watched, the numbers began to run backward. He must have done it, he thought. The video screen switched off.

Still looking at all the instruments, a thought occurred to

him: in an emergency, could he operate this sub? He slipped into the pilot's chair, faced the bewildering dials and switches of the instrument array. There didn't seem to be any steering apparatus, no wheel or joystick. How did you work the damned thing?

The video screen switched on:

DEEPSTAR III - COMMAND MODULE

Do you require help?
Yes   No   Cancel

Yes, he thought. I require help. He looked around for a "YES" button near the screen, but there wasn't any that he could see. Finally he thought to touch the screen, pressing "YES."

DEEPSTAR III - CHECKLIST OPTIONS

Descend   Ascend
Secure   Shutdown
Monitor   Cancel

He pressed "ASCEND." The screen changed to a small drawing of the instrument panel. One particular section of the drawing blinked on and off. Beneath the picture were the words:

DEEPSTAR III - ASCEND CHECKLIST

1. Set Ballast Blowers To: On
Proceed To Next   Cancel

So that was how it worked, Norman thought. A step-by-step checklist stored in the sub's computer. All you had to do was follow directions. He could do that.

A small surge of current moved the sub, swaying it at its tether.

He pressed the "CANCEL" and the screen went blank. It flashed:

Timer Reset - Counting 11:53:04

The counter was still running backward. He thought, Have I really been here seven minutes? Another surge of current, and the sub swayed again. It was time to go.

He moved to the hatch, climbed out into the dome, and closed the hatch. He lowered himself down the side of the sub, touched the bottom. Out from beneath the shielding metal, his radio immediately crackled.

"—you there? Norman, are you there? Answer, please!"

It was Harry, on the radio.

"I'm here," Norman said.

"Norman, for God's sake—"

In that moment, Norman saw the greenish glow, and he knew why the sub had surged and rocked at its moorings. The squid was just ten yards away, its glowing tentacles writhing out toward him, churning up the sediment along the ocean floor.

"—Norman, will you—"

There was no time to think. Norman took three steps, jumped, and pulled himself through the open hatch into DH-7.

HE SLAMMED THE hatch door down behind him but the flat, spade-like tentacle was already reaching in. He pinned the tentacle in the partially closed hatch, but the tentacle didn't withdraw. It was incredibly strong and muscular, writhing as he watched, the suckers like small puckered mouths opening and closing. Norman stomped down on the hatch, trying to force the tentacle to withdraw. With a muscular flip, the hatch flew open, knocking him backward, and the tentacle reached up into the habitat. He smelled the strong odor of ammonium.

Norman fled, climbing higher into the cylinder. The second tentacle appeared, splashing up through the hatch. The two tentacles swung in circles beneath him, searching. He came to a porthole and looked out, saw the great body of the animal, the huge round staring eye. He clambered higher, getting away from the tentacles. Most of the cylinder seemed to be given over to storage; it was crammed with equipment, boxes, tanks. Many of the boxes were bright red with stencils: "CAUTION NO SMOKING NO ELECTRONICS TE-VAC EXPLOSIVES." There were a hell of a lot of explosives in here, he thought, stumbling upward.

The tentacles rose higher behind him. Somewhere, in a detached, logical part of his brain, he thought: The cylinder is only forty feet high, and the tentacles are at least forty feet long. There will be no place for me to hide.

He stumbled, banged his knee, kept going. He heard the slap of the tentacles as they struck the walls, swung upward toward him.

A weapon, he thought. I have to find a weapon.

He came to the small galley, metal counter, some pots and pans. He pulled the drawers open hastily, looking for a knife. He could find only a small paring knife, threw it away in disgust. He heard the tentacles coming closer. The next moment he was knocked down, his helmet banging on the deck. Norman scrambled to his feet, dodged the tentacle, moved up the cylinder.

A communications section: radio set, computer, a couple of monitors. The tentacles were right behind him, slithering up like nightmarish vines. His eyes burned from the ammonia fumes.

He came to the bunks, a narrow space near the top of the cylinder.

No place to hide, he thought. No weapons, and no place to hide.

The tentacles reached the top of the cylinder, slapped against the upper curved surface, swung sideways. In a moment they would have him. He grabbed the mattress from one bunk, held it up as flimsy protection. The two tentacles were swinging erratically around him. He dodged the first.

And then with a *whump* the second tentacle coiled around him, holding both him and the mattress in a cold, slimy grip. He felt a sickening slow squeeze, the dozens of suckers gripping his body, cutting into his skin. He moaned in horror. The second tentacle swung back to grip him along with the first. He was trapped in a vise.

Oh God, he thought.

The tentacles swung away from the wall, lifting him high in the air, into the middle of the cylinder. This is it, he thought, but in the next moment he felt his body sliding downward past the mattress, and he slipped through the grip and fell through the air. He grabbed the tentacles for support, sliding down the giant evil-smelling vines, and then he crashed down onto the deck near the galley, his head banging on the metal deck. He rolled onto his back.

He saw the two tentacles above, gripping the mattress, squeezing it, twisting it. Did the squid realize what had happened, that he had gotten free?

Norman looked around desperately. A weapon, a weapon. This was a Navy habitat. There must be a weapon somewhere.

The tentacles tore the mattress apart. Shreds of white padding drifted down through the cylinder. The tentacles released the mattress, the big pieces falling. Then the tentacles started swinging around the habitat again.

Searching.

It knows, he thought. It knows I have gotten away, and that I am still in here somewhere. It is hunting me.

But how did it know?

Norman ducked behind the galley as one of the flat tentacles came crashing through the pots and pans, sweeping around, feeling for him. Norman scrambled back, coming up against a large potted plant. The tentacle was still searching, moving restlessly across the floor, banging the pans. Norman pushed the plant forward, and the tentacle gripped it, uprooted it easily, sweeping it away into the air.

The distraction allowed Norman to scramble forward.

A weapon, he thought. A weapon.

He looked down to where the mattress had fallen, and he saw, lining the wall near the bottom hatch, a series of silver vertical bars. Spear guns! Somehow he had missed them on the way up. Each spear gun was tipped in a fat bulb like a hand grenade. Explosive tips? He started to climb down.

The tentacles were sliding down, too, following him. How did the squid know where he was? And then, as he passed a porthole, he saw the eye outside and he thought, He can see me, for God's sake.

Stay away from the portholes.

Not thinking clearly. Everything happening fast. Crawling down past the explosive crates in the storage hold, thinking, I better not miss in here, and he landed with a *clang* on the air-lock deck.

The arms were slithering down, moving down the cylinder toward him. He tugged at one of the spear guns. It was strapped to the wall with a rubber cord. Norman pulled at it, tried to release it. The tentacles drew closer. He yanked at the rubber, but it wouldn't release. What was wrong with these snaps?

The tentacles were closer. Coming down swiftly.

Then he realized the cords had safety catches: you had to pull the guns *sideways*, not out. He did; the rubber popped free. The spear gun was in his hand. He turned, and the tentacle knocked him down. He flipped onto his back and saw the great flat suckered palm of the tentacle coming straight down on him, and the tentacle wrapped over his helmet, everything was black, and he fired.

There was tremendous pain in his chest and abdomen. For a horrified moment he thought he had shot himself. Then he gasped and he realized it was just the concussion; his chest was burning, but the squid released him.

He still couldn't see. He pulled the palm off his face and it fell heavily onto the deck, writhing, severed from the squid arm. The interior walls of the habitat were splattered with blood. One tentacle was still moving, the other was a bloody, ragged stump. Both arms pulled out through the hatch, slipped into the water.

Norman ran for the porthole; the squid moved swiftly away, the green glow diminishing. He had done it! He'd beaten it off.

He'd done it.

DH-8

"How many did you bring?" Harry said, turning the spear gun over in his hands.

"Five," Norman said. "That was all I could carry."

"But it worked?" He was examining the bulbous explosive tip.

"Yeah, it worked. Blew the whole tentacle off."

"I saw the squid going away," Harry said. "I figured you must have done something."

"Where's Beth?"

"I don't know. Her suit's gone. I think she may have gone to the ship."

"Gone to the ship?" Norman said, frowning.

"All I know is, when I woke up she was gone. I figured you were over at the habitat, and then I saw the squid, and I tried to get you on the radio but I guess the metal blocked the transmission."

"Beth left?" Norman said. He was starting to get angry. Beth was supposed to stay at the communications console, watching the sensors for him while he was outside. Instead, she had gone to the ship?

"Her suit's gone," Harry said again.

"Son of a bitch!" Norman said. He was suddenly furious—really, deeply furious. He kicked the console.

"Careful there," Harry said.

"Damn it!"

"Take it easy," Harry said, "come on, take it easy, Norman."

"What the hell does she think she's doing?"

"Come on, sit down, Norman." Harry steered him to a chair. "We're all tired."

"Damn right we're tired!"

"Easy, Norman, easy . . . Remember your blood pressure."

"My blood pressure's fine!"

"Not now, it's not," Harry said. "You're purple."

"How could she let me go outside and then just leave?"

"Worse, go out herself," Harry said.

"But she wasn't watching out for me any more," Norman said. And then it came to him, why he was so angry—he was angry because he was afraid. At a moment of great personal danger, Beth had abandoned him. There were only three of them left down there, and they needed each other—they needed to depend on each other. But Beth was unreliable, and that made him afraid. And angry.

"Can you hear me?" her voice said, on the intercom. "Anybody hear me?"

Norman reached for the microphone, but Harry snatched it away. "I'll do this," he said. "Yes, Beth, we can hear you."

"I'm in the ship," she said, her voice crackling on the intercom. "I've found another compartment, aft, behind the crew bunks. It's quite interesting."

Quite interesting, Norman thought. Jesus, quite interesting. He grabbed the microphone from Harry. "Beth, what the hell are you doing over there?"

"Oh, hi, Norman. You made it back okay, huh?"

"Barely."

"You have some trouble?" She didn't sound concerned.

"Yes, I did."

"Are you all right? You sound mad."

"You bet I'm mad. Beth, why did you leave while I was out there?"

"Harry said he'd take over for me."

"He what?" Norman looked at Harry. Harry was shaking his head no.

"Harry said he'd take over at the console for me. He told me to go ahead to the ship. Since the squid wasn't around, it seemed like a good time."

Norman cupped his hand over the microphone. "I don't remember that," Harry said.

"Did you talk to her?"

"I don't remember talking to her."

Beth said, "Just ask him, Norman. He'll tell you."

"He says he never said that."

"Well, then, he's full of it," Beth said. "What do you think, I'd abandon you when you were *outside*, for Christ's sake?" There was a pause. "I'd never do that, Norman."

"I swear," Harry said to Norman. "I never had any conversation with Beth. I never talked to her at all. I'm telling you, she was gone when I woke up. There was nobody here. If you ask me, she always intended to go to the ship."

Norman remembered how quickly Beth had agreed to let Norman go to the sub, how surprised he had been. Perhaps Harry was right, he thought. Perhaps Beth had been planning it all along.

"You know what I think?" Harry said. "I think she's cracking up."

Over the intercom, Beth said, "You guys get it straightened out?"

Norman said, "I think so, Beth, yes."

"Good," Beth said. "Because I have made a discovery over here, in the spaceship."

"What's that?"

"I've found the crew."

"YOU BOTH CAME," Beth said. She was sitting on a console in the comfortable beige flight deck of the spacecraft.

"Yes," Norman said, looking at her. She looked okay. If anything, she looked better than ever. Stronger, clearer. She actually looked rather beautiful, he thought. "Harry thought that the squid wouldn't come back."

"The *squid* was out there?"

Norman briefly told her about his attack.

"Jesus. I'm sorry, Norman. I'd never have left if I had any idea."

She certainly didn't sound like somebody who was cracking up, Norman thought. She sounded appropriate and sincere.

"Anyway," he said, "I injured it, and Harry thought it wouldn't come back."

Harry said, "And we couldn't decide who should stay behind, so we both came."

"Well, come this way," Beth said. She led them back, through the crew quarters, past the twenty bunks for the crew, the large galley. Norman paused at the galley. So did Harry.

"I'm hungry," Harry said.

"Eat something," Beth said. "I did. They have some sort of nut bars or something, they taste okay." She opened a drawer in the galley, produced bars wrapped in metal foil, gave them each one. Norman tore the foil and saw something that looked like chocolate. It tasted dry.

"Anything to drink?"

"Sure." She threw open a refrigerator door. "Diet Coke?"

"You're kidding. . . ."

"The can design is different, and I'm afraid it's warm, but it's Diet Coke, all right."

"I'm buying stock in that company," Harry said. "Now that we know it'll still be there in fifty years." He read the can. "Official drink of the Star Voyager Expedition."

"Yeah, it's a promo," Beth said.

Harry turned the can around. The other side was printed in Japanese. "Wonder what this means?"

"It means, don't buy that stock after all," she said.

Norman sipped the Coke with a sense of vague unease. The galley seemed subtly changed from the last time he had seen it. He wasn't sure—he'd only glanced briefly at the room before—

but he usually had a good memory for room layouts, and his wife had always joked that Norman could find his way around any kitchen. "You know," he said, "I don't remember a refrigerator in the galley."

"I never really noticed, myself," Beth said.

"As a matter of fact," Norman said, "this whole room looks different to me. It looks bigger, and—I don't know—different."

"It's 'cause you're hungry." Harry grinned.

"Maybe," Norman said. Harry could actually be right. In the sixties, there had been a number of studies of visual perception which demonstrated that subjects interpreted blurred slides according to their predispositions. Hungry people saw all the slides as food.

But this room really did look different. For instance, he didn't remember the door to the galley being to the left, as it was now. He remembered it as being in the center of the wall separating the galley from the bunks.

"This way," Beth said, leading them farther aft. "Actually, the refrigerator was what got me thinking. It's one thing to store a lot of food on a test ship being sent through a black hole. But to stock a refrigerator—why bother to do that? It made me think, there might be a crew after all."

They entered a short, glass-walled tunnel. Deep-purple lights glowed down on them. "Ultraviolet," Beth said. "I don't know what it's for."

"Disinfection?"

"Maybe."

"Maybe it's to get a suntan," Harry said. "Vitamin D."

Then they came into a large room unlike anything Norman had ever seen. The floor glowed purple, bathing the room in ultraviolet light from beneath. Mounted on all four walls were a series of wide glass tubes. Inside each tube was a narrow silver mattress. The tubes all appeared empty.

"Over here," Beth said.

They peered through one glass tube. The naked woman had once been beautiful. It was still possible to see that. Her skin was dark brown and deeply wrinkled, her body withered.

"Mummified?" Harry said.

Beth nodded. "Best I can figure out. I haven't opened the tube, considering the risk of infection."

"What was this room?" he said, looking around.

"It must be some kind of hibernation chamber. Each tube is separately connected to a life-support system—power supply, air handlers, heaters, the works—in the next room."

Harry counted. "Twenty tubes," he said.

"And twenty bunks," Norman said.

"So where is everybody else?"

Beth shook her head. "I don't know."

"This woman is the only one left?"

"Looks like it. I haven't found any others."

"I wonder how they all died," Harry said.

"Have you been to the sphere?" Norman asked Beth.

"No. Why?"

"Just wondered."

"You mean, you wondered if the crew died after they picked up the sphere?"

"Basically, yes."

"I don't think the sphere is aggressive or dangerous in any sense," Beth said. "It's possible that the crew died of natural causes in the course of the journey itself. This woman, for example, is so well preserved it makes you wonder about radiation. Maybe she got a large dose of radiation. There's tremendous radiation around a black hole."

"You think the crew died going through the black hole, and the sphere was picked up automatically by the spacecraft later?"

"It's possible."

"She's pretty good-looking," Harry said, peering through the glass. "Boy, the reporters would go crazy with this, wouldn't they? Sexy woman from the future found nude and mummified. Film at eleven."

"She's tall, too," Norman said. "She must be over six feet."

"An Amazon woman," Harry said. "With great tits."

"All right," Beth said.

"What's wrong—offended on her behalf?" Harry said.

"I don't think there's any need for comments of that kind."

"Actually, Beth," Harry said, "she looks a little like you."

Beth frowned.

"I'm serious. Have you looked at her?"

"Don't be ridiculous."

Norman peered through the glass, shielding his hand against the reflection of the purple UV tubes in the floor. The mummified woman did indeed look like Beth—younger, taller, stronger, but like Beth, nevertheless. "He's right," Norman said.

"Maybe she's you, from the future," Harry said.

"No, she's obviously in her twenties."

"Maybe she's your granddaughter."

"Pretty unlikely," Beth said.

"You never know," Harry said. "Does Jennifer look like you?"

"Not really. But she's at that awkward stage. And she doesn't look like that woman. And neither do I."

Norman was struck by the conviction with which Beth denied any resemblance or association to the mummified woman. "Beth," he said, "what do you suppose happened here? Why is this woman the only one left?"

"I think she was important to the expedition," Beth said. "Maybe even the captain, or the co-captain. The others were mostly men. And they did something foolish—I don't know what—something she advised them against—and as a result they all died. She alone remained alive in this spacecraft. And she piloted it home. But there was something wrong with her—something she couldn't help—and she died."

"What was wrong with her?"

"I don't know. Something."

Fascinating, Norman thought. He'd never really considered it before, but this room—for that matter, this entire spacecraft—was one big Rorschach. Or more accurately, a TAT. The Thematic Apperception Test was a psychological test that consisted of a series of ambiguous pictures. Subjects were supposed to tell what they thought was happening in the pictures. Since no clear story was implied by the pictures, the subjects supplied the stories. And the stories told much more about the storytellers than about the pictures.

Now Beth was telling them her fantasy about this room: that a woman had been in charge of the expedition, the men had failed to listen to her, they had died, and she alone had remained alive, the sole survivor.

It didn't tell them much about this spaceship. But it told them a lot about Beth.

"I get it," Harry said. "You mean she's the one who made the mistake and piloted the ship back too far into the past. Typical woman driver."

"Do you have to make a joke of everything?"

"Do you have to take everything so seriously?"

"This *is* serious," Beth said.

"I'll tell you a different story," Harry said. "This woman screwed up. She was supposed to do something, and she forgot to do it, or else she made a mistake. And then she went into hibernation. As a result of her mistake, the rest of the crew died, and she never woke up from the hibernation—never realized what she had done, because she was so unaware of what was really happening."

"I'm sure you like that story better," Beth said. "It fits with your typical black-male contempt for women."

"Easy," Norman said.

"You resent the power of the female," Beth said.

"What power? You call lifting weights power? That's only strength—and it comes out of a feeling of weakness, not power."

"You skinny little weasel," Beth said.

"What're you going to do, beat me up?" Harry said. "Is that your idea of power?"

"I know what power is," Beth said, glaring at him.

"Easy, easy," Norman said. "Let's not get into this."

Harry said, "What do you think, Norman? Do you have a story about the room, too?"

"No," Norman said. "I don't."

"Oh, come on," Harry said. "I bet you do."

"No," Norman said. "And I'm not going to mediate between you two. We've all got to stay together on this. We have to work as a team, as long as we're down here."

"It's Harry who's divisive," Beth said. "From the beginning of this trip, he's tried to make trouble with everybody. All those snide little comments . . ."

"What snide little comments?" Harry said.

"You know perfectly well what snide little comments," Beth said.

Norman walked out of the room.

"Where're you going?"

"Your audience is leaving."

"Why?"

"Because you're both boring."

"Oh," Beth said, "Mr. Cool Psychologist decides we are boring?"

"That's right," Norman said, walking through the glass tunnel, not looking back.

"Where do you get off, making all these judgments of other people?" Beth shouted at him.

He kept walking.

"I'm speaking to you! Don't you walk away while I'm speaking to you, Norman!"

He came into the galley once more and started opening the drawers, looking for the nut bars. He was hungry again, and the search took his mind off the other two. He had to admit he was disturbed by the way things were going. He found a bar, tore the foil, ate it.

Disturbed, but not surprised. In studies of group dynamics he had long ago verified the truth of the old statement "Three's a crowd." For a high-tension situation, groups of three were inherently unstable. Unless everybody had clearly defined responsibilities, the group tended to form shifting allegiances, two against one. That was what was happening now.

He finished the nut bar, and immediately ate another one. How much longer did they have down here? At least thirty-six hours more. He looked for a place to carry additional nut bars, but his polyester jumpsuit had no pockets.

Beth and Harry came into the galley, much chagrined.

"Want a nut bar?" he said, chewing.

"We want to apologize," she said.

"For what?"

"For acting like children," Harry said.

"I'm embarrassed," Beth said. "I feel terrible about losing my temper that way, I feel like a complete idiot. . . ." Beth was hanging her head, staring at the floor. Interesting how she flipped, he thought, from aggressive self-confidence to the complete opposite, abject self-apology. Nothing in between.

"Let's not take it too far," he said. "We're all tired."

"I feel just awful," Beth continued. "Really awful. I feel as if I've let you both down. I shouldn't be here in the first place. I'm not worthy to be in this group."

Norman said, "Beth, have a nut bar and stop feeling sorry for yourself."

"Yes," Harry said. "I think I like you better angry."

"I'm sick of those nut bars," Beth said. "Before you came here, I ate eleven of them."

"Well, make it an even dozen," Norman said, "and we'll go back to the habitat."

WALKING BACK ACROSS the ocean floor, they were tense, watching for the squid. But Norman derived comfort from the fact that they were armed. And something else: some inner confidence that came from his earlier confrontation with the squid.

"You hold that spear gun like you mean it," Beth said.

"Yes. I guess so." All his life he had been an academic, a university researcher, and had never conceived of himself as a man of action. At least, nothing beyond the occasional game of golf. Now, holding the spear gun ready, he found he rather liked the feeling.

As he walked he noticed the profusion of sea fans on the path between the spacecraft and the habitat. They were obliged to walk around the fans, which were sometimes four and five feet tall, gaudy purple and blue in their lights. Norman was quite sure that the fans had not been down here when they first arrived at the habitat.

Now there were not only colorful fans, but schools of large fish, too. Most of the fish were black with a reddish stripe across the back. Beth said they were Pacific surgeonfish, normal for the region.

Everything is changing, he thought. It's all changing around us. But he wasn't sure about that. He didn't really trust his memory down here. There were too many other things to alter his perceptions—the high-pressure atmosphere, the injuries he had received, and the nagging tension and fear he lived with.

Something pale caught his eye. Shining his light down on the bottom, he saw a wriggling white streak with a long thin fin and black stripes. At first he thought it was an eel. Then he saw the tiny head, the mouth.

"Just wait," Beth said, putting her arm on him.

"What is it?"

"Sea snake."

"Are they dangerous?"

"Not usually."

"Poisonous?" Harry said.

"Very poisonous."

The snake stayed close to the bottom, apparently looking for food. The snake ignored them entirely, and Norman found it quite beautiful to watch, particularly as it moved farther away.

"It gives me the creeps," Beth said.

"Do you know what kind it is?" Norman said.

"It may be a Belcher's," Beth said. "Pacific sea snakes are all poisonous, but Belcher's sea snake is the most poisonous. In fact, some researchers think it's the deadliest reptile in the world, with venom a hundred times more powerful than the venom of a king cobra or the black tiger snake."

"So if it bit you . . ."

"Two minutes, tops."

They watched the snake slither away among the fans. Then it was gone.

"Sea snakes are not usually aggressive," Beth said. "Some divers even touch them, play with them, but I never would. God. *Snakes*."

"Why are they so poisonous? Is it for immobilizing prey?"

"You know, it's interesting," Beth said, "but the most toxic creatures in the world are all water creatures. The venom of land animals is nothing in comparison. And even among land animals, the most deadly poison is derived from an amphibian, a toad, *Bufotene marfensis*. In the sea, there are poisonous fish, like the blowfish, which is a delicacy in Japan; there are poisonous shells, like the star cone, *Alaverdis lotensis*. Once I was on a boat in Guam and a woman brought up a star cone. The shells are very beautiful, but she didn't know you have to keep your fingers away from the point. The animal extruded its poison spine and stung her in the palm. She took three steps before she collapsed in convulsions, and she died within an hour. There are also poisonous plants, poisonous sponges, poisonous corals. And then the snakes. Even the weakest of the sea snakes are invariably lethal."

"Nice," Harry said.

"Well, you have to recognize that the ocean is a much older living environment than the land. There's been life in the oceans for three and a half billion years, much longer than on land. The methods of competition and defense are much more highly developed in the ocean—there's been more time."

"You mean a few billion years from now, there will be tremendously poisonous animals on land, too?"

"If we get that far," she said.

"Let's just get back to the habitat," Harry said.

The habitat was now very close. They could see all the streaming bubbles rising from the leaks.

"Leaking like a bastard," Harry said.

"I think we've got enough air."

"I think I'll check."

"Be my guest," Beth said, "but I did a thorough job."

Norman thought another argument was about to start, but Beth and Harry dropped it. They came to the hatch and climbed up into DH-8.

The Console

"Jerry?"

Norman stared at the console screen. It remained blank, just a blinking cursor.

"Jerry, are you there?"

The screen was blank.

"I wonder why we aren't hearing from you, Jerry," Norman said.

The screen remained blank.

"Trying a little psychology?" Beth said. She was checking the controls for the external sensors, reviewing the graphs. "If you ask me, the person you should use your psychology on is Harry."

"What do you mean?"

"What I mean is, I don't think Harry should be screwing around with our life-support systems. I don't think he's stable."

"Stable?"

"That's a psychologist's trick, isn't it? To repeat the last word in a sentence. It's a way to keep the person talking."

"Talking?" Norman said, smiling at her.

"Okay, maybe I am a little stressed out," she said. "But, Norman, seriously. Before I left for the ship, Harry came into this room and said he would take over for me. I told him you were at the sub but there weren't any squid around and that I wanted to go to the ship. He said fine, he'd take over. So I left. And now he doesn't remember any of that. Doesn't that strike you as pretty screwy?"

"Screwy?" Norman said.

"Stop it, be serious."

"Serious?" Norman said.

"Are you trying to avoid this conversation? I notice how you avoid what you don't want to talk about. You keep everybody on an even keel, steer the conversation away from hard topics. But I think you should listen to what I'm saying, Norman. There's a problem with Harry."

"I'm listening to what you're saying, Beth."

"And?"

"I wasn't present for this particular episode, so I don't really know. What I see of Harry now looks like the same old Harry—arrogant, disdainful, and very, very intelligent."

"You don't think he's cracking up?"

"No more than the rest of us."

"Jesus! What do I have to do to convince you? I had a *whole conversation* with the man and now he denies it. You think that's normal? You think we can trust a person like that?"

"Beth. I wasn't there."

"You mean it might be me."

"I wasn't there."

"You think I might be the one who's cracking up? I say there was a conversation when there really wasn't?"

"Beth."

"Norman, I'm telling you. There is a problem about Harry and you aren't facing up to it."

They heard footsteps approaching.

"I'm going to my lab," she said. "You think about what I've said."

She climbed the ladder as Harry walked in. "Well, guess what? Beth did an excellent job with the life-support systems. Everything looks fine. We have air for fifty-two hours more at present rates of consumption. We should be fine. You talking to Jerry?"

"What?" Norman said.

Harry pointed to the screen:

HELLO NORMAN.

"I don't know when he came back. He wasn't talking earlier."

"Well, he is now," Harry said.

HELLO HARRY.

"How's it going, Jerry?" Harry said.

FINE THANK YOU. HOW ARE YOU? I AM WANTING SO MUCH TO TALK WITH YOUR ENTITIES. WHERE IS THE CONTROL ENTITY HARALD C. BARNES?

"Don't you know?"

I DO NOT SENSE THAT ENTITY NOW.

"He's, uh, gone."

I SEE. HE WAS NOT FRIENDLY. HE DID NOT ENJOY TO TALK WITH ME.

Norman thought, What is he telling us? Did Jerry get rid of Barnes because he thought he was unfriendly?

"Jerry," Norman said, "what happened to the control entity?"

HE WAS NOT FRIENDLY. I DID NOT LIKE HIM.

"Yes, but what *happened* to him?"

HE IS NOT NOW.

"And the other entities?"

AND THE OTHER ENTITIES. THEY DID NOT ENJOY TO TALKING WITH ME.

Harry said, "You think he's saying he got rid of them?"

I AM NOT HAPPY TO TALKING WITH THEM.

"So he got rid of all the Navy people?" Harry said.

Norman was thinking, That's not quite correct. He also got rid of Ted, and Ted was trying to communicate with him. Or with the squid. Was the squid related to Jerry? How would Norman ask that?

"Jerry . . ."

YES NORMAN. I AM HERE.

"Let's talk."

GOOD. I LIKE THAT MUCH.

"Tell us about the squid, Jerry."

THE ENTITY SQUID IS A MANIFESTATION.

"Where did it come from?"

DO YOU LIKE IT? I CAN MANIFEST IT MORE FOR YOU.

"No, no, don't do that," Norman said quickly.

YOU DO NOT LIKE IT?

"No, no. We like it, Jerry."

THIS IS TRUE?

"Yes, true. We like it. Really we do."

GOOD. I AM PLEASED YOU LIKE IT. IT IS A VERY IMPRESSIVE ENTITY OF LARGE SIZE.

"Yes, it is," Norman said, wiping sweat from his forehead. Jesus, he thought, this is like talking to a child with a loaded gun.

IT IS DIFFICULT FOR ME TO MANIFEST THIS LARGE ENTITY. I AM PLEASED THAT YOU LIKE IT.

"Very impressive," Norman agreed. "But you do not need to repeat that entity for us."

YOU WISH A NEW ENTITY MANIFESTED FOR YOU?

"No, Jerry. Nothing right now, thank you."

MANIFESTING IS HAPPY FOR ME.

"Yes, I'm sure it is."

I AM ENJOYING TO MANIFEST FOR YOU NORMAN. AND ALSO FOR YOU HARRY.

"Thank you, Jerry."

I AM ENJOYING YOUR MANIFESTATIONS ALSO.

"*Our* manifestations?" Norman said, glancing at Harry. Apparently Jerry thought that the people on the habitat were manifesting something in return. Jerry seemed to consider it an exchange of some kind.

YES I AM ENJOYING YOUR MANIFESTATIONS ALSO.

"Tell us about our manifestations, Jerry," Norman said.

THE MANIFESTATIONS ARE SMALL AND THEY DO NOT EXTEND BEYOND YOUR ENTITIES BUT THE MANIFESTATIONS ARE NEW FOR ME. THEY ARE HAPPY FOR ME.

"What's he talking about?" Harry said.

YOUR MANIFESTATIONS HARRY.

"What manifestations, for Christ's sake?"

"Don't get mad," Norman warned. "Stay calm."

I AM LIKING THAT ONE HARRY. DO AN OTHER.

Norman thought: Is he reading emotions? Does he regard our emotions as manifestations? But that didn't make sense. Jerry couldn't read their minds; they'd already determined that. Maybe he'd better check again. Jerry, he thought, can you hear me?

I AM LIKING HARRY. HIS MANIFESTATIONS ARE RED. THEY ARE WITFUL.

"Witful?"

WITFUL = FULL OF WIT?

"I see," Harry said. "He thinks we're funny."

FUNNY = FULL OF FUN?

"Not exactly," Norman said. "We entities have the concept of . . ." He trailed off. How was he going to explain "funny"? What was a joke, anyway? "We entities have the concept of a situation which causes discomfort and we call this situation humorous."

HUME OR US?

"No. One word." Norman spelled it for him.

I SEE. YOUR MANIFESTATIONS ARE HUMOR-

OUS. THE ENTITY SQUID MAKES MANY HUMOR-OUS MANIFESTATIONS FROM YOU.

"We don't think so," Harry said.

I THINK SO.

AND THAT ABOUT summed it up, Norman thought, sitting at the console. Somehow he had to make Jerry understand the seriousness of his actions. "Jerry," Norman explained, "your manifestations injure our entities. Some of our entities are already gone."

YES I KNOW.

"If you continue your manifestations—"

YES I AM LIKING TO MANIFEST. IT IS HUMOR-OUS FOR YOU.

"—then pretty soon all our entities will be gone. And then there will be no one to talk to you."

I DO NOT WISH THAT.

"I know that. But many entities are gone already."

BRING THEM BACK.

"We can't do that. They are gone forever."

WHY?

"We cannot bring them back."

WHY?

Just like a kid, Norman thought. Just exactly like a kid. Telling the kid you can't do what he wants, you can't play the way he wants to play, and he refuses to accept it.

"We do not have the power, Jerry, to bring them back."

I WISH YOU TO BRING THE OTHER ENTITIES BACK NOW.

"He thinks we're refusing to play," Harry said.

BRING BACK THE ENTITY TED.

Norman said, "We can't, Jerry. We would if we could."

I AM LIKING THE ENTITY TED. HE IS VERY HUMOROUS.

"Yes," Norman said. "Ted liked you, too. Ted was trying to talk to you."

YES I AM LIKING HIS MANIFESTATIONS. BRING BACK TED.

"We can't."

There was a long pause.

I AM OFFENDED YOU?

"No, not at all."

WE ARE FRIENDS NORMAN AND HARRY.

"Yes, we are."

THEN BRING BACK THE ENTITIES.

"He just refuses to understand," Harry said. "Jerry, for God's sake, we can't do it!"

YOU ARE HUMOROUS HARRY. MAKE IT AGAIN.

He's definitely reading strong emotional reactions as some kind of manifestation, Norman thought. Was this his idea of play—to make a provocation to the other party, and then to be amused by their responses? Was he delighted to see the vivid emotions brought on by the squid? Was this his idea of a game?

HARRY MAKE IT AGAIN. HARRY MAKE IT AGAIN.

"Hey, man," Harry said angrily. "Get off my back!"

THANK YOU. I AM LIKING THAT. IT WAS RED ALSO. NOW YOU WILL PLEASE BRING BACK THE ENTITIES GONE.

Norman had an idea. "Jerry," he said, "if you wish the entities back, why don't *you* bring them back?"

I AM NOT PLEASED TO DO THIS.

"But you could do it, if you wanted to."

I CAN DO ANY THING.

"Yes, of course you can. So why don't you bring back the entities you desire?"

NO. I AM NOT HAPPY TO DO THIS.

"Why not?" Harry said.

HEY MAN GET OFF MY BACK.

"No offense, Jerry," Norman said quickly.

There was no reply on the screen.

"Jerry?"

The screen did not respond.

"He's gone again," Harry said. He shook his head. "God knows what the little bastard will do next."

Further Analysis

Norman went up to the lab to see Beth, but she was asleep, curled up on her couch. In sleep, she looked quite beautiful. It was odd after all the time down here she should seem so radiant. It was as if the harshness had gone out of her features. Her nose did not seem so sharp any more; the line of the mouth was softer, fuller. He looked at her arms, which had been sinewy, veins bulging. The muscles seemed smoother, more feminine somehow.

Who knows? he thought. After so many hours down here, you're no judge of anything. He climbed back down the ladder and went to his bunk. Harry was already there, snoring loudly.

Norman decided to take another shower. As he stepped under the spray, he made a startling discovery.

The bruises which had covered his body were gone.

Anyway, almost gone, he thought, staring down at the remaining patches of yellow and purple. They had healed within hours. He moved his limbs experimentally and realized that the pain had gone, too. Why? What had happened? For a moment he thought this was all a dream, or a nightmare, and then he thought: No, it's just the atmosphere. Cuts and bruises healing faster in the high-pressure environment. It wasn't anything mysterious. Just an atmospheric effect.

He toweled himself as dry as he could with the damp towel, and then went back to his bunk. Harry was still snoring, as loud as ever.

Norman lay on his back, stared at the red humming coils of the ceiling heater. He had an idea, and got out of bed, and shifted Harry's talker from the base of his throat to one side. Immediately the snores changed to a soft, high-pitched hiss.

Much better, he thought. He lay on the damp pillow, and was almost immediately asleep. He awoke with no sense of passing time—it might have been only a few seconds—but he felt refreshed. He stretched and yawned, and got out of bed.

Harry still slept. Norman moved the talker back, and the snores resumed. He went into D Cyl, to the console. Still on the screen were the words:

HEY MAN GET OFF MY BACK.

"Jerry?" Norman said. "Are you there, Jerry?"

The screen did not respond. Jerry wasn't there. Norman looked at the stack of printouts to one side. I really should go over this stuff, he thought. Because something troubled him about Jerry. Norman couldn't put his finger on it, but even if one imagined the alien as a spoiled child-king, Jerry's behavior didn't make sense. It just didn't add up. Including the last message.

HEY MAN GET OFF MY BACK.

Street talk? Or just imitating Harry? In any case it wasn't Jerry's usual mode of communication. Usually Jerry was ungrammatical and sort of spacy, talking about entities and awareness. But from time to time he would become sharply colloquial. Norman looked at the sheets.

WE'LL BE RIGHT BACK AFTER A SHORT BREAK FOR THESE MESSAGES FROM OUR SPONSOR.

That was one example. Where had that come from? It sounded like Johnny Carson. Then why didn't Jerry sound like Johnny Carson all the time? What caused the shift?

Then, too, there was the problem of the squid. If Jerry liked to scare them, if he enjoyed rattling their cage and seeing them jump, why use a squid? Where had that idea come from? And why only a squid? Jerry seemed to enjoy manifesting different things. So why hadn't he produced giant squid one time, great white sharks another time, and so on? Wouldn't that provide a greater challenge to his abilities?

Then there was the problem of Ted. Ted had been playing with Jerry at the time he was killed. If Jerry liked to play so much, why would he kill off a player? It just didn't make sense.

Or did it?

Norman sighed. His trouble lay in his assumptions. Norman was assuming that the alien had logical processes similar to his own. But that might not be true. For one thing, Jerry might operate at a much faster metabolic rate, and thus have a different sense of time. Kids played with a toy only until they got tired of it; then they changed to another. The hours that seemed so painfully long to Norman might be only a few seconds in the consciousness of Jerry. He might just be playing with the squid for a few seconds, until he dropped it for another toy.

Kids also had a poor idea about breaking things. If Jerry didn't know about death, then he wouldn't mind killing Ted, because he would think the death was just a temporary event, a "humorous" manifestation by Ted. He might not realize he was actually breaking his toys.

And it was also true, when he thought about it, that Jerry *had* manifested different things. Assuming that the jellyfish and the shrimps and the sea fans and now the sea snakes were his manifestations. Were they? Or were they just normal parts of the environment? Was there any way to tell?

And the Navy seaman, he thought suddenly. Let's not forget the seaman. Where had he come from? Was that seaman another of Jerry's manifestations? Could Jerry manifest his playmates at will? In that case, he really wouldn't care if he killed them all.

But I think that's clear, Norman thought. Jerry doesn't care if he kills us. He just wants to play, and he doesn't know his own strength.

Yet there was something else. He scanned the sheets of printout, feeling instinctively some underlying organization to everything. Something he wasn't getting, some connection he wasn't making.

As he thought about it, he kept coming back to one question: Why a squid? Why a squid?

Of course, he thought. They had been talking about a squid, during the conversation at dinner. Jerry must have overheard that. He must have decided that a squid would be a provocative item to manifest. And he was certainly right about that.

Norman shifted the papers, and came upon the very first message that Harry had decoded.

HELLO. HOW ARE YOU? I AM FINE. WHAT IS YOUR NAME? MY NAME IS JERRY.

That was as good a place to begin as any. It had been quite a feat for Harry to decode it, Norman thought. If Harry hadn't succeeded with that, they would never have ever started talking to Jerry at all.

Norman sat at the console, stared at the keyboard. What had Harry said? The keyboard was a spiral: the letter G was one, and B was two, and so on. Very clever to figure it out. Norman would never have figured that out in a million years. He started trying to find the letters in the first sequence.

```
00032125252632 032629 301321 04261037 18 3016 06180
82132 29033005 1822 04261013 0830162137 1604 083016
21 1822 033013130432
```

Let's see . . . 00 marked the beginning of the message, Harry had said. And 03, that was H. And then 21, that was E, then 25 was L, and 25 was another L, and just above it, 26, was O. . . .

HELLO.

Yes, it all fitted. He continued translating. 032629 was HOW. . . .

HOW ARE YOU?

So far, so good. Norman experienced a certain pleasure, almost as if he were decoding it himself for the first time. Now, 18. That was I. . . .

I AM FINE.

He moved more quickly, writing down the letters.

WHAT IS YOUR NAME?

Now, 1604 was MY. . . . MY NAME IS . . . But then he found a mistake in one letter. Was that possible? Norman kept going, found a second mistake, then wrote out the message, and stared at it in growing shock.

MY NAME IS HARRY.

"Jesus Christ," he said.

He went over it again, but there was no mistake. Not by him. The message was perfectly clear.

HELLO. HOW ARE YOU? I AM FINE. WHAT IS YOUR NAME? MY NAME IS HARRY.

THE
POWER

The Shadow

Beth sat up in her bed in the laboratory and stared at the message Norman had given her. "Oh my God," she said. She pushed her thick dark hair away from her face. "How can it be?" she said.

"It all goes together," Norman said. "Just think. When did the messages start? After Harry came out of the sphere. When did the squid and the other animals first appear? After Harry came out of the sphere."

"Yes, but—"

"—At first there were little squid, but then, when we were going to eat them, suddenly there were shrimps, too. Just in time for dinner. Why? Because Harry doesn't like to eat squid."

Beth said nothing; she just listened.

"And who, as a child, was terrified by the giant squid in *Twenty Thousand Leagues Under the Sea*?"

"Harry was," she said. "I remember he said that."

Norman went on in a rush. "And when does Jerry appear on the screen? When Harry is present. Not at other times. And when does Jerry answer us as we talk? When Harry is in the room to hear what we're saying. And why can't Jerry read our minds? Because Harry can't read our minds. And remember how Barnes kept asking for the name, and Harry wouldn't ask for the name? Why? Because he was afraid the screen would say 'Harry,' not 'Jerry.'"

"And the crewman . . ."

"Right. The black crewman. Who shows up just as Harry is having a dream of being rescued? A black crewman shows up to rescue us."

Beth was frowning, thinking. "What about the giant squid?"

"Well, in the middle of its attack, Harry hit his head and was knocked unconscious. Immediately the squid disappeared. It didn't come back again until Harry woke up from his nap, and told you he'd take over."

"My God," Beth said.

"Yes," Norman said. "It explains a lot."

She was silent for a while, staring at the message. "But how is he doing it?"

"I doubt if he is. At least, not consciously." Norman had been thinking about this. "Let's assume," he said, "that something happened to Harry when he went inside the sphere—he acquired some kind of power while in the sphere."

"Like what?"

"The power to make things happen just by thinking of them. The power to make his thoughts real."

Beth frowned. "Make his thoughts real . . ."

"It's not so strange," he said. "Just think: if you were a sculptor, first you would get an idea, and then you would carve it in stone or wood, to make it real. The idea comes first, then the execution follows, with some added effort to create a reality that reflects your prior thoughts. That's the way the world works for us. We imagine something, and then we try to make it happen. Sometimes the way we make it happen is unconscious—like the guy who just happens to go home unexpectedly at lunchtime and catches his wife in bed with another man. He doesn't consciously plan it. It just sort of happens by itself."

"Or the wife who catches the husband in bed with another woman," Beth said.

"Yes, of course. The point is, we manage to make things happen all the time without thinking about them too much. I don't think of every word when I talk to you. I just intend to say something and it comes out okay."

"Yes . . ."

"So we can make complicated creations like sentences without effort. But we can't make other complicated creations like sculptures without effort. We believe we have to *do* something besides simply have an idea."

"And we do," Beth said.

"Well, Harry doesn't. Harry's gone one step further. He doesn't have to carve the statue any more. He just gets the idea, and things happen by themselves. He manifests things."

"Harry imagines a frightening squid, and suddenly we have a frightening squid outside our window?"

"Exactly. And when he loses consciousness, the squid disappears."

"And he got this power from the sphere?"

"Yes."

Beth frowned. "Why is he doing this? Is he trying to kill us?"

Norman shook his head. "No. I think he's in over his head."

"How do you mean?"

"Well," Norman said, "we've considered lots of ideas of what the sphere from another civilization might be. Ted thought it was a trophy or a message—he saw it as a present. Harry thought it had something inside—he saw it as a container. But I wonder if it might be a mine."

"You mean, an explosive?"

"Not exactly—but a defense, or a test. An alien civilization could strew these things around the galaxy, and any intelligence that picks them up would get to experience the power of the sphere. Which is that whatever you think comes true. If you think positive thoughts, you get delicious shrimp for dinner. If you think negative thoughts, you get monsters trying to kill you. Same process, just a matter of content."

"So, the same way a land mine blows up if you step on it, this sphere destroys people if they have negative thoughts?"

"Or," he said, "if they simply aren't in control of their consciousness. Because, if you're in control of your consciousness, the sphere would have no particular effect. If you're not in control, it gets rid of you."

"How can you control a negative thought?" Beth said. She

seemed suddenly very agitated. "How can you say to someone, 'Don't think of a giant squid'? The minute you say that, they automatically think of the squid in the course of trying *not* to think of it."

"It's possible to control your thoughts," Norman said.

"Maybe for a yogi or something."

"For anybody," Norman said. "It's possible to deflect your attention from undesirable thoughts. How do people quit smoking? How do any of us ever change our minds about anything? By controlling our thoughts."

"I still don't see why Harry is doing this."

"Remember your idea that the sphere might strike us below the belt?" Norman said. "The way the AIDS virus strikes our immune system below the belt? AIDS hits us at a level we aren't prepared to deal with. So, in a sense, does the sphere. Because we believe that we can think whatever we want, without consequence. 'Sticks and stones can break my bones, but names can never hurt me.' We have sayings like that, which emphasize the point. But now suddenly a name is as real as a stick, and it can hurt us in the same way. Our thoughts get manifested—what a wonderful thing—except that *all* our thoughts get manifested, the good ones and the bad ones. And we simply aren't prepared to control our thoughts. We've never had to do it before."

"When I was a child," Beth said, "I was angry with my mother, and when she got cancer, I was terribly guilty. . . ."

"Yes," Norman said. "Children think this way. Children all believe that their thoughts have power. But we patiently teach them that they're wrong to think that. Of course," he said, "there has always been another tradition of belief about thoughts. The Bible says not to covet your neighbor's wife, which we interpret to mean that the act of adultery is forbidden. But that's not really what the Bible is saying. The Bible is saying that the *thought* of adultery is as forbidden as the act itself."

"And Harry?"

"Do you know anything about Jungian psychology?"

Beth said, "That stuff has never struck me as relevant."

"Well, it's relevant *now*," Norman said. He explained. "Jung broke with Freud early in this century, and developed his own psychology. Jung suspected there was an underlying structure to the human psyche that was reflected in an underlying similarity to our myths and archetypes. One of his ideas was that everybody had a dark side to his personality, which he called the 'shadow.' The shadow contained all the unacknowledged personality aspects—the hateful parts, the sadistic parts, all that. Jung thought people had the obligation to become acquainted with their shadow side. But very few people do. We all prefer to think we're nice guys and we don't ever have the desire to kill and maim and rape and pillage."

"Yes . . ."

"As Jung saw it, if you didn't acknowledge your shadow side, it would rule you."

"So we're seeing Harry's shadow side?"

"In a sense, yes. Harry needs to present himself as Mr. Arrogant Know-It-All Black Man," Norman said.

"He certainly does."

"So, if he's afraid to be down here in this habitat—and

who isn't?—then he can't admit his fears. But he has the fears anyway, whether he admits them or not. And so his shadow side justifies the fears—creating things that prove his fears to be valid."

"The squid exists to justify his fears?"

"Something like that, yes."

"I don't know," Beth said. She leaned back and turned her head up, and her high cheekbones caught the light. She looked almost like a model, elegant and handsome and strong. "I'm a zoologist, Norman. I want to touch things and hold them in my hands and see that they're real. All these theories about manifestations, they just . . . They're so . . . *psychological.*"

"The world of the mind is just as real, and follows rules just as rigorous, as the world of external reality," Norman said.

"Yes, I'm sure you're right, but . . ." She shrugged. "It isn't very satisfying to me."

"You know everything that has happened since we got down here," Norman said. "Tell me another hypothesis that explains it all."

"I can't," she admitted. "I've been trying, all the time you've been talking. I can't." She folded the paper in her hands and considered it for a while. "You know, Norman, I think you've made a brilliant series of deductions. Absolutely brilliant. I'm seeing you in a whole different light."

Norman smiled with pleasure. For most of the time he had been down in the habitat, he'd felt like a fifth wheel, an unnecessary person in this group. Now someone was acknowledging his contribution, and he was pleased. "Thank you, Beth."

She looked at him, her large eyes liquid and soft. "You're a very attractive man, Norman. I don't think I ever really noticed before." Absently, she touched her breast, beneath the clinging jumpsuit. Her hands pressed the fabric, outlining the hard nipples. She suddenly stood and hugged him, her body close to him. "We have to stay together on this," she said. "We have to stay close, you and I."

"Yes, we do."

"Because, if what you are saying is true, then Harry is a very dangerous man."

"Yes."

"Just the fact that he is walking around, fully conscious, makes him dangerous."

"Yes."

"What are we going to do about him?"

"Hey, you guys," Harry said, coming up the stairs. "Is this a private party? Or can anybody join in?"

"Sure," Norman said, "come on up, Harry," and he moved away from Beth.

"Was I interrupting something?" Harry said.

"No, no."

"I don't want to get in the way of anybody's sex life."

"Oh, Harry," Beth said. She sat at the lab bench, moving away from Norman.

"Well, you two sure look all charged up about *something*."

"Do we?" Norman said.

"Yeah, especially Beth. I think she gets more beautiful every day she's down here."

"I've noticed that, too," Norman said, smiling.

"I'll bet you have. A woman in love. Lucky you." Harry turned to Beth. "Why are you staring at me like that?"

"I'm not staring," Beth said.

"You are, too."

"Harry, I'm not staring."

"I can tell when someone is staring at me, for Christ's sake."

Norman said, "Harry—"

"—I just want to know why you two are looking at me like that. You're looking at me like I'm a criminal or something."

"Don't get paranoid, Harry."

"Huddling up here, whispering . . ."

"We weren't whispering."

"You *were*." Harry looked around the room. "So it's two white people and one black person now, is that it?"

"Oh, Harry . . ."

"I'm not stupid, you know. Something's going on between you. I can tell."

"Harry," Norman said, "nothing is going on."

And then they heard a low insistent beeping, from the communications console downstairs. They exchanged glances, and went downstairs to look.

THE CONSOLE SCREEN was slowly printing out letter groups.

CQX VDX MOP LKI

"Is that Jerry?" Norman asked.

"I don't think so," Harry said. "I don't think he would go back to code."

"Is it a code?"

"I would say so, definitely."

"Why is it so slow?" Beth said. A new letter was added every few seconds in a steady, rhythmic way.

"I don't know," Harry said.

"Where is it coming from?"

Harry frowned. "I don't know, but the transmission speed is the most interesting characteristic. The slowness. Interesting."

Norman and Beth waited for him to figure it out. Norman thought: How can we ever get along without Harry? We need him. He is both the most important intelligence down here, and the most dangerous. But we need him.

CQX VDX MOP LKI XXC VRW TGK PIU YQA

"Interesting," Harry said. "The letters are coming about every five seconds. So I think it's safe to say that we know where it's coming from. Wisconsin."

Norman could not have been more surprised. "Wisconsin?"

"Yeah. This is a Navy transmission. It may or may not be directed to us, but it is coming from Wisconsin."

"How do you know that?"

"Because that's the only place in the world it *could* be coming from," Harry said. "You know about ELF? No? Well, it's like this. You can send radio waves through the air, and, as you know, they travel pretty well. But you can't send radio far through water. Water is a bad medium, so you need an incredibly powerful signal to go even a short distance."

"Yes . . ."

"But the ability to penetrate is a function of wavelength. An ordinary radio wave is short—shortwave radio, all of that. The length of the waves are tiny, thousands or millions of little waves to an inch. But you can also make ELF, extremely low-frequency waves, which are long—each individual wave is maybe twenty feet long. And those waves, once generated, will go a very great distance, thousands of miles, through water, no problem. The only trouble is that, since the waves are long, they're also slow. That's why we're getting one character every five seconds. The Navy needed a way to communicate with their submarines underwater, so they built a big ELF antenna in Wisconsin to send these long waves. And that's what we're getting."

"And the code?"

"It must be a compression code—three-letter groupings which stand for a long section of predefined message. So it won't take so long to send a message. Because if you sent a plain text message, it would literally take hours."

CQX VDX MOP LKI XXC VRW TGK PIU YQA IYT EEQ FVC ZNB TMK EXE MMN OPW GEW

The letters stopped.

"Looks like that's it," Harry said.

"How do we translate it?" Beth said.

"Assuming it's a Navy transmission," Harry said, "we don't."

"Maybe there's a codebook here somewhere," Beth said.

"Just hold on," Harry said.

The screen shifted, translating groups one after another.

2340 HOURS 7-07 CHIEF CINCCOMPAC TO BARNES DEEPHAB-8

"It's a message to Barnes," Harry said. They watched as the other letter groups were translated.

SURFACE SUPPORT VESSELS STEAMING NANDI

AND VIPATI TO YOUR LOCATION ETA 1600 HOURS
7-08 DEEP WITHDRAW AUTOSET ACKNOWLEDGE
GOOD LUCK SPAULDING END

"Does that mean what I think it means?" Beth said.

"Yeah," Harry said. "The cavalry is on the way."

"Hot damn!" Beth clapped her hands.

"The storm must be calming down. They've sent the surface ships and they'll be here in a little more than sixteen hours."

"And autoset?"

They had the answer immediately. Every screen in the habitat flickered. In the upper right corner of each appeared a small box with numbers: 16:20:00. The numbers ran backward.

"It's automatically counting down for us."

"Is there some kind of countdown we're supposed to follow for leaving the habitat?" Beth said.

Norman watched the numbers. They were rolling backward, just as they had on the submarine. Then he said, "What about the submarine?"

"Who cares about the submarine," Harry said.

"I think we should keep it with us," Beth said. She checked her watch. "We have another four hours before it has to be reset."

"Plenty of time."

"Yes."

Privately, Norman was trying to gauge whether they could survive for sixteen more hours.

Harry said, "Well, this is great news! Why are you two so hangdog?"

"Just wondering if we'll make it," Norman said.

"Why shouldn't we make it?" Harry said.

"Jerry might do something first," Beth said. Norman felt a burst of irritation with her. Didn't she realize that by saying that, she was planting the idea in Harry's mind?

"We can't survive another attack on the habitat," Beth said.

Norman thought, Shut up, Beth. You're making suggestions.

"An attack on the habitat?" Harry said.

Quickly, Norman said, "Harry, I think you and I should talk to Jerry again."

"Really? Why?"

"I want to see if I can reason with him."

"I don't know if you can," Harry said. "Reason with him."

"Let's try anyway," Norman said, with a glance at Beth. "It's worth a try."

NORMAN KNEW HE would not really be talking to Jerry. He would be talking to a part of Harry. An unconscious part, a shadow part. How should he go about it? What could he use?

He sat in front of the monitor screen, thinking, What do I know about Harry, really? Harry, who had grown up in Philadelphia as a thin, introverted, painfully shy boy, a mathematical prodigy, his gifts denigrated by his friends and family. Harry had said once that when he cared about mathematics, everybody else cared about slamdunking. Even now, Harry hated all games, all sports. As a young man he had been humiliated and neglected, and when he finally got proper recognition for his gifts, Norman suspected, it came too late. The damage was already done. Certainly it came too late to prevent the arrogant, braggart exterior.

I AM HERE. DO NOT BE AFRAID.

"Jerry."

YES NORMAN.

"I have a request to make."

YOU MAY DO SO.

"Jerry, many of our entities are gone, and our habitat is weakened."

I KNOW THIS. MAKE YOUR REQUEST.

"Would you please stop manifesting?"

NO.

"Why not?"

I DO NOT WISH TO STOP.

Well, Norman thought, at least we got right down to it. No wasting time. "Jerry, I know that you have been isolated for a long time, for many centuries, and that you have felt alone during all that time. You have felt that nobody cared about you. You have felt that nobody wanted to play with you, or shared your interests."

YES THIS IS TRUE.

"And now at last you can manifest, and you are enjoying this. You like to show us what you can do, to impress us."

THIS IS TRUE.

"So that we will pay attention to you."

YES. I LIKE IT.

"And it works. We do pay attention to you."

YES I KNOW IT.

"But these manifestations injure us, Jerry."

I DO NOT CARE.

"And they surprise us, too."

I AM GLAD.

"We're surprised, Jerry, because you are merely playing a game with us."

I DO NOT LIKE GAMES. I DO NOT PLAY GAMES.

"Yes. This is a game for you, Jerry. It is a sport."

NO, IT IS NOT.

"Yes, it is," Norman said. "It is a *stupid sport.*"

Harry, standing beside Norman, said, "Do you want to contradict him that way? You might make him mad. I don't think Jerry likes to be contradicted."

I'm sure you don't, Norman thought. But he said, "Well, I have to tell Jerry the truth about his own behavior. He isn't doing anything very interesting."

OH? NOT INTERESTING?

"No. You are being spoiled and petulant, Jerry."

DO YOU DARE TO SPEAK TO ME IN THIS FASHION?

"Yes. Because you are acting stupidly."

"Jeez," Harry said. "Take it easy with him."

I CAN EASILY MAKE YOU REGRET YOUR WORDS, NORMAN.

Norman was noticing, in passing, that Jerry's vocabulary and syntax were now flawless. All pretense of naïveté, of an alien quality, had been dropped. But Norman felt stronger, more confident, as the conversation progressed. He knew whom he was talking to now. He wasn't talking to any alien. There weren't any unknown assumptions. He was talking to a childish part of another human being.

I HAVE MORE POWER THAN YOU CAN IMAGINE.

"I know you have power, Jerry," Norman said. "Big deal."

Harry became suddenly agitated. "Norman. For Christ's sake. You're going to get us all killed."

LISTEN TO HARRY. HE IS WISE.

"No, Jerry," Norman said. "Harry is not wise. He is only afraid."

HARRY IS NOT AFRAID. ABSOLUTELY NOT.

Norman decided to let that pass. "I'm talking to *you*, Jerry. Only to you. You are the one who is playing games."

GAMES ARE STUPID.

"Yes, they are, Jerry. They are not worthy of you."

GAMES ARE NOT OF INTEREST TO ANY INTELLIGENT PERSON.

"Then stop, Jerry. Stop the manifestations."

I CAN STOP WHENEVER I WANT.

"I am not sure you can, Jerry."

YES. I CAN.

"Then prove it. Stop this sport of manifestations."

There was a long pause. They waited for the response.

NORMAN YOUR TRICKS OF MANIPULATION ARE CHILDISH AND OBVIOUS TO THE POINT OF TEDIUM. I AM NOT INTERESTED IN TALKING WITH YOU FURTHER. I WILL DO EXACTLY AS I PLEASE AND I WILL MANIFEST AS I WISH.

"Our habitat cannot withstand more manifestations, Jerry."

I DO NOT CARE.

"If you injure our habitat again, Harry will die."

Harry said, "Me and everybody else, for Christ's sake."

I DO NOT CARE NORMAN.

"Why would you kill us, Jerry?"

YOU SHOULD NOT BE DOWN HERE IN THE FIRST PLACE. YOU PEOPLE DO NOT BELONG HERE. YOU ARE ARROGANT CREATURES WHO INTRUDE EVERYWHERE IN THE WORLD AND YOU HAVE TAKEN A GREAT FOOLISH RISK AND NOW YOU MUST PAY THE PRICE. YOU ARE AN UN-CARING UNFEELING SPECIES WITH NO LOVE FOR ONE ANOTHER.

"That's not true, Jerry."

DO NOT CONTRADICT ME AGAIN, NORMAN.

"I'm sorry, but the unfeeling, uncaring person is you, Jerry. You do not care if you injure us. You do not care for our predicament. It is you who are uncaring, Jerry. Not us. You."

ENOUGH.

"He's not going to talk to you any more," Harry said. "He's really mad, Norman."

And then the screen printed:

I WILL KILL YOU ALL.

NORMAN WAS SWEATING; he wiped his forehead, turned away from the words on the screen.

"I don't think you can talk to this guy," Beth said. "I don't think you can reason with him."

"You shouldn't have made him angry," Harry said. He was

almost pleading. "Why did you make him angry like that, Norman?"

"I had to tell him the truth."

"But you were so mean to him, and now he's angry."

"It doesn't matter, angry or not," Beth said. "Harry attacked us before, when he wasn't angry."

"You mean *Jerry*," Norman said to her. "Jerry attacked us."

"Yes, right, Jerry."

"That's a hell of a mistake to make, Beth," Harry said.

"You're right, Harry. I'm sorry."

Harry was looking at her in an odd way. Norman thought, Harry doesn't miss a trick, and he isn't going to let that one go by.

"I don't know how you could make that confusion," Harry said.

"I know. It was a slip of the tongue. It was stupid of me."

"I'll say."

"I'm sorry," Beth said. "Really I am."

"Never mind," Harry said. "It doesn't matter."

There was a sudden flatness in his manner, a complete indifference in his tone. Norman thought: Uh-oh.

Harry yawned and stretched. "You know," he said, "I'm suddenly very tired. I think I'll take a nap now."

And he went off to the bunks.

1600 Hours

W e have to do something," Beth said. "We can't talk him out of it."

"You're right," Norman said. "We can't."

Beth tapped the screen. The words still glowed: I WILL KILL YOU ALL.

"Do you think he means it?"

"Yes."

Beth stood, clenched her fists. "So it's him or us."

"Yes. I think so."

The implications hung in the air, unspoken.

"This manifesting process of his," Beth said. "Do you think he has to be completely unconscious to prevent it from happening?"

"Yes."

"Or dead," Beth said.

"Yes," Norman said. That had occurred to him. It seemed so

improbable, such an unlikely turn of events in his life, that he would now be a thousand feet under the water, contemplating the murder of another human being. Yet that was what he was doing.

"I'd hate to kill him," Beth said.

"Me, too."

"I mean, I wouldn't even know how to begin to do it."

"Maybe we don't have to kill him," Norman said.

"Maybe we don't have to kill him unless he starts something," Beth said. Then she shook her head. "Oh hell, Norman, who're we kidding? This habitat can't survive another attack. We've got to kill him. I just don't want to face up to it."

"Neither do I," Norman said.

"We could get one of those explosive spear guns and have an unfortunate accident. And then just wait for our time to be up, for the Navy to come and get us out of here."

"I don't want to do that."

"I don't, either," Beth said. "But what else can we do?"

"We don't have to kill him," Norman said. "Just make him unconscious." He went to the first-aid cabinet, started going through the medicines.

"You think there might be something there?" Beth said.

"Maybe. An anesthetic, I don't know."

"Would that work?"

"I think anything that produces unconsciousness will work. I think."

"I hope you're right," Beth said, "because if he starts dreaming and then manifests the monsters from his dreams, that wouldn't be very good."

"No. But anesthesia produces a dreamless, total state of unconsciousness." Norman was looking at the labels on the bottles. "Do you know what these things are?"

"No," Beth said, "but it's all in the computer." She sat down at the console. "Read me the names and I'll look them up for you."

"Diphenyl paralene."

Beth pushed buttons, scanned a screen of dense text. "It's, uh . . . looks like . . . something for burns."

"Ephedrine hydrochloride."

Another screen. "It's . . . I guess it's for motion sickness."

"Valdomet."

"It's for ulcers."

"Sintag."

"Synthetic opium analogue. It's very short-acting."

"Produces unconsciousness?" Norman asked.

"No. Not according to this. Anyway, it only lasts a few minutes."

"Tarazine."

"Tranquilizer. Causes drowsiness."

"Good." He set the bottle to one side.

"'And may also cause bizarre ideation.'"

"No," he said, and put the bottle back. They didn't need to have any bizarre ideation. "Riordan?"

"Antihistamine. For bites."

"Oxalamine?"

"Antibiotic."

"Chloramphenicol?"

"Another antibiotic."

"Damn." They were running out of bottles. "Parasolutrine?"

"It's a soporific. . . ."

"What's that?"

"Causes sleep."

"You mean it's a sleeping pill?"

"No, it's—it says you can give it in combination with paracin trichloride and use it as an anesthetic."

"Paracin trichloride . . . Yes. I have it here," Norman said.

Beth was reading from the screen. "Parasolutrine twenty cc's in combination with paracin six cc's given IM produces deep sleep suitable for emergency surgical procedures . . . no cardiac side effects . . . sleep from which the subject can be awakened only with difficulty . . . REM activity is suppressed. . . ."

"How long does it last?"

"Three to six hours."

"And how fast does it take effect?"

She frowned. "It doesn't say. 'After appropriate depth of anesthesia is induced, even extensive surgical procedures may be begun. . . .' But it doesn't say how long it takes."

"Hell," Norman said.

"It's probably fast," Beth said.

"But what if it isn't?" Norman said. "What if it takes twenty minutes? And can you fight it? Fight it off?"

She shook her head. "Nothing about that here."

In the end they decided on a mixture of parasolutrine, paracin, dulcinea, and sintag, the opiate. Norman filled a large syringe with the clear liquids. The syringe was so big it looked like something for horses.

"You think it might kill him?" Beth said.

"I don't know. Do we have a choice?"

"No," Beth said. "We've got to do it. Have you ever given an injection before?"

Norman shook his head. "You?"

"Only lab animals."

"Where do I stick it?"

"Do it in the shoulder," Beth said. "While he's asleep."

Norman turned the syringe up to the light, and squirted a few drops from the needle into the air. "Okay," he said.

"I better come with you," Beth said, "and hold him down."

"No," Norman said. "If he's awake and sees both of us coming, he'll be suspicious. Remember, you don't sleep in the bunks any more."

"But what if he gets violent?"

"I think I can handle this."

"Okay, Norman. Whatever you say."

THE LIGHTS IN the corridor of C Cyl seemed unnaturally bright. Norman heard his feet padding on the carpet, heard the constant hum of the air handlers and the space heaters. He felt the weight of the syringe concealed in his palm. He came to the door to the sleeping quarters.

Two female Navy crewmen were standing outside the bulkhead door. They snapped to attention as he approached.

"Dr. Johnson, sir!"

Norman paused. The women were handsome, black, and muscular-looking. "At ease, men," Norman said with a smile.

They did not relax. "Sorry, sir! We have our orders, sir!"

"I see," Norman said. "Well, carry on, then." He started to move past them into the sleeping area.

"Beg your pardon, Dr. Johnson, sir!"

They barred his way.

"What is it?" Norman asked, as innocently as he could manage.

"This area is off-limits to all personnel, sir!"

"But I want to go to sleep."

"Very sorry, Dr. Johnson, sir! No one may disturb Dr. Adams while he sleeps, sir!"

"I won't disturb Dr. Adams."

"Sorry, Dr. Johnson, sir! May we see what is in your hand, sir!"

"In my hand?"

"Yes, there is something in your hand, sir!"

Their snapping, machine-gun delivery, always punctuated by the "sir!" at the end, was getting on his nerves. He looked at them again. The starched uniforms covered powerful muscles. He didn't think he could force his way past them. Beyond the door he saw Harry, lying on his back, snoring. It was a perfect moment to inject him.

"Dr. Johnson, may we see what is in your hand, sir!"

"No, damn it, you may not."

"Very good, sir!"

Norman turned, and walked back to D Cyl.

"I SAW," BETH said, nodding to the monitor.

Norman looked at the monitor, at the two women in the corridor. Then he looked at the adjacent monitor, which showed the sphere.

"The sphere has changed!" Norman said.

The convoluted grooves of the doorway were definitely altered, the pattern more complex, and shifted farther up. Norman felt sure it was changed.

"I think you're right," Beth said.

"When did that happen?"

"We can run the tapes back later," she said. "Right now we'd better take care of those two."

"How?" Norman said.

"Simple," Beth said, bunching her fists again. "We have five explosive spearheads in B Cyl. I'll go into B, get two of them, blow the guardian angels away. You run in and jab Harry."

Her cold-blooded determination would have been chilling if she didn't look so beautiful. There was a refined quality to her features now. She seemed to grow more elegant by the minute.

"The spearguns are in B?" Norman said.

"Sure. Look on the video." She pressed a button. "Hell."

In B Cyl the spearguns were missing.

"I think the son of a bitch has covered his bases," Norman said. "Good old Harry."

Beth looked at him thoughtfully. "Norman, are you feeling okay?"

"Sure, why?"

"There's a mirror in the first-aid kit. Go look."

He opened the white box of the kit and looked at himself in the mirror. He was shocked by what he saw. Not that he expected to look good; he was accustomed to the pudgy contours of his own face, and the gray stubble of his beard when he didn't shave on weekends.

But the face staring back at him was lean, with a coarse, jet-black beard. There were dark circles beneath smoldering, bloodshot eyes. His hair was lank and greasy, hanging over his forehead. He looked like a dangerous man.

"I look like Dr. Jekyll," he said. "Or, rather, Mr. Hyde."

"Yeah. You do."

"You're getting more beautiful," he said to Beth. "But I'm the man who was mean to Jerry. So I'm getting meaner."

"You think Harry's doing this?"

"I think so," Norman said. Adding to himself: I hope so.

"You feel different, Norman?"

"No, I feel exactly the same. I just look like hell."

"Yes. You look a little frightening."

"I'm sure I do."

"You really feel fine?"

"Beth . . ."

"Okay," Beth said. She turned, looked back at the monitors. "I have one last idea. We both get to A Cyl, put on our suits, get into B Cyl, and shut down the oxygen in the rest of the habitat. Make Harry unconscious. His guards will disappear, we can go in and jab him. What do you think?"

"Worth a try."

Norman put down the syringe. They headed off toward A Cyl.

In C Cyl, they passed the two guards, who again snapped to attention.

"Dr. Halpern, sir!"

"Dr. Johnson, sir!"

"Carry on, men," Beth said.

"Yes, sir! May we ask where you are going, sir!"

"Routine inspection tour," Beth said.

There was a pause.

"Very good, sir!"

They were allowed to pass. They moved into B Cyl, with its array of pipes and machinery. Norman glanced at it nervously; he didn't like screwing around with the life-support systems, but he didn't see what else they could do.

In A Cyl, there were three suits left. Norman reached for his. "You know what you're doing?" he asked.

"Yes," Beth said. "Trust me."

She slipped her foot into her suit, and started zipping it up.

And then the alarms began to sound throughout the habitat, and the red lights flashed again. Norman knew, without being told, that it was the peripheral alarms.

Another attack was beginning.

1520 Hours

They ran back through the lateral connecting corridor directly from B Cyl into D. Norman noticed in passing that the crewmen had gone. In D, the alarms were clanging and the peripheral sensor screens glowed bright red. Norman glanced at the video monitors.

I AM COMING.

Beth quickly scanned the screens.

"Inner thermals are activated. He's coming, all right."

They felt a thump, and Norman turned to look out the porthole. The green squid was already outside, the huge suckered arms coiling around the base of the habitat. One great arm slapped flat against the porthole, the suckers distorted against the glass.

I AM HERE.

"*Harryyy!*" Beth shouted.

There was a tentative jolt, as squid arms gripped the habitat. The slow, agonizing creak of metal.

Harry came running into the room.

"What is it?"

"You know what it is, Harry!" Beth shouted.

"No, no, what is it?"

"It's the squid, Harry!"

"Oh my God, no," Harry moaned.

The habitat shook powerfully. The room lights flickered and went out. There was only flashing red now, from the emergency lights.

Norman turned to him. "Stop it, Harry."

"What are you talking about?" he cried plaintively.

"You know what I'm talking about, Harry."

"I don't!"

"Yes, you do, Harry. It's *you*, Harry," Norman said. "You're doing it."

"No, you're wrong. It's not me! I swear it's not me!"

"Yes, Harry," Norman said. "And if you don't stop it, we'll all die."

The habitat shook again. One of the ceiling heaters exploded, showering fragments of hot glass and wire.

"Come on, Harry. . . ."

"No, no!"

"There's not much time. You know you're doing it."

"The habitat can't take much more, Norman," Beth said.

"It can't be me!"

"Yes, Harry. Face it, Harry. Face it now."

Even as he spoke, Norman was looking for the syringe. He had left it somewhere in this room, but papers were sliding off the desktops, monitors crashing to the floor, chaos all around him. . . .

The whole habitat rocked again, and there was a tremendous explosion from another cylinder. New, rising alarms sounded, and a roaring vibration that Norman instantly recognized—water, under great pressure, rushing into the habitat.

"Flooding in C!" Beth shouted, reading the consoles. She ran down the corridor. He heard the metal *clang* of bulkhead doors as she shut them. The room was filled with salty mist.

Norman pushed Harry against the wall. "Harry! Face it and stop it!"

"It can't be me, it can't be me," Harry moaned.

Another jolting impact, staggering them.

"It can't be me!" Harry cried. *"It has nothing to do with me!"*

And then Harry screamed, and his body twisted, and Norman saw Beth withdraw the syringe from his shoulder, the needle tipped with blood.

"What are you doing?" Harry cried, but already his eyes were glassy and vacant. He staggered at the next impact, fell drunkenly on his knees to the floor. "No," he said softly. "No . . ."

And he collapsed, falling face-down on the carpet. Immediately the wrenching of metal stopped. The alarms stopped. Everything became ominously silent, except for the soft gurgle of water from somewhere within the habitat.

BETH MOVED SWIFTLY, reading one screen after another.

"Inner off. Peripherals off. Everything off. *All right!* No readings!"

Norman ran to the porthole. The squid had disappeared. The sea bottom outside was deserted.

"Damage report!" Beth shouted. "Main power out! E Cylinder out! C Cylinder out! B Cylinder . . ."

Norman spun, looked at her. If B Cyl was gone, their life support would be gone, they would certainly die. "B Cylinder holding," she said finally. Her body sagged. "We're okay, Norman."

Norman collapsed on the carpet, exhausted, suddenly feeling the strain and tension in every part of his body.

It was over. The crisis had passed. They were going to be all right, after all. Norman felt his body relax.

It was over.

1230 Hours

The blood had stopped flowing from Harry's broken nose and now he seemed to be breathing more regularly, more easily. Norman lifted the icepack to look at the swollen face, and adjusted the flow of the intravenous drip in Harry's arm. Beth had started the intravenous line in Harry's hand after several unsuccessful attempts. They were dripping an anesthetic mixture into him. Harry's breath smelled sour, like tin. But otherwise he was okay. Out cold.

The radio crackled. "I'm at the submarine," Beth said. "Going aboard now."

Norman glanced out the porthole at DH-7, saw Beth climbing up into the dome beside the sub. She was going to press the "Delay" button, the last time such a trip would be necessary. He turned back to Harry.

The computer didn't have any information about the effects of keeping a person asleep for twelve hours straight, but that was what they would have to do. Either Harry would make it, or he wouldn't.

Same as the rest of us, Norman thought. He glanced at the monitor clocks. They showed 1230 hours, and counted backward. He put a blanket over Harry and went over to the console.

The sphere was still there, with its changed pattern of grooves. In all the excitement he had almost forgotten his initial fascination with the sphere, where it had come from, what it meant. Although they understood now what it meant. What had Beth called it? A mental enzyme. An enzyme was something that made chemical reactions possible without actually participating in them. Our bodies needed to perform chemical reactions, but our body temperatures were too cold for most chemical reactions to proceed smoothly. So we had enzymes to help the process along, speed it up. The enzymes made it all possible. And she had called the sphere a mental enzyme.

Very clever, he thought. Clever woman. Her impulsiveness had turned out to be just what was needed. With Harry unconscious, Beth still looked beautiful, but Norman was relieved to find that his own features had returned to pudgy normalcy. He saw his own familiar reflection in the screen as he stared at the sphere on the monitor.

That sphere.

With Harry unconscious, he wondered if they would ever know exactly what had happened, exactly what it had been like. He remembered the lights, like fireflies. And what had Harry said? Something about foam. The foam. Norman heard a whirring sound, and looked out the porthole.

The sub was moving.

Freed of its tethers, the yellow minisub glided across the bottom, its lights shining on the ocean floor. Norman pushed the intercom button: "Beth? Beth!"

"I'm here, Norman."

"What're you doing?"

"Just take it easy, Norman."

"What're you doing in the sub, Beth?"

"Just a precaution, Norman."

"Are you leaving?"

She laughed over the intercom. A light, relaxed laugh. "No, Norman. Just take it easy."

"Tell me what you're doing."

"It's a secret."

"Come on, Beth." This was all he needed, he thought, to have Beth crack up now. He thought again of her impulsiveness, which moments before he had admired. He did not admire it any more. "Beth?"

"Talk to you later," she said.

The sub turned in profile, and he saw red boxes in its claw arms. He could not read the lettering on the boxes, but they looked vaguely familiar. As he watched, the sub moved past the high fin of the spacecraft, and then settled to the bottom. One of the boxes was released, plumping softly on the muddy floor. The sub started up again, churning sediment, and glided forward a hundred yards. Then it stopped again, and released another box. It continued this way along the length of the spacecraft.

"Beth?"

No answer. Norman squinted at the boxes. There was lettering on them, but he could not read them at this distance.

The sub had turned now, and was coming directly toward DH-8. The lights shone at him. It moved closer and the sensor alarms went off, clanging and flashing red lights. He hated these alarms, he thought, going over to the console, looking at the buttons. How the hell did you turn them off? He glanced at Harry, but Harry remained unconscious.

"Beth? Are you there? You set off the damn alarms."

"Push F8."

What the hell was F8? He looked around, finally saw a row of keys on the keyboard, numbered F1 to F20. He pushed F8 and the alarms stopped. The sub was now very close, lights shining into the porthole windows. In the high bubble, Beth was clearly visible, instrument lights shining up on her face. Then the sub descended out of view.

He went to the porthole and looked out. *Deepstar III* was resting on the bottom, depositing more boxes from its claw hands. Now he could read the lettering on the boxes:

CAUTION NO SMOKING NO ELECTRONICS TEVAC EXPLOSIVES

"Beth? What the hell are you doing?"

"Later, Norman."

He listened to her voice. She sounded okay. Was she cracking up? No, he thought. She's not cracking up. She sounds okay. I'm sure she's okay.

But he wasn't sure.

The sub was moving again, its lights blurred by the cloud

of sediment churned up by the propellors. The cloud drifted up past the porthole, obscuring his vision.

"Beth?"

"Everything's fine, Norman. Back in a minute."

As the sediment drifted down to the bottom again, he saw the sub, heading back to DH-7. Moments later, it docked beneath the dome. Then he saw Beth climb out, and tether the sub fore and aft.

1100 Hours

I t's very simple," Beth said.

"Explosives?" He pointed to the screen. "It says here, 'Tevacs are, weight for weight, the most powerful conventional explosives known.' What the hell are you doing putting them around the habitat?"

"Norman, take it easy." She rested her hand on his shoulder. Her touch was soft and reassuring. He relaxed a little, feeling her body so close.

"We should have discussed this together first."

"Norman, I'm not taking any chances. Not any more."

"But Harry is unconscious."

"He might wake up."

"He won't, Beth."

"I'm not taking any chances," she said. "This way, if something starts to come out of that sphere, we can blow the hell out of the whole ship. I've put explosives along the whole length of it."

"But why around the habitat?"

"Defense."

"How is it defense?"

"Believe me, it is."

"Beth, it's dangerous to have that stuff so close to us."

"It's not wired up, Norman. In fact, it's not wired up around the ship, either. I have to go out and do that by hand." She glanced at the screens. "I thought I'd wait a while first, maybe take a nap. Are you tired?"

"No," Norman said.

"You haven't slept in a long time, Norman."

"I'm not tired."

She gave him an appraising look. "I'll keep an eye on Harry, if that's what you're worried about."

"I'm just not tired, Beth."

"Okay," she said, "suit yourself." She brushed her luxuriant hair back from her face with her fingers. "Personally, I'm exhausted. I'm going to get a few hours." She started up the stairs to her lab, then looked down at him. "Want to join me?"

"What?" he said.

She smiled at him directly, knowingly. "You heard me, Norman."

"Maybe later, Beth."

"Okay. Sure."

She ascended the staircase, her body swinging smoothly, sensuously in the tight jumpsuit. She looked good in that jumpsuit. He had to admit it. She was a good-looking woman.

Across the room, Harry snored in a regular rhythm. Norman checked Harry's icepack, and thought about Beth. He heard her moving around in the lab upstairs.

"Hey, Norm?"

"Yes . . ." He moved to the bottom of the stairs, looked up.

"Is there another one of these down there? A clean one?" Something blue dropped into his hands. It was her jumpsuit.

"Yes. I think they're in storage in B."

"Bring me one, would you, Norm?"

"Okay," he said.

Going to B Cyl, he found himself inexplicably nervous. What was going on? Of course, he thought, he knew exactly what was going on, but why now? Beth was exerting a powerful attraction, and he mistrusted it. In her dealings with men, Beth was confrontational, energetic, direct, and angry. Seduction wasn't her method at all.

It is now, he thought, fishing a new jumpsuit out of the storage locker. He took it back to D Cyl and climbed the ladder. From above, he saw a strange bluish light.

"Beth?"

"I'm here, Norm."

He came up and saw her lying naked on her back, beneath a bank of ultraviolet sunlamps hinged out from the wall. She wore opaque cups over her eyes. She twisted her body seductively.

"Did you bring the suit?"

"Yes," he said.

"Thanks a lot. Just put it anywhere, by the lab bench."

"Okay." He draped it over her chair.

She rolled back to face the glowing lamps, sighed. "I thought I'd better get a little vitamin D, Norm."

"Yes . . ."

"You probably should, too."

"Yeah, probably." But Norman was thinking that he didn't remember a bank of sunlamps in the lab. In fact, he was sure that there wasn't one. He had spent a lot of time in that room; he would have remembered. He went back down the stairs quickly.

In fact, the staircase was new, too. It was black anodized metal. It hadn't been that way before. This was a new descending staircase.

"Norm?"

"In a minute, Beth."

He went to the console and started punching buttons. He had seen a file before, on habitat parameters or something like that. He finally found it:

DEEPHAB-8 MIPPR DESIGN PARAMETERS

5.024A Cylinder A
5.024B Cylinder B
5.024C Cylinder C
5.024D Cylinder D
5.024E Cylinder E

Choose one:

He chose Cyl D, and another screen appeared. He chose design plans. He got page after page of architectural drawings. He flicked through them, stabbing at the keys, until he came to the detail plans for the biological laboratory at the top of D Cyl.

Clearly shown in the drawings was a large sunlamp bank, hinged to fold back against the wall. It must have been there all the time; he just hadn't ever noticed it. There were lots of other details he hadn't noticed—like the emergency escape hatch in the domed ceiling of the lab. And the fact that there was a second foldout bunk near the floor entrance. And a black anodized descending staircase.

You're in a panic, he thought. And it has nothing to do with sunlamps and architectural drawings. It doesn't even have to do with sex. You're in a panic because Beth is the only one left besides you, and Beth isn't acting like herself.

In the corner of the screen, he watched the small clock tick backward, the seconds clicking off with agonizing slowness. Twelve more hours, he thought. I've just got to last twelve more hours, and everything will be all right.

He was hungry, but he knew there wasn't any food. He was tired, but there wasn't any place for him to sleep. Both E and C Cylinders were flooded, and he didn't want to go upstairs with Beth. Norman lay down on the floor of D Cyl, beside Harry on the couch. It was cold and damp on the floor. For a long time he couldn't sleep.

0900 **Hours**

The pounding, that terrifying pounding, and the shaking of the floor awakened him abruptly. He rolled over and got to his feet, instantly alert. He saw Beth standing by the monitors. "What is it?" he cried. "What is it?"

"What is what?" Beth said.

She seemed calm. She smiled at him. Norman looked around. The alarms hadn't gone off; the lights weren't flashing.

"I don't know, I thought—I don't know . . ." He trailed off.

"You thought we were under attack again?" she said.

He nodded.

"Why would you think that, Norman?" she said.

Beth was looking at him again in that odd way. An appraising way, her stare very direct and cool. There was no hint of seductiveness to her. If anything, she conveyed the suspiciousness of the old Beth: You're a man, and you're a problem.

"Harry's still unconscious, isn't he? So why would you think we were being attacked?"

"I don't know. I guess I was dreaming."

Beth shrugged. "Maybe you felt the vibration of me walking on the floor," she said. "Anyway, I'm glad you decided to sleep."

That same appraising stare. As if there were something wrong with him.

"You haven't slept enough, Norman."

"None of us have."

"You, particularly."

"Maybe you're right." He had to admit he felt better now that he had slept for a couple of hours. He smiled. "Did you eat all the coffee and Danish?"

"There isn't any coffee and Danish, Norman."

"I know."

"Then why would you say that?" she asked seriously.

"It was a joke, Beth."

"Oh."

"Just a joke. You know, a humorous reflection on our condition?"

"I see." She was working with the screens. "By the way, what did you find out about the balloon?"

"The balloon?"

"The surface balloon. Remember we talked about it?"

He shook his head. He didn't remember.

"Before I went out to the sub, I asked about the control codes to send a balloon to the surface, and you said you'd look in the computer and see if you could find how to do it."

"I did?"

"Yes, Norman. You did."

He thought back. He remembered how he and Beth had

lifted Harry's inert, surprisingly heavy body off the floor, setting him on the couch, and how they had staunched the flow of blood from his nose while Beth had started an intravenous line, which she knew how to do from her work with lab animals. In fact, she had made a joke, saying she hoped Harry fared better than her lab animals, since they usually ended up dead. Then Beth had volunteered to go to the sub, and he had said he'd stay with Harry. That was what he remembered. Nothing about any balloons.

"Sure," Beth said. "Because the communication said we were supposed to acknowledge transmission, and that means a radio balloon sent to the surface. And we figured, with the storm abating, the surface conditions must be calm enough to allow the balloon to ride without snapping the wire. So it was a question of how to release the balloons. And you said you'd look for the control commands."

"I really don't remember," he said. "I'm sorry."

"Norman, we have to work together in these last few hours," Beth said.

"I agree, Beth. Absolutely."

"How are you feeling now?" she said.

"Okay. Pretty good, in fact."

"Good," she said. "Hang in there, Norman. It's only a few more hours."

She hugged him warmly, but when she released him, he saw in her eyes that same detached, appraising look.

AN HOUR LATER, they figured out how to release the balloon. They distantly heard a metallic sizzle as the wire unwound from the outside spool, trailing behind the inflated balloon as it shot toward the surface. Then there was a long pause.

"What's happening?" Norman said.

"We're a thousand feet down," Beth said. "It takes a while for the balloon to get to the surface."

Then the screen changed, and they got a readout of surface conditions. Wind was down to fifteen knots. Waves were running six feet. Barometric pressure was 20.9. Sunlight was recorded.

"Good news," Beth said. "The surface is okay."

Norman was staring at the screen, thinking about the fact that sunlight was recorded. He had never longed for sunlight before. It was funny, what you took for granted. Now the thought of seeing sunlight struck him as unbelievably pleasurable. He could imagine no greater joy than to see sun and clouds, and blue sky.

"What are you thinking?"

"I'm thinking I can't wait to get out of here."

"Me, too," Beth said. "But it won't be long now."

PONG! PONG! PONG! pong!

Norman was checking Harry, and he spun at the sound. "What is it, Beth?"

Pong! pong! pong! pong!

"Take it easy," Beth said, at the console. "I'm just figuring out how to work this thing."

Pong! pong! pong! pong!

"Work what?"

"The side-scanning sonar. False-aperture sonar. I don't

know why they call it 'false-aperture.' Do you know what that refers to, 'false-aperture'?"

Pong! pong! pong! pong!

"No, I don't," Norman said. "Turn it off, please." The sound was unnerving.

"It's marked 'FAS,' which I think stands for 'false-aperture sonar,' but it also says 'side-scanning.' It's very confusing."

"Beth, turn it off!"

Pong! pong! pong! pong!

"Sure, of course," Beth said.

"Why do you want to know how to work that, anyway?" Norman said. He felt irritable, as if she'd intentionally annoyed him with that sound.

"Just in case," Beth said.

"In case *what*, for Christ's sake? You said yourself that Harry's unconscious. There aren't going to be any more attacks."

"Take it easy, Norman," Beth said. "I want to be prepared, that's all."

0720 Hours

He couldn't talk her out of it. She insisted on going outside and wiring the explosives around the ship. It was an absolutely fixed idea in her mind.

"But *why*, Beth?" he kept saying.

"Because I'll feel better after I do it," she said.

"But there isn't any reason to do it."

"I'll feel better if I do," she insisted, and in the end he couldn't stop her.

He saw her now, a small figure with a single glowing light from her helmet, moving from one crate of explosives to another. She opened each crate and removed large yellow cones which looked rather like the cones that highway repair trucks used. These cones were wired together, and when the wiring was completed a small red light glowed at the tip.

He saw small red lights all up and down the length of the ship. It made him uneasy.

When she left, he had said to her, "But you won't wire up the explosives near the habitat."

"No, Norman. I won't."

"Promise me."

"I told you, I won't. If it's going to upset you, I won't."

"It's going to upset me."

"Okay, okay."

Now the red lights were strung along the length of the ship, starting at the dimly visible tail, which rose out of the coral bottom. Beth moved farther north, toward the rest of the unopened crates.

Norman looked at Harry, who snored loudly but who remained unconscious. He paced back and forth in D Cyl, and then went to the monitors.

The screen blinked.

I AM COMING.

Oh God, he thought. And in the next moment he thought, How can this be happening? It can't be happening. Harry was still out cold. How could it be happening?

I AM COMING FOR YOU.

"Beth!"

Her voice sounded tinny on the intercom. "Yes, Norman."

"Get the hell out of there."

DO NOT BE AFRAID, the screen said.

"What is it, Norman?" she said.

"I'm getting something on the screen."

"Check Harry. He must be waking up."

"He's not. Get back here, Beth."

I AM COMING NOW.

"All right, Norman, I'm heading back," she said.

"Fast, Beth."

But he didn't need to say that; already he could see her light bouncing as she ran across the bottom. She was at least a hundred yards from the habitat. He heard her breathing hard on the intercom.

"Can you see anything, Norman?"

"No, nothing." He was straining to look toward the horizon, where the squid had always appeared. The first thing had always been a green glow on the horizon. But he saw no glow now.

Beth was panting.

"I can feel something, Norman. I feel the water . . . surging . . . strong. . . ."

The screen flashed: I WILL KILL YOU.

"Don't you see anything out here?" Beth said.

"No. I don't see anything at all." He saw Beth, alone on the muddy bottom. Her light the solitary focus of his attention.

"I can *feel* it, Norman. It's *close*. Jesus God. What about the alarms?"

"Nothing, Beth."

"Jesus." Her breath came in hissing gasps as she ran. Beth was in good shape, but she couldn't exert herself like that in this atmosphere. Not for long, he thought. Already he could see she was moving more slowly, the helmet lamp bobbing more slowly.

"Norman?"

"Yes, Beth. I'm here."

"Norman, I don't know if I can make it."

"Beth, you can make it. Slow down."

"It's *here*, I can feel it."

"I don't see anything, Beth."

He heard a rapid sharp clicking sound. At first he thought it was static on the line, and then he realized it was her teeth chattering as she shivered. With this exertion she should be getting overheated, but instead she was getting cold. He didn't understand.

"—cold, Norman."

"Slow down, Beth."

"Can't—talking—close—"

She was slowing down, despite herself. She had come into the area of the habitat lights, and she was no more than ten yards from the hatch, but he could see her limbs moving slowly, clumsily.

And now at last he could see something swirling the muddy sediment behind her, in the darkness beyond the lights. It was like a tornado, a swirling cloud of muddy sediment. He couldn't see what was inside the cloud, but he sensed the power within it.

"Close—Nor—"

Beth stumbled, fell. The swirling cloud moved toward her.

I WILL KILL YOU NOW.

Beth got to her feet, looked back, saw the churning cloud bearing down on her. Something about it filled Norman with a deep horror, a horror from childhood, the stuff of nightmares.

"Normannnnnn . . ."

Then Norman was running, not really knowing what he was going to do, but propelled by the vision he had seen, thinking only that he had to do something, he had to take some action, and he went through B into A and looked at his suit but there wasn't time and the black water in the open hatch was spitting and swirling and he saw Beth's gloved hand below the surface, flailing, she was right there beneath him, and she was the only other one, and without thinking he jumped into the black water and went down.

THE SHOCK OF the cold made him want to scream; it tore at his lungs. His whole body was instantly numb, and he felt a second of hideous paralysis. The water churned and tossed him like a great wave; he was powerless to fight it; his head banged on the underside of the habitat. He could see nothing at all.

He reached for Beth, throwing his arms blindly in all directions. His lungs burned. The water spun him in circles, up-ended him.

He touched her, lost her. The water continued to spin him.

He grabbed her. Something. An arm. He was already losing feeling, already feeling slower and stupider. He pulled. He saw a ring of light above him: the hatch. He kicked his legs but he did not seem to move. The circle came no closer.

He kicked again, dragging Beth like a dead weight. Perhaps she was dead. His lungs burned. It was the worst pain he had ever felt in his life. He fought the pain, and he fought the angry churning water and he kept kicking toward the light, that was his only thought, to kick to the light, to come closer to the light, to reach the light, the light, the light. . . .

The light.

The images were confusing. Beth's suited body clanging on the metal, inside the airlock. His own knee bleeding on the metal of the hatch, the drops of blood spattering. Beth's shaking hands reaching for her helmet, twisting it, trying to get the helmet unlocked. Hands shaking. Water in the hatch, sucking, surging. Lights in his eyes. A terrible pain somewhere. Rust very close to his face, a sharp edge of metal. Cold metal. Cold air. Lights in his eyes, dimming. Fading. Blackness.

THE SENSATION OF warmth was pleasant. He heard a hissing roar in his ears. He looked up and saw Beth, out of her suit, looming large above him, adjusting the big space heater, turning the power up. She was still shivering, but she was turning up the heat. He closed his eyes. We made it, he thought. We're still together. We're still okay. We made it.

He relaxed.

There was a crawly sensation over his body. From the cold, he thought, his body warming from the cold. The crawly sensation was not pleasant. And the hissing was not pleasant, either; it was sibilant, intermittent.

Something slithered softly under his chin as he lay on the deck. He opened his eyes and saw a silvery white tube, and then he focused and saw the tiny beady eyes, and the flicking tongue. It was a snake.

A sea snake.

He froze. He looked down, moving only his eyes.

His entire body was covered with white snakes.

The crawly sensation came from dozens of snakes, coiling around his ankles, sliding between his legs, over his chest. He felt a cool slithering motion across his forehead. He closed his eyes, feeling horror as the snake body moved over his face, down his nose, brushed over his lips, then moved away.

He listened to the hissing of the reptiles and thought of how poisonous Beth had said they were. Beth, he thought, where is Beth?

He did not move. He felt snakes coiling around his neck, slipping over his shoulder, sliding between the fingers of his hands. He did not want to open his eyes. He felt a surge of nausea.

God, he thought. I'm going to throw up.

He felt snakes under his armpit, and felt snakes slipping past his groin. He burst into a cold sweat. He fought nausea.

Beth, he thought. He did not want to speak. Beth . . .

He listened to the hissing and then, when he couldn't stand it any more, he opened his eyes and saw the mass of coiling, writhing white flesh, the tiny heads, the flicking forked tongues. He closed his eyes again.

He felt one crawling up the leg of his jumpsuit, moving against his bare skin.

"Don't move, Norman."

It was Beth. He could hear the tension in her voice. He looked up, could not see her, only her shadow.

He heard her say, "Oh God, what time is it?" and he thought, The hell with the time, who cares what time it is? It didn't make any sense to him. "I have to know the time," Beth was saying. He heard her feet moving on the deck. "The time . . ."

She was moving away, leaving him!

The snakes slid over his ears, under his chin, past his nostrils, the bodies damp and slithering.

Then he heard her feet on the deck, and a metallic *clang* as she threw open the hatch. He opened his eyes to see her bending over him, grabbing the snakes in great handfuls, throwing them down the hatch into the water. Snakes writhed in her hands, twisted around her wrists, but she shook them off, tossed them aside. Some of the snakes didn't land in the water and coiled on the deck. But most of the snakes were off his body now.

One more crawling up his leg, toward his groin. He felt it moving quickly backward—she was pulling it out by the tail!

"Jesus, careful—"

The snake was out, flung over her shoulder.

"You can get up, Norman," she said.

He jumped to his feet, and promptly vomited.

0700 Hours

He had a murderous, pounding headache. It made the habitat lights seem unpleasantly bright. And he was cold. Beth had wrapped him in blankets and had moved him next to the big space heaters in D Cyl, so close that the hum of the electrical elements was very loud in his ears, but he was still cold. He looked down at her now, as she bandaged his cut knee.

"How is it?" he said.

"Not good," she said. "It's right down to the bone. But you'll be all right. It's only a few more hours now."

"Yes, I—ouch!"

"Sorry. Almost done." Beth was following first-aid directions from the computer. To distract his mind from the pain, he read the screen.

"That's what I need," he said. "Some microsleep. Or better yet, some serious macrosleep."

"Yes, we all do."

MINOR MEDICAL (NON-LETHAL) COMPLICATIONS

7.113 Trauma
7.115 Microsleep
7.118 Helium Tremor
7.119 Otitis
7.121 Toxic Contaminants
7.143 Synovial Pain

Choose one:

A thought occurred to him. "Beth, remember when you were pulling the snakes off me? What was all that you were saying about the time of day?"

"Sea snakes are diurnal," Beth said. "Many poisonous snakes are alternately aggressive and passive in twelve-hour cycles, corresponding to day and night. During the day, when they're passive, you can handle them and they will never bite. For example, in India, the highly poisonous banded krait has never been known to bite during the day, even when children play with them. But at night, watch out. So I was trying to determine which cycle the sea snakes were on, until I decided that this must be their passive daytime cycle."

"How'd you figure that?"

"Because you were still alive." Then she had used her bare hands to remove the snakes, knowing that they wouldn't bite her, either.

"With your hands full of snakes, you looked like Medusa."

"What is that, a rock star?"

"No, it's a mythological figure."

"The one who killed her children?" she asked, with a quick suspicious glance. Beth, ever alert to a veiled insult.

"No, that's somebody else. That was Medea. Medusa was a mythical woman with a head full of snakes who turned men to stone if they looked at her. Perseus killed her by looking at her reflection in his polished shield."

"Sorry, Norman. Not my field."

It was remarkable, he thought, that at one time every educated Western person knew these figures from mythology and the stories behind them intimately—as intimately as they knew the stories of families and friends. Myths had once represented the common knowledge of humanity, and they served as a kind of map of consciousness.

But now a well-educated person such as Beth knew nothing of myths at all. It was as if men had decided that the map of human consciousness had changed. But had it really changed? He shivered.

"Still cold, Norman?"

"Yeah. But the worst thing is the headache."

"You're probably dehydrated. Let's see if I can find something for you to drink." She went to the first-aid box on the wall.

"You know, that was a hell of a thing you did," Beth said. "Jumping in like that without a suit. That water's only a couple of degrees above freezing. It was very brave. Stupid, but brave." She smiled. "You saved my life, Norman."

"I didn't think," Norman said. "I just did it." And then he told her how, when he had seen her outside, with the churning cloud of sediment approaching her, he had felt an old and childish horror, something from distant memory.

"You know what it was?" he said. "It reminded me of the tornado in *The Wizard of Oz*. That tornado scared the bejesus out of me when I was a kid. I just didn't want to see it happen again."

And then he thought, Perhaps these are our new myths. Dorothy and Toto and the Wicked Witch, Captain Nemo and the giant squid . . .

"Well," Beth said, "whatever the reason, you saved my life. Thank you."

"Any time," Norman said. He smiled. "Just don't do it again."

"No, I won't be going out again."

She brought back a drink in a paper cup. It was syrupy and sweet.

"What is this?"

"Isotonic glucose supplement. Drink it."

He sipped it again, but it was unpleasantly sweet. Across the room, the console screen still said I WILL KILL YOU NOW. He looked at Harry, still unconscious, with the intravenous line running into his arm.

Harry had been unconscious all this time.

He hadn't faced the implications of that. It was time to do it now. He didn't want to do it, but he had to. He said, "Beth, why do you think all this is happening?"

"All what?"

"The screen, printing words. And another manifestation coming to attack us."

Beth looked at him in a flat, neutral way. "What do you think, Norman?"

"It's not Harry."

"No. It's not."

"Then why is it happening?" Norman said. He got up, pulling the blankets tighter around him. He flexed his bandaged knee; it hurt, but not too badly. Norman moved to the porthole and looked out the window. In the distance he could see the string of red lights, from the explosives Beth had set and armed. He had never understood why she had wanted to do that. She had acted so strangely about the whole thing. He looked down toward the base of the habitat.

Red lights were glowing there, too, just below the porthole. *She had armed the explosives around the habitat.*

"Beth, what have you done?"

"Done?"

"You armed the explosives around DH-8."

"Yes, Norman," she said. She stood watching him, very still, very calm.

"Beth, you promised you wouldn't do that."

"I know. I had to."

"How are they wired? Where's the button, Beth?"

"There is no button. They're set on automatic vibration sensors."

"You mean they'll go off *automatically?*"

"Yes, Norman."

"Beth, this is crazy. Someone is still making these manifestations. *Who is doing that, Beth?*"

She smiled slowly, a lazy, cat smile, as if he secretly amused her. "Don't you really know?"

He did know. Yes, he thought. He knew, and it chilled him. "You're making these manifestations, Beth."

"No, Norman," she said, still calm. "I'm not doing it. You are."

0640 Hours

He thought back years ago, to the early days of his training, when he had worked in the state hospital at Borrego. Norman had been sent by his supervisor to make a progress report on a particular patient. The man was in his late twenties, pleasant and well educated. Norman talked to him about all sorts of things: the Oldsmobile Hydramatic transmission, the best surfing beaches, Adlai Stevenson's recent presidential campaign, Whitey Ford's pitching, even Freudian theory. The man was quite charming, although he chain-smoked and seemed to have an underlying tension. Finally Norman got around to asking him why he had been sent to the hospital.

The man didn't remember why. He was sorry, he just couldn't seem to recall. Under repeated questioning from Norman, the man became less charming, more irritable. Finally he turned threatening and angry, pounding the table, demanding that Norman talk about something else.

Only then did it dawn on Norman who this man was: Alan Whittier, who as a teenager had murdered his mother and sister in their trailer in Palm Desert, and then had gone on to kill six people at a gas station and three others in a supermarket parking lot, until he finally turned himself in to the police, sobbing, hysterical with guilt and remorse. Whittier had been in the state hospital for ten years, and he had brutally attacked several attendants during that time.

This was the man who was now enraged, standing up in front of Norman, and kicking the table, flinging his chair back against the wall. Norman was still a student; he didn't know how to handle it. He turned to flee the room, but the door behind him was locked. They had locked him in, which is what they always did during interviews with violent patients. Behind him, Whittier lifted the table and threw it against the wall; he was coming for Norman. Norman had a moment of horrible panic until he heard the locks rattling, and then three huge attendants dashed in, grabbed Whittier, and dragged him away, still screaming and swearing.

Norman went directly to his supervisor, demanded to know why he had been set up. The supervisor said to him, Set up? Yes, Norman had said, *set up*. The supervisor said, But weren't you told the man's name beforehand? Didn't the name mean anything to you? Norman replied that he hadn't really paid attention.

You better pay attention, Norman, the supervisor had said. You can't ever let down your guard in a place like this. It's too dangerous.

Now, looking across the habitat at Beth, he thought: Pay attention, Norman. You can't let down your guard. Because you're dealing with a crazy person and you haven't realized it.

"I see you don't believe me," Beth said, still very calm. "Are you able to talk?"

"Sure," Norman said.

"Be logical, all of that?"

"Sure," he said, thinking: I'm not the crazy one here.

"All right," Beth said. "Remember when you told me about Harry—how all the evidence pointed to Harry?"

"Yes. Of course."

"You asked me if I could think of another explanation, and I said no. But there *is* another explanation, Norman. Some points you conveniently overlooked the first time. Like the jellyfish. Why the jellyfish? It was *your* little brother who was stung by the jellyfish, Norman, and *you* who felt guilty afterward. And when does Jerry speak? When *you're* there, Norman. And when does the squid stop its attack? When *you* were knocked unconscious, Norman. Not Harry, *you*."

Her voice was so calm, so reasonable. He struggled to consider what she was saying. Was it possible she was right?

"Step back. Take the long view," Beth said. "You're a psychologist, down here with a bunch of scientists dealing with hardware. There's nothing for you to do down here—you said so yourself. And wasn't there a time in your life when you felt similarly professionally bypassed? Wasn't that an uncomfortable time for you? Didn't you once tell me that you hated that time in your life?"

"Yes, but—"

"When all the strange things start to happen, the problem isn't hardware any more. Now it's a psychological problem. It's right up your alley, Norman, your particular area of expertise. Suddenly you become the center of attention, don't you?"

No, he thought. This can't be right.

"When Jerry starts to communicate with us, who notices that he has emotions? Who insists we deal with Jerry's emotions? None of us are interested in emotions, Norman. Barnes only wants to know about armaments, Ted only wants to talk science, Harry only wants to play logical games. You're the one who's interested in emotions. And who manipulates Jerry—or fails to manipulate him? You, Norman. It's all you."

"It can't be," Norman said. His mind was reeling. He struggled to find a contradiction, and found it. "It can't be me—because I haven't been inside the sphere."

"Yes, you have," Beth said. "You just don't remember."

HE FELT BATTERED, repeatedly punched and battered. He couldn't seem to get his balance, and the blows kept coming.

"Just the way you don't remember that I asked you to look up the balloon codes," Beth was saying in her calm voice. "Or the way Barnes asked you about the helium concentrations in E Cyl."

He thought, what helium concentrations in E Cyl? When did Barnes ask me about that?

"There's a lot you don't remember, Norman."

Norman said, "When did I go to the sphere?"

"Before the first squid attack. After Harry came out."

"I was asleep! I was sleeping in my bunk!"

"No, Norman. You weren't. Because Fletcher came to get you and you were gone. We couldn't find you for about two hours, and then you showed up, yawning."

"I don't believe you," he said.

"I know you don't. You prefer to make it somebody else's problem. And you're clever. You're skilled at psychological manipulation, Norman. Remember those tests you conducted? Putting unsuspecting people up in an airplane, then telling them the pilot had a heart attack? Scaring them half to death? That's pretty ruthless manipulation, Norman.

"And down here in the habitat, when all these things started happening, you needed a monster. So you made Harry the monster. But Harry wasn't the monster, Norman. You are the monster. That's why your appearance changed, why you became ugly. Because you're the monster."

"But the message. It said 'My name is Harry.'"

"Yes, it did. And as you yourself pointed out, the person causing it was afraid that the real name would come out on the screen."

"Harry," Norman said. "The name was *Harry*."

"And what's your name?"

"Norman Johnson."

"Your full name."

He paused. Somehow his mouth wasn't working. His brain was blank.

"I'll tell you what it is," Beth said. "I looked it up. It's Norman *Harrison* Johnson."

NO, HE THOUGHT. No, no, no. She *can't* be right.

"It's hard to accept," Beth was saying in her slow, patient, almost hypnotic voice. "I understand that. But if you think about it, you'll realize you wanted it to come to this. You wanted me to figure it out, Norman. Why, just a few minutes ago, you even told me about *The Wizard of Oz*, didn't you? You helped me along when I wasn't getting the point—or at least your unconscious did. Are you still calm?"

"Of course I'm calm."

"Good. Stay calm, Norman. Let's consider this logically. Will you cooperate with me?"

"What do you want to do?"

"I want to put you under, Norman. Like Harry."

He shook his head.

"It's only for a few hours, Norman," she said, and then she seemed to decide; she moved swiftly toward him, and he saw the syringe in her hand, the glint of the needle, and he twisted away. The needle plunged into the blanket, and he threw it off and ran for the stairs.

"Norman! Come back here!"

He was climbing the stairs. He saw Beth running forward with the needle. He kicked with his foot, got upstairs into her lab, and slammed the hatch down on her.

"Norman!"

She pounded on the hatch. Norman stood on it, knowing that she could never lift his weight. Beth continued to pound.

"Norman Johnson, you open that hatch this minute!"

"No, Beth, I'm sorry."

He paused. What could she do? Nothing, he thought. He was safe here. She couldn't get to him up here, she couldn't do anything to him as long as he remained here.

Then he saw the metal pivot move in the center of the hatch between his feet. On the other side of the hatch, Beth was spinning the wheel.

Locking him in.

0600 Hours

The only lights in the laboratory shone on the bench, next to a row of neatly bottled specimens: squid, shrimps, giant squid eggs. He touched the bottles absently. He turned on the laboratory monitor and punched buttons until he saw Beth, downstairs, on the video. Beth was working at the main D Cyl console. To one side, he saw Harry, still lying unconscious.

"Norman, can you hear me?"

He said aloud, "Yes, Beth. I hear you."

"Norman, you are acting irresponsibly. You are a menace to this entire expedition."

Was that true? he wondered. He didn't think he was a menace to the expedition. It didn't *feel* true to him. But how often in his life had he confronted patients who refused to acknowledge what was happening in their lives? Even trivial examples—a man, another professor at the university, who was terrified of elevators but who steadfastly insisted he always took the stairs because it was good exercise. The man would climb fifteen-story buildings; he would decline appointments in taller buildings; he arranged his entire life to accommodate a problem he would not admit he had. The problem remained concealed from him until he finally had a heart attack. Or the woman who was exhausted from years of caring for her disturbed daughter; she gave her daughter a bottle of sleeping pills because she said the girl needed a rest; the girl committed suicide. Or the novice sailor who cheerfully packed his family off on a sailing excursion to Catalina in a gale, nearly killing them all.

Dozens of examples came to mind. It was a psychological truism, this blindness about self. Did he imagine that he was immune? Three years ago, there had been a minor scandal when one of the assistant professors in the Psychology Department had committed suicide, sticking a gun in his mouth over the Labor Day weekend. There had been headlines for that one: "PSYCH PROF KILLS SELF, Colleagues Express Surprise, Say Deceased Was 'Always Happy.'"

The dean of the faculty, embarrassed in his fund-raising, had berated Norman about that incident, but the difficult truth was that psychology had severe limitations. Even with professional knowledge and the best of intentions, there remained an enormous amount you never knew about your closest friends, your colleagues, your wives and husbands and children.

And your ignorance about yourself was even greater than that. Self-awareness was the most difficult of all. Few people attained it. Or perhaps nobody attained it.

"Norman, are you there?"

"Yes, Beth."

"I think you are a good person, Norman."

He said nothing. He just watched her on the monitor.

"I think you have integrity, and that you believe in telling the truth. This is a difficult moment for you, to face the reality about yourself. I know your mind is struggling now to find excuses, to blame someone else. But I think you can do it, Norman. Harry couldn't do it, but you can. I think you can admit the hard truth—that so long as you remain conscious, the expedition is menaced."

He felt the strength of her conviction, heard the quiet force of her voice. As Beth spoke, it felt almost as if her ideas were clothing being draped over his body. He began to see things her way. She was so calm, she must be right. Her ideas had such power. Her thoughts had such power. . . .

"Beth, have you been in the sphere?"

"No, Norman. That's your mind, trying to evade the point again. I haven't been in the sphere. *You* have."

He honestly couldn't remember going into the sphere. He had no recollection at all. And when Harry had been in the sphere, he remembered afterward. Why would Norman forget? Why would he block it?

"You're a psychologist, Norman," she was saying. "You, of all people, do not want to admit you have a shadow side. You have a professional stake in believing in your own mental health. Of course you will deny it."

He didn't think so. But how to resolve it? How to determine if she was right or not? His mind wasn't working well.

His cut knee throbbed painfully. At least there was no doubt about that—his injured knee was real.

Reality testing.

That was how to resolve it, he thought. Reality testing. What was the objective evidence that Norman had gone to the sphere? They had made tapes of everything that occurred in the habitat. If Norman had gone to the sphere many hours ago, somewhere there was a tape showing him in the airlock, alone, getting dressed, slipping away. Beth should be able to show him that tape. Where was that tape?

In the submarine, of course.

It would long ago have been taken to the submarine. Norman himself might have taken it, when he made his excursion to the sub.

No objective evidence.

"Norman, give up. Please. For all our sakes."

Perhaps she was right, he thought. She was so sure of herself. If he was evading the truth, if he was putting the expedition in jeopardy, then he had to give himself up and let her put him under. Could he trust her to do that? He would have to. There wasn't any choice.

It must be me, he thought. It must be. The thought was so horrible to him—that in itself was suspicious. He was resisting it so violently—not a good sign, he thought. Too much resistance.

"Norman?"

"Okay, Beth."

"Will you do it?"

"Don't push. Give me a minute, will you?"

"Sure, Norman. Of course."

He looked at the video recorder next to the monitor. He remembered how Beth had used this recorder to play the same tape, again and again, the tape in which the sphere had opened by itself. That tape was now lying on the counter beside the recorder. He pushed the tape into the slot, clicked the recorder on. Why bother to look at it now? he thought. You're just delaying. You're wasting time.

The screen flickered, and he waited for the familiar image of Beth eating cake, her back to the monitor. But this was a different tape. This was a direct monitor feed showing the sphere. The gleaming sphere, just sitting there.

He watched for a few seconds, but nothing happened. The sphere was immobile, as always. Polished, perfect, immobile. He watched a while longer, but there was nothing to see.

"Norman, if I open the hatch now, will you come down quietly?"

"Yes, Beth."

He sighed, sat back in the chair. How long would he be unconscious? A little less than six hours. It would be okay. But in any case, Beth was right, he had to give himself up.

"Norman, why are you watching that tape?"

He looked around quickly. Was there a video camera in the room allowing her to see him? Yes: high up in the ceiling, next to the upper hatch.

"Why are you watching that tape, Norman?"

"It was here."

"Who said you could watch that tape?"

"Nobody," Norman said. "It was just here."

"Turn the tape off, Norman. Turn it off now."

She didn't sound so calm any more. "What's the matter, Beth?"

"Turn that damned tape off, Norman!"

He was about to ask her why, but then he saw Beth enter the video image, stand next to the sphere. Beth closed her eyes and clenched her fists. The convoluted grooves of the sphere parted, revealing blackness. And as he watched, Beth stepped inside the sphere.

And the door of the sphere closed behind her.

"YOU GODDAMNED MEN," Beth said in a tight, angry voice. "You're all the same; you can't leave well enough alone, none of you."

"You lied to me, Beth."

"Why did you watch that tape? I *begged* you not to watch that tape. It could only hurt you to watch that tape, Norman." She wasn't angry any more; now she was pleading, near tears. She was undergoing rapid emotional shifts. Unstable, unpredictable.

And she was in control of the habitat.

"Beth."

"I'm sorry, Norman. I can't trust you any more."

"Beth."

"I'm turning you off, Norman. I'm not going to listen to—"

"—Beth, wait—"

"—you any more. I know how dangerous you are. I saw what you did to Harry. How you twisted the facts so that it was Harry's fault. Oh yes, it was *Harry's* fault, by the time you got through. And now you want to make it *Beth's* fault, don't you? Well, let me tell you, Norman, you won't be able to do it, because I have *shut you off*, Norman. I can't hear your soft, convincing words. I can't hear your manipulation. So don't waste your breath, Norman."

He stopped the tape. The monitor now showed Beth at the console in the room below.

Pushing buttons on the console.

"Beth?" he said.

She didn't reply; she just went on working at the console, muttering to herself.

"You're a real son of a bitch, Norman, do you know that? You feel so terrible that you need to make everybody else just as low as you are."

She was talking about herself, he thought.

"You're so big on the unconscious, Norman. The unconscious *this*, the unconscious *that*. Jesus Christ, I'm sick of you. *Your* unconscious probably wants to kill us all, just because you want to kill yourself and you think everybody else should die with you."

He felt a shuddering chill. Beth, with her lack of self-esteem, her deep core of self-hate, had gone inside the sphere, and now she was acting with the power of the sphere, but without stability to her thoughts. Beth saw herself as a victim who struggled against her fate, always unsuccessfully. Beth was victimized by men, victimized by the establishment, victimized by research, victimized by reality. In every case she failed to see how she had done it to herself. And she's put explosives all around the habitat, he thought.

"I won't let you do it, Norman. I'm going to stop you before you kill us all."

Everything she said was the reverse of the truth. He began to see the pattern now.

Beth had figured out how to open the sphere, and she had gone there in secret, because she had always been attracted to power—she always felt she lacked power and needed more. But Beth wasn't prepared to handle power once she had it. Beth still saw herself as a victim, so she had to deny the power, and arrange to be victimized by it.

It was very different from Harry. Harry had denied his fears, and so fearful images had manifested themselves. But Beth denied her power, and so she manifested a churning cloud of formless, uncontrolled power.

Harry was a mathematician who lived in a conscious world of abstraction, of equations and thoughts. A concrete form, like a squid, was what Harry feared. But Beth, the zoologist who dealt every day with animals, creatures she could touch and see, created an abstraction. A power that she could not touch or see. A formless abstract power that was coming to get her.

And to defend herself, she had armed the habitat with explosives. It wasn't much of a defense, Norman thought.

Unless you secretly wanted to kill yourself.

The horror of his true predicament became clear to him.

"You won't get away with this, Norman. I won't let it happen. Not to *me*."

She was punching keys on the console. What was she planning? What could she do to him? He had to think.

Suddenly, the lights in the laboratory went off. A moment

later, the big space heater died, the red elements cooling, turning dark.

She had shut off the power.

With the heater turned off, how long could he last? He took the blankets from her bed, wrapped himself in them. How long, without heat? Certainly not six hours, he thought grimly.

"I'm sorry, Norman. But you understand the position I'm in. As long as you're conscious, I'm in danger."

Maybe an hour, he thought. Maybe I can last an hour.

"I'm sorry, Norman. But I have to do this to you."

He heard a soft hiss. The alarm on his chest badge began to beep. He looked down at it. Even in the darkness, he could see it was now gray. He knew immediately what had happened.

Beth had turned off his air.

0535 Hours

Huddled in the darkness, listening to the beep of his alarm and the hiss of the escaping air. The pressure diminishing rapidly: his ears popped, as if he were in an airplane taking off.

Do something, he thought, feeling a surge of panic.

But there was nothing he could do. He was locked in the upper chamber of D Cyl. He could not get out. Beth had control of the entire facility, and she knew how to run the life-support systems. She had shut off his power, she had shut off his heat, and now she had shut off his air. He was trapped.

As the pressure fell, the sealed specimen bottles exploded like bombs, shooting fragments of glass across the room. He ducked under the blankets, feeling the glass rip and tug at the cloth. Breathing was harder now. At first he thought it was tension, and then he realized that the air was thinner. He would lose consciousness soon.

Do something.

He couldn't seem to catch his breath.

Do something.

But all he could think about was breathing. He needed air, needed oxygen. Then he thought of the first-aid cabinet. Wasn't there emergency oxygen in the cabinet? He wasn't sure. He seemed to remember. . . . As he got up, another specimen bottle exploded, and he twisted away from the flying glass.

He was gasping for breath, chest heaving. He started to see gray spots before his eyes.

He fumbled in the darkness, looking for the cabinet, his hands moving along the wall. He touched a cylinder. Oxygen? No, too large—it must be the fire extinguisher. Where was the cabinet? His hands moved along the wall. Where?

He felt the metal case, the embossed cover with the raised cross. He pulled it open, thrust his hands inside.

More spots swam before his eyes. There wasn't much time.

His fingers touched small bottles, soft bandage packs. There was no air bottle. Damn! The bottles fell to the floor, and then something large and heavy landed on his foot with a thud. He bent down, touched the floor, felt a shard of glass cut his finger, paid no attention. His hand closed over a cold metal cylinder. It was small, hardly longer than the palm of his hand. At one end was some fitting, a nozzle. . . .

It was a spray can—some kind of damn spray can. He threw it aside. Oxygen. He needed oxygen!

By the bed, he remembered. Wasn't there emergency oxygen by every bed in the habitat? He felt for the couch where

Beth had slept, felt for the wall above where her head would have been. Surely there was oxygen nearby. He was dizzy now. He wasn't thinking clearly.

No oxygen.

Then he realized this wasn't a regular bed. It wasn't intended for sleeping. They wouldn't have placed any oxygen here. Damn! And then his hand touched a metal cylinder, clipped to the wall. At one end was something soft. Soft . . .

An oxygen mask.

Quickly he pushed the mask over his mouth and nose. He felt the bottle, twisted a knurled knob. He heard a hissing, breathed cold air. He felt a wave of intense dizziness, and then his head cleared. Oxygen! He was fine!

He felt the shape of the bottle, gauging its size. It was an emergency bottle, only a few hundred cc's. How long would it last? Not long, he thought. A few minutes. It was only a temporary reprieve.

Do something.

But he couldn't think of anything to do. He had no options. He was locked in a room.

He remembered one of his teachers, fat old Dr. Temkin. "You always have an option. There is always something you can do. You are never without choice."

I am now, he thought. No choices now. Anyway, Temkin had been talking about treating patients, not escaping from sealed chambers. Temkin didn't have any experience escaping from sealed chambers. And neither did Norman.

The oxygen made him lightheaded. Or was it already running out? He saw a parade of his old teachers before him. Was this like seeing your life running before you, before you died? All his teachers: Mrs. Jefferson, who told him to be a lawyer instead. Old Joe Lamper, who laughed and said, "Everything is sex. Trust me. It always comes down to sex." Dr. Stein, who used to say, "There is no such thing as a resistant patient. Show me a resistant patient and I'll show you a resistant therapist. If you're not making headway with a patient, then do something else, do anything else. But do something."

Do something.

Stein advocated crazy stuff. If you weren't getting through to a patient, get crazy. Dress up in a clown suit, kick the patient, squirt him with a water pistol, do any damned thing that came into your head, but *do something.*

"Look," he used to say. "What you're doing now isn't working. So you might as well do something else, no matter how crazy it seems."

That was fine back then, Norman thought. He'd like to see Stein assess this problem. What would Dr. Stein tell him to do?

Open the door. I can't; she's locked it.

Talk to her. I can't; she won't listen.

Turn on your air. I can't; she has control of the system.

Get control of the system. I can't; she is in control.

Find help inside the room. I can't; there is nothing left to help me.

Then leave. I can't; I—

He paused. That wasn't true. He could leave by smashing a porthole, or, for that matter, by opening the hatch in the ceiling. But there was no place to go. He didn't have a suit.

The water was freezing. He had been exposed to that freezing water for only a few seconds and he had nearly died. If he were to leave the room for the open ocean, he would almost surely die. He'd probably be fatally chilled before the chamber even filled with water. He would surely die.

In his mind he saw Stein raise his bushy eyebrows, give his quizzical smile. *So? You'll die anyway. What have you got to lose?*

A plan began to form in Norman's mind. If he opened the ceiling hatch, he could go outside the habitat. Once outside, perhaps he could make his way down to A Cyl, get back in through the airlock, and put his suit on. Then he would be okay.

If he could make it to the airlock. How long would that take? Thirty seconds? A minute? Could he hold his breath that long? Could he withstand the cold that long?

You'll die anyway.

And then he thought, You damn fool, you're holding an oxygen bottle in your hand; you have enough air if you don't stay here, wasting time worrying. Get on with it.

No, he thought, there's something else, something I'm forgetting. . . .

Get on with it!

So he stopped thinking, and climbed up to the ceiling hatch at the top of the cylinder. Then he held his breath, braced himself, and spun the wheel, opening the hatch.

"Norman! Norman, what are you doing? Norman! You are insa—" he heard Beth shout, and then the rest was lost in the roar of freezing water pouring like a mighty waterfall into the habitat, filling the room.

• • •

THE MOMENT HE was outside, he realized his mistake. He needed weights. His body was buoyant, tugging him up toward the surface. He sucked a final breath, dropped the oxygen bottle, and desperately gripped the cold pipes on the outside of the habitat, knowing that if he lost his grip, there would be nothing to stop him, nothing to grab onto, all the way to the surface. He would reach the surface and explode like a balloon.

Holding the pipes, he pulled himself down, hand over hand, looking for the next pipe, the next protrusion to grab. It was like mountain-climbing in reverse; if he let go, he would fall upward and die. His hands were long since numb. His body was stiff with cold, slow with cold. His lungs burned.

He had very little time.

He reached the bottom, swung under D Cyl, pulled himself along, felt in the darkness for the airlock. It wasn't there! The airlock was gone! Then he saw he was beneath B Cyl. He moved over to A, felt the airlock. The airlock was closed. He tugged the wheel. It was shut tight. He pulled on it, but he could not move it.

He was locked out.

The most intense fear gripped him. His body was almost immobile from cold; he knew he had only a few seconds of consciousness remaining. He had to open the hatch. He pounded it, pounded the metal around the rim, feeling nothing in his numb hands.

The wheel began to spin by itself. The hatch popped open. There must have been an emergency button, he must have—

He burst above the surface of the water, gasped air, and sank again. He came back up, but he couldn't climb out into the cylinder. He was too numb, his muscles frozen, his body unresponsive.

You have to do it, he thought. You have to do it. His fingers gripped metal, slipped off, gripped again. *One pull*, he thought. One last pull. He heaved his chest over the metal rim, flopped onto the deck. He couldn't feel anything, he was so cold. He twisted his body, trying to pull his legs up, and fell back into the icy water.

No!

He pulled himself up again, one last time—again over the rim, again onto the deck, and he twisted, twisted, one leg up, his balance precarious, then the other leg, he couldn't really feel it, and then he was out of the water, and lying on the deck.

He was shivering. He tried to stand, and fell over. His whole body was shaking so hard he could not keep his balance.

Across the airlock he saw his suit, hanging on the wall of the cylinder. He saw the helmet, "JOHNSON" stenciled on it. Norman crawled toward the suit, his body shaking violently. He tried to stand, and could not. The boots of his suit were directly in front of his face. He tried to grip them in his hands, but his hands could not close. He tried to bite the suit, to pull himself up with his teeth, but his teeth were chattering uncontrollably.

The intercom crackled.

"Norman! I know what you're doing, Norman!"

Any minute, Beth would be here. He had to get into the suit. He stared at it, inches from him, but his hands still shook, he could not hold anything. Finally he saw the fabric loops near the waist to clip instruments. He hooked one hand into the loop, managed to hold on. He pulled himself upright. He got one foot into the suit, then the other.

"Norman!"

He reached for the helmet. The helmet drummed in a staccato beat against the wall before he managed to get it free of the peg and drop it over his head. He twisted it, heard the click of the snap-lock.

He was still very cold. Why wasn't the suit heating up? Then he realized, no power. The power was in the tank pack. Norman backed up against the tank, shrugged it on, staggered under the weight. He had to hook the umbilicus—he reached behind him, felt it—held it—hook it into the suit—at the waist—hook it—

He heard a click.

The fan hummed.

He felt long streaks of pain all over his body. The electrical elements were heating, painful against his frozen skin. He felt pins and needles all over. Beth was talking—he heard her through the intercom—but he couldn't listen to her. He sat heavily on the deck, breathing hard.

But already he knew that he was going to be all right; the pain was lessening, his head was clearing, and he was no longer shaking so badly. He had been chilled, but not long enough for it to be central. He was recovering fast.

The radio crackled.

"You'll never get to me, Norman!"

He got to his feet, pulled on his weight belt, locked the buckles.

"Norman!"

He said nothing. He felt quite warm now, quite normal.

"Norman! I am surrounded by explosives! If you come anywhere near me, I will blow you to pieces! You'll die, Norman! You'll never get near me!"

But Norman wasn't going to Beth. He had another plan entirely. He heard his tank air hiss as the pressure equalized in his suit.

He jumped back into the water.

0500 **Hours**

The sphere gleamed in the light. Norman saw himself reflected in its perfectly polished surface, then saw his image break up, fragmented on the convolutions, as he moved around to the back.

To the door.

It looked like a mouth, he thought. Like the maw of some primitive creature, about to eat him. Confronted by the sphere, seeing once again the alien, unhuman pattern of the convolutions, he felt his intention dissolve. He was suddenly afraid. He didn't think he could go through with it.

Don't be silly, he told himself. Harry did it. And Beth did it. They survived.

He examined the convolutions, as if for reassurance. But there wasn't any reassurance to be obtained. Just curved grooves in the metal, reflecting back the light.

Okay, he thought finally. I'll do it. I've come this far, I've survived everything so far. I might as well do it.

Go ahead and open up.

But the sphere did not open. It remained exactly as it was, a gleaming, polished, perfect shape.

What was the purpose of the thing? He wished he understood its purpose.

He thought of Dr. Stein again. What was Stein's favorite line? "Understanding is a delaying tactic." Stein used to get angry about that. When the graduate students would intellectualize, going on and on about patients and their problems, he would interrupt in annoyance, "Who cares? Who cares whether we understand the psychodynamics in this case? Do you want to understand how to swim, or do you want to jump in and start swimming? Only people who are afraid of the water want to understand it. Other people jump in and get wet."

Okay, Norman thought. Let's get wet.

He turned to face the sphere, and thought, *Open up.*

The sphere did not open.

"Open up," he said aloud.

The sphere did not open.

Of course he knew that wouldn't work, because Ted had tried it for hours. When Harry and Beth went in, they hadn't said anything. They just did something in their minds.

He closed his eyes, focused his attention, and thought, Open up.

He opened his eyes and looked at the sphere. It was still closed.

I am ready for you to open up, he thought. I am ready now.

Nothing happened. The sphere did not open.

NORMAN HADN'T CONSIDERED the possibility that he would be unable to open the sphere. After all, two others had already done it. How had they managed it?

Harry, with his logical brain, had been the first to figure it out. But Harry had only figured it out *after* he had seen Beth's tape. So Harry had discovered a clue in the tape, an important clue.

Beth had also reviewed the tape, watching it again and again, until she finally figured it out, too. Something in the tape . . .

Too bad he didn't have the tape here, Norman thought. But he had seen it often, he could probably reconstruct it, play it back in his mind. How did it go? In his mind he saw the images: Beth and Tina talking. Beth eating cake. Then Tina had said something about the tapes being stored in the submarine. And Beth said something back. Then Tina had moved away, out of the picture, but she had said, "Do you think they'll ever get the sphere open?"

And Beth said, "Maybe. I don't know." And the sphere had opened at that moment.

Why?

"Do you think they'll ever get the sphere open?" Tina had asked. And in response to such a question, Beth must have imagined the sphere open, must have seen an image of the open sphere in her mind—

There was a deep, low rumble, a vibration that filled the room.

The sphere was open, the door gaping wide and black.

THAT'S IT, HE thought. Visualize it happening and it happens. Which meant that if he also visualized the sphere door closed—

With another deep rumble, the sphere closed.

—or open—

The sphere opened again.

"I'd better not press my luck," he said aloud. The door was still open. He peered in the doorway but saw only deep, undifferentiated blackness. It's now or never, he thought.

He stepped inside.

The sphere closed behind him.

THERE IS DARKNESS, and then, as his eyes adjust, something like fireflies. It is a dancing, luminous foam, millions of points of light, swirling around him.

What is this? he thinks. All he sees is the foam. There is no structure to it and apparently no limit. It is a surging ocean, a glistening, multifaceted foam. He feels great beauty and peace. It is restful to be here.

He moves his hands, scooping the foam, his movements making it swirl. But then he notices that his hands are becoming transparent, that he can see the sparkling foam through his own flesh. He looks down at his body. His legs, his torso, everything is becoming transparent to the foam. He is part of the foam. The sensation is very pleasant.

He grows lighter. Soon he is lifted, and floats in the limitless ocean foam. He puts his hands behind his neck and floats. He feels happy. He feels he could stay here forever.

He becomes aware of something else in this ocean, some other presence.

"Anybody here?" he says.

I am here.

He almost jumps, it is so loud. Or it seems loud. Then he wonders if he has heard anything at all.

"Did you speak?"

No.

How are we communicating? he wonders.

The way everything communicates with everything else.

Which way is that?

Why do you ask if you already know the answer?

But I don't know the answer.

The foam moves him gently, peacefully, but he receives no answer for a time. He wonders if he is alone again.

Are you there?

Yes.

I thought you had gone away.

There is nowhere to go.

Do you mean you are imprisoned inside this sphere?

No.

Will you answer a question? Who are you?

I am not a who.

Are you God?

God is a word.

I mean, are you a higher being, or a higher consciousness?

Higher than what?

Higher than me, I suppose.

How high are you?

Pretty low. At least, I imagine so.

Well, then, that's your trouble.

Riding in the foam, he is disturbed by the possibility that God is making fun of him. He thinks, Are you making a joke?

Why do you ask if you already know the answer?

Am I talking to God?

You are not talking at all.

You take what I say very literally. Is this because you are from another planet?

No.

Are you from another planet?

No.

Are you from another civilization?

No.

Where are you from?

Why do you ask if you already know the answer?

In another time, he thinks, he would be irritated by this repetitive answer, but now he feels no emotions. There are no judgments. He is simply receiving information, a response.

He thinks, But this sphere comes from another civilization.

Yes.

And maybe from another time.

Yes.

And aren't you a part of this sphere?

I am now.

So, where are you from?

Why do you ask if you already know the answer?

The foam gently shifts him, rocking him soothingly.

Are you still there?

Yes. There is nowhere to go.

I'm afraid I am not very knowledgeable about religion. I am a psychologist. I deal with how people think. In my training, I never learned much about religion.

Oh, I see.

Psychology doesn't have much to do with religion.

Of course.

So you agree?

I agree with you.

That's reassuring.

I don't see why.

Who is I?

Who indeed?

He rocks in the foam, feeling a deep peace despite the difficulties of this conversation.

I am troubled, he thinks.

Tell me.

I am troubled because you sound like Jerry.

That is to be expected.

But Jerry was really Harry.

Yes.

So are you Harry, too?

No. Of course not.

Who are you?

I am not a who.

Then why do you sound like Jerry or Harry?

Because we spring from the same source.

I don't understand.

When you look in the mirror, who do you see?

I see myself.

I see.

Isn't that right?

It's up to you.

I don't understand.

What you see is up to you.

I already know that. Everybody knows that. That is a psychological truism, a cliché.

I see.

Are you an alien intelligence?

Are you an alien intelligence?

I find you difficult to talk to. Will you give me the power?

What power?

The power you gave to Harry and Beth. The power to make things happen by imagination. Will you give it to me?

No.

Why not?

Because you already have it.

I don't feel as if I have it.

I know.

Then how is it that I have the power?

How did you get in here?

I imagined the door opening.

Yes.

Rocking in the foam, waiting for a further response, but there is no response, there is only gentle movement in the foam, a peaceful timelessness, and a drowsy sensation.

After a passage of time, he thinks, I am sorry, but I wish you would just explain and stop speaking in riddles.

On your planet you have an animal called a bear. It is a large animal, sometimes larger than you, and it is clever and has ingenuity, and it has a brain as large as yours. But the bear differs from you in one important way. It cannot perform the activity you call imagining. It cannot make mental images of how reality might be. It cannot envision what you call the past and what you call the future. This special ability of imagination is what has made your species as great as it is. Nothing else. It is not your ape-nature, not your tool-using nature, not language or your violence or your caring for young or your social groupings. It is none of these things, which are all found in other animals. Your greatness lies in imagination.

The ability to imagine is the largest part of what you call intelligence. You think the ability to imagine is merely a useful step on the way to solving a problem or making something happen. But imagining it is what makes it happen.

This is the gift of your species and this is the danger, because you do not choose to control your imaginings. You imagine wonderful things and you imagine terrible things, and you take no responsibility for the choice. You say you have inside you both the power of good and the power of evil, the angel and the devil, but in truth you have just one thing inside you—the ability to imagine.

I hope you enjoyed this speech, which I plan to give at the next meeting of the American Association of Psychologists and Social Workers, which is meeting in Houston in March. I feel it will be quite well received.

What? he thinks, startled.

Who did you think you were talking to? God?

Who is this? he thinks.

You, of course.

But you are somebody different from me, separate. You are not me, he thinks.

Yes I am. You imagined me.

Tell me more.

There is no more.

● ● ●

HIS CHEEK RESTED on cold metal. He rolled onto his back and looked at the polished surface of the sphere, curving above him. The convolutions of the door had changed again.

Norman got to his feet. He felt relaxed and at peace, as if he had been sleeping a long time. He felt as if he had had a wonderful dream. He remembered everything quite clearly.

He moved through the ship, back to the flight deck, and then down the hallway with the ultraviolet lights to the room with all the tubes on the wall.

The tubes were filled. There was a crewman in each one.

Just as he thought: Beth had manifested a single crewman—a solitary woman—as a way of warning them. Now Norman was in charge, and he found the room full.

Not bad, he thought.

He looked at the room and thought: Gone, one at a time.

One by one, the crew members in the tubes vanished before his eyes, until they were all gone.

Back, one at a time.

The crew members popped back in the tubes, materializing on demand.

All men.

The women were changed into men.

All women.

They all became women.

He had the power.

0200 Hours

Norman."

Beth's voice over the loudspeakers, hissing through the empty spacecraft.

"Where are you, Norman? I know you're there somewhere. I can *feel* you, Norman."

Norman was moving through the kitchen, past the empty cans of Coke on the counter, then through the heavy door and into the flight deck. He saw Beth's face on all the console screens, Beth seeming to see him, the image repeated a dozen times.

"Norman. I know where you've been. You've been inside the sphere, haven't you, Norman?"

He pressed the consoles with the flat of his hand, trying to turn off the screens. He couldn't do it; the images remained.

"Norman. Answer me, Norman."

He moved past the flight deck, going toward the airlock.

"It won't do you any good, Norman. I'm in charge now. Do you hear me, Norman?"

In the airlock, he heard a click as his helmet ring locked; the air from the tanks was cool and dry. He listened to the even sound of his own breathing.

"Norman." Beth, on the intercom in his helmet. "Why don't you speak to me, Norman? Are you afraid, Norman?"

The repetition of his name irritated him. He pressed the buttons to open the airlock. Water began to flood in from the floor, rising swiftly.

"Oh, *there you are*, Norman. I see you now." And she began to laugh, a high, cackling laugh.

Norman turned around, saw the video camera mounted on the robot, still inside the airlock. He shoved the camera, spinning it away.

"That won't do any good, Norman."

He was back outside the spacecraft, standing by the airlock. The Tevac explosives, rows of glowing red dots, extended away in erratic lines, like an airplane runway laid out by some demented engineer.

"Norman? Why don't you answer me, Norman?"

Beth was unstable, erratic. He could hear it in her voice. He had to deprive her of her weapons, to turn off the explosives, if he could.

Off, he thought. Let's have the explosives off and disarmed.

All the red lights immediately went off.

Not bad, he thought, with a burst of pleasure.

A moment later, the red lights blinked back on.

"You can't do it, Norman," Beth said, laughing. "Not to me. I can fight you."

He knew she was right. They were having an argument, a test of wills, turning the explosives on and off. And the argument couldn't ever be resolved. Not that way. He would have to do something more direct.

He moved toward the nearest of the Tevac explosives. Up close, the cone was larger than he had thought, four feet high, with a red light at the top.

"I can see you, Norman. *I see what you're doing.*"

There was writing on the cone, yellow letters stenciled on the gray surface. Norman bent to read it. His faceplate was slightly fogged, but he could still make out the words.

DANGER-TEVAC EXPLOSIVES

U.S.N. CONSTRUCTION/DEMOLITION USE ONLY
DEFAULT DETONATE SEQUENCE 20:00
CONSULT MANUAL USN/VV/512-A
AUTHORIZED PERSONNEL ONLY

DANGER-TEVAC EXPLOSIVES

There was still more writing beneath that, but it was smaller, and he couldn't make it out.

"Norman! What're you doing with my explosives, Norman?"

Norman didn't answer her. He looked at the wiring. One thin cable ran into the base of the cone, and a second cable ran out. The second cable went along the muddy bottom to the next cone, where there were again just two cables—one in, and one out.

"Get away from there, Norman. You're making me nervous."

One cable in, and one cable out.

Beth had wired the cones together *in series*, like Christmas-tree bulbs! By pulling out a single cable, Norman would disconnect the entire line of explosives. He reached forward and gripped the cable in his gloved hand.

"Norman! Don't touch that wire, Norman!"

"Take it easy, Beth."

His fingers closed around the cable. He felt the soft plastic coating, gripped it tightly.

"Norman, if you pull that cable you'll set off the explosives. I swear to you—it'll blow you and me and Harry and everything to hell, Norman."

He didn't think it was true. Beth was lying. Beth was out of control and she was dangerous and she was lying to him again.

He drew his hand back. He felt the tension in the cable.

"Don't do it, Norman. . . ."

The cable was now taut in his hand. "I'm going to shut you down, Beth."

"For God's sake, Norman. Believe me, will you? You'll kill us all!"

Still he hesitated. Could she be telling the truth? Did she know about wiring explosives? He looked at the big gray cone at his feet, reaching up to his waist. What would it feel like if it exploded? Would he feel anything at all?

"The hell with it," he said aloud.

He pulled the cable out of the cone.

THE SHRIEK OF the alarm, ringing inside his helmet, made him jump. There was a small liquid-crystal display at the top of his faceplate blinking rapidly: "EMERGENCY" . . . "EMER-GENCY" . . .

"Oh, Norman. God damn it. Now you've done it."

He barely heard her voice over the alarm. The red cone lights were blinking, all down the length of the spacecraft. He braced himself for the explosion.

But then the alarm was interrupted by a deep, resonant male voice that said, "Your attention, please. Your attention, please. All construction personnel clear the blast area immediately. Tevac explosives are now activated. The countdown will begin . . . now. Mark twenty, and counting."

On the cone, a red display flashed 20:00. Then it began counting backward: 19:59 . . . 19:58 . . .

The same display was repeated on the crystal display at the top of his helmet.

It took him a moment to put it together, to understand. Staring at the cone, he read the yellow lettering once again: U.S.N. CONSTRUCTION/DEMOLITION USE ONLY.

Of course! Tevac explosives weren't weapons, they were made for construction and demolition. They had built-in safety timers—a programmed twenty-minute delay before they went off, to allow workers to get away.

Twenty minutes to get away, he thought. That would give him plenty of time.

Norman turned, and began striding quickly toward DH-7 and the submarine.

0140 Hours

He walked evenly, steadily. He felt no strain. His breath came easily. He was comfortable in his suit. All systems working smoothly.

He was leaving.

"Norman, please . . ."

Now Beth was pleading with him, another erratic shift of mood. Norman ignored her. He continued on toward the submarine. The deep recorded voice said, "Your attention, please. All Navy personnel clear the blast area. Nineteen minutes and counting."

Norman felt an enormous sense of purposefulness, of power. He had no illusions any more. He had no questions. He knew what he had to do.

He had to save himself.

"I don't believe you're doing this, Norman. I don't believe you're abandoning us."

Believe it, he thought. After all, what choice did he have?

Beth was out of control and dangerous. It was too late to save her now—in fact, it was crazy to go anywhere near her. Beth was homicidal. She'd already tried to kill him once, and had nearly succeeded.

And Harry had been drugged for thirteen hours; by now he was probably clinically dead, brain-dead. There was no reason for Norman to stay. There was nothing for him to do.

The sub was close now. He could see the fittings on the yellow exterior.

"Norman, please . . . I need you."

Sorry, he thought. I'm getting out of here.

He moved around beneath the twin propellor screws, the name painted on the curved hull, *Deepstar III.* He climbed the footholds, moving up into the dome.

"Norman—"

Now he was out of contact with the intercom. He was on his own. He opened the hatch, climbed inside the submarine. He unlocked his helmet, pulled it off.

"Your attention, please. Eighteen minutes and counting."

Norman sat in the pilot's padded seat, faced the controls. The instruments blinked on, and the screen directly before him glowed.

DEEPSTAR III - COMMAND MODULE

Do you require help?
Yes   No   Cancel

He pressed "YES." He waited for the next screen to flash up.

It was too bad about Harry and Beth; he was sorry to leave

them behind. But they had both, in their own ways, failed to explore their inner selves, thus making them vulnerable to the sphere and its power. It was a classic scientific error, this so-called triumph of rational thought over irrational thought. Scientists refused to acknowledge their irrational side, refused to see it as important. They dealt only with the rational. Everything made sense to a scientist, and if it didn't make sense, it was dismissed as what Einstein called the "merely personal."

The merely personal, he thought, in a burst of contempt. People killed each other for reasons that were "merely personal."

DEEPSTAR III - CHECKLIST OPTIONS

Descend	Ascend
Secure	Shutdown
Monitor	Cancel

Norman pressed "ASCEND." The screen changed to the drawing of the instrument panel, with the flashing point. He waited for the next instruction.

Yes, he thought, it was true: scientists refused to deal with the irrational. But the irrational side didn't go away if you refused to deal with it. Irrationality didn't atrophy with disuse. On the contrary, left unattended, the irrational side of man had grown in power and scope.

And complaining about it didn't help, either. All those scientists whining in the Sunday supplements about man's inherent destructiveness and his propensity for violence, throwing up their hands. That wasn't dealing with the irrational side. That was just a formal admission that they were giving up on it.

The screen changed again:

DEEPSTAR III - ASCEND CHECKLIST

1. Set Ballast Blowers To: On
Proceed To Next   Cancel

Norman pushed buttons on the panel, setting the ballast blowers, and waited for the next screen.

After all, how did scientists approach their own research? The scientists all agreed: scientific research can't be stopped. If we don't build the bomb, someone else will. But then pretty soon the bomb was in the hands of new people, who said, If we don't *use* the bomb, someone else will.

At which point, the scientists said, those other people are terrible people, they're irrational and irresponsible. We scientists are okay. But those other people are a real problem.

Yet the truth was that responsibility began with each individual person, and the choices he made. Each person had a choice.

Well, Norman thought, there was nothing he could do for Harry or Beth any longer. He had to save himself.

He heard a deep hum as the generators turned on, and the throb of the propellors. The screen flashed:

DEEPSTAR III - PILOT INSTRUMENTS ACTIVATED

Here we go, he thought, resting his hands confidently on the controls. He felt the submarine respond beneath him.

"Your attention, please. Seventeen minutes and counting."

Muddy sediment churned up around the canopy as the

screws engaged, and then the little submarine slipped out from beneath the dome. It was just like driving a car, he thought. There was nothing to it.

He turned in a slow arc, away from DH-7, toward DH-8. He was twenty feet above the bottom, high enough for the screws to clear the mud.

There were seventeen minutes left. At a maximum ascent rate of 6.6 feet per second—he did the mental calculation quickly, effortlessly—he would reach the surface in two and a half minutes.

There was plenty of time.

He moved the submarine close to DH-8. The exterior habitat floodlights were yellow and pale. Power must be dropping. He could see the damage to the cylinders—streams of bubbles rising from the weakened A and B Cylinders; the dents in the D; and the gaping hole in E Cyl, which was flooded. The habitat was battered, and dying.

Why had he come so close? He squinted at the portholes, then realized he was hoping to catch sight of Harry and Beth, one last time. He wanted to see Harry, unconscious and unresponsive. He wanted to see Beth standing at the window, shaking her fist at him in maniacal rage. He wanted confirmation that he was right to leave them.

But he saw only the fading yellow light inside the habitat. He was disappointed.

"Norman."

"Yes, Beth." He felt comfortable answering her now. He had his hands on the controls of the submarine, ready to make his ascent. There was nothing she could do to him now.

"Norman, you really are a son of a bitch."

"You tried to kill me, Beth."

"I didn't *want* to kill you. I had no choice, Norman."

"Yeah, well. Me, too. I have no choice." As he spoke, he knew he was right. Better for one person to survive. Better than nothing.

"You're just going to leave us?"

"That's right, Beth."

His hand moved to the ascent-rate dial. He set it to 6.6 feet. Ready to ascend.

"You're just going to run away?" He heard the contempt in her voice.

"That's right, Beth."

"You, the one who kept talking about how we had to stay together down here?"

"Sorry, Beth."

"You must be very afraid, Norman."

"I'm not afraid at all." And indeed he felt strong and confident, setting the controls, preparing for his ascent. He felt better than he had felt for days.

"Norman," she said. "Please help us. *Please.*"

Her words struck him at some deep level, arousing feelings of caring, of professional competence, of simple human kindness. For a moment he felt confusion, his strength and conviction weakened. But then he got a grip on himself, and shook his head. The strength flew back into his body.

"Sorry, Beth. It's too late for that."

And he pressed the "ASCEND" button, heard the roar as the ballast tanks blew, and *Deepstar III* swayed. The habitat slipped away below him, and he started toward the surface, a thousand feet above.

BLACK WATER, NO sense of movement except for the readings on the glowing green instrument panel. He began to review the events in his mind, as if he were already facing a Navy inquiry. Had he done the right thing, leaving the others behind?

Unquestionably, he had. The sphere was an alien object which gave a person the power to manifest his thoughts. Well and good, except that human beings had a split in their brains, a split in their mental processes. It was almost as if men had two brains. The conscious brain could be consciously controlled, and presented no problem. But the unconscious brain, wild and abandoned, was dangerous and destructive when its impulses were manifested.

The trouble with people like Harry and Beth was that they were literally unbalanced. Their conscious brains were overdeveloped, but they had never bothered to explore their unconscious. That was the difference between Norman and them. As a psychologist, Norman had some acquaintance with his unconscious. It held no surprises for him.

That was why Harry and Beth had manifested monsters, but Norman had not. Norman knew his unconscious. No monsters awaited him.

No. Wrong.

He was startled by the suddenness of the thought, the abruptness of it. Was he really wrong? He considered carefully, and decided once again that he was correct after all. Beth and Harry were at risk from the products of their unconscious, but Norman was not. Norman knew himself; the others did not.

"The fears unleashed by contact with a new life form are not understood. The most likely consequence of contact is absolute terror."

The statements from his own report popped into his head. Why should he think of them now? It had been years since he had written his report.

"Under circumstances of extreme terror, people make decisions poorly."

Yet Norman wasn't afraid. Far from it. He was confident and strong. He had a plan, he was carrying it out. Why should he even think of that report? At the time, he'd agonized over it, thinking of each sentence. . . . Why was it coming to mind now? It troubled him.

"Your attention, please. Sixteen minutes and counting."

Norman scanned the gauges before him. He was at nine hundred feet, rising swiftly. There was no turning back now.

Why should he even think of turning back?

Why should it enter his mind?

As he rose silently through black water, he increasingly felt a kind of split inside himself, an almost schizophrenic internal division. Something *was* wrong, he sensed. There was something he hadn't considered yet.

But what could he have overlooked? Nothing, he decided, because, unlike Beth and Harry, I am fully conscious; I am aware of everything that is happening inside me.

Except Norman didn't really believe that. Complete awareness might be a philosophical goal, but it was not really attainable. Consciousness was like a pebble that rippled the surface of the unconscious. As consciousness widened, there was still more unconsciousness beyond. There was always more, just beyond reach. Even for a humanistic psychologist.

Stein, his old professor: "You always have your shadow."

What was Norman's shadow side doing now? What was happening in the unconscious, denied parts of his own brain?

Nothing. Keep going up.

He shifted uneasily in the pilot's chair. He wanted to go to the surface so badly, he felt such conviction. . . .

I hate Beth. I hate Harry. I hate worrying about these people, caring for them. I don't want to care any more. It's not my responsibility. I want to save myself. I hate them. I hate them.

He was shocked. Shocked by his own thoughts, the vehemence of them.

I must go back, he thought.

If I go back I will die.

But some other part of himself was growing stronger with each moment. What Beth had said was true: Norman had been the one who kept saying that they had to stay together, to work together. How could he abandon them now? He couldn't. It was against everything he believed in, everything that was important and human.

He had to go back.

I am afraid to go back.

At last, he thought. There it is. Fear so strong he had denied its existence, fear that had caused him to rationalize abandoning the others.

He pressed the controls, halting his ascent. As he started back down, he saw that his hands were shaking.

0130 Hours

The sub came to rest gently on the bottom beside the habitat. Norman stepped into the submarine airlock, flooded the chamber. Moments later, he climbed down the side and walked toward the habitat. The Tevac explosives' cones with their blinking red lights looked oddly festive.

"Your attention, please. Fourteen minutes and counting."

He estimated the time he would need. One minute to get inside. Five, maybe six minutes to dress Beth and Harry in the suits. Another four minutes to reach the sub and get them aboard. Two or three minutes to make the ascent.

It was going to be close.

He moved beneath the big support pylons, under the habitat.

"So you came back, Norman," Beth said, over the intercom.

"Yes, Beth."

"Thank God," she said. She started to cry. He was beneath

A Cyl, hearing her sobs over the intercom. He found the hatch cover, spun the wheel to open it. It was locked shut.

"Beth, open the hatch."

She was crying over the intercom. She didn't answer him.

"Beth, can you hear me? Open the hatch."

Crying like a child, sobbing hysterically. "Norman," she said. "Please help me. *Please.*"

"I'm trying to help you, Beth. Open the hatch."

"I can't."

"What do you mean, you can't?"

"It won't do any good."

"Beth," he said. "Come on, now. . . ."

"I can't do it, Norman."

"Of course you can. Open the hatch, Beth."

"You shouldn't have come back, Norman."

There was no time for this now. "Beth, pull yourself together. Open the hatch."

"No, Norman, I can't."

And she began crying again.

HE TRIED ALL the hatches, one after another. B Cyl, locked. C Cyl, locked. D Cyl, locked.

"Your attention, please. Thirteen minutes and counting."

He was standing by E Cyl, which had been flooded in an earlier attack. He saw the gaping, jagged tear in the outer cylinder surface. The hole was large enough for him to climb through, but the edges were sharp, and if he tore his suit . . .

No, he decided. It was too risky. He moved beneath E Cyl. Was there a hatch?

He found a hatch, spun the wheel. It opened easily. He pushed the circular lid upward, heard it clang against the inner wall.

"Norman? Is that you?"

He hauled himself up, into E Cyl. He was panting from the exertion, on his hands and knees on the deck of E Cyl. He shut the hatch and locked it again, then took a moment to get his breath.

"Your attention, please. Twelve minutes and counting."

Jesus, he thought. Already?

Something white drifted past his faceplate, startling him. He pulled back, realized it was a box of corn flakes. When he touched it, the cardboard disintegrated in his hands, the flakes like yellow snow.

He was in the kitchen. Beyond the stove he saw another hatch, leading to D Cyl. D Cyl was not flooded, which meant that he must somehow pressurize E Cyl.

He looked up, saw an overhead bulkhead hatch, leading to the living room with the gaping tear. He climbed up quickly. He needed to find gas, some kind of tanks. The living room was dark, except for the reflected light from the floodlights, which filtered in through the tear. Cushions and padding floated in the water. Something touched him and he spun and saw dark hair streaming around a face, and as the hair moved he saw part of the face was missing, torn away grotesquely.

Tina.

Norman shuddered, pushed her body away. It drifted off, moving upward.

"Your attention, please. Eleven minutes and counting."

It was all happening too fast, he thought. There was hardly

enough time left. He needed to be inside the habitat now.

No tanks in the living room. He climbed back down to the kitchen, shutting the hatch above. He looked at the stove, the ovens. He opened the oven door, and a burst of gas bubbled out. Air trapped in the oven.

But that couldn't be right, he thought, because gas was still coming out. A trickle of bubbles continued to come from the open oven.

A steady trickle.

What had Barnes said about cooking under pressure? There was something unusual about it, he couldn't remember exactly. Did they use gas? Yes, but they also needed more oxygen. That meant—

He pulled the stove away from the wall, grunting with exertion, and then he found it. A squat bottle of propane, and two large blue tanks.

Oxygen tanks.

He twisted the Y-valves, his gloved fingers clumsy. Gas began to roar out. The bubbles rushed up to the ceiling, where the gas was trapped, the big air bubble that was forming.

He opened the second oxygen tank. The water level fell rapidly, to his waist, then his knees. Then it stopped. The tanks must be empty. No matter, the level was low enough.

"Your attention, please. Ten minutes and counting."

Norman opened the bulkhead door to D Cyl, and stepped through, into the habitat.

THE LIGHT WAS dim. A strange green, slimy mold covered the walls.

On the couch, Harry lay unconscious, the intravenous

line still in his arm. Norman pulled the needle out with a spurt of blood. He shook Harry, trying to rouse him.

Harry's eyelids fluttered, but he was otherwise unresponsive. Norman lifted him, put him over his shoulder, carried him through the habitat.

On the intercom, Beth was still crying. "Norman, you shouldn't have come."

"Where are you, Beth?"

On the monitors, he read:

DETONATION SEQUENCE 09:32.

Counting backward. The numbers seemed to move too fast.

"Take Harry and go, Norman. Both of you go. Leave me behind."

"Tell me where you are, Beth."

He was moving through the habitat, from D to C Cyl. He didn't see her anywhere. Harry was a dead weight on his shoulder, making it difficult to get through the bulkhead doors.

"It won't do any good, Norman."

"Come on, Beth. . . ."

"I know I'm bad, Norman. I know I can't be helped."

"Beth . . ." He was hearing her through the helmet radio, so he could not locate her by the sound. But he could not risk removing his helmet. Not now.

"I deserve to die, Norman."

"Cut it out, Beth."

"Attention, please. Nine minutes and counting."

A new alarm sounded, an intermittent beeping that became louder and more intense as the seconds ticked by.

He was in B Cyl, a maze of pipes and equipment. Once clean and multicolored, now the slimy mold coated every surface. In some places fibrous mossy strands hung down. B Cyl looked like a jungle swamp.

"Beth . . ."

She was silent now. She must be in this room, he thought. B Cyl had always been Beth's favorite place, the place where the habitat was controlled. He put Harry on the deck, propped him against a wall. But the wall was slippery and Harry slid down, banged his head. He coughed, opened his eyes.

"Jesus. Norman?"

Norman held his hand up, signaling Harry to be quiet.

"Beth?" Norman said.

No answer. Norman moved among the slimy pipes.

"Beth?"

"Leave me, Norman."

"I can't do that, Beth. I'm taking you, too."

"No. I'm staying, Norman."

"Beth," he said, "there's no time for this."

"I'm staying, Norman. I deserve to stay."

He saw her.

Beth was huddled in the back, wedged among pipes, crying like a child. She held one of the explosive-tipped spearguns in her hand. She looked at him tearfully.

"Oh, Norman," she said. "You were going to *leave* us. . . ."

"I'm sorry. I was wrong."

He started toward her, holding out his hands to her. She swung the speargun around. "No, you were right. You were right. I want you to leave now."

Above her head he saw a glowing monitor, the numbers clicking inexorably backward: 08:27 . . . 08:26 . . .

He thought, I can change this. *I want the numbers to stop counting.*

The numbers did not stop.

"You can't fight me, Norman," she said, huddled in the corner. Her eyes blazed with furious energy.

"I can see that."

"There isn't much time, Norman. I want you to leave."

She held the gun, pointed firmly toward him. He had a sudden sense of the absurdity of it all, that he had come back to rescue someone who didn't want to be rescued. What could he do now? Beth was wedged back in there, beyond his reach, beyond his help. There was barely enough time for him to get away, let alone to take Harry. . . .

Harry, he thought suddenly. Where was Harry now?

I want Harry to help me.

But he wondered if there was time; the numbers were clicking backward, there was hardly more than eight minutes, now. . . .

"I came back for you, Beth."

"Go," she said. "Go now, Norman."

"But, Beth—"

"—No, Norman! I mean it! Go! Why don't you go?" And then she began to get suspicious; she started to look around; and at that moment Harry stood up behind her, and swung the big wrench down on her head, and there was a sickening thud, and she fell.

"Did I kill her?" Harry said.

And the deep male voice said, "Attention, please. Eight minutes and counting."

NORMAN CONCENTRATED ON the clock as it ticked backwards. Stop. Stop the countdown.

But when he looked again, the clock was still ticking backwards. And the alarm: Was the alarm interfering with his concentration? He tried again.

Stop now. The countdown will stop now. The countdown has stopped.

"Forget it," Harry said. "It won't work."

"But it *should* work," Norman said.

"No," Harry said. "Because she's not completely unconscious."

On the floor at their feet, Beth groaned. Her leg moved.

"She's still able to control it, somehow," Norman said. "She's very strong."

"Can we inject her?"

Norman shook his head. There was no time to go back for the syringe. Anyway, if they injected her and it didn't work, it would be time wasted—

"Hit her again?" Harry said. "Harder? Kill her?"

"No," Norman said.

"Killing her is the only way—"

"—No," Norman said, thinking, We didn't kill you, Harry, when we had the chance.

"If you won't kill her, then you can't do anything about that timer," Harry said. "So we better get the hell out."

They ran for the airlock.

• • •

"HOW MUCH TIME is left?" Harry said. They were in the A Cyl airlock, trying to put the suit on Beth. She was groaning; blood was matted on the back of her head. Beth struggled a little, making it more difficult.

"Jesus, Beth—how much time, Norman?"

"Seven and a half minutes, maybe less."

Her legs were in; they quickly pushed her arms in, zipped up the chest. They turned on her air. Norman helped Harry with his suit.

"Attention, please. Seven minutes and counting."

Harry said, "How much time you figure to get to the surface?"

"Two and a half minutes, after we get inside the sub," Norman said.

"Great," Harry said.

Norman snapped Harry's helmet locked. "Let's go."

Harry descended into the water, and Norman lowered Beth's unconscious body. She was heavy with the tank and weights.

"Come on, Norman!"

Norman plunged into the water.

AT THE SUBMARINE, Norman climbed up to the hatch entrance, but the untethered sub rolled unpredictably with his weight. Harry, standing on the bottom, tried to push Beth up toward Norman, but Beth kept bending over at the waist. Norman, grabbing for her, fell off the sub and slid to the bottom.

"Attention, please. Six minutes and counting."

"Hurry, Norman! Six minutes!"

"I heard, damn it."

Norman got to his feet, climbed back on the sub, but now his suit was muddy, his gloves slippery. Harry was counting: "Five twenty-nine ... five twenty-eight ... five twenty-seven ..." Norman caught Beth's arm, but she slipped away again.

"Damn it, Norman! Hold on to her!"

"I'm trying!"

"Here. Here she is again."

"Attention, please. Five minutes and counting."

The alarm was now high-pitched, beeping insistently. They had to shout over it to be heard.

"Harry, give her to me—"

"Well, here, take her—"

"Missed—"

"Here—"

Norman finally caught Beth's air hose in his hand, just behind the helmet. He wondered if it would pull out, but he had to risk it. Gripping the hose, he hauled Beth up, until she lay on her back on the top of the sub. Then he eased her down into the hatch.

"Four twenty-nine ... four twenty-eight ..."

Norman had trouble keeping his balance. He got one of Beth's legs into the hatch, but the other knee was bent, jammed against the lip of the hatch. He couldn't get her down. Every time he leaned forward to unbend her leg, the whole submarine tipped, and he would start to lose his balance again.

"Four sixteen ... four fifteen ..."

"Would you stop counting and *do something!*"

Harry pressed his body against the side of the submarine, countering the rolling with his weight. Norman leaned forward and pressed Beth's knee straight; she slid easily into the open hatch. Norman climbed in after her. It was a one-man airlock, but Beth was unconscious, and could not work the controls.

He would have to do it for her.

"Attention, please. Four minutes and counting."

He was cramped in the airlock, his body pressed up against Beth, chest to chest, her helmet banging against his. With difficulty he pulled the hatch closed over his head. He blew out the water in a furious rush of compressed air; unsupported by the water, Beth's body now sagged heavily against him.

He reached around her for the handle to the inner hatch. Beth's body blocked his way. He tried to twist her around sideways. In the confined space, he couldn't get any leverage on the body. Beth was like a dead weight; he tried to shift her body around, to get to the hatch.

The whole submarine began to sway: Harry was climbing up the side.

"What the hell's going on in there?"

"Harry, *will you shut up!*"

"Well, what's the delay?"

Norman's hand closed on the inner latch handle. He shoved it down, but the door didn't move: the door was hinged to swing *inward*. He couldn't open it with Beth in the hatch with him. It was too crowded; her body blocked the movement of the door.

"Harry, we've got a problem."

"Jesus Christ . . . Three minutes thirty."

Norman began to sweat. They were really in trouble now.

"Harry, I've got to pass her out to you, and go in alone."

"Jesus, Norman . . ."

Norman flooded the airlock, opened the upper hatch once again. Harry's balance atop the submarine was precarious. He grabbed Beth by the air hose, dragged her up.

Norman reached up to close the hatch.

"Harry, can you get her feet out of the way?"

"I'm trying to keep my balance here."

"Can't you see her feet are blocking—" Irritably, Norman pushed Beth's feet aside. The hatch clanged down. The air blasted past him. The hatch pressurized.

"Attention, please. Two minutes and counting."

He was inside the submarine. The instruments glowed green.

He opened the inner hatch.

"Norman?"

"Try and get her down," Norman said. "Do it as fast as you can."

But he was thinking they were in terrible trouble: at least thirty seconds to get Beth into the hatch, and thirty seconds more for Harry to come down. A minute all together—

"She's in. Vent it."

Norman jumped for the air vent, blew out the water.

"How'd you get her in so fast, Harry?"

"Nature's way," Harry said, "to get people through tight spaces." And before Norman could ask what that meant, he had opened the hatch and saw that Harry had pushed Beth into the airlock head first. He grabbed her shoulders and eased her onto the floor of the submarine, then slammed the hatch shut. Moments later, he heard the blast of air as Harry, too, vented the airlock.

THE SUBMARINE HATCH clanged. Harry came forward.

"Christ, one minute forty," Harry said. "Do you know how to work this thing?"

"Yes."

Norman sat in the seat, placed his hands on the controls.

They heard the whine of the props, felt the rumble. The sub lurched, moved off the bottom.

"One minute thirty seconds. How long did you say to the surface?"

"Two thirty," Norman said, cranking up the ascent rate. He pushed it past 6.6, to the far end of the dial.

They heard a high-pitched shriek of air as the ballast tanks blew. The sub nosed up sharply, began to rise swiftly.

"Is this as fast as it goes?"

"Yes."

"Jesus."

"Take it easy, Harry."

Looking back down, they could see the habitat with its lights. And then the long lines of explosives set over the spaceship itself. They rose past the high fin of the spacecraft, leaving it behind, seeing only black water now.

"One minute twenty."

"Nine hundred feet," Norman said. There was very little

sensation of movement, only the changing dials on the instrument panel to tell them they were moving.

"It's not fast enough," Harry said. "That's a hell of a lot of explosive down there."

It is fast enough, Norman thought, correcting him.

"The shock wave will crush us like a can of sardines," Harry said, shaking his head.

The shock wave will not harm us.

Eight hundred feet.

"Forty seconds," Harry said. "We'll never make it."

"We'll make it."

They were at seven hundred feet, rising fast. The water now had a faint blue color: sunlight filtering down.

"Thirty seconds," Harry said. "Where are we? Twenty-nine . . . eight . . ."

"Six hundred twenty feet," Norman said. "Six ten."

They looked back down the side of the sub. They could barely discern the habitat, faint pinpricks of light far beneath them.

Beth coughed. "It's too late now," Harry said. "I knew from the beginning we'd never make it."

"Yes we will," Norman said.

"Ten seconds," Harry said. "Nine . . . eight . . . Brace yourself!"

Norman pulled Beth to his chest as the explosion rocked the submarine, spinning it like a toy, upending it, then righting it again, and lifting it in a giant upward surge.

"Mama!" Harry shouted, but they were still rising, they were okay. "We did it!"

"Two hundred feet," Norman said. The water outside was now light blue. He pushed buttons, slowing the ascent. They were going up very fast.

Harry was screaming, pounding Norman on the back. "We did it! God damn it, you son of a bitch, we did it! We survived! I never thought we would! We survived!"

Norman was having trouble seeing the instruments for tears in his eyes.

And then he had to squint as bright sunlight streamed into the bubble canopy as they surfaced, and they saw calm seas, sky, and fluffy clouds.

"Do you see that?" Harry cried. He was screaming in Norman's ear. "Do you see that? *It is a perfect goddamned day!*"

0000 Hours

Norman awoke to see a brilliant shaft of light, streaming through the single porthole, shining down on the chemical toilet in the corner of the decompression chamber. He lay on his bunk and looked around the chamber, a horizontal cylinder fifty feet long: bunks, a metal table and chairs in the center of the cylinder, toilet behind a small partition. Harry snored in the bunk above him. Across the chamber, Beth slept, one arm flung over her face. Faintly, from a distance, he heard men shouting.

Norman yawned, and swung off the bunk. His body was sore but he was otherwise all right. He walked to the shining porthole and looked out, squinting in the bright Pacific sun.

He saw the rear deck of the research ship *John Hawes*: the white helicopter pad, heavy coiled cables, the tubular metal frame of an underwater robot. A Navy crew was lowering a second robot over the side, with a lot of shouting and swearing and waving of hands; Norman had heard their voices faintly through the thick steel walls of the chamber.

Near the chamber itself, a muscular seaman rolled a large green tank marked "Oxygen" alongside a dozen other tanks on the deck. The three-man medical crew which supervised the decompression chamber played cards.

Looking through the inch-thick glass of the porthole, Norman felt as if he were peering into a miniature world to which he had little connection, a kind of terrarium populated by interesting and exotic specimens. This new world was as alien to him as the dark ocean world had once seemed from inside the habitat.

He watched the crew slap down their cards on a wooden packing crate, watched them laugh and gesture as the game proceeded. They never glanced in his direction, never looked at the decompression chamber. Norman didn't understand these young men. Were they supposed to be paying attention to the decompression? They looked young and inexperienced to Norman. Focused on their card game, they seemed indifferent to the huge metal chamber nearby, indifferent to the three survivors inside the chamber—and indifferent to the larger meaning of the mission, to the news the survivors had brought back to the surface. These cheerful Navy card-players didn't seem to give a damn about Norman's mission. But perhaps they didn't know.

He turned back to the chamber, sat down at the table. His knee throbbed, and the skin was swollen around the white bandage. He had been treated by a Navy physician during their transfer from the submarine to the decompression chamber. They had been taken off the minisub *Deepstar III* in a pressurized diving bell, and from there had been transferred to the large chamber on the deck of the ship—the SDC, the Navy called it, the surface decompression chamber. They were going to spend four days here. Norman wasn't sure how long he had been here so far. They had all immediately gone to sleep, and there was no clock in the chamber. The face of his own wristwatch was smashed, although he didn't remember it happening.

On the table in front of him, someone had scratched "U.S.N. SUCKS" into the surface. Norman ran his fingers over the grooves, and remembered the grooves in the silver sphere. But he and Harry and Beth were in the hands of the Navy now.

And he thought: What are we going to tell them?

"WHAT ARE WE going to tell them?" Beth said.

It was several hours later; Beth and Harry had awakened, and now they were all sitting around the scarred metal table. None of them had made any attempt to talk to the crew outside. It was, Norman thought, as if they shared an unspoken agreement to remain in isolation a while longer.

"I think we'll have to tell them everything," Harry said.

"I don't think we should," Norman said. He was surprised by the strength of his conviction, the firmness of his own voice.

"I agree," Beth said. "I'm not sure the world is ready for that sphere. *I* certainly wasn't."

She gave Norman a sheepish look. He put his hand on her shoulder.

"That's fine," Harry said. "But look at it from the stand-point of the Navy. The Navy has mounted a large and expensive operation; six people have died, and two habitats have been destroyed. They're going to want answers—and they're going to keep asking until they get them."

"We can refuse to talk," Beth said.

"That won't make any difference," Harry said. "Remember, the Navy has all the tapes."

"That's right, the tapes," Norman said. He had forgotten about the videotapes they had brought up in the submarine. Dozens of tapes, documenting everything that had happened in the habitat during their time underwater. Documenting the squid, the deaths, the sphere. Documenting everything.

"We should have destroyed those tapes," Beth said.

"Perhaps we should have," Harry said. "But it's too late now. We can't prevent the Navy from getting the answers they want."

Norman sighed. Harry was right. At this point there was no way to conceal what had happened, or to prevent the Navy from finding out about the sphere, and the power it conveyed. That power would represent a kind of ultimate weapon: the ability to overcome your enemies simply by imagining it had happened. It was frightening in its implications, and there was nothing they could do about it. Unless—

"I think we *can* prevent them from knowing," Norman said.

"How?" Harry said.

"We still have the power, don't we?"

"I guess so."

"And that power," Norman said, "consists of the ability to make anything happen, simply by thinking it."

"Yes . . ."

"Then we can prevent the Navy from knowing. We can decide to forget the whole thing."

Harry frowned. "That's an interesting question: whether we have the power to forget the power."

"I think we should forget it," Beth said. "That sphere is too dangerous."

They fell silent, considering the implications of forgetting the sphere. Because forgetting would not merely prevent the Navy from knowing about the sphere—it would erase all knowledge of it, including their own. Make it vanish from human consciousness, as if it had never existed in the first place. Remove it from the awareness of the human species, forever.

"Big step," Harry said. "After all we've been through, just to forget about it . . ."

"It's because of all we've been through, Harry," Beth said. "Let's face it—we didn't handle ourselves very well." Norman noticed that she spoke without rancor now, her previous combative edge gone.

"I'm afraid that's true," Norman said. "The sphere was built to test whatever intelligent life might pick it up, and we simply failed that test."

"Is that what you think the sphere was made for?" Harry said. "I don't."

"Then what?" Norman said.

"Well," Harry said, "look at it this way: Suppose you were

an intelligent bacterium floating in space, and you came upon one of our communication satellites, in orbit around the Earth. You would think, What a strange, alien object this is, let's explore it. Suppose you opened it up and crawled inside. You would find it very interesting in there, with lots of huge things to puzzle over. But eventually you might climb into one of the fuel cells, and the hydrogen would kill you. And your last thought would be: This alien device was obviously made to test bacterial intelligence and to kill us if we make a false step.

"Now, that would be correct from the standpoint of the dying bacterium. But that wouldn't be correct at all from the standpoint of the beings who made the satellite. From our point of view, the communications satellite has nothing to do with intelligent bacteria. We don't even know that there are intelligent bacteria out there. We're just trying to communicate, and we've made what we consider a quite ordinary device to do it."

"You mean the sphere might not be a message or a trophy or a trap at all?"

"That's right," Harry said. "The sphere may have nothing to do with the search for other life forms, or testing life, as we might imagine those activities to occur. It may be an accident that the sphere causes such profound changes in us."

"But why would someone build such a machine?" Norman said.

"That's the same question an intelligent bacterium would ask about a communications satellite: Why would anyone build such a thing?"

"For that matter," Beth said, "it may not be a machine. The sphere may be a life form. It may be alive."

"Possible," Harry said, nodding.

Beth said, "So, if the sphere is alive, do we have an obligation to keep it alive?"

"We don't know if it *is* alive."

Norman sat back in the chair. "All this speculation is interesting," he said, "but when you get down to it, we don't really know *anything* about the sphere. In fact, we shouldn't even be calling it *the* sphere. We probably should just call it 'sphere.' Because we don't know what it is. We don't know where it came from. We don't know whether it's living or dead. We don't know how it came to be inside that spaceship. We don't know anything about it except what we imagine—and what we imagine says more about us than it does about the sphere."

"Right," Harry said.

"Because it's literally a sort of mirror for us," Norman said.

"Speaking of which, there's another possibility," Harry said. "It may not be alien at all. It may be man-made."

That took Norman completely by surprise. Harry explained.

"Consider," Harry said. "A ship from our own future went through a black hole, into another universe, or another part of our universe. We cannot imagine what would happen as a result of that. But suppose there were some major distortion of time. Suppose that ship, which left with a human crew in the year 2043, actually has been in transit for thousands and thousands of years. Couldn't the human crew have invented it during that time?"

"I don't think that's likely," Beth said.

"Well, let's consider for a moment, Beth," Harry said gently. Norman noticed that Harry wasn't arrogant any more. They were all in this together, Norman thought, and they were working together in a way they never had before. All the time underwater they had been at odds, but now they functioned smoothly together, coordinated. A team.

"There is a real problem about the future," Harry was saying, "and we don't admit it. We assume we can see into the future better than we really can. Leonardo da Vinci tried to make a helicopter five hundred years ago; and Jules Verne predicted a submarine a hundred years ago. From instances like that, we tend to believe that the future is predictable in a way that it really isn't. Because neither Leonardo nor Jules Verne could ever have imagined, say, a computer. The very concept of a computer implies too much knowledge that was simply inconceivable at the time those men were alive. It was, if you will, information that came out of nowhere, later on.

"And we're no wiser, sitting here now. We couldn't have guessed that men would send a ship through a black hole—we didn't even suspect the existence of black holes until a few years ago—and we certainly can't guess what men might accomplish thousands of years in the future."

"Assuming the sphere was made by men."

"Yes. Assuming that."

"And if it wasn't? If it's really a sphere from an alien civilization? Are we justified in erasing all human knowledge of this alien life?"

"I don't know," Harry said, shaking his head. "If we decide to forget the sphere . . ."

"Then it'll be gone," Norman said.

Beth stared at the table. "I wish we could ask someone," she said finally.

"There isn't anybody to ask," Norman said.

"But *can* we really forget it?" Beth said. "Will it work?"

There was a long silence.

"Yes," Harry said, finally. "There's no question about it. And I think we already have evidence that we *will* forget about it. That solves a logical problem that bothered me from the beginning, when we first explored the ship. Because something very important was missing from that ship."

"Yes? What?"

"Any sign that the builders of the ship already knew travel through a black hole was possible."

"I don't follow you," Norman said.

"Well," Harry said, "the three of us have already seen a spaceship that has been through a black hole. We've walked through it. So we know that such travel is possible."

"Yes . . ."

"Yet, fifty years from now, men are going to build that ship in a very tentative, experimental way, with apparently no knowledge that the ship has already been found, fifty years in their past. There is no sign on the ship that the builders already know of its existence in the past."

"Maybe it's one of those time paradoxes," Beth said. "You

know, how you can't go back and meet yourself in the past. . . ."

Harry shook his head. "I don't think it's a paradox," he said. "I think that all knowledge of that ship is going to be lost."

"You mean, we are going to forget it."

"Yes," Harry said. "And, frankly, I think it's a much better solution. For a long time while we were down there, I assumed none of us would ever get back alive. That was the only explanation I could think of. That's why I wanted to make out my will."

"But if we decide to forget . . ."

"Exactly," Harry said. "If we decide to forget, that will produce the same result."

"The knowledge will be gone forever," Norman said quietly. He found himself hesitating. Now that they had arrived at this moment, he was strangely reluctant to proceed. He ran his fingertips over the scarred table, touching the surface, as if it might provide an answer.

In a sense, he thought, all we consist of is memories. Our personalities are constructed from memories, our lives are organized around memories, our cultures are built upon the foundation of shared memories that we call history and science. But now, to give up a memory, to give up knowledge, to give up the past . . .

"It's not easy," Harry said, shaking his head.

"No," Norman said. "It's not." In fact he found it so difficult he wondered if he was experiencing a human characteristic as fundamental as sexual desire. He simply could not give up this knowledge. The information seemed so important to

him, the implications so fascinating. . . . His entire being re-
belled against the idea of forgetting.

"Well," Harry said, "I think we have to do it, anyway."

"I was thinking of Ted," Beth said. "And Barnes, and the
others. We're the only ones who know how they really died.
What they gave their lives for. And if we forget . . ."

"*When* we forget," Norman said firmly.

"She has a point," Harry said. "If we forget, how do we
handle all the details? All the loose ends?"

"I don't think that's a problem," Norman said. "The unconscious has tremendous creative powers, as we've seen.
The details will be taken care of unconsciously. It's like the
way we get dressed in the morning. When we dress, we don't
necessarily think of every detail, the belt and the socks and so
on. We just make a basic overall decision about how we want
to look, and then we get dressed."

"Even so," Harry said. "We still better make the overall
decision, because we all have the power, and if we imagine
different stories, we'll get confusion."

"All right," Norman said. "Let's agree on what happened.
Why did we come here?"

"I thought it was going to be an airplane crash."

"Me, too."

"Okay, suppose it *was* an airplane crash."

"Fine. And what happened?"

"The Navy sent some people down to investigate the
crash, and a problem developed—"

"—Wait a minute, what problem?"

"The squid?"

"No. Better a technical problem."

"Something to do with the storm?"

"Life-support systems failed during the storm?"

"Yes, good. Life-support systems failed during the storm."

"And several people died as a result?"

"Wait a minute. Let's not go so fast. What made the life-support systems fail?"

Beth said, "The habitat developed a leak, and sea water corrupted the scrubber canisters in B Cyl, releasing a toxic gas."

"Could that have happened?" Norman said.

"Yes, easily."

"And several people died as a result of that accident."

"Okay."

"But we survived."

"Yes."

"Why?" Norman said.

"We were in the other habitat?"

Norman shook his head. "The other habitat was destroyed, too."

"Maybe it was destroyed later, with the explosives."

"Too complicated," Norman said. "Let's keep it simple. It was an accident which happened suddenly and unexpectedly. The habitat sprang a leak and the scrubbers failed, and as a result most of the people died, but we didn't because—"

"We were in the sub?"

"Okay," Norman said. "We were in the sub when the systems failed, so we survived and the others didn't."

"Why were we in the sub?"

"We were transferring the tapes according to the schedule."

"And what about the tapes?" Harry said. "What will they show?"

"The tapes will confirm our story," Norman said. "Everything will be consistent with the story, including the Navy people who sent us down in the first place, and including us, too—we won't remember anything but this story."

"And we won't have the power any more?" Beth said, frowning.

"No," Norman said. "Not any more."

"Okay," Harry said.

Beth seemed to think about it longer, biting her lip. But finally she nodded. "Okay."

Norman took a deep breath, and looked at Beth and Harry. "Are we ready to forget the sphere, and the fact that we once had the power to make things happen by thinking them?"

They nodded.

Beth became suddenly agitated, twisting in her chair. "But how do we do it, exactly?"

"We just do it," Norman said. "Close your eyes and tell yourself to forget it."

Beth said, "But are you sure we should do it? *Really* sure?" She was still agitated, moving nervously.

"Yes, Beth. You just . . . give up the power."

"Then we have to do it all together," she said. "At the same time."

"Okay," Harry said. "On the count of three."

They closed their eyes.

"One . . ."

With his eyes closed, Norman thought, People always forget that they have power, anyway.

"Two . . ." Harry said.

And then Norman focused his mind. With a sudden intensity he saw the sphere again, shining like a star, perfect and polished, and he thought: I want to forget I ever saw the sphere.

And in his mind's eye, the sphere vanished.

"THREE," HARRY SAID.

"Three what?" Norman said. His eyes ached and burned. He rubbed them with his thumb and forefinger, then opened them. Beth and Harry were sitting around the table in the decompression chamber with him. They all looked tired and depressed. But that was to be expected, he thought, considering what they had all been through.

"Three what?" Norman said again.

"Oh," Harry said, "I was just thinking out loud. Only three of us left."

Beth sighed. Norman saw tears in her eyes. She fumbled in her pocket for a Kleenex, blew her nose.

"You can't blame yourselves," Norman said. "It was an accident. There was nothing we could do about it."

"I know," Harry said. "But those people suffocating, while we were in the submarine . . . I keep hearing the screams. . . . God, I wish it had never happened."

There was a silence. Beth blew her nose again.

Norman wished it had never happened, too. But wishing wasn't going to make a difference now.

"We can't change what happened," Norman said. "We can only learn to accept it."

"I know," Beth said.

"I've had a lot of experience with accident trauma," he said. "You simply have to keep telling yourself that you have no reason to be guilty. What happened happened—some people died, and you were spared. It isn't anybody's fault. It's just one of those things. It was an accident."

"I know that," Harry said, "but I still feel bad."

"Keep telling yourself it's just one of those things," Norman said. "Keep reminding yourself of that." He got up from the table. They ought to eat, he thought. They ought to have food. "I'm going to ask for food."

"I'm not hungry," Beth said.

"I know that, but we should eat anyway."

Norman walked to the porthole. The attentive Navy crew saw him at once, pressed the radio intercom. "Do anything for you, Dr. Johnson?"

"Yes," Norman said. "We need some food."

"Right away, sir."

Norman saw the sympathy on the faces of the Navy crew. These senior men understood what a shock it must be for the three survivors.

"Dr. Johnson? Are your people ready to talk to somebody now?"

"Talk?"

"Yes, sir. The intelligence experts have been reviewing the videotapes from the submarine, and they have some questions for you."

"What about?" Norman asked, without much interest.

"Well, when you were transferred to the SDC, Dr. Adams mentioned something about a squid."

"Did he?"

"Yes, sir. Only there doesn't seem to be any squid recorded on the tapes."

"I don't remember any squid," Norman said, puzzled. He turned to Harry. "Did you say something about a squid, Harry?"

Harry frowned. "A squid? I don't think so."

Norman turned back to the Navy man. "What do the videotapes show, exactly?"

"Well, the tapes go right up to the time when the air in the habitat . . . you know, the accident . . ."

"Yes," Norman said. "I remember the accident."

"From the tapes, we think we know what happened. Apparently there was a leak in the habitat wall, and the scrubber cylinders got wet. They became inoperable, and the ambient atmosphere went bad."

"I see."

"It must have happened very suddenly, sir."

"Yes," Johnson said. "Yes, it did."

"So, are you ready to talk to someone now?"

"I think so. Yes."

Norman turned away from the porthole. He put his hands in the pockets of his jacket, and felt a piece of paper. He pulled out a picture and stared at it curiously.

It was a photograph of a red Corvette. Norman wondered where the picture had come from. Probably a car that belonged to someone else, who had worn the jacket before Norman. Probably one of the Navy people who had died in the underwater disaster.

Norman shivered, crumpled the picture in his fist, and tossed it into the trash. He didn't need any mementos. He remembered that disaster only too well. He knew he would never forget it for the rest of his life.

He glanced back at Beth and Harry. They both looked tired. Beth stared into space, preoccupied with her own thoughts. But her face was serene; despite the hardships of their time underwater, Norman thought she looked almost beautiful.

"You know, Beth," he said, "you look lovely."

Beth did not seem to hear, but then she turned toward him slowly. "Why, thank you, Norman," she said.

And she smiled.

ABOUT THE AUTHOR

MICHAEL CRICHTON has sold over 200 million books, which have been translated into thirty-six languages; thirteen of his books have been made into films. His novels include *Next, State of Fear, Timeline, Jurassic Park*, and *The Andromeda Strain*. Also known as a filmmaker and the creator of *ER*, he remains the only writer to have had the number one book, movie, and TV show simultaneously. He died in 2008 at the age of sixty-six.